Annabelle sighed. "What are you doing here?"

He wished he knew. It had seemed so simple when his mother had suggested it. Help get Annie out of town. But being around her messed with more than his mind. "I'm going to help you pack up the house and take what you don't want to the dump—unless you want to argue about that, too?"

"I know you think I'm a charity case that you have to—"

"You never were graceful when it came to taking help from anyone," he interrupted. "Just say thank you and let's leave it at that."

She clamped her jaw shut for a moment. "I'm also not graceful when people pity me."

He let out a bark of a laugh. "You think that's what this is? Sorry, sister, but you are the last person I feel sorry for. You need to get your grandmother's house ready to sell. You want to sell this house and clear out of town? Fine with me. I had some things to take to the dump. I thought I'd take some of yours." He gave her a challenging look. "But if you don't want my help—"

B.J. Daniels is a *New York Times* and *USA TODAY* bestselling author. She wrote her first book after a career as an award-winning newspaper journalist and author of thirty-seven published short stories. She lives in Montana with her husband, Parker, and three springer spaniels. When not writing, she quilts, boats and plays tennis. Contact her at bjdaniels.com, on Facebook or on Twitter, @bjdanielsauthor.

Books by B.J. Daniels

Harlequin Intrigue

Whitehorse, Montana: The Clementine Sisters

Hard Rustler

The Montana Cahills

Cowboy's Redemption

Whitehorse, Montana: The McGraw Kidnapping

Dark Horse
Dead Ringer
Rough Rider

HQN Books

The Montana Cahills

Renegade's Pride
Outlaw's Honor
Hero's Return
Rancher's Dream

Visit the Author Profile page
at Harlequin.com for more titles.

B.J. DANIELS

HARD RUSTLER
&
SHOTGUN BRIDE

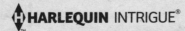

ISBN-13: 978-1-335-54271-7

Hard Rustler & Shotgun Bride

Copyright © 2018 by Harlequin Books S.A.

The publisher acknowledges the copyright holder
of the individual works as follows:

Hard Rustler
Copyright © 2018 by Barbara Heinlein

Shotgun Bride
Copyright © 2009 by Barbara Heinlein

Recycling programs
for this product may
not exist in your area.

Printed in U.S.A.

www.Harlequin.com

CONTENTS

This book is for Julie Simundson Nagy, a true fan, who has been a bright spot in so many of my days. Writing is such a solitary endeavor with lots of stress. I will see Julie and she will remind me that I'm not alone in this. Her smile and enthusiasm keep me grounded. Thank you, Julie!

HARD RUSTLER

Chapter One

As her sports car topped the rise, Annabelle Clementine looked out at the rugged country spread before her and felt her heart drop. She'd never thought she'd see so many miles of wild winter Montana landscape ever again. At least, she'd hoped not.

How could she have forgotten the remoteness? The vastness? The isolation? There wasn't a town in sight. Or a ranch house. Or another living soul.

She glanced down at her gas gauge. It hovered at empty. She'd tried to get gas at the last station, but her credit card wouldn't work and she'd gone through almost all of her cash. She'd put in what fuel she could with the change she was able scrape up, but it had barely moved the gauge. If she ran out of gas before she reached Whitehorse…well, it would just be her luck, wouldn't it?

She let the expensive silver sports car coast down the mountain toward the deep gorge of the Missouri River, thankful that most of the snow was high in the mountains and not on the highway. She didn't know what she would have done if the roads had been icy since she hadn't seen a snow tire since she'd left Montana.

The motor coughed. She looked down at the gauge.

The engine had to be running on fumes. What was she going to do? It was still miles to Whitehorse. Tears burned her eyes, but she refused to cry. Yes, things were bad. Really bad. But—

She was almost to the river bottom when she saw it. At a wide spot where the river wound on its way through Montana east to the Mississippi, a pickup and horse trailer were pulled off to the side of the highway. Her pulse jumped at just the thought of another human being—let alone the possibility of getting some fuel. If she could just get to Whitehorse...

But as she descended the mountain, she didn't see anyone around the pickup or horse trailer. What if the rig had been left beside the road and the driver was no-where to be found? Maybe there would be a gas can in the back of the pickup or—*Have you stooped so low that now you would steal gas?*

Fortunately, she wasn't forced to answer that. She spotted a cowboy standing on the far side of the truck. Her instant of relief was quickly doused as she looked around and realized how alone the two of them were, out here in the middle of nowhere.

Don't be silly. What are the chances the cowboy is a serial killer, rapist, kidnapper, ax murderer...? The motor sputtered as if taking its last gasp as she slowed. It wasn't as if she had a choice. She hadn't seen another car for over an hour. For miles she'd driven through open country dotted occasionally with cows but no people. And she knew there was nothing but rugged country the rest of the way north to Whitehorse.

If there had been any other way to get where she was

headed, she would have taken it. But her options had been limited for some time now.

And today, it seemed, her options had come down to this cowboy and possible serial killer rapist kidnapper ax murderer.

She let the car glide into the spot next to where the cowboy had pulled off the highway. *I'll just bum a little fuel and be on my way. Nothing to worry about.* Just the thought made her laugh. Her life was one big worry right now, she fretted, as she took in the rangy-looking cowboy standing by his truck.

"What's the worst that could happen?" She groaned. *Taking risks is what got you into this mess.* Like she had to be reminded.

The engine let out a final cough and died. Committed now, she had no choice as she braked next to the horse trailer. Turning off the key in the ignition, she checked her makeup and hair in the mirror. *You're Annabelle Clementine. You can do this.* The woman who stared back at her from the mirror looked skeptical at best.

Bucking up her courage, she stepped out of the car, careful not to let her last pair of expensive heels get muddy. "Excuse me?" she called, determined also not to get too far away from her open car door. "I'm afraid I have a small problem and really could use some help."

She was ready to make a hasty retreat back into the car, if need be. Not that she would be going far if things went south. But at least she could lock herself in. She instantly regretted the fact that she'd bought a canvas-topped convertible, which had been perfect in Southern California.

The cowboy had his back to her and hadn't looked

up from where he'd been digging around in the back of his pickup bed.

"Excuse me?" she tried again. He had to have heard her. But so far, he hadn't acknowledged her presence in any way.

Forced to move away from the car, she took in the cowboy as she approached and wasn't impressed with what she saw. But then again, she'd grown up with cowboys so she'd never understood the fascination. Admittedly, this one was tall, broad shouldered, slim hipped, long legged and not bad from the backside.

Unfortunately, everything else about him looked worn and dirty, from his jeans, boots and canvas jacket to the Stetson on the too-long dark hair curling at the nape of his red neck.

At her approach, he gave her a quick glance over his shoulder. She could see little of his face. He wore mirrored sunglasses against the winter glare, his hat pulled low. Under the dark shadow of his Stetson, she glimpsed several week's growth of beard, making him look even more craggy and unkempt. No designer stubble on this cowboy.

Either he'd been on the range for days or this was as good as it got with him.

You're not marrying him. You're just bumming fuel.
"Hello?" she said louder and with more attitude as he went back to what he was doing.

"There a problem?" he drawled in a low, lazy tone as he finally finished and turned, seemingly reluctantly, to give her his attention. She saw that he'd been feeding his dog in the back of the pickup. The dog—little more than a puppy—was a furry mutt with one blue eye and one brown one circled by a patch of black. He didn't look much better than his owner.

She shifted her gaze back to the cowboy who was looking at her car as if he'd never seen one like it before. *Probably doesn't get off the ranch much.*

He slowly slid his gaze back to her with a nonchalance that made her grind her teeth.

"Yes, there is a problem." She'd thought she'd already told him that.

He lifted the brim of his hat, dropped his sunglasses down to look over them for a moment. She caught a glimpse of brown eyes as he surveyed her, making her feel nearly naked under the black cashmere sweater and slacks she was wearing, before he lifted his sunglasses again.

"I'm afraid I forgot to buy gas at the last station," she said, wanting to get this over with as quickly as possible—even if it did make her look like a fool. She had worse problems. "I was wondering if you might have some gas that I could borrow? Just enough to get me into town?"

"Borrow?" He chuckled at that. "And town being?"

She hated to even admit where she was headed. "Whitehorse."

"That's another hour up the road."

As if she didn't know that. "My car used more gas than I thought it would." She gave a nervous laugh, hating that she had to resort to acting as if she didn't have a brain. Back when she was making money, fuel was never an issue. She hadn't realized how much a lot of things cost—until she couldn't pay for them anymore.

He nodded, glancing toward the river as if considering her request. "I suppose I could siphon some out of one of my tanks." He didn't sound thrilled about it. Nor had he moved.

"I would appreciate that so much." She glanced at her watch.

"Got some place to be, do you?"

"I have an appointment."

"In Whitehorse?" From under the brim of his hat and behind the mirrored sunglasses, he studied her a few moments more before he sighed. "Best pull up next to my pickup while I grab a hose."

She feared the car wouldn't start, let alone move. But there must have been just enough fumes left for her to pull up before it died again. She shut off the engine, staying in the car to pop the gas compartment open and watch him move slow as molasses. He acted as if he had all day. *He* probably did.

Patience had never been one of her strong suits. She tapped a toe as she heard him talking to his dog, mumbling so she couldn't make out a word. As if she didn't know he was giving the dog an earful about her.

The dog, still in the pickup bed, wagged its tail enthusiastically at whatever the cowboy said. Whatever he was saying, he certainly found it amusing from that hint of a grin under the beard. Annabelle consoled herself with the thought that the mutt was probably the closest thing the cowboy could get to a female companion.

After a good five to ten minutes, he finished. She hadn't thought past getting enough gas to get to Whitehorse. Now her stomach clenched at a thought. Not only should she offer him money, but he also might demand it. And since she had no money and doubted he took credit cards—even ones that weren't frozen for lack of payment...

She watched him walk to his pickup to put the hose away and knew what she had to do. It was the coward's way out. But she told herself that she had no choice. She'd been telling herself that for months now. Not that it made her feel any better as she quickly started her car and threw it into reverse.

Whirring down the passenger side window, she called out, "Thank you so much. If you're ever in White-horse..." With that she took off, torn between guilt and glee over seeing that he'd given her almost a full tank of gas.

When she dared look back, she saw him standing by his pickup shaking his head as he watched her leave. She thought of that glimpse of golden brown. Even shaded under the brim of his old Stetson, those eyes... They'd almost seemed...familiar.

Chapter Two

Dawson Rogers swore as he pulled off his worn Stetson. Raking a hand through his hair, he watched the silver sports car take off like a bat out of hell.

"Annabelle Clementine." He said the name like a curse. For years, he'd only seen her staring back at him from glossy women's magazine ads. He'd been just fine knowing there was no chance that he'd ever lay eyes on her in the flesh again. She'd been real clear about never setting foot in this state again when she'd left all those years ago.

So what was she doing headed for Whitehorse?

That his heart was still pounding only made him more furious with himself. When he'd heard her voice behind him…he couldn't believe it. He'd thought for sure that his worn-out, dog-weary body was playing tricks on him. He'd frozen in place, counting to ten and then ten again, afraid to turn around for fear he'd be wrong—or worse—right.

Now he swore, remembering his reaction to just the sound of her voice. Could he be a bigger fool?

And yet that voice had brought it all back. The ache in his belly, the stompin' she'd done on his heart. Worse, the hope that set a fire inside him at just the sound of it. In that instant, he'd wanted it to be her more than he'd wanted his next breath. After everything she'd done to him, he'd actually felt a spike of joy at the thought of seeing her again.

And still he hadn't turned around, because he'd known once he did, the disappointment would be as painful as the last time he'd seen her.

Turning, he'd seen her standing there and thought, *Damn, the woman is even more beautiful than when she'd hightailed it out of here.*

He'd been shocked—and still was. Annie. In the flesh. That she hadn't changed except to become more gorgeous had left him shaken. A dust devil of emotions whirled inside him as he watched her drive away.

"What is she doing back here?" he demanded as the pup came over to the side of the pickup bed to lick his hand.

Sadie wagged her tail in response. "What am I doing asking you?" He ruffled the dog's fur. Still, he found himself squinting after the sports car as it climbed the mountain on the other side of the river and disappeared around a curve. "What's a woman who said she'd never set foot in Whitehorse doing back here? If I hadn't seen her with my own eyes..."

For just a moment there, earlier, before she'd asked for gas, he'd thought...

Hell, he didn't want to think about what he'd thought as he shoved his hat back on. "Let's get on home," he said to the pup as he reminded himself that Annabelle Clementine's coming back had nothing to do with him.

He told himself that he shouldn't have been surprised

that she hadn't changed. Still, it galled him. Her clothes might be more expensive and she drove a much fancier car, but she was still the same girl who'd looked down her nose at him—and Whitehorse—all those years ago.

It nagged at him. What could have brought her back? He shook his head, telling himself it was obviously none of his business. Best thing he could do was to forget about her—something he'd been working on for some time now.

After two weeks in hunting camp, he recalled that before he'd seen her, all he'd wanted was to get home, have a hot shower and climb into a warm, soft bed. If he hadn't stopped beside the road to take a leak, let Sadie out and give the pup a snack…well, he might not have seen her at all.

The only thing that didn't surprise him, he told himself as he lifted Sadie into the pickup's front seat and climbed behind the wheel, was that the woman hadn't given him the time of day. Hell, he couldn't even be sure she remembered him. After all, it had been… How many years *had* it been? He wondered with a frown as he started the truck engine.

Thirteen. He let out a low whistle. Sadie's ears perked up, but she lay back down and closed her eyes for the ride home.

And it wasn't like Annie had ever given him a thought since she'd been gone, he reminded himself. She'd made it perfectly clear that they had no future before she'd left right after high school to find fame and fortune.

Dawson pointed the pickup toward Whitehorse, all the time trying to imagine what could have brought her back. Certainly not her grandmother's funeral. Only her two sisters had made it back for that. Of course, they'd attended the funeral and left right away, but at least they'd shown up. He shook his head, thinking that he'd expected better of the girl he'd fallen in love with all those years ago. Given how much her grandmother had doted on her...

But he reminded himself that he'd *always* been wrong about the woman. He could no more predict what Annabelle was going to do than predict the Montana weather. He thought of that young fool cowboy who'd saved every dime he made that year to promise her something that would make her stay. He growled under his breath at the memory.

Well, he wasn't that young fool anymore. Which was why he was going to give her a wide berth as long as she was in town. Not that he suspected it would be for long. Knowing her, she would be hightailing it back to California as fast as she could. Back to her fancy life in the spotlight.

"Which is just fine with us, huh, Sadie," he said to his pup. "Don't need the likes of her around here messing with our minds." Sadie barked in answer and curled closer to him, making him laugh. "This was before your time," he said to the dog, "But that woman was once nothing but walking heartache for this cowboy. Fortunately, I'm not that man anymore."

His words sounded hollow, even to him. He felt his face flush at how much gas he'd given her and mentally kicked himself. He should have left her beside the road to fend for herself. But then, he'd never been able to say no to her—even when he should have known that a girl like her wanted something better than a cowboy like him.

ANNABELLE PUT THE cowboy and his dog behind her as she drove north. She was determined that nothing would get in her way. Once she did what she'd come for, she was out of here. Another one of those limited options.

She took the back way into the small Western town. The first settlement of Whitehorse had been nearer the Missouri River. But when the railroad came through, the town migrated north, taking the name with it. Old Town Whitehorse, as it was now known, was little more than a ghost town to the south.

Not that Whitehorse proper was a thriving metropolis. The whole town was only ten blocks square. Nothing but a siding along the railroad tracks more than a hundred years ago, it had become a small rural town like a lot of small rural Montana towns.

Why her grandmother had settled here was still a mystery, but when Annabelle's parents had been killed, Grandma Frannie had taken Annabelle and her two sisters in without hesitation. Annabelle had grown up here, dreaming of a life she envisioned far from this dusty old Western town.

As she drove down the tree-lined street with the large houses that backed onto the Milk River, images of her childhood flickered like the winter sun coming through the leafless cottonwood trees. From as far back as she could remember, she'd grown up with one thing in mind: getting out of this town and making something of her life.

That sick feeling she'd become acquainted with over the past few months now settled in her stomach. Right now, she couldn't face even thinking about how she'd messed up. Sitting up a little straighter behind the wheel of the car, she assured herself that everything was going to be fine.

She would just take care of business and put all the unpleasantness behind her. As she tried to look for a silver lining in all this, she noticed that she still had plenty of gas. It should last her for what little time she would be here, thanks to that cowboy. She shoved away the guilt. If she ever saw him again…

Down the block, she spotted the house. Her foot came off the gas pedal, the car slowing as she felt a rush of déjà vu. The house hadn't changed—just like she doubted the town had—and for a moment it was as if she'd never left. So much had happened to her, she'd expected this part of her past would have changed, somehow.

Instead, it looked so much the same, she almost expected Frannie to come out on the porch as Annabelle pulled up in front of the large, two-story house and shut off the engine. The key to the front door was in her pocket, but she wasn't ready to go inside. Not yet. Glancing at her watch, she saw that she'd gotten here early. There was no sign of the Realtor. Taking a breath, she let it out and tried to relax as she studied the house.

The white siding could use an overall paint job and the emerald trim needed a touch-up. But if she closed her eyes, she could picture herself and her sisters, the three Clementine girls, on that wide porch drinking Grandma Frannie's lemonade and giggling like the schoolgirls they'd been.

She hadn't realized that she'd closed her eyes until she felt them burn with tears. Her guilt was like one of her grandmother's knitting needles to her heart. Yes, she should have made it to Frannie's funeral. She'd had her reasons, and they hadn't all been out of embarrassment for the way her life had turned out.

Her grandmother would have understood because Annabelle had always been the favorite. At least, that's what she told herself.

"You're so much like me, Annabelle Clementine, that sometimes I swear you'll be the death of me." Then Grandma Frannie's expression would soften and she'd press a cool palm to Annabelle's cheek. "So much like me. It's like seeing myself at your age."

"That's why I'm your favorite," she'd say, and her grandmother would shake her head and laugh before telling her to run along outside.

But it had to have been true. Otherwise, why would Frannie have left her the only thing she had of any value—this house. And left it only to her instead of to all three sisters?

A tap on the passenger-side window startled her. Her eyes flew open, but it took a moment to chase away the bittersweet memories along with the guilt and the tears.

REALTOR MARY SUE LINTON glanced at the silver sports car and shook her head. Leave it to Annabelle to show up in something like that. She shouldn't have been surprised since this was the Annabelle Clementine she'd known since grade school.

She had been surprised, though, when her former classmate had called and asked Mary Sue to represent her in the sale. Not surprised. Shocked. The two of them had never been friends, traveling in a completely different circle of friends, even as small as the classes had been. The truth was that Annabelle hadn't uttered two words to her throughout four years of high school. Did people still say stuck-up?

Blonde and blue-eyed, with a figure that Mary Sue would have killed for, Annabelle was The Girl Most Likely to Become Famous. At least, that's what it had said in their senior class yearbook. Everyone knew Annabelle was going to be somebody. Annabelle had said it enough times.

But, then again, she'd also said that she would never come back to Whitehorse. And here she was.

Still, why come all this way to sell her grandmother's house? Mary Sue had told her on the phone that she could deal with everything but the paperwork and save her the trip. She had expected Annabelle to jump at it. Instead, the woman had insisted on coming back to "handle" things.

"If you don't trust me to get you the best price..." Mary Sue had started to say, "you can kiss my—"

But Annabelle had interrupted with, "It's *my* grandmother's house."

Right. Just like it had been *her* grandmother's funeral. Everyone in town had turned out. Annabelle's two sisters had flown in and out. No Annabelle, though. So was Mary Sue supposed to believe the house had sentimental value to this woman? Not likely.

After tapping on the sports car window, she bent down and looked in. One glance and it was clear that her former classmate had aged well. She looked better than she had in high school. Mary Sue felt that old stab of jealousy.

She started to tap again, but to her surprise, Annabelle appeared to be furtively wiping away tears. Shocked at such a sign of emotion, Mary Sue was taken aback. Maybe she was wrong about Annabelle. Maybe she did have a heart. Maybe she did care about her grandmother. Maybe she even cared about this house and Whitehorse and the people she'd once snubbed.

The thought almost made her laugh though as her former classmate climbed out of the convertible sports car saying, "Okay, let's get this over with so I can get out of this one-horse town."

DAWSON UNLOADED THE horse trailer, parked it and went into the ranch house he'd built himself. He'd worked hard the past thirteen years and now had a place he was proud of on the family ranch. The oldest son of two, he'd had to take over helping his mother run the ranch after his father had died. He'd worked hard and was proud of what he'd been able to accomplish. Annabelle wasn't the only one who'd done well over the years, he told himself with no small amount of defensiveness.

"Got a chip on your shoulder, do you?" he grumbled with a curse. He'd been thinking about her again. All the way to town he'd been trying to exorcize her from his thoughts with little luck. Before she'd left town, she'd made him feel as if he was never going to amount to anything. It still stuck in his craw.

He kept seeing her sitting in her car while he refueled it. She hadn't even had the good grace to look at him— not to mention acknowledge that she'd once known him. Known him damned well, too.

Dawson gave that memory an angry shove away. When Annabelle Clementine had left town in a cloud of dust years ago, she'd said she was never looking back. Well, today proved that, didn't it?

Worked up over his run-in with her, he told himself he just needed a hot shower and clean clothes. But as he caught his reflection in the bathroom mirror, he came to a startled stop and had to laugh. He wouldn't even recognize himself after two weeks in a hunting camp in the Missouri Breaks.

He stared at his grizzled face and filthy, camp-worn clothes, seeing what she'd seen today. Even if she had recognized him, seeing him like that would only have confirmed what she'd thought of him all those years ago. He looked like a man who wasn't going anywhere.

Stripping down, he turned on the shower and stepped in. The warm water felt like heaven as he began to suds up in a fury. He just wanted that woman out of his hair—and his head. But his thoughts went straight as an arrow to that image of her standing beside the river. Her long blond hair gleaming in the sunlight and that black outfit hugging every unforgettable curve he'd once known so well. Growling, he turned the water to cold.

Out of the shower and toweling himself off, he looked at his reflection in the mirror again. Was it really possible that she hadn't known him? He reached for his razor, telling himself it didn't matter. With a curse, he acknowledged that he'd been lying to himself for years about his feelings for her—ever since that day he'd rescued her from his tree house when she was five.

And he'd rescued her again today, he thought with a curse. He just never learned.

ANNABELLE TOOK THE key from her pocket and opened her grandmother's front door, Mary Sue Linton at her elbow. Taking a deep breath, she stepped inside, bracing herself for more painful memories. Instead, shock stopped her cold just inside the door.

"You can't sell the house like this," Mary Sue said, stating the obvious next to her. "I thought you said your sisters cleaned everything out?"

"They said they took what they wanted." She couldn't believe what she was seeing. Her grandmother hadn't been a packrat, she'd been a hoarder. The house was crammed full of...stuff. She could barely see the floor. The rooms appeared to be filled with furniture, knick-knacks, stacks of newspapers and magazines, bags of clothing and clutter. The house looked more like a crowded old antique shop than a home. Unfortunately it didn't take a trained eye to see that all of this wasn't even junkshop worthy.

"What am I supposed to do with all of this?" she demanded. "I can't very well have a garage sale this time of year. If there was anything in all this mess worth selling." It was late November. Christmas was only weeks away.

Mary Sue shrugged. "You could hire someone to help you pack it all up. Unfortunately, the local charity shop can't take most of this. If there are things you want to save—"

"No."

"I was going to say that you could put them into a storage shed."

Annabelle was shaking her head, overwhelmed as they worked their way along the paths through the house.

"Otherwise, I could give you some names of people who might be able to help you at least haul it out to the dump."

"Great. How long is that going to take? I need to get this house on the market right away." She followed the narrow trails, going from room to room, Mary Sue on her heels, until she reached what had once been a bedroom but now looked more like a storage room where a bomb had gone off.

"This is no normal hoarding," Mary Sue said. "It looks like someone ransacked this room."

Annabelle agreed it did appear that someone had torn into all the boxes and dumped the contents on the floor. Her grandmother before she died? Her sisters when they'd come back for the funeral?

"Look at the window," Mary Sue said in a hoarse whisper as she grabbed Annabelle's arm, her fingernails digging into tender flesh.

"Ouch." She jerked free and kicked aside some of the mess to move to the window, which was now half open, the screen torn. "The lock is broken."

Behind her, Mary Sue let out a shudder. "Someone broke in."

That was the way it appeared, although she couldn't imagine in her wildest dreams why they would want to. She closed the window and turned to find Mary Sue hugging herself.

"Whoever broke in isn't here anymore," she tried to assure the Realtor. "Let's look upstairs. Maybe it's better." Unfortunately, the upstairs wasn't any better; both bedrooms were stacked full of clutter, including her grandmother's old room.

Back downstairs, she took another look at the front downstairs bedroom. It wasn't quite as full as the others. She checked the closet, found what must be her grandmother's clothing and assumed that, as Frannie got older, she'd moved downstairs.

"Could this be anymore outdated?" Mary Sue called from the kitchen.

"I think I can clean out one of the downstairs bedrooms so at least I'll have a place I can stay," Annabelle said as she joined her in the kitchen. The front bedroom downstairs had been hers growing up.

Mary Sue didn't seem to hear her. Instead, she was frowning at the clipboard she had in her hands.

"What?" Annabelle demanded. "Don't tell me there is another problem."

"No, not exactly. But it is strange. This is a layout of the house I got from the records department at the courthouse," she said, indicating the sheet on her clipboard. "That wall shouldn't be there."

"What?"

"This shows an alcove."

"An alcove? Maybe it's back there behind all the junk and you just can't see it."

Mary Sue's frown deepened. "Do you remember an alcove from when you were growing up here?"

She was supposed to remember an alcove? Seriously? "No. The plans for the house must be outdated."

"Not according to the courthouse. Your grandmother bought this house when she was in her twenties so she had it for…"

"She was seventy-six when she died, so she had it for more than fifty years." Annabelle hadn't realized how long Frannie had lived in Whitehorse until she'd seen it in the obituary that one of her sisters had sent her. It hadn't been out of kindness that Chloe had mailed it to her. Her older sister had never been that subtle. Both Chloe and Tessa Jane—TJ—had tried to make her feel guilty about their grandmother leaving her the house— let alone Annabelle missing the funeral.

"Frannie owned this house almost from the time it was built," Mary Sue was saying. "So if anyone made the changes, it had to have been your grandmother. Why would she wall up an alcove? I wonder what's behind it?"

"Okay, you're giving me the creeps now," Annabelle said. "Clearly, you have the plans for the wrong house. Aren't there a bunch of houses along this street with similar floor plans?"

Mary Sue nodded, but didn't look convinced. "I can check at the courthouse again I guess. But you have to admit, if the plans are right, then it is more than a little odd to wall up the alcove, let alone—"

"You're letting your imagination run away with you. You *knew* my grandmother."

With a lift of one eyebrow, Mary Sue said, "She said her husband died before she moved to Whitehorse, but what if—"

"Seriously? You think my grandfather's body is stuffed in there?"

"Ever seen the play *Arsenic and Old Lace*?"

"Frannie Clementine was one of the most kind and generous people in town. She wouldn't hurt a fly." Standing just over five feet, Frannie had been a tiny, sweet-tempered woman who loved kids, garage sales and cooking. She attended church every Sunday, come rain or shine or snow.

Annabelle could tell that Mary Sue was enjoying trying to scare her. Was it any wonder that they hadn't been friends in high school?

"Just sayin'," the Realtor said, clearly trying to hide a grin. "Did you know that since her death right before Halloween last month, kids are saying that this house is haunted?"

"That's ridiculous. Just because she died in this house…" Annabelle tried to hide the shudder that moved through her at the thought. If one of her neighbors, old Inez Gilbert, hadn't come over to check on Frannie, she would have been lost in all this mess for weeks. That thought did nothing to improve the situation.

"On Halloween some kids saw what they said was a ghost moving around in the house. They said it looked like an old woman dressed in all white and—"

"Stop," Annabelle snapped, having had enough. The house was creepy as it was with all the memories, not to mention being filled to overflowing with collected junk. She really didn't need this. "It was probably Inez from next door. The woman is a horrible busybody and always has been."

If Mary Sue thought she could scare her, then she didn't know what scary was. Unfortunately, Annabelle did. It was losing a dream job and a fabulous lifestyle, and being forced to do things she'd told herself she would never do, like return to this town and all the memories that came with it.

"The house isn't haunted. There never was an alcove—"

Mary Sue tapped her clipboard. "But the plans—"

"The alcove isn't here now so that's all I care about. I need to get packing and you need to get this house sold. Just get me the names of people who will help clean it out."

Right now, though, she needed a breath of fresh air and Whitehorse had plenty of that. She stepped out onto the front porch, letting the door close behind her. She'd known this wouldn't be easy, but it was turning out to be more difficult than she could have imagined. The memories, the stories, the stupid missing alcove, not to mention all that junk. She definitely had more pressing things to worry about than a bunch of local kids thinking the house was haunted.

The clock was ticking, she thought, looking at her car, the last vestige of her former life other than the clothes on her back. She had to get this house sold.

MARY SUE GRITTED her teeth. Annabelle annoyed her to no end. "Hasn't changed a bit," she muttered. "Get me this, do this for me." She looked around the house, her gaze going to the kitchen and the missing alcove. "I hope there is a body walled up in there—and a vindictive ghost who hates blondes." That would serve Annabelle right.

She felt guilty, but only a little, for trying to scare her former classmate. But she was still puzzling over the missing alcove as she stepped out onto the porch. Her mother had been a Realtor. Maybe she'd ask her if she knew anything about the old Clementine house, as it was known around town. It sat along with a half dozen others on a street locally and affectionately known as

Millionaire's Row. The houses were large, a lot of them the same basic floor plan.

Mary Sue moved to the end of the porch to look back at the rock wall that marked the property line. On the other side of the wall was the Milk River. Between the house and the river, though, were large trees and an expanse of grass broken only by some cracked sidewalk that ended at an old garage that had seen better days.

"That should come down," she said of the dilapidated structure and marked it on her sheet on her clipboard. Through the trees, she could make out only a portion of the neighboring house's eaves in the distance. These really were beautiful old houses along this street, so private because of the old-growth trees and the huge lots. Not exactly Millionaire's Row now, but definitely prime real estate in this town.

"So where can I reach you?" Mary Sue asked, turning to Annabelle who appeared distracted. Not that she could blame her. The supermodel had quite a job before her.

"You have my cell number and you know where to find me. I'll be staying here."

"In the house?" Mary Sue couldn't help her surprise.

Annabelle turned to look at her. "Why *wouldn't* I stay here?"

"No reason, except..." She remembered all the clutter and the fact that Frannie had died here. Not that unusual for a woman her age, but still, add to that the walled-up alcove... Mary Sue shivered.

While she had been trying to scare Annabelle earlier, she had to admit that the house had an odd feel to it. Maybe it was just her, but there was something... Or maybe she had managed to scare herself more than she had Annabelle and all because of that discrepancy in the floor plan—and the fact that someone had broken into the house and might come back.

She mentioned this to Annabelle who only waved away the idea. "It was probably kids. You know how teenagers are, an empty house, ghost story dares…"

Mary Sue didn't know, but she had a feeling that Annabelle was all too aware of how kids like *that* acted because she'd been one. "I just thought you'd want to stay at the hotel, since that's where your sisters stayed when they came home for the funeral."

Annabelle made an angry sound under her breath. "*They didn't stay here?* No wonder they didn't take much—let alone tell me how full this house was. I thought they were here going through things. From what I can see, they didn't take anything. You were the one who let them into the house with the key I sent you, right?"

Mary Sue sighed, wondering if Annabelle was going to blame her. "Yes, but I didn't come inside. The house was left to you. I was the one who was responsible for opening the door and making sure it was locked when they left. That was all. I wouldn't have felt comfortable going in the house without you."

"So did they take *anything*?"

"Not as far as I could tell." She shrugged. "I let them in, they went into the house, but only for a short period of time, they sat on the porch steps for a little while and then they left and I locked up. From what I saw, they took a few framed photographs, but I think that was about all."

Annabelle looked as if she was going to blow a gasket. "I should have known they wouldn't be of any help. That's just great. Well, they're not getting anything now. Not that there is anything worth keeping in there. From what I've seen, most of the stuff is on the way to the dump just as soon as I can get it loaded up. I'll need help right away. Did you make those calls yet?"

Mary Sue tried not to bristle. "You do realize that tomorrow is Thanksgiving, right?" she asked. "And the day after that is Black Friday, when a lot of people in town will be shopping, either locally or driving the three hours to Billings." Billings was the largest city in Montana and two hundred miles to the south. Mary Sue was planning to go down to shop with a couple of friends, spending the night at a hotel and making a trip out of it.

"Your point?"

"It's going to be hard to find anyone to help this time of year," she said, and added quickly before Annabelle could argue. "But let me make a few quick calls." She hurriedly stepped off the porch and walked down the cracked driveway toward her car, phone in hand. Even though it was now close to freezing outside, she didn't want to go back into the house. Nor did she want Annabelle to hear her phone conversations. When she told people who they would be working for, she expected them to balk.

A few minutes later, she returned to the porch where Annabelle was pacing. The model looked cold, but no wonder, since she was inappropriately dressed for Montana weather. Mary Sue guessed that she wasn't anxious to go back inside the house, either. "I found a couple of men who are willing to help for thirty dollars an hour."

"*Thirty dollars an hour?* I'm not asking them to remodel the house." Annabelle looked through the window with a shake of the head as if calculating how many hours work was in there. "Forget it," she said with a sigh. "I'll do the packing myself. Where can I find some boxes?"

"Behind the town recycling center. But you aren't going to be able to get very many into that car of yours. Are you sure you don't want—"

"I'll figure it out."

"Okay, but once you get everything boxed up, you're going to need a truck to take it either to the dump or a storage unit, if you decide to keep some of it."

"Got it. I'll deal with all that once it's boxed up."

"I have plans, otherwise…" Otherwise what? Did she really feel guilty about not offering to help? If Annabelle was too cheap to hire help, that was her problem.

With a wave of her hand, her former classmate dismissed her.

"All right, then let me know when the house is ready to go on the market," Mary Sue said, not about to mention that the place would need to be cleaned. A nice coat of fresh paint in the rooms would also help. But she didn't feel that Annabelle was up to hearing more bad news right now and Mary Sue wasn't up to giving it.

Anyway, she was anxious to talk to her mother. As she walked to her car, her clipboard in hand, she tried to convince herself that she'd gotten the wrong floor plan from the courthouse.

Except she knew better. She prided herself on being thorough. Frannie had walled up the alcove. But why? And what was in the closed-up space?

"SHOULDN'T YOU BE ASLEEP?" the assisted-living nurse asked from his doorway.

Bernard "Bernie the Hawk" McDougal gave her the smile that had worked on women since he was a boy. Even at eighty-nine, the old mobster still could make a woman blush with no more than a wink and a grin. There might be snow on the roof, but it was still plenty hot down in the furnace.

"Just finishing up here," he told her from his desk and waited until she moved on before he picked up the scissors again.

He pulled the newspaper clipping toward him, still shocked that he'd discovered it online while surfing for obits of women of a certain age. The moment he'd seen this one, he'd printed it out, but the resolution wasn't good so he'd called the newspaper where it had run— the *Milk River Courier*—and had the paper overnighted to him.

It had arrived this afternoon while he was napping. When he'd awakened, he'd seen the envelope waiting for him on his desk and quickly torn into it. Inside he'd found the complete edition of that week's Whitehorse, Montana, newspaper—all four pages of it.

Now he studied the face in the obituary mug shot. The photo didn't do her justice. The one he'd seen on the internet had been much more flattering.

But no photo of his Baby Doll could hold a candle to the woman in the flesh—especially back when she was young. She'd been a blonde beauty. Tiny and gorgeous, she'd been exquisite. The kind of woman who stopped traffic and turned heads. She'd certainly turned is, he thought with a curse. And the things she'd put him through from the first time he'd laid eyes on her.

That was something else about her that had attracted her to him. She wasn't intimidated by him or any of his goons. Oh, that woman had a mouth on her. She could cut a man down to size as if her tongue was a switchblade.

He chuckled to himself. He'd wanted her and would have married her, but she wasn't having any of that. She liked being mysterious. Hell, he'd never known her real name. That first night at the party, he'd seen right away that she and her friend had crashed his little gettogether on the posh rooftop of his favorite New York City restaurant. He'd thought about booting the two of them, but there was something about her.

She'd flirted with him but refused to tell him who she was, as if she thought he'd call her daddy to have her picked up and taken home. A few minutes with her and that was the last thing he planned to do.

"Okay, you want to play it coy? You'll just be my Baby Doll, then," he'd said, knowing even then that he had to have her.

"Baby Doll? I like that," she'd said, coming off older than she was. She hadn't been more than seventeen. Jailbait. Like that had stopped him. He had a reputation for going after whatever he wanted—and getting it. But then, so did Baby Doll as it turned out.

Opening the scissors, he began to slice the paper around her mug shot. Bernie couldn't stand sloppiness. He liked things done a certain way. It had saved his life more than once and kept him from being behind bars.

Now he found himself looking into her eyes, remem-

bering. This was her. There was no doubt about it. He'd
thought he found her before, but this time… He wished
he had been able to find a photograph of her when she
was younger but there was nothing on the internet. Francesca Marie Clementine had kept a low profile. Another reason he was convinced that this woman was his
Baby Doll.

Oh, those blue eyes. The memories of her in his arms.
Just being with her had felt like living on the edge, she'd
been that kind of woman. She kept his blood revved up.
He'd known he could never get enough of her. He'd asked
her to marry him more times than he liked to remember.
He shook his head. While he'd only known her a short
while, he'd thought he could trust her with his life, his
secrets—and his loot. His first mistake.

That was the problem, wasn't it? he thought as he
clipped the photo free from the newspaper. He'd trusted
a woman who hadn't even trusted him enough to tell
him her real name.

"Come on, Baby Doll, tell me your name," he used
to tease her. "We can't get married until I know exactly
who you are."

"Oh, you know who I am." She'd smiled that coy
smile of hers and said, "I'm Bernie McDougal's Baby
Doll. That's enough. For now." Her look had been a
promise of a lot more to come and he'd been a goner.
Oh, the swanky parties they'd attended, the fur coats and
fancy dresses he'd clothed her in, the expensive champagne they'd guzzled, the money they'd burned through.
Nothing was too good for his Baby Doll.

His stomach roiled at the memory. She'd blindsided
him from the beginning, he thought, able to admit it now,

more than fifty years later. He'd thought she was young and naïve. He'd never seen it coming.

The obit was short, but it did provide some useful information, such as where she'd been all these years—and that she was survived by her three granddaughters, Annabelle Clementine, Tessa Jane Clementine (TJ St. Clair) and Chloe Clementine. No husband. That didn't surprise him.

He'd had to look up the town on the internet. Whitehorse, Montana. It surprised him that she'd disappeared to some wide spot out West. He'd always thought of her living it up in Paris or London, or even New York City where it had all begun. It was why he'd looked for her in the faces of every woman he'd passed all these years.

But Baby Doll had always been full of surprises, hadn't she? He still couldn't believe that she'd evaded him. He'd had his men looking for her as well as his associates. He'd put a price on her pretty head. And still nothing. It was as if she'd stepped off the face of the earth.

But he'd finally found her. The problem was, it seemed too late. She was dead. Which meant that she'd probably taken their secret to the grave. It filled him with regret. He would have loved to look into her eyes one last time before he killed her.

He took her photo, stuck a pin between her eyes and put it up on the bulletin board next to his desk. As he started to throw the rest of the newspaper away, his gaze lit on the name *Clementine* again.

It appeared to be a real estate ad. Moving the paper where he could see the ad, he saw that it read *Clementine Place*. His breath came out on a laugh. Of course.

She'd owned a house and now it was for sale. A house where she'd kept her secrets. He told himself not to get his hopes up, and yet he was reaching for his phone since it was still early out in Montana.

Francesca's house was for sale? Why hadn't he thought of that? There were some things she wouldn't have been able to take with her. That is, if she'd still had them when she'd died. She could have gone through everything a long time ago. Probably had. But there was only one way to find out.

He dialed the number of the Realtor who was selling the house. The newspaper was a week old. The house could have sold by now.

A woman named Mary Sue Linton answered on the third ring.

"I'm calling about a house you have for sale," he said. "I believe it's called Clementine Place?"

"That's right. It just went on the market. What can I tell you about it?"

He had the photo of the house in front of him. But he couldn't imagine Baby Doll living somewhere like that. It was too common after the penthouse they'd shared. It all came down to that one question that had niggled at him all these years. Why? Why take off like she had—let alone end up where she had? Which led to his second big question. What had she done with what she'd stolen from him?

"I'd like to send someone to look at it in the next few days," he said. "Is that possible?"

"It's not quite ready to show."

Really? "I don't care what kind of shape it's in."

"One of the relatives is in the process of cleaning everything out. I'm afraid Frannie was a…collector." Yes, she'd collected a few things from him before she'd left. "But the house will be pristine in a few weeks if you'd like to see it then."

Frannie? "You say a relative is cleaning it out?"

"Her granddaughter, Annabelle."

His old heart thumped hard against his ribs. What if she'd already thrown it out? She had to be stopped. "Then I'll check back with you."

"That would be ideal."

He hung up and made a call. "I need to see you. *Now*."

Oh, Baby Doll, he said to himself as he disconnected. The woman had thought she'd outfoxed him. Soon she would be turning over in her grave. As for her granddaughter, she could be joining Frannie very soon.

Chapter Three

Dawson hadn't driven by the old Clementine place in years. After he'd cleaned up, he'd driven into town since there was still some daylight left in the winter day and his brother had called wanting to hear about his hunting trip. He'd told himself he wasn't going near Annabelle's grandmother's house, but it was as if his pickup had a mind of its own.

There was a time that this neighborhood had been his second home. That was back when his best friend lived two doors down from Frannie Clementine's house. Back when he and his best friend had built a tree house only to find five-year-old Annabelle in it and unable to get down.

With a bark of a laugh, he reminded himself that she hadn't been filled with gratitude that time he'd saved her, either.

He slowed his pickup, surprised how long it had been since he'd driven through this neighborhood. His best friend had moved away years ago and once Annabelle left…

The house, on so-called Millionaire's Row on the west side of town, sat on a huge lot surrounded by massive trees. Behind it, the water of the Milk River curved slowly past. An old single-car garage stood off to the side, looking like it needed to be torn down.

He pulled up on the opposite side of the street. There was a For Sale sign in the yard, which shouldn't have come as a surprise. Mystery solved. Of course that was what had brought Annabelle back. She was planning to get rid of the house—the only thing still tethering her to Whitehorse now that her grandmother was gone.

Pulling under the protective boughs of a huge evergreen, he left the engine running and took in the home. He was wondering what Annabelle could get for the place when he saw a woman in a bandanna, a gaudy sweatshirt and a pair of baggy jeans come out. She carried a large box out the front door to the side of the porch closest to the driveway. Even from a distance, he could tell that the woman was covered in dust and dirt. So Annabelle had hired help. That, too, shouldn't have surprised him, although he didn't recognize the woman.

As she set the box at the open end of the porch, she stood to stretch, as if her back bothered her. A lock of blond hair escaped from beneath the bandanna. With a shock, he realized what he was seeing. *Annabelle?*

The sight of the supermodel looking like a janitor made him laugh and shake his head in disbelief. He was tempted to take a photo with his cell phone. But he could just imagine how horrified she would be if he did. He had barely recognized her, and not just because he suspected Annabelle had never done a day's manual labor in her life. Surely she wasn't packing up the entire house by herself.

But as he looked around, he saw that the only vehicle

near the place was the silver sports car. Nor did anyone else emerge from the house carrying boxes as he sat watching, truck engine running. Why hadn't she hired help? It was so unlike her.

A thought struck him like a swift kick to the shin. She'd said she'd forgotten to get gas, but what if… The idea was so preposterous that he laughed out loud as he put his pickup into gear to drive away. Whatever Annabelle was up to, it had nothin' to do with him. He didn't even know why he'd driven by.

His cell phone rang, making him jump. He really wasn't good at this cloak-and-dagger stuff. He hit the brakes and quickly answered as he watched Annabelle put down another box, stretch and go back inside. As she glanced in his direction, he slowly let out the clutch and eased the pickup down the street, making sure he kept his head turned. The last thing he wanted was for her to think that he had any interest in her.

"You on your way?" his brother asked without pre-amble.

He'd lost track of time. "I am. Be right there." He disconnected, hoping his brother's invitation was only about having a beer. The way news traveled around this county, by now everyone could know that Annabelle Clementine was back in town—his brother Luke included. And that was a subject he didn't want to discuss.

Luke was already sitting on a bar stool at the Mint when he walked in. Seeing him coming, Luke ordered him a Moose Drool and patted the stool next to him. "Some pretty nice weather for November, huh?"

"Uh-huh," Dawson said, groaning inside. Luke was

grinning like a jackass and it had nothing to do with the weather.

"Annabelle Clementine is back in town," his brother blurted, as if unable to hold it in a second longer.

"Who?" Dawson asked innocently and took a sip of the beer the bartender set in front of him. Luke was as subtle as a horseshoe to the head. At least he'd been smart enough to know that Dawson would need a beer.

"Who?" Luke echoed. "Annabelle Clementine, or as you used to call her… Annie. You aren't going to tell me that you've forgotten about the woman who—" His brother stopped and gave him a you-had-me-there-for-a-minute grin. "So, you already heard?" He sounded disappointed.

"Actually, I saw her."

"No kiddin'? She still gorgeous? She say why she's back?"

Dawson ran his thumb around the top of his beer bottle for a moment. Something stopped him from telling his brother about siphoning gas out of his pickup to practically fill her fancy sports car. "Saw her packing up at her grandmother's house. She's got the place for sale." He took a sip of his beer.

"You just happened to be in that neighborhood, did you?" Luke couldn't seem to get that goofy grin off his face. "She say how long she's staying?"

"I said I *saw* her. Didn't say I made a point of talking to her. So I wouldn't know, but I think it's a pretty good assumption that she'll be hightailing it out of town just as quickly as she can," he said without looking at his brother.

"Why didn't you talk to her?" Luke asked.

"Why would I?"

"After all these years, I would think you'd be curious. Maybe it isn't just her grandmother's house that brought her back. Maybe—"

"It's just her grandmother's house."

"You can't know that. Maybe—"

"So, what's the plan for tomorrow?" Dawson asked, hoping to change the subject. Thinking about Annabelle gave him a headache. Talking about her was even worse. It had been years since he'd called her Annie, let alone allowed himself to even say the word. Annie was the woman he fell in love with. Annabelle was…well, she was a supermodel he didn't know, didn't want to know.

"Tomorrow?" Luke asked, as if confused by the quick change of subject.

"Thanksgiving Day."

"Don't remind me." Luke took a drink of his beer, clearly upset that this was all he was going to get. He sighed. "I haven't gotten my deer yet. But you know Mom. Said not to be late. She's invited some of the neighbors."

Dawson nodded, smiling to himself at the thought of their mother. There was no one quite like Wilhelmina "Willie" Rogers. She'd managed to raise both of her sons on her own after their father died when they were boys—and run the ranch, as well. When it came to anyone who needed a hot meal, Willie was always ready to rustle something up. His mother equated love with food. She spent half her time making casseroles for anyone who'd fallen on hard times or families who'd had an illness. Anyone in town die? The family would have a dish on their doorstep within the hour.

"Mom said we both better be there," Luke said. "She already read me the riot act about going deer hunting beforehand. Speaking of hunting, how'd you do down in the Breaks? Get anything worth bringing home and stringin' up?"

Dawson shook his head. "I saw one big buck, but didn't get a shot." The truth was, he loved hiking around looking for deer and elk, but when he still had plenty of meat in the freezer, he wasn't much for killing anything. He wasn't a trophy hunter.

Two weeks in hunting camp with some buddies, though, was a tradition he wasn't apt to miss. He liked sleeping out under the stars, working his way through rugged country during the day, eating food cooked over a camp stove and sitting around the fire later, listening to his friends' outrageous stories before climbing into his bedroll. He always slept like the dead at hunting camp.

Not that he wasn't glad to get home to a hot shower and his own bed.

"Any idea how much the old Clementine place might go for?" Luke asked.

"Haven't given it any thought."

"Still, you have to admit it's strange that Annabelle wouldn't let Mary Sue handle it so she didn't have to come back here," Luke said. His brother was dating Mary Sue's younger sister, Sally. "Unless the house wasn't the only reason she's back," he said, clearly baiting him. "Kinda makes you wonder, doesn't it?"

"What makes me wonder is what *your* interest in all this is," Dawson said and looked over at his brother.

"Actually, I find your apparent so-called *lack* of interest more fascinating. You don't think I didn't know how you felt about her? Now she's back. You aren't even going to stop by her place and talk to her?" Luke shook his head. "My big brother, as it turns out, is a coward."

"It's not going to work," Dawson said and drained the rest of his beer.

"The brother I knew would have given his left arm for that woman," Luke said. "He wouldn't pass up a possible second chance to be with her. You telling me you don't still feel somethin'?"

Dawson shook his head as he stood. "I'm not tellin' you anything. I'll let my walkin' out of here speak for itself. Thanks for the beer."

Luke sighed. "Fine, have it your way, you stubborn jackass. But you're going to be sorry."

"I've been sorry before. Tell Mom I'll stop by early tomorrow to see if she needs any help."

"You always have to be the good son, don't you? I'm going deer huntin'. Save me a place at the table just in case I get something and run late." The door closed on his last words.

Even as Dawson started his pickup, he knew he was going to do it. And it made him madder than hell. He turned down the street. It wasn't late, but it was already dark this time of year. Deep shadows hunkered in the trees. The temperature had dropped.

As he drove by her house, he saw that the light was on. There were more boxes stacked up under the porch roof. He turned out his headlights as he stopped across the street again. Several large pines blocked most of the house, but he would get glimpses of her inside working.

There was still no sign of anyone helping her. "What's going on, Annie?" he asked in the dark cab of his truck.

If she didn't get out of town before the next snowstorm, she probably wouldn't be able to in that impractical car of hers. He doubted she had snow tires on it since she'd been living in California. Not that they would help much. A car like that would get high-centered on the first snowdrift across the highway. Hell, she'd be lucky if she could get out of her driveway.

Dawson reminded himself that it wasn't his problem. And yet he couldn't help thinking about what his brother had said back at the bar. Unfortunately, he'd already been a fool when it came to her. He liked to think he was too smart to do it again as he watched her pass in front of the large picture window. She looked exhausted. How many hours had she been packing up her grandmother's things by herself?

But even from this distance, he could see the determination in her expression, in the way she moved. There had never been a more stubborn woman, he thought, as he turned on his headlights again and headed for the ranch.

ANNABELLE HURT ALL OVER. She closed another box on more of her grandmother's chipped and cracked knick-knacks, but realized she was too tired to take it out to the porch. For hours, she'd been boxing up her grandmother's junk. Now she looked around the room with growing discouragement. She'd thought she was making progress, but she hadn't even made a dent in all this…stuff.

Earlier she'd removed what she could from the front bedroom. Her grandmother had been using the one in the back of the house opposite the shared bathroom. Apparently, she'd turned the bedroom Annabelle had chosen into an extra wardrobe. An array of ugly, gaudy sweat-shirts was hanging in the closet. Each was bedazzled with anything shiny you could tack onto it. Where did the woman find these horrific things? A lot of them were seasonal, with Santas, elves, Christmas lights, overdeco-rated wreaths, even an Easter egg one that was so bright it could put an eye out.

Not wanting to ruin the last of the good clothes that she hadn't sold to pay for the trip north, she'd changed into one of the less garish ones, a sweatshirt with a be-jeweled clown face, along with a pair of her grandmoth-er's pull-on jeans that she had to tie around her waist so they'd stay up, a pair of sneakers and socks with lacy tops. They'd do to work in.

After she'd decluttered the bedroom, she cleaned. She'd discovered some laundered sheets and made the bed so it would be ready for tonight. Then she'd gone down to the recycling building in town and loaded as many boxes as she could into her car by putting smaller ones into larger ones and holding some out the window as she drove.

Back at the house, she'd started dumping the worst of the junk into boxes and carrying them out to the porch.

Now she just wanted to sit down. *You were so right, Mary Sue. I really could have used some help.* But not at thirty dollars an hour. And no one was going to work for her with only the promise of getting paid *after* the house sold.

She wandered into the kitchen, one of the only rooms that had chairs that weren't covered with junk. As full as the place was, she couldn't help but be thankful to her grandmother. Frannie had never had a lot of money, but in the will she'd made sure that the taxes and utilities were paid six months in advance.

Clearly, she'd known what a job it was going to be to clean out this house and sell it.

Brushing an errant lock of hair back from her dirty face, Annabelle wondered if her grandmother had also somehow figured that she was going to need financial help. Six months was generous. Frannie had to have known that Annabelle wouldn't be staying that long. But it definitely allowed her time to get the house sold.

She glanced around the kitchen, tempted to fill another box with the ceramic knickknacks that crowded the windowsill. Her grandmother had saved *everything*. Was it an old lady thing? Or had her grandmother lost her mind before the end? She couldn't understand how the woman had been able to live here with junk piled waist high throughout the house. It seemed at odds with the woman who'd raised Annabelle most of her life.

But it was also odd that her grandmother had willed the house to her and not her sisters. It still bothered her. "Why, Grandma Frannie? Why leave the house to just me?" she asked the knickknacks. Several frogs looked back at her with big, dusty eyes. Maybe TJ was right. Frannie had left the house to the granddaughter she thought would need the most help.

At the time, Annabelle had been furious at such an insinuation. Now she wondered if her grandmother hadn't been the only one who'd expected her to fail. Maybe everyone had seen it coming but Annabelle herself.

For whatever the reason, this house was now hers and unless she got it sold and soon… She shook her head, stood and reached for the ceramic bric-a-brac.

Her stomach rumbled. She hadn't even thought about food—until this moment. For years she'd had to watch her weight. She still wasn't used to being able to eat anything she wanted. Now she could give in to her hunger. It was a new feeling. One that signaled more than anything that she would never be modeling again. Too bad she couldn't afford to eat.

She pushed that thought away. Looking down at the hideous clothes she was wearing, she told herself that she couldn't go to the grocery store, even in Whitehorse, in this outfit—even if she had any cash. She stood for a moment, feeling lost and close to tears. As she put one of the ceramic creatures into the box she was loading, she spied a container that her grandmother had used for her grocery money.

She was reminded of the time Grandma Frannie had caught her red-handed with her fingers in it and felt a stab of remorse for even having thought about taking the money, let alone getting caught. But mostly what she felt was regret that she hadn't come back to see the grandmother who'd loved her so much.

That day, her hand literally in the cookie jar, Annabelle had fished around for an excuse. Her grandmother had stopped her and said, "If you're going to steal, then own it. Same with getting caught," her grandmother had said. "Lying and sniveling makes you look weak."

With a sigh, she now lifted the lid of the container, telling herself it would be empty. Reaching inside, her fingers brushed something. She pulled out a handful of crinkled-up twenties and began to cry.

"Grandma," she said, her voice breaking. She swallowed the lump in her throat and wiped at her tears.

Frannie had known she was going to need money. She *was* the one her grandmother had known would fail. As much as that hurt, her heart filled to bursting with love for her grandmother, who was still looking out for her after all these years. Because someone needed to, that was for sure.

There were enough bills to keep her from going hungry for a while. She said a whispered thank-you to her grandmother and glanced at her watch. Did she really have the energy to shower and change to go to the grocery store to get something to eat?

The answer was a resounding no. If she sneaked in and out of the only grocery store in town quickly, hopefully she wouldn't see anyone she knew.

ROBERT "ROB" MCDOUGAL saw that it was his uncle calling and ignored the call. The old mobster probably just wanted to bitch about the way-too-expensive assisted-living facility where he'd been the past four years.

Since Rob was paying almost twenty grand a month to keep him in the resort-like place, he didn't have much sympathy. It was a deal his old man had made with the "family."

Rob wasn't stupid enough to renege on the agreement, since that would get him killed. But he didn't have to listen to the old man's constant complaining. Nor was he in the mood to indulge his uncle.

But when his phone rang once again and he saw that it was Bernie calling yet another time, he finally listened to the original message his uncle had left.

"I have a job for you. A real one. Get your butt out here. This is urgent family business."

Urgent family business? Rob groaned. What now? He didn't bother to call his uncle back. He simply texted that he was on his way to Golden Years Retirement Living and Spa.

The moment he walked into his uncle's room, the old codger patted the arm of his wheelchair and said, "Let's take a walk."

In his uncle's generation that might have meant he was about to die. But he didn't think Bernie had a gun on him or a garrote or even a butter knife from the kitchen. But you never knew.

"What's this about?" Rob asked impatiently as he pushed the old man's wheelchair out to the canal after getting a special pass at the main desk to do so. It was hot as hell, even though it was late at night, but it often was this far south. Florida. He hated it. He missed the change of seasons up north. But as long as Bernie was alive… And the old codger didn't seem to be aging in the least.

"Isn't this far enough?" Rob asked, swatting at a mosquito as he kept an eye out for alligators. Each year down here alligators attacked ten people on average. They snatched pets from the sides of pools, grabbed little kids and even ate a few adults, twenty-three since 1948, he'd read. Walking along the canal always made him nervous.

His uncle finally signaled they could stop. Looking around he checked to make sure they were alone. They were. Rob was losing patience. His shirt was soaked with sweat and sticking to his back. He swatted at another bug flying around his head and swore under his breath.

"The Marco Polo Heist," Bernie said.

Rob felt his stomach twist. He'd grown up without a father because of that heist. Everything had gone perfectly until an off-duty guard had shown up. His father and one of the other thieves had been killed. Only one of the thieves had gotten away clean—Bernie. The cops had known Bernie was involved but they'd never been able to prove it.

Bernie had walked away with the loot—which was never recovered since, according to his uncle, it had been stolen right out from under his nose. It had been the only black stain on the mobster's otherwise glowing criminal career—and something that remained stuck in the old man's craw.

"I have a lead on the goods," his uncle said.

After more than fifty years and a lot of blind alleys and wild-goose chases? Rob stared at him. "It just came to you?"

Bernie cuffed him in the back. "Don't be a damned fool. I know you think I'm getting senile, but I'm as sharp as a shank."

Right, Rob thought as he watched the old man dig a newspaper clipping out of his pocket.

"That's her," his uncle said, handing him the black-and-white photo. "Francesca Clementine." When Rob had no reaction, he added impatiently, "Baby Doll."

The notorious Baby Doll. Rob wanted to laugh. He'd had to hear about her all of his adult life. The moll who'd broken Bernie's heart and stolen a king's fortune from him.

"That's her?" He couldn't help being skeptical. They'd been here before.

His uncle nodded and handed him the obit. He read

it, trying not to roll his eyes. "Whitehorse, Montana?" He couldn't be serious.

Bernie smiled. "Her house is coming up for sale."

"You want me to buy the house?"

"Hell, no. Too obvious. We don't want to call attention to any of this. The Feds are still watching me." Rob doubted this but said nothing. "There are too many people still looking for the loot, you know what I'm saying?"

Just like they were still looking for Jimmy Hoffa.

"You need to leave right away," Bernie said, keeping his voice down, apparently afraid the Feds were listening from the mangroves beyond the canal. They'd had to come all the way out here by the canal with the wild alligators because his uncle was convinced that his room was bugged. "I think you can handle this alone. Better that way."

Rob nodded, telling himself he wasn't going to Montana on some wild-goose chase.

"I'm depending on you," Bernie said and grabbed his hand to squeeze it hard. "I trust you, Robby."

"Rob," he corrected for the millionth time. Nor had he been chosen because his uncle trusted him. There was no one else who would do it. He had been appointed his uncle's babysitter. Not that the family didn't still fear Bernie. The old man had his connections. It was why Rob came when his uncle called, eventually. But Montana?

The doctor had said Bernie didn't have more than a year to live. But that was four years ago. Tough as old pigskin and meaner than a junkyard dog, the old man had defied modern science with just stubborn determination alone, Rob thought.

"I'm honored that you would trust me to take care of this," he said.

His uncle chuckled and met his eye. "Honored. And smart. You know what will happen to you if you don't come back with my goods."

His goods. Arrogant bastard. "Let's say this dame is your... Baby Doll."

"Don't call her a dame, okay?"

"What if she still didn't have any of it when she died?" Rob asked for the sake of argument. "What if she's been selling it off? After all, it's been over fifty years."

Bernie shook his head. "I would have heard if any of it had turned up. She took all of it, the cash, the jewels, the gold. I'm betting she still had it when she died. Just to show me," he said, admiration in his tone. "She willed the house to one of her granddaughters, someone named Annabelle Clementine. The Realtor made it sound like I should know who she was."

Rob shrugged. "Never heard of her."

"Apparently she's getting the house ready to sell. Take care of her and soon. She might throw out something not realizing what it is. Just don't call attention to yourself or her. I shouldn't have to spell it out for you."

"No," Rob said. But he hadn't done any wet work in years. He didn't want to start again. "Tomorrow is Thanksgiving—"

His uncle shot him a look of disbelief and the rest of the words in Rob's mouth dried up. "When you find my loot you'll want to take off with the whole lot, but you won't. You know why?"

He shook his head even though they'd had this discussion before, since his uncle never got tired of telling him.

"Because there's a curse on the loot, but nothing like the curse that would be on you. Take me back to my room and then get on a plane. You can't waste any time. If that house sells before you get there…or the grand-daughter finds the goods…"

Rob nodded since there was nothing else he could do.

"There's one more thing," Bernie said. "I doubt I'm the only one to recognize Baby Doll. Nor am I the only one who's been looking all these years." Rob doubted that was the case but kept his trap shut. "Which means you won't be alone even if the Feds aren't wise to her. There's the insurance company guy who had to pay out all those years ago, not to mention the museum cura-tor who swore he'd get his priceless jewels back and see me in prison."

Rob didn't bother to mention that both of those guys were probably dead by now.

"So watch your back," his uncle said. "If they rec-ognized Baby Doll like I did… You know our photos were all over the society pages. Me and Baby Doll at the swankiest parties. She was some woman."

DAWSON KICKED AROUND his house, unable to settle more than a few minutes in any one place. He'd cleaned the kitchen after making himself some dinner, washed his hunting clothing, unpacked all his gear and even put clean sheets on his bed.

He'd been looking forward to that bed all the way from the hunting camp, but even though he was bone-weary tired, he knew he wouldn't be able to sleep. Sadie didn't have that problem. She was curled up on her bed in front of the fireplace, snoring softly.

At a hard knock on his door, he started. His first thought was Annabelle. She'd come to thank him for the gas and apologize for not saying something earlier. His heart began to pound until he reminded himself how unlikely that was. He told himself it better not be Luke with more news about Annabelle. He thought about not answering the door, but the knock was so insistent...

He opened the door and blinked when he saw that it was his neighbor from the adjoining county. "Cull?"

"Sorry to bother you so late," the cowboy and horse rancher said. "I was riding fence earlier and you've got some barbed wire down that I thought I better warn you about. I did what I could, but I'm worried you're going to have cattle out on the county road if you can't get it fixed soon."

"Thanks for the heads-up." He liked Cull McGraw. He liked all the McGraws, actually, and was glad to have them as neighbors. Anyone else might not have bothered to tell him until his cattle were running wild. "You want to come in? I think there's a couple of beers in the fridge." Suddenly he didn't want to be alone.

"Thanks, but I need to get on home," Cull said, and he realized his neighbor was probably anxious to get home to his wife. "Maybe some other time."

He closed the door and turned back to his empty house. Empty. Funny, but he'd never thought of it that way until... He swore. Until Annabelle's return. Cursing himself, he began to turn out lights. After making sure the screen was on the fireplace, he headed for bed.

Behind him, he heard the soft patter of four feet as Sadie decided to join him. He told himself the pup was all he needed for company as he heard her lie down on the floor at the foot of his bed.

But the moment he was between the cool sheets, his thoughts spun back to Annabelle, his first love, his first lover. What was he going to have to do to get her out of his system?

Chapter Four

Whitehorse, Montana. Rob swore as he sat for a moment in the dark in the parking lot of the expensive nursing home. Unfortunately, this wasn't the first time Bernie had been convinced he'd found Baby Doll. Before, it had been some old woman in Maine. Then one in California. Another in Maryland. Oh, and that one in Tennessee.

Now Whitehorse, Montana? He'd gone on too many wild-goose chases, all of them dead ends. None of the women had been Baby Doll. None of them had had the loot. All they had in common was that they were six feet under now.

He pulled the photocopied snapshot and obit from his pocket and looked at them again. Francesca Clementine? At least he wouldn't have to kill this one—she was already dead. But the granddaughter wasn't, he reminded himself.

He debated not going and telling the old man that he had and that Francesca Clementine wasn't his Baby Doll. It would break the old man's heart, but it wasn't the first time. After all, what were the chances that this Francesca Clementine had even been to New York City, let alone had a love affair with a mobster and stolen a king's ransom in already stolen loot? Less than nil.

So why waste his time? Just give it a few days and then report back to Bernie… It was a gamble, though. He suspected the old man had Alzheimer's or dementia and his brain was more pickled than his aunt's canned beets.

But that didn't mean Bernie wasn't dangerous. He still could make Rob's life a living hell. That's if he didn't just cut bait and have Rob killed.

He considered what to do. The old man was crazy. If he found out that Rob hadn't gone to Montana…

Swearing, he pulled out his cell phone and called the airport for a ticket to the closest airport—Billings, Montana, some three hours away from Whitehorse.

This, he thought, was going to be the worst wildgoose chase ever. Montana in the winter. For the granddaughter's sake, he hoped the old man had gotten it wrong again and he could prove it quickly.

ANNABELLE'S PLAN, WHEN SHE left California had been to sneak back into town, if at all possible. She'd thought she could sell her grandmother's house and be gone before anyone noticed. Now, as she drove the few blocks to the grocery, she realized how foolish that had been.

Whitehorse was so small that it didn't even have a stoplight. The closest big-box store was three hours away—and that was when the roads weren't icy or under construction. To say that the small rural town was in the middle of nowhere was an understatement. Sometimes in the winter the highways out of town would close because of a blizzard and they'd be trapped until the plows could get through.

That was one of Annabelle's worries. That she would get snowed in here before she could sell her grandmother's house and she ran completely out of money. Meanwhile, she just hoped she didn't see anyone she knew. But the way she was dressed, she hardly recognized herself, she thought, as she straightened the bandanna she'd decided to leave covering her blond hair.

Parking at the side of the grocery store, she turned off the engine and sat for a moment. Only a few people came and went. It was late and the store would close soon. She saw a few older people who could have been familiar but they didn't pay her any mind. A couple of teenaged boys eyed her car, but didn't give her a second glance.

Her stomach growling, she finally climbed out, locked her car and headed inside. Whitehorse was the kind of place where everyone returned the grocery carts. No one would dream of leaving theirs outside for fear someone would see them and they'd be the talk of the town.

Once inside the store, everyone was always very polite. There was no cart bumping, no angry looks, let alone words. This was Whitehorse. People here were beyond civilized.

Fortunately, the first aisle she went down was empty of people. She considered what she needed. Some time ago, on one of those rare occasions when she'd had too much to drink and was feeling nostalgic, she'd called home. Her grandmother had told her that the biggest news in town was that the grocery store had expanded to include a deli.

But the store still seemed small, the aisles narrow, and at one corner of the store, she swore the floor dropped a good three inches toward the back wall. Now that she was here, she felt overwhelmed. She'd never cooked, even though her grandmother had encouraged her to learn.

"You might be hungry someday," Frannie had said, making Annabelle realize that her grandmother had apparently seen this all coming.

Her sister TJ loved to cook. Chloe loved to bake. Annabelle had realized early on that there was no need for her to learn either skill if someone else cooked and baked. Even at a young age, she'd believed she would never have to cook for herself—not with the life she had planned—and that had been the case. For a while.

Faced with fending for herself in the kitchen now, she didn't know where to begin. Her grandmother had gone down to the senior center for her meals. Food-wise, the cupboards were bare.

Catching a whiff of something that smelled already cooked, she followed her nose and was delighted to find the new deli. She peered through the glass, her mouth watering, even though the deli was a far cry from the grocery stores she was used to.

"I'll take some of that," she said pointing at the breaded chicken. "And some of that," she said of chopped salad. Not having to worry about calories anymore, she feared she wouldn't be able to stop once she started eating real food again. She pointed out a few more things and happily put the containers in her cart.

"I should get something for breakfast," she said to herself spying the pastries. Lemon-filled donuts. Cream-cheese-laced rolls. Maple sticks. She hadn't faced such tough decisions in years.

"Annabelle?"

The voice behind her made her freeze in mid-drool. The years seemed to disappear and she was a tongue-tied, knobby-kneed teen again.

As she turned, Wilhelmina Rogers said, "If it isn't my favorite almost daughter-in-law." Dawson's mother threw her arms around her, hugging her as if she hadn't seen her in years. She hadn't.

Almost daughter-in-law. "Willie." It was all she could get out. Willie's reaction to seeing her again was surprising. Shocking, actually. Annabelle had just assumed that Willie would hate her after what she did to Dawson. The woman's greeting made her feel…loved and forgiven and guilty. Tears filled her eyes as she was enveloped by the long and lean ranchwoman's strong arms.

"Let me look at you," Willie said as she held Annabelle at arm's length and gave her the once-over. "You look good enough to eat, although I'm going to have to fatten you up before I do," she said with a hearty laugh. She instantly sobered. "Seriously, it is so good to see you."

All Annabelle could do was nod and fight tears. She'd always loved Dawson's mom. Maybe if things had been different… Who was she kidding? Maybe if *she'd* been different. Maybe if she'd wanted something different. But back then, staying in Whitehorse hadn't been an option. It would have felt like settling. It would have felt as if she wasn't good enough to leave and make it. Like she would have failed without even trying. Did she really feel all that different, even now?

"I expect to see you at my house tomorrow at 11:45 a.m. on the dot," Willie ordered.

"Tomorrow?" Annabelle parroted, feeling off-balance and confused.

"Thanksgiving! Don't even bother arguing. You don'̶
show up, I'll send one of my ranch hands to get you. ̶
mean it. You're coming." Willie patted Annabelle's arm.
"I'm so glad you're back. You remember the way out to
the ranch, don't you?"

She nodded, choked up. The last thing she wanted
to do was have Thanksgiving at the ranch with her ex-
almost-fiancé.

"Luke said something about them going huntin' so
I'll need your help," Willie said, as if to let her know
Dawson probably wouldn't be there. Apparently thinking it was all settled, Willie breezed off with a cart overflowing with food. She'd made it sound as if Annabelle
showing up for Thanksgiving was doing *her* the favor.
That was Willie.

But just the thought of one of Willie's meals made
her stomach rumble. Also, she had no doubt that the
woman would do exactly what she said she would, send
a hired hand after her. So Annabelle knew she had no
choice. She'd be back on the Rogers Ranch tomorrow
for Thanksgiving—just like old times.

Except Dawson would be hunting with his brother
instead of sitting next to her.

What had she just agreed to? Reaching into the bak-
ery display, she grabbed a package of assorted donuts,
one each of all her favorites. Now if she could just get
out of this store without anyone else recognizing her.

Mary Sue had tried a half dozen times to reach her
mother. When Carla answered, she recalled that her
mother had gone shopping in Havre for the day.

"I just saw all your messages," her mother said.

"What was so important that I had to call you the moment I got home?"

In the background she could hear that her mother was putting away groceries. "The old Clementine place. Have you ever been inside it?"

"No, why? I heard it's a mess and that Frannie collected everything under the sun. Is it in terrible shape inside?"

"Full to the brim, but there is something odd. On the plans from the county office, it shows that there was once an alcove off the kitchen."

"So, what is there now?" her mother asked as she worked.

"A wall."

Carla stopped putting away her groceries. "A wall?"

"It's as if there never was an alcove."

She heard her mother sit down heavily. "Why would someone close off an alcove?"

"That's what I want to know."

"You sure the planning office didn't give you the wrong house?"

"I'm sure. I even went back down there this afternoon and double-checked. There was definitely an alcove there about three wide by six feet long and eight foot high." Just large enough to hide a body. Or more bodies, if you stacked them, she thought, but didn't say.

"That is definitely odd," her mother agreed. "It shouldn't hurt the sale of the house, though. Annabelle is going to leave the wall, isn't she?"

"I got that impression. Still, it's kind of spooky, don't you think?"

"Oh, Mary Sue," her mother said, clearly hefting

herself to her feet again. "Stop watching those zombie shows all the time. Why don't you come over and help me bake the pies? I'm dead on my feet."

Why not? "Do you need me to bring anything?"

Her mother had grown quiet, as if thinking about the question Mary Sue had asked her. But when she spoke it had nothing to do with Thanksgiving pies.

"You know, it didn't come out until she died, but Frannie never married."

"But I thought her husband died before she moved to Whitehorse?"

"But there'd been a man in her life, her son's father. So who was he?"

"Don't know. As far as I heard, Frannie never even dated, although Inez told me that she saw a man over there one time. Never saw him again."

Mary Sue was more interested in why Frannie had closed up that alcove. "Maybe she killed the man and walled him up in the alcove."

"Oh, Mary Sue, Frannie wouldn't hurt a fly."

"That's what Annabelle said." But Mary Sue couldn't help but wonder what—or who—might be behind that wall. People often surprised you, especially the innocent-looking ones, she'd found.

Chapter Five

Annabelle felt sick as she pulled into her driveway. She glanced over at the box of donuts on the passenger seat next to her. The box was almost empty. She hadn't even waited until she got home before she'd started in on them. Seeing Willie had upset her. It had brought back too many memories of Dawson. Too many memories in general.

She couldn't take her eyes off the remaining donuts, especially the last lemon-filled one. It had been years since she'd had a donut. Now that she had...

Hurriedly she slammed the lid closed on the ones that were left. Had she really thought she could sneak into town, sell the house, take care of her problems and slip out in the dead of night before anyone learned the truth?

"I'm such a fool," she said as she grabbed the donut box and the bag of food she'd ended up buying and exited her car. Earlier, she hadn't bothered locking the front door of the house and was glad now. Juggling everything, she managed to open the door and get inside without dropping the donut box.

Kicking the door closed behind her, she moved through the dark house toward the kitchen. Moonlight fingered its way through the open blinds, painting the floor and walls with bands of light and dark. She was fumbling for the kitchen light switch when she thought she heard something.

Suddenly the hair stood up on the back of her neck. She felt her eyes widen in alarm as her gaze slowly shifted to the far side of the kitchen and that stupid wall that wasn't supposed to be there. Enough moonlight came through the window over the sink to throw a ghostly white haze over the dated kitchen.

But it was the dark spot that held her gaze. She stared at *the wall* as her heart began to hammer in her chest. There appeared to be a stain on the lower half of it. Dark like…blood, she could hear Mary Sue say, as if something had leaked through from the other side.

That was impossible after all these years. But still… Annabelle took a step back and bumped into the counter making her drop one of the bags of groceries and let out a stifled scream. The bag with the milk, orange juice and coffee hit the floor with a loud crash.

Still her eyes were on the spot with the stain. It had to be just a trick of the moonlight. Just a strange shadow. She groped for the light switch, anxious to prove that that was all it was.

She managed to put down the rest of the groceries and the donut box on the counter, all the time keeping an eye on the stain as if she thought it might grow. Or worse, begin to seep out onto the faded linoleum floor.

Pulling out her cell phone, she dialed her sister Chloe as she kept looking for the overhead light switch. "Why didn't you and TJ stay at the house?" she demanded the moment her sister answered.

"Annabelle? Are you drunk? What time is it?" Chloe ,ounded as if she'd been asleep.

She glanced at the clock. It was only ten. But ten in Montana was midnight back East. "You heard me. Why didn't you stay in Grandmother's house?"

"So it's Grandmother's house now? I thought it was yours? You're the one who inherited it, as you are fond of telling us."

"You're not answering my question." She moved cautiously along the counter until she reached the wall with the light switch—right where she now remembered it being. She snapped it on, blinded for a moment by the sudden light that filled the kitchen. The spot on the wall disappeared. Disappeared as if it had never been there at all.

Her relief made her go weak, even as she felt foolish. Of course it had been just a trick of the light and dark. A shadow. What had made her think blood? Mary Sue. She shivered, though, since she still had a wall where an alcove had once been.

"We didn't want to stay in the house." Her sister sounded defensive.

"Why?"

"Why do you care?" Chloe demanded. "We don't talk for months and this is what you have to say to me?"

"Was there something in the house that…unnerved you?" Annabelle forced herself to ask. Forced herself to admit that the house spooked her. She wanted to throttle Mary Sue for telling her about the missing alcove, about old ladies who killed people and buried them who knew where, about school kids avoiding the place on Halloween night after her grandmother had died because they saw her ghost in the window.

"What's going on, Annabelle?"

She shook her head, exhausted, dirty and donut sick. She hadn't called her sisters when she'd gotten in trouble because they'd had a fight over the house and weren't talking. But she also hadn't wanted to admit that her career was over and she was flat broke. So there hadn't been anyone close to her to confide in, since her circle of so-called friends already knew and had disappeared. Disappeared like the stain on the wall, leaving her scared and alone.

"It's nothing. Everything is fine," she said, remembering her sisters' reactions when they'd gotten the news about their grandmother's will. She was still hurt and angry about the snotty things they'd said—even if they'd been true.

"So, you've sold the house."

"Not yet, but soon. I'm sorry I bothered you." She disconnected and stood staring at the wall. Why would her grandmother close off the alcove? What if there had never been an alcove?

She swore that if Mary Sue showed up tomorrow and admitted she'd had the wrong set of house plans, Annabelle would throttle her.

Chapter Six

"Did he get on a plane?" Bernie said into the phone as he pushed out of the wheelchair to the window.

"He did. I'm babysitting his cat."

"He has a cat?" Bernie realized how little he knew about his nephew, and yet he felt good about this errand he'd sent Robby on. This time he wasn't wrong. This time the woman really was Baby Doll. It surprised him that, more than getting back what she'd taken from him, he wanted to know why. Why she left him. Had it always only been about the money for her?

Bernie shook his gray head. He knew in his heart that couldn't be true. He'd loved her. Baby Doll had to have loved him. Robby had to find proof. Bernie couldn't die in peace until he knew.

"If you hear anything, let me know. I'm like on another planet in this place." As he disconnected, he happened to look down at his wastebasket. It hadn't been emptied, but the newspaper, the one from Whitehorse, Montana, was gone.

He was positive that he'd put it in the trash. But maybe he'd only thought about it. Getting old annoyed the devil out of him. His memory...it played tricks on him. He glanced around the room, sure the newspaper had to be here. Who would take the paper—with holes in it where he'd carefully, almost surgically removed sections?

His heart began to pound. The paper wasn't here. Realization settled in like crowbar to his gut. Someone had taken it from his wastebasket. He glanced toward the hall, thinking of his pretty, nice nurse. He shook his head. It hadn't been her. But he hadn't been paying close attention lately to new employees, new patients and their visitors, strangers on the property.

Damned if he wasn't getting old. He'd let his guard down, a mistake he would never have made when he was younger.

His legs suddenly felt weak. He moved to the wheelchair and dropped into it. His pulse thundered in his ears as he looked out toward the canal. Past it, he saw a boat moving slowly down the canal with two men in it and swore. Feds.

ANNABELLE WOKE AT daylight after a night of tossing and turning. The old bed sagged and groaned under her as she flung her feet over the side. Her head hurt and her stomach didn't feel all that great, either. But then again, that could have been the donuts.

After seeing what looked like a bloodstain on the wall in the kitchen and calling her sister, half in hysterics, she'd lost her appetite and gone straight to bed. Had she really eaten almost all of the donuts? Just the thought made her nauseous.

As she opened the bedroom door and padded across the hall to the bathroom, she couldn't shake off the weird dreams she'd had during the night. They seemed to float in and fade out like a weak radio station.

She shivered as she sat down on the cold toilet seat. One dream was more real than any of the other bits and pieces that kept coming back to her. Grandma Frannie had been standing at the end of her bed last night, looking so real and alive that Annabelle had been terrified. Worse, her grandmother had spoken to her.

I know you wonder why I left the house only to you. I'm sorry, but you're the only one can handle it. You're the one most like me. Your sisters can't deal with the truth about what's behind that wall.

Now Annabelle laughed with a shake of her head. It was obvious where that dream had come from. Mary Sue and all those crazy things she'd been saying.

Finishing her business, she padded back to the bedroom and pulled on the same dirty clothes as yesterday. She didn't see much reason to look for more ugly clothes to wear to clean out this place.

As she padded barefoot across the bedroom floor, one of the boards creaked loudly, reminding her of all the moaning and groaning the house had done last night. She didn't remember it being this bad when she was young. Or maybe that, too, had been part of the dream.

She took another step and felt the floorboard under her give a little. Looking down, she saw that the board appeared to be loose. Leaning closer, she made out a scratch mark at the end where it looked as if someone had used a screwdriver on it. To pry it up?

Kneeling down, she tried to work it free with her fingers. It moved enough that she had no doubt it would come loose—with a little help. In the kitchen she didn't locate a screwdriver, but she did find a butter knife.

Back in the bedroom, she knelt on the floor again and pried at the end where she'd noticed the scratches in the wood. The board popped up, bringing with it an old-house smell. She hesitated. There could be all kinds of creepy-crawly things under there.

Still, she carefully lifted the floorboard, aware of the spiderwebs stuck to it. Setting it aside, she cautiously peered down into the space below. Under the floorboards was another board. While the space was dusty and filled with cobwebs, she thought she saw something pushed back out of sight. Grimacing, she reached down and pulled out a battered metal box.

With a cleaning rag she'd been using yesterday, she removed the spiderwebs and dust on the box. Sitting down she pulled it between her legs and tried to open it. Locked.

She picked up the butter knife and had just gone to work on the lock when she heard the doorbell ring. As she looked out, she saw an old man standing out there. He wore a baseball cap on his short white hair. His coat was red-and-black checked wool, and he appeared to be wearing a dress shirt under it.

He rang the bell again. She thought about staying where she was behind the corner of the curtains until he went away, but he seemed determined as he rang the bell yet another time. He glanced toward her car and seemed ready to keep ringing until someone answered.

With a groan, Annabelle got to her feet. She stuck the box into one of the dresser drawers and went to the front door, patting at her hair as she went. Whatever the man was selling, she wasn't buying.

"Yes?" she asked briskly as she flung open the door. "I'm sorry but I'm really busy and—"

"You must be Annabelle," the man said as he smiled and leaned on his cane. She hadn't seen the cane from the window. Nor had she been able to see his face clearly. He looked to be in his late seventies or early eighties, though fit.

"You're just as your grandmother described you," he was saying.

It was worse than she'd originally thought. He wasn't just some random passerby. The slacks and dress shoes should have been a dead giveaway. Men in Whitehorse wore dressy boots and jeans to everything from a wedding to a funeral.

This man must be the pastor from the church her grandmother attended. Or a well-meaning member of the congregation who wanted to invite her to Sunday services.

"I'm sensing that your grandmother didn't tell you about me," the man said. "Where are my manners? I'm Lawrence Clarkston. Your grandmother's…boyfriend."

"Boyfriend?"

The man laughed. "Male companion?"

"You and grandmother…" She didn't know what to say. Frannie had a beau? After all these years? Clearly, he wasn't from around here. Something about the man made her nervous. He kept trying to see past her into the house. "I should get back to work."

"I can see that you're busy." He glanced over her shoulder again. "Packing up her things, huh? Looks like quite a job. I'd be happy to help. If I could just come in for a minute—"

"Thanks, but I have it."

"If you're sure," he said. "I'll come some other time." The man turned back toward the street, leaning heavily on his cane as he headed for a dark car parked at the curb, making her wonder how many secrets her grandmother had kept from her.

DAWSON TOOK OFF his Stetson to shoo the last of the cows back onto Rogers Ranch property before going to work on the fence. The sun was barely up, just hitting the tops of the Little Rockies. The November air was cold enough that he wished he were in front of his kitchen woodstove having another cup of coffee.

But he'd been awake for hours after a long night of tossing and turning. He didn't need to search for a reason for his unrest. Annabelle Clementine. That she'd haunted his dreams only made him more angry with himself. He'd thought he'd put that woman out of his life for good and now she showed up back in town?

He cursed under his breath as he pulled his chain saw from the bed of his truck and cranked it up. A tree had fallen and taken out a portion of his barbed-wire fence. He made short work of cutting up the tree and tossing the firewood into the back of the pickup. Sadie watched from inside the cab, barking at the cows that came over to see what was going on.

As he was loading the chain saw, his brother drove up. For a moment, he thought Luke had come to help. But then he noticed that Luke wasn't alone. His girlfriend,

Sally, was with him, and his brother was clad in hunter orange and winter boots.

He wondered how much hunting Luke would get done with Sally along. No wonder his brother hadn't gotten his deer yet.

Dawson leaned against the side of his pickup as Luke approached, telling himself to keep that thought to himself. "I wondered what you were doing up so early," he said as his brother pulled alongside and whirred down his window.

"Mom said you were mending fence." Luke quickly lost interest, his gaze going to the Little Rockies. "Heard about a big buck that was seen on up the road. We thought we'd check it out." His baby brother's gaze finally lit on him again. "You look like hell. Rough night?" There was humor in his brother's tone as if enjoying the moment. Not that Luke wanted him to lose sleep over Annabelle Clementine's return. But Luke wouldn't mind seeing proof that his big brother cared more than he'd said he did.

"Just worried the cattle would get out with the fence down," Dawson said noncommittally. He might look like hell, but he wasn't about to admit who had kept him awake most of the night. "Some of us put work ahead of..." he shot Sally a look "...hunting."

"Uh-huh," Luke said, not taking the bait.

"I need to get this finished." Dawson pushed off the side of his pickup. "Good luck finding that big buck."

Had he really thought he could make his brother feel guilty enough to help him? Luke drove off toward the Little Rockies with a honk of his horn, a wave of his hand and a shouted, "Save me some turkey."

CLOSING THE FRONT door as Lawrence Clarkston left, Annabelle went back into the house and immediately resumed filling boxes. Her grandmother had a boyfriend? In all the years she'd lived with her grandmother, Frannie had steered clear of men, saying that her husband had been the love of her life. That there was no other man for her.

And then along comes Lawrence Clarkston? Annabelle tried to figure out why he'd made her nervous. Because he wasn't Frannie's type, she thought, frowning, as she carried the full box of junk out to the porch. But, then again, who *was* Frannie's type?

It wasn't until later, when Dawson's mother called to tell her again that she was depending on her to show up at the house at eleven forty-five, that Annabelle quit working and went into the bedroom to start getting ready.

As she entered, she saw the gaping hole where she'd removed the floorboard and now quickly replaced it. All she needed to do was step into that hole and break her leg. Seeing the hole, she remembered the metal box. The surprise of meeting Frannie's boyfriend had caused her to forget all about it.

She took the box out of the drawer and, butter knife in hand, went to work on the lock. As she worked, she thought of Willie's call. She really couldn't be late. She hadn't planned on going out to the Rogers Ranch for Thanksgiving. Yesterday, even as she was nodding agreement, she was thinking of an excuse for when she would call her today to get out of it.

Now, though, she realized she had little choice but to show up. She knew the woman well enough to know that Willie didn't make idle threats. She would send someone after Annabelle. And what was the harm with Dawson and his brother out hunting? It wasn't like Willie was playing matchmaker, hoping to get her and Dawson back together.

Also, she remembered other Thanksgivings she'd shared at the Rogers Ranch. Willie put on a feast. Just the thought made her stomach growl. But she doubted Willie needed her help. She'd always admired Dawson's mom and had felt close to her. Maybe Willie felt the same. Why else would the woman forgive her for hurting her oldest son and invite her to Thanksgiving dinner?

The lock finally gave on the metal box. Putting down the butter knife, Annabelle carefully and slowly pried open the lid. Who had hidden this under the floorboards? The first people who owned the house? Or her grandmother? But if it had been Frannie, why hide a locked box under the floorboards?

The hinges groaned as the lid rose. An even mustier scent than the house rose from the metal box. She'd been worried about what she would find and was a little disappointed to see that the box was only filled with old photos and some yellowed newspaper clippings.

She picked up a few of the black-and-white photos, thumbed through them and realized that she didn't recognize any of the faces. Who knew how long they'd been under the house? She doubted they were even Frannie's, given the way the people in the photos were dressed. Either way, Annabelle didn't have time to go through them right now.

Hearing the coffeemaker shut off, she carried the box into the kitchen and absently put it on the table out of the way while she poured herself a cup of strong coffee before taking a shower and getting ready.

It had been years since she'd driven out to the Rogers Ranch, not that she could ever forget how to get there. It would feel strange being there, though. At least Dawson wouldn't be around, although she feared it was only a matter of time before he'd hear she was back. Or worse, that she'd run into him.

She couldn't help but wonder how much he'd changed in the past thirteen years. He could be bald with a potbelly. The thought made her laugh. She wondered if she would even recognize him.

WALKING INTO THE large ranch house on Thanksgiving Day, Dawson saw that the table was set for at least a dozen people. He shook his head, smiling. His mother. Around the holidays, she took in every stray who crossed her path.

"Nothing like offering people a decent meal," Willie would say. "It's a small thing, opening your kitchen to those who can use it." Every year, his mother found those who could use it and filled every seat, and then some, at their huge ranch-house table.

He followed the aroma of turkey and dressing, passing a dozen pies on the sideboard. How many people had she invited? He found Willie in the kitchen laughing with one of the neighbor ladies. His mother was in her element in this kitchen, her face glowing, her eyes bright.

"Well, look who's here!" Willie announced when she saw him and hurried over to give him a kiss on the cheek. She was a tall, lean woman with a warm face that was tanned year-round and seemed backlit with sunshine. Her smile had warmed more hearts than even he could imagine.

She'd had dozens of offers to remarry since Dawson's father had died, but she'd laughed them off, saying the last thing she needed was a husband. He often worried that she had turned down some good ones because she hadn't wanted to install a stepfather for her sons.

His mother motioned to the other women in the kitchen. "You know Kay from down the road," she said, indicating a gray-haired woman in her seventies. "And Patricia." The fiftysomething spinster who belonged to his mother's church nodded at him. Whitehorse, as small as it was, had a half dozen churches—and as many bars.

He smiled. "Yes, Mother, I've known Kay since I was two. Hello, Mrs. Welch. And I've known Patricia for only half my life."

His mother laughed. "And I guess I don't have to introduce you to this woman," she said as Annabelle Clementine came out of the pantry holding a huge bowl of cranberry relish. "I believe you've known her since you were…ten."

"Seven," he corrected as his gaze met Annabelle's. She looked as startled as he was to see *her*. Had she thought he wouldn't be here? "She was five."

She wore the black outfit that he'd seen her in by the river just the day before. She looked sexy as hell, but then, she'd looked good even in the sweatshirt and baggy jeans she'd been cleaning in yesterday.

"Seven," his mother repeated. "My mistake. Just put that on the table," she said to Annabelle. "Dawson, you can take this out." She reached into the refrigerator and handed him several plates with sticks of butter on them.

He shot her a Mother-how-could-you? look.

She gave him an impatient look back. "I was delighted to learn that Annabelle was back in town. I'm just happy she could join us for Thanksgiving dinner." His mother cocked her head and narrowed her eyes as if to say, *You'd better be polite, or else*, and then shooed him out to the dining room. No son of Wilhelmina Rogers would dream of being impolite to a guest at her house.

He followed Annabelle out to the dining room and out of earshot of his mother. "What are you doing here?" he asked under his breath.

"What are *you* doing here? I thought you'd be hunting."

"I was. Until *yesterday*." He waited for her to say something about their meeting on the highway. When she didn't, he added, "Which was a good thing or you could still be sitting beside the road in your fancy silver sports car without a drop of gas."

Her eyes widened in alarm and her cheeks flushed. "That was...*you*?"

He let out a bitter laugh. "How easily she forgets."

Chapter Seven

Those golden-brown eyes. She felt a shiver. How could she not have recognized him? She hadn't gotten a good look at him, not that she'd been trying. The cowboy had looked so.. scruffy, so filthy, so rough.

She groaned inwardly and lied, since she would have run out of gas not a half mile up the road if he hadn't helped her. "I wouldn't have stopped if I'd known it was you."

"Thanks."

"No, what I meant was…"

"Don't worry, I got the message." His gaze locked with hers. "Just like I got it thirteen years ago."

"Dawson—" She stopped. Just saying his name was a painful reminder of the intimacy they'd shared—and she'd thrown away. "I never—"

"Please don't."

No matter what she said, there was no way she could take it all back. She looked into those warm brown eyes, now so familiar in that handsome face. He was clean-shaven today, accentuating the razor edge of his unyield-ing jaw. Dawson looked damned good. The Western shirt he wore stretched over the taut muscles of his wide shoulders. She didn't need to see his abs to know they would be rock hard and still tanned from a summer spent bare chested on the ranch.

She swallowed, remembering the feel of his body against hers. "I'm sorry. I should have at least offered to pay you something for the gas."

"Seriously?" He looked even more disappointed in her. "Girl, you've been livin' in the big city for too long," he said with a shake of his head. "Out here in this part of Montana we help each other without expecting anything in return. I thought maybe you might have remembered that from growing up here, but then again, you couldn't wait to get out of here, could you? What was it you said to me? Unlike me, you were going to make something of yourself."

She felt her cheeks flame again. "Daw—"

"Don't bother. You were real clear when you left town. You didn't stutter," he said and turned on his boot heel to stride off, all long legs and attitude.

She watched him go, swamped with a wave of regret that she hadn't expected. For years she'd told herself that she hadn't left behind anything in Whitehorse. She hadn't even come back for her grandmother's funeral. What kind of woman was she?

"I understand that you need to spread your wings, Annabelle," Grandma Frannie had said the day she'd packed to leave. "There's nothing for you here. You need space to find what it is you're looking for. I was just like you when I was your age. I wanted to take a big bite out of the world. I craved it so much, it was eating me up inside. Fame, fortune, whatever it is, I know if anyone can find it, it will be you. I just hope it's everything you expect it to be."

"But I hate to leave you."

"Don't be ridiculous. It's time for this little bird to fly the nest." She'd hugged Annabelle. "I have great hopes for you no matter what happens."

"That's because I'm your favorite."

Frannie had laughed. "You're the one, all right," she'd said with a wink. "You're the one I'm depending on in the end."

Annabelle realized now that Patricia had come into the dining room and said something to her. "I'm sorry. My mind was a million miles away."

"I gathered that," the woman said. "I was saying that I hadn't realized you and Dawson had a history. Willie was just telling me that she always thought you'd be her daughter-in-law."

There was that pain again. She'd left this life behind without a backward glance and yet... She thought of the tree house two doors down from her grandmother's and the first time she'd laid eyes on Dawson. Being the way she'd always been, she had climbed up the ladder to the tree house even though she could read the sign: Do Not Enter. She'd been reading since she was three.

Earlier, she'd sneaked away from her sisters. They'd been told not to let her leave the yard, but they often got to playing with their dolls and not paying any attention to her.

Once up in the tree house, she hadn't been able to get down. She'd been five. "Precocious for your age," is what Frannie always said. "A brat," is what her older sisters contended.

Seven-year-old Dawson had come along and seen her up there. "Get down from there right now!" he'd ordered. "The sign says—"

"I know what the sign says," she'd said, surprised by how scared she was about being this high off the ground. Her words had come out in a stutter.

"What's your name?" he'd asked as he started up the ladder.

She'd watched him, feeling sick to her stomach and wishing she hadn't looked down. She tried to say her name but it came out "Anna."

"All right, Annie, you just have to trust me, okay?" He had been almost to her by then. He was nice, nothing like those boys her sisters made goggle eyes over.

Instinctively, she had trusted him. She'd let him help her down from the tree house, saving her. Just like he'd saved her on the highway yesterday.

"We used to play together as kids, that's all," she said to Pamela now, feeling the pinch of the lie. Dawson had always been there for her when she'd needed him. But while his feet had been firmly planted in this county's soil, hers had itched to kick the dust off her shoes and put this town in her rearview mirror. Too bad it hadn't turned out quite like she'd planned it.

"You look like a woman who could use a drink," said a male voice behind her. She turned to see Dawson's best friend, Jason Reynolds. "Welcome back to Whitehorse."

She felt a surge of relief. "I can't tell you how great it is to see a friendly face." Jason had always been nice to her and was one of the few people who had seemed to understand her need to leave Whitehorse—and Dawson.

He laughed now and hugged her. "I heard you were back, but I didn't believe it."

"Just long enough to sell my grandmother's house."

"Oh," he said and glanced toward the kitchen where Dawson was leaning against the counter scowling. "That explains a lot, then. What do you say when we're done here today we meet at the Mint Bar?"

She hesitated, but only for a moment. "One drink. I have a lot of work to do, but you're on."

DAWSON DID HIS best to be civil during the meal, but having Annabelle there just like old times had ruined his appetite. His mother had acted as if his high school girlfriend was part of the family.

"Jason flirted with her the entire meal," Dawson snapped after he and his brother had helped take dishes to the kitchen. Their mother had shooed them out to the family room where there was a game on the television. Jason had left right after the meal, saying he had to stop by the nursing home to see his grandmother. Annabelle had cut out shortly after that when their mother wouldn't let her help with the dishes.

His brother now grinned from the couch. His girlfriend, Sally, was having Thanksgiving with her own family. Willie and an assortment of guests were in the kitchen, finishing up. "It's your own fault. You're the one who gave Jason your seat next to Annabelle. Looked like the two of them were having a fine time."

Dawson growled under his breath. He hadn't missed a moment of it. "It wasn't my idea, having her over for Thanksgiving. It was Mother's. All I need is Willie playing matchmaker."

Luke laughed. "Well, if it makes you feel any better, Mom wasn't all that happy that Jason and Annabelle hit it off at dinner."

Dawson got to his feet, unable to sit another moment.

"Oh, come on. What's the harm if Jason flirted with her? Like you said, she isn't staying. So lighten up. Anyway, once she gets her grandmother's house sold, she'll be gone."

"Just not soon enough."

"I thought you were over her?" Luke said. "That you didn't care she was back. That—where are you headed?"

"I need a stiff drink."

"I think Mom's got some brandy that she uses for her fruitcakes. I know where she hides it."

Dawson shook his head. "I need to get out of here. Want to go to the Mint?"

THE MOMENT HE and his brother walked in, Dawson spotted Annabelle and almost turned back around and left. He would have if his brother hadn't stopped him.

"You can't keep dodging her," Luke argued. "You two are going to see each other. If you really don't care, then what's the big deal?"

He knew he was being manipulated, but he wanted a drink more than he wanted to argue with his brother. The band was finishing up a cheating song. Just the sight of Annabelle there with Jason… He was moving toward the bar when Jason saw him and called him over to their table.

"Everything all right?" his friend asked. Dawson ordered a shot of whiskey and a beer from the waitress who appeared.

"Why wouldn't everything be all right?" he snapped as he looked at Annabelle. She was pretending interest in the couples out on the dance floor.

"Your mama outdid herself on that Thanksgiving dinner," Jason said, as if ignoring the tension at the table.

"You should know. You've been showing up there every year since we were kids."

His friend smiled. "Got up on the wrong side of the bed, did you?"

Dawson glared at him, feeling like a jackass. Jason was his best friend and part of the Rogers family. The waitress brought his drinks. He picked up the shot of whiskey, downed it and chased it with some of the beer. As the band wrapped up their song and broke into a slow one, he turned to Annabelle.

"Let's dance," he said and reached for her hand.

She hesitated, but he caught her fingers and pulled her up from her seat and out on the dance floor. "Dawson, what are you doing?" she demanded once they were away from the table.

"Dancing." He leaned closer, caught a whiff of her perfume and felt his head spin. Did she still wear his favorite? Or had she just put it on for the dinner, thinking he'd be there? Or had she known Jason would be there? Hadn't she said she thought Dawson would be out hunting?

He hated being jealous, but he couldn't seem to help himself. "Don't you think you at least owe me a dance?"

"For the gas?"

He shook his head as they began to move to the music. "One dance for breaking my heart. It's a cheap deal at twice the price."

ANNABELLE COULD HEAR the hurt in his voice, the anger and something she couldn't put her finger on. They hadn't spoken at dinner after that short discussion in the dining room before the turkey was served. But she'd felt him watching her throughout the meal.

"I broke your heart?" she asked, wondering if that was true. He'd been furious, that much she'd known. And hurt. But he hadn't even bothered to stop by the day she'd left. Nor had she heard from him since.

"What do you think?" He locked eyes with her.

She felt them drilling into her. Surprisingly, as angry as he was, it felt intimate. She swallowed and looked away, thinking he'd given up pretty easily when she'd said she was leaving town. "If that's true, I'm sorry."

"Don't be. You proved that leaving was your best choice. If you'd stayed here and married me…well, as you said, you weren't cut out to be a Montana ranch-woman. Clearly you made the right choice."

Her smile hurt her. "I didn't think I had a choice back then. It felt like leaving was something I had to do."

"And look how it turned out."

"Yes." She glanced away, her eyes burning with tears. Yes, look how it had turned out. "It hasn't been easy."

"But then, no one is stronger or more determined than you are."

He made that sound like a compliment. She looked into his handsome face. Those warm brown eyes had always been her downfall. "Whether you believe it or not, it wasn't easy to leave you."

Dawson laughed. "Oh, you didn't seem to have that much trouble doing it." He brushed a lock of her hair back from her forehead. His fingertips felt hot against her sensitive skin. She trembled even though it was warm on the dance floor. Dawson's hand on her waist seemed to burn the tender flesh under her blouse.

She looked into those eyes and remembered all of it—from their first kiss to the last time they'd made love. Leaving him was the hardest thing she'd ever done. She hadn't wanted him to make it easy. Had she wanted him to fight for her? To beg her to stay? Well, he hadn't. He'd let her go and walked away.

Not that she would have stayed, she told herself. But they would never know, would they? "Dawson." The slow country song was coming to an end. His gaze shifted to her lips and she knew he was going to kiss her. The ache at her center intensified as he brushed his mouth over hers. "Dawson," she breathed.

His arms tightened around her and she was drawn into his rock-hard body. Her lips parted as his mouth took possession of hers.

Had the song not died away, she could have stayed right there in his arms, captured in the elixir of that kiss. But the music stopped and so did the kiss. She looked at the handsome cowboy and felt the full weight of the lie she was living. If he only knew how she'd traded him for a life she'd thought she wanted more than her next breath only to fail so miserably—

She stepped out of his arms, saw the hurt and experienced a loss like none she had ever felt before. She couldn't hurt this man again. But walking away from him broke her heart one more time. She'd compared every man she'd met in the past thirteen years to Dawson—and they'd all come up lacking.

She tore herself away and headed for the door. She

was almost there when someone grabbed her arm. She turned, thinking it would be Dawson. It was Jason.

"Dawson just left by the back way," he said, drawing her back to the table. "One drink," he reminded her. "It will give Dawson a chance to make a clean getaway and I think he needs that right now."

Annabelle felt unsteady on her feet as she let him lead her back to the table. The last thing she wanted was a drink. But she couldn't bear running into Dawson in the parking lot. Tears burned her eyes. She touched the tip of her tongue to her lower lip. Her mouth still tingled from his kiss. She bit down on her lip and tried not to cry.

"I should never have come back here," she said, picking up the drink Jason pushed in front of her as they sat down.

"It will get easier," he told her.

She shook her head. "I'm not staying that long. Once I get that house cleaned out…" The magnitude of what she still had to do overwhelmed her. The band was taking a break but had punched in some songs on the jukebox.

"I can't let you hurt Dawson again," Jason said, taking her by surprise. "He was a mess for a long time after you left. I'm not sure he's tough enough to go through that again."

She realized that he'd seen her and Dawson kissing. "He's the one who made me dance with him and the kiss…" She was going to say it was all Dawson, but that would have been another lie.

"It's taken him years to get over you. You hurt him bad," Jason said, not unkindly. "He spent months saving up for that engagement ring."

Wanting to disappear under the table, she took a gulp

of her drink. It tasted bitter on her tongue and it felt as if she was trying to wash away the memory of the kiss. Another lie. She wanted to take that kiss to her grave.

"I'm only telling you this because he's my friend and so are you," Jason was saying. "I really thought you'd come back. You know, that day you left, I thought you'd realize what you were giving up. But then I saw your photograph on a billboard down in Denver a year later. I said, 'Wow, I used to know that girl.' You really showed Dawson. Hell, you showed everyone in town."

She felt like crying. "I didn't show anyone anything," she said under her breath. "Don't worry. I'm leaving just as soon as I can. In the meantime, I will stay as far away from Dawson as possible, and I'm sure he feels the same way." She pushed the remainder of the drink away. Alcohol was the last thing she needed. "I have to go. Thank you. For the drink. For…" She reached for his hand and squeezed it. "For the advice." For telling her that she'd broken Dawson's heart and warning her not to do it again?

"I don't want to see you hurt, either," Jason said. "Dawson is never leaving Montana. He's a cowboy. He'd die in California."

She nodded. "I know." Why hadn't she just let Mary Sue sell the house and send her the money? Why had she come back here?

DAWSON LEFT THE BAR, needing fresh air and distance. He should never have danced with Annabelle—let alone kissed her. He was mentally kicking himself for that impulsive moment of weakness when he noticed her fancy sports car. What called his attention to the vehicle was the man hooking it to a wrecker.

As he walked closer, he realized he didn't recognize the towing company. Nor had there seemed to be anything wrong with Annabelle's car. Other than running out of gas. That couldn't be the problem, since he'd given her almost a full tank.

"Hey," he said as he approached. "Why are you towing that car?"

"Stay out of it," the man said. "Just doing my job. I don't want any trouble. I have the paperwork right here." He reached into his jacket pocket and pulled out some folded sheets of paper.

Paperwork? "I know the woman who owns that car. I want to see those," Dawson said.

The man sighed, but stepped to him, unfolded the papers and handed them to him.

Reading under the streetlight, Dawson couldn't believe what he was seeing. *Her car was being repossessed for lack of payment?* He looked toward the bar, then at the wrecker operator. "There must be some mistake. Do you know who Annabelle Clementine is?"

"No mistake. She's a deadbeat like any other deadbeat."

He bristled at the man's words. "Look…" He glanced at the name on the paperwork: Chet's Retrieval Service. "Look, Chet. Come on, give the lady a break."

Chet gave Dawson an impatient look. "She's been given all kinds of breaks and now I had to come all this way to get the car. She's used up all her breaks."

"What does she owe?"

Chet kept hooking up the car.

"Just give me the amount." He withdrew a loose check from his wallet. "You have a pen?"

The wrecker operator stopped to look at him for a long moment, then sighed and took the papers from his hand, thumbed through them to a page and pointed at a figure at the bottom.

The amount took Dawson's breath away. How could she have gotten so far behind in her car payments? What had she been thinking, buying such an expensive car to begin with if she couldn't afford it?

The wrecker operator grinned, seeing Dawson's surprise. "Still want to bail her out?"

"Yes." He ground his teeth as he wrote the check for the full amount and handed to it him. "Unhook it."

The wrecker operator looked at the check. "I'm staying in town at the motel and cashing this first thing in the morning. If this bounces—"

"It isn't going to bounce," Dawson said indignantly. "Unhook it."

"I'll be going to your bank as soon as it opens in the morning. Don't make me have to look for this car again."

"I'll transfer the funds tonight online to my checking account. Don't worry. The owner of this car isn't going anywhere, anyway." He doubted she could afford money for gas to leave town right now. Things were beginning to make sense. Like the reason she was so anxious to get her grandmother's house sold. Why she was packing it up by herself, instead of hiring help. Why he'd seen her in the same outfit twice.

"But we keep this between us," Dawson added.

Chet gave him a pitying look as if he was the biggest sucker he'd ever met. "It's your money." The man folded the check, pocketed it and began to unhook Annabelle's car.

From behind him he heard a door slam, then a plaintive wail. "Wait!"

Dawson groaned as he turned to see Annabelle come out of the bar. She saw him, eyes narrowing as she stormed toward them.

ANNABELLE WAS IN the middle of her worst nightmare. At first, all she'd seen was her car dangling from the back of the wrecker. After months of avoiding the repo man, he'd caught up with her. She ran across the parking lot, telling herself she had to talk him out of taking her car. She needed it desperately if she hoped to get her grandmother's house sold.

What she hadn't seen at first was Dawson standing in the shadows. When he turned, her heart had dropped like a sack of potatoes. Instantly, she went on the defensive, since that was all she had. That and her badly damaged pride.

"What's going on?" she demanded, hands on her not-so-slim hips.

"I took care of it," Dawson said.

Annabelle looked from him to the wrecker driver who only gave her a satisfied grin and a shrug. She realized what had happened and felt her face burn with shame followed quickly by anger.

"How dare you?" she snapped, turning on Dawson. "How dare you take it upon yourself to pay my bills?"

Dawson pulled off his Stetson and raked a hand through his hair. "I couldn't let him take your car."

"It was none of your business."

"You're right." He put his hat back on and held up both hands in surrender. "I thought I was helping, but clearly…" He cursed under his breath before she swung back around on the repo man.

"This is just a misunderstanding between me and my bank. I will take care of it."

"Sure it is." The wrecker operator nodded with a grin that made her want to retch. "Out of my hands now. Take it up with…" he glanced toward Dawson "…your… friend."

She swung back around to find Dawson studying his boots. Tears burned her eyes but she willed herself not to cry. Just when she'd thought things couldn't get any worse. She didn't have to look into Dawson's brown-eyed gaze to see the truth. He knew.

On top of that, he'd just saved her again. She thought she would die of embarrassment. If only the parking lot pavement would open up and swallow her.

"This must give you a lot of satisfaction," she said, biting off each word.

He glanced up, looking confused.

"I was so full of myself, leaving here to go make something of my life."

"You did what you set out to do."

She shook her head fighting tears. "Only to fail and come back here broke and—" The words caught in her throat as it constricted.

As the wrecker drove off, Dawson closed the distance between them, taking her shoulders in his hands. "You didn't fail."

She let out a strangled laugh and had to look away.

"I got fired. Worse, blackballed. I'll never be able to get another modeling job."

"So?"

"So?" she demanded returning her gaze to him. "It's the only thing I know how to do, the only thing I ever planned to do."

"Plans change. I know you. You can do anything you set our mind to."

"Right."

"Don't sell yourself short. You just need a new plan."

She wiped at her tears. "Why are you being so nice to me?"

He released her shoulders. "Why wouldn't I be?"

"Seriously?"

"I was angry for a while, I'll admit it." His voice softened. "I was devastated when you left. But you were right. You needed to go off and follow your dream. And, Annie, you did it."

She heard what sounded like pride in his voice. And he'd called her Annie, his pet name for her.

"So it didn't work out quite like you thought it would. So what?"

So what? She looked away as she tried to swallow the lump in her throat.

"You were right about me, as well. I'm just a cowboy. I'm never going to set the world on fire. I'm happy chasing cows, mending fence, working on my old tractor."

She felt chagrin heat her face as she remembered saying he would be working on some old tractor the rest of his life. "I'm sorry for the awful things I said to you."

"Hell, girl, it forced me to buy a new tractor." He

grinned and shrugged. "But I also got the old one running, as well."

She couldn't help but smile at him. "I'm glad you haven't changed. I'm even glad Whitehorse hasn't changed."

"That's only because you'll be selling your grandmother's house and leaving this one-horse town on your next adventure." He smiled when he said it, but the words still stung because she remembered saying them to Mary Sue. It had all been bravado and she felt ashamed.

What if she didn't want to leave? What was there for her here if she stayed? Those were the words she wanted to say, but they were stuck in her throat.

She opened her mouth, aching for the feel of his arms around her, and closed it again. When she finally spoke, her voice broke. "I will pay you back every dime." With that she turned, and with as much dignity as she could muster, walked to her car and drove away.

Back at the house, she stood for a moment just inside the door. She didn't want to go into the kitchen. She didn't want to see the blood spot on the wall where there might or might not have been an alcove.

But she needed a drink of water. Forcing herself to go into the kitchen, she quickly snapped on the light before glancing toward the wall. A laugh escaped her.

She was exhausted from packing boxes, from worry. From trying to ignore Dawson. From fighting emotions that seemed to overwhelm her at every turn. From living a lie.

But as she stood there, she remembered. There *had* been an alcove there growing up. The reason she hadn't remembered was because her grandmother had kept a hutch there that had filled up the space.

Why hadn't she remembered the hutch? Because it had been covered with knickknacks, plants, newspapers. Her grandmother had always been a collector. A hoarder.

So, when had Frannie gotten rid of the hutch? And why? Why close up that space? It made no sense. She shuddered. Was it possible there was something behind that wall? But what?

"This is silly," she said to the empty room. Anyone who knew grandmother wouldn't suspect her of…of what?

She hugged herself, blaming the crazy thoughts on her exhaustion. Sleep, that's what she needed. Tomorrow everything would look brighter. That made her laugh again because she knew better. Tomorrow she would again be faced with filling boxes and lugging them out to the porch. After that—

Determined not to think about it, she turned off the kitchen light but stood for a moment longer staring at the wall. No dark shadow resembling blood appeared. That was at least something.

ROB STARED OUT at the wide-open spaces in his headlights feeling nervous. It was so isolated out here in the middle of Montana. He hadn't seen another set of headlights for miles on the two-lane highway and that after flying for hours. It was next to impossible to get a decent flight from Florida to Montana—on Thanksgiving Day, no less. He'd been on four different planes, endured hours of layovers and had barely made the connection for the ast one. Tired and irritable, he couldn't have felt worse about this so-called job.

Now he wasn't sure he was even on the right road. The rental car had a navigation system, but he hated those things. The rental agent had given him a paper map that now lay on the passenger seat.

According to the map, he just kept going north. If he hit Canada, well, then he'd gone too far. He hoped to find a town, a gas station, someplace he could stop and ask. But he'd driven miles without seeing a soul. Lots of cows, but little else.

Finally, as the sun was coming up, he spotted a gas station ahead and what was reportedly the town of Grass Range though he didn't see much town. He pulled in, bought gas, asked for directions.

"Just keep going up the road. Can't miss Whitehorse," the clerk told him after taking his money.

"Tell me it's bigger than this burg," Rob said.

The clerk, a young woman with red hair and freckles, laughed. "It's bigger."

"There a motel in Whitehorse?"

"Four, I think."

Four? Well, that was better than none, he thought as he climbed back into the rental car. He'd bought some large cookies, two peanut butter and two chocolate chip. He chased them down with a liter of cola as he drove.

He couldn't wait to get to Whitehorse, find out that the dead woman wasn't Bernie's Baby Doll, then head home. He'd missed Thanksgiving, not that he'd ever liked turkey.

As he drove, the country became wilder and more forbidding. He thought about Baby Doll, the woman who'd fooled the family kingpin, the great Bernard "Bernie the Hawk" McDougal.

Was it possible she had been hiding out all these years in this Wild West–looking country? Not the broad the family had described to him. She'd been one cagey woman. Rob couldn't see her way out here in Montana. If he could prove that this Francesca Marie Clementine wasn't Baby Doll, he would be on the first plane out of here.

He relaxed a little, turning on the radio and searching for a station. He found only one. "Shit-kicking music," his friend Murph would have called it. Normally, the two of them did the jobs together. It had surprised Rob when his uncle had wanted him to handle this one alone. Bernie really did think this old chick had been Baby Doll, which also meant he believed that she'd held on to the loot.

Yep, his uncle had to be losing it.

He decided to listen to the country music station. "When in Montana," Rob said as he watched the rental car eat up the miles of rolling ranch land, rugged river bottom and, finally, open prairie.

By the time he reached the outskirts of Whitehorse, he was tired enough that all he wanted to do was find a motel and get some sleep. But he knew his uncle would be calling, wanting an update.

The Grass Range convenience store clerk had been right about one thing. This town was a little bigger. But not much. Which made it almost too easy to find the Clementine place.

Chapter Eight

Annabelle woke to daylight, blinked and covered her head with the duvet at the memory of the night before. Dawson knew everything now about her dire straits. Worse, he'd paid for her car not to be towed. She couldn't have been more mortified.

Even worse than that, she couldn't spend the day under the covers hiding out. She had to get up. This house had to be emptied out before she could sell it. Just the thought of another day loading junk into boxes made her groan. How could this now be her life?

That was a question she didn't want to contemplate. She'd rather fill boxes and lug them out to the porch, she thought as she threw back the covers and got out of bed. Feeling sorry for herself wasn't going to get her anywhere.

Last night she'd hated to face coming back to this place. It was much creepier after dark, especially with a breeze in the bare limbs of the cottonwoods and the pine boughs. The house had creaked and groaned more than the first night.

She started toward the kitchen to make coffee. She wouldn't have a car if it wasn't for Dawson. She wouldn't

even have made it to Whitehorse if he hadn't given her
fuel. Tears welled in her eyes. She quickly wiped them
away with the back of her hand, ashamed of the way
she'd been acting. She'd yelled at Dawson for keeping
her car from being towed. She'd just been so embarrassed. Maybe pushing people away was her one true
talent, she thought as she stepped into the kitchen and
got the coffee going.

She tried to think of what needed to be done this
morning instead of mentally beating herself up. She
needed to make another box run and then get back to
work. Pouring herself a cup of coffee, she wandered
into the living room and stood looking everything that
remained. She felt overwhelmed. Not even the coffee
helped.

But if she was anything, it was determined. She lifted
her chin, telling herself she could do this. Like she had a
choice. Finishing her coffee, she returned her cup to the
kitchen then went to get dressed in her "work" clothes.

She reminded herself how hard it had been to suc-
ceed in the modeling business. Not discounting luck,
she'd worked hard to get where she'd been. *Where she'd
been.* It still hurt to think that she'd thrown it all away.

Shaking her head to dislodge those thoughts, she went
to work, determined to put Dawson out of her mind. But
it was so like Dawson to bail her out. Of course he'd
want to know why. It had been a perfect opportunity to
say *I told you so.*

But he hadn't. If anything he'd been kind. *Too kind.*
She grumbled under her breath. She didn't need his pity.
She didn't need anyone's pity.

The thought of her dire circumstances—and worse,

that Dawson knew—turned her stomach. This was what she'd hoped to avoid. She'd left this town so smug, so sure of herself, so determined to be someone... Now it made her laugh. She was a joke, and the only man she'd ever loved now knew it.

The knock at the door made her jump. For a moment, she thought it would be Dawson, as if just thinking about him had conjured him up.

But it was a pinch-faced little old gray-haired woman who was now peering in the window. She had her hands cupped around her watery eyes and her nose pressed to the glass.

"Can I help you?" Annabelle demanded, opening the door.

"There was a man looking in your windows last night," the woman said. "I live right next door and I looked out—"

"Mrs. Gilbert?" It had been years since she'd seen her grandmother's nosey neighbor.

"You're the trouble one, right?"

"Trouble one?" she echoed.

"The granddaughter Frannie worried about all the time."

"That would be me," she said—as her grandmother would have insisted, owning it.

"I ran him off. The man who was peeking in your windows. Might want to keep your blinds drawn. Those types often come back," Inez Gilbert said as she turned, cane in hand.

Seeing the cane reminded her of the man who'd stopped by yesterday morning. "Did my grandmother have a boyfriend?"

The elderly woman stopped to peer back at her.

"A distinguished-looking man who carries a cane? Said his name was Lawrence Clarkston."

"I saw him. Yesterday morning at your door," Inez said. "Never seen him before in my life. Nor was it him last night."

"So Frannie didn't—"

"She did not," her neighbor said, as she wobbled down the stairs and took off down the sidewalk. "If she had, I would have known."

"I'm sure you would have," Annabelle said under her breath.

Going back inside, she hugged herself. So, who was the man pretending to be her grandmother's boyfriend? Maybe more scary, who was the man Inez had seen peering in her windows last night?

Catching her reflection and the hideous outfit she was wearing, Annabelle promised herself she would go uptown and buy herself a pair of jeans and a couple of T-shirts.

In the meantime… She looked at the mess—not just in the house but in her life and burst into tears.

DAWSON DIDN'T THINK he had slept a wink. Not long after the sun rose, he drove over to the main ranch house to find his mother and brother in the kitchen.

"Rough night?" his mother asked and handed him a cup of coffee. "I could make you some breakfast."

He shook his head. "Thanks, but I'm not hungry."

"Well, something's gotten under your hide." She motioned to a chair at the table.

He hesitated, even though he knew the reason he'd

driven over here so early in the morning was that he needed to talk to her. She'd been his sounding board since he was a kid. Nothing had changed. He glanced at his younger brother already sitting at the table.

"You want me to leave?" Luke asked, pretending to be insulted. "Hell, we both know what's bothering you."

"Language," their mother said as Luke shoved back his chair and started to get up.

"You can stay," Dawson said with a sigh, and his brother dropped back down, grinning. "But not a word of this leaves this room. Agreed?"

Luke nodded. His mother didn't bother. She knew how to keep a secret better than anyone he knew.

Without preamble, he said, "Annabelle's broke. That's why she's back."

His brother laughed. "Annabelle Clementine? What are you talking about? She was just on the cover of one of those fancy women's magazines."

"You read fancy women's magazines?" his mother asked.

Luke's face reddened. "I saw it at Sally's house." He turned to his brother. "This sounds like you just being jealous again, big brother. She left and made something of herself and you stayed here. You've always resented being forced to stay behind to take care of the ranch. Now you're taking it out on her. Why don't you admit it? You're still hung up on her."

"I was wrong. I should have let you leave," Dawson said.

"Your brother means well." Their mother sent a withering look at Luke. "What do you mean, broke?"

"Flat broke." He told her about crossing paths with Annabelle south of town by the river.

"You didn't tell me that," Luke said.

Ignoring him, Dawson continued, "Last night at the bar, her car was almost repossessed. Apparently she hasn't been making her car payment for months." He didn't mention that Annabelle had been wearing the same outfit he'd first seen her in again yesterday at Thanksgiving dinner.

Willie shook her head. "Oh, the poor dear. Something must have happened. You have no idea what?"

"No, but it seems the only reason she's back is to sell her grandmother's house as quickly as possible to get herself out of trouble financially," he said. "More than likely she got in over her head with her supermodel lifestyle." He hated the bitterness he heard in his tone.

"What are you going to do about it?" his mother asked.

Dawson frowned and held up his hands. "Do about it? I gave her gas, I paid to keep her car from being repossessed—at least temporarily, and she told me to stay out of her business."

"She must be so embarrassed," Willie said. "You're the last person she'd want bailing her out."

"Exactly," he said.

"Well, there's a simple solution," Luke said, looking pleased with himself. "Sounds like it will take a while for her to get the house ready to sell, since it's packed with junk that has to be hauled to the dump. Also, Mary Sue doesn't think it will sell fast, especially this close to Christmas. There's time to tell her how you feel."

Dawson groaned. "If I did still have feelings for her,

which I don't, what would be the point? I'm a Montana rancher. She's…whatever it is she is. There's a reason we broke up all those years ago. Not to mention that once she has money again, she'll be gone. She isn't interested in Montana or me. The sooner she gets out of town, the better." He finished his coffee and stood.

"Well, if that's the case," his mother said, "then you need to help her."

He stopped in his tracks. "What?"

"You want her out of town? She wants out of town. The solution is right in front of you. Help her get the house ready to sell. Otherwise, who knows how long she'll be around, running out of money."

Dawson stared at his mother. "If this is you match-making—"

"Not at all," Willie assured him. "I can see how Annabelle being in town is upsetting you—not to mention costing you money. Help her get the house sold, and if you're right, she'll be gone."

He eyed her suspiciously for a long moment, hating to admit that she might have a point. "Fine. But little brother, you're going to help. Bring the flatbed truck to Annabelle's this afternoon along with some of your friends. We're going to make a trip to the dump."

"Hey, don't involve me in this," Luke complained. "My solution requires a lot less lifting. Also I'm helping the neighbor this morning with his fence."

"Two this afternoon," Dawson said pointing a finger at his brother. "You're the one who is so interested in Annabelle…" He slammed out of the house, letting the door bang behind him.

"Help your brother," Willie said as she rose to get more coffee.

"There's no help for him. He's in love and too stubborn to admit it, as if you didn't know that when you invited Annabelle to Thanksgiving dinner."

Willie looked after her oldest son who was now driving away. "Did he only stay because he thinks I need him to help run the ranch?"

"No, Mom," Luke said, putting an arm around her shoulder. "I was just giving him a hard time. He's a born Montana cowboy and rancher. He's just mad because he didn't put up more of a fight thirteen years ago."

"I'm not sure it would have helped," she said with a sigh. "You need to cut him some slack. For some people, there is only that one person in life. Annabelle has always been the one for your brother."

Luke shook his head. "Guess he's going to be a bachelor till he dies, then."

"Maybe."

He shot her a look. "Don't pretend that you aren't hoping his helping her will make them both realize they love each other."

"Don't be ridiculous. Have I ever interfered in your lives?"

"You really want me to answer that?" he said to her retreating back, but she merely laughed.

Chapter Nine

"What did Annabelle say when she called you?" TJ asked distractedly as she walked with her cell phone to her ear to peek through the curtains at the street below. She'd been writing all day on her latest thriller. That was enough to spook her, a Montana girl living in New York City.

"That's just it," her sister Chloe said with a sigh. "She didn't say anything, really. She just wanted to know why we didn't stay in the house when we were in Whitehorse for Grandma's funeral."

TJ could hear sounds of the newsroom behind Chloe. Like her, she was still at work at the large newspaper where she worked as an investigative reporter. "What did you tell her?"

"That we didn't want to."

"It takes a lot of nerve to call you and demand to know why we stayed at the hotel," TJ said. "She didn't even attend Grandma's funeral. I hope Grandma comes back and haunts her."

"Annabelle did sound scared. I can't imagine staying in that house. You felt it, too. But I wasn't about to tell Annabelle that was the reason we stayed at the hotel."

TJ shivered and hugged herself with her free arm. "Why didn't you tell her?"

"Tell her what? I'm not sure what I felt—let alone what we might have heard upstairs. I was feeling emotional with grandmother's funeral and remembering going to live there as a girl…and everything."

"We both heard a noise upstairs," TJ said. "It could have been the wind, a branch rubbing against the side of the house or just the house settling. Even though I write this stuff, staying in the house just felt…wrong."

"We are as bad as Annabelle when it comes to sticking our heads in the sand and pretending nothing is wrong," Chloe said. "What if there is something…dangerous going on up there and now Annabelle is in that house?"

"Look, you know Annabelle. She always overreacts to everything. So has she sold the house?"

"She says it will be soon and then she'll be out of there. But you know what it looked like. I would think it would take months just to clean it out, let alone get it ready to sell."

"Chloe, don't you wonder why Grandmother left the house to her and not us?"

"Not really. Annabelle's right. She always was grandmother's favorite. Anyway, if Frannie had left it to all three of us, we would have killed each other over it. The three of us have never gotten along."

"We did once. After high school our lives just kind of went in all different directions. But we're still sisters and Christmas is coming." Chloe said nothing. "I'm glad Frannie left the house to Annabelle."

Her sister chuckled. "I was, too, once that I saw what

a mess it was. I like to think it was Grandma teaching her a lesson." TJ laughed. "Can you imagine Annabelle's face when she saw the place?"

Chloe laughed, too, but TJ could hear the hurt in her voice. "The house isn't worth much, so what does it matter?" she asked, letting the curtain drop back into place. It had mattered enough that they'd gotten in a huge fight with their sister and hadn't really spoken for months.

"I suppose you're right."

"I was thinking about going to Whitehorse for Christmas," Chloe said, as if it had just come to her. "Surprise Annabelle. She should have the house ready to sell by then, but if she didn't, maybe help her?"

"Seriously?" TJ glanced outside again, then moved away from the window.

"Remember Christmas in Montana? I wonder if they still have that Christmas dance at the old gym."

"You're really thinking about going?" TJ asked.

"You have to come, too. It's been so long since we've been together. Christmas is the perfect time to patch things up between the three of us."

"I don't know. I have a book out then. My publisher wants me to do a book tour." But TJ was balking at the idea and now that Chloe mentioned it, she was definitely considering Christmas in Montana. Not for the reasons Chloe would have liked, though. "I'll think about it. I have to go." She took another look out the window as she disconnected.

Just the thought of whatever they'd heard upstairs in their grandmother's house—footsteps, the creaking of floorboards, what sounded like their grandmother's walker... The memory made her shudder and she let the curtain drop back again. Frannie's ghost? she thought with a laugh.

Unfortunately there were worse things than ghosts, she thought, as she checked her apartment door to make sure all the locks were engaged.

ONE LOOK AT Annabelle and Dawson could see she'd been crying. He hated that her tears could still affect him the way they did. How had he not seen how hurt and alone she was?

Annabelle leaned against the doorjamb, eyes narrowing. "If you came to get your money back…"

His earlier moment of weakness vanished. He reached over and flicked at her shoulder, making her flinch. "Just trying to knock that chip off your shoulder. I told you. I'm not worried about the money."

"I'll pay you back when I sell the house."

"Fine." He wished he hadn't come here, but the sooner she got the house ready to sell, the sooner it would be bought, even if he had to buy it himself, and then she'd be out of here and things could get back to normal.

Annabelle sighed. "What are you doing here?"

He wished he knew. It had seemed so simple when his mother had suggested it. Help get Annie out of town. But being around her messed with more than his mind or his money. "I'm going to help you pack up the house and take what you don't want to the dump—unless you want to argue about that, too?"

"I know you think I'm a charity case that you have to—"

"You never were graceful when it came to taking

help from anyone," he interrupted with a sigh. "Just say thank-you and let's leave it at that."

She clamped her jaw shut for a moment. "I'm also not graceful when people pity me."

He let out a bark of a laugh. "You think that's what this is? Sorry, sister, but you are the last person I feel sorry for. You need to get your grandmother's house ready to sell. You want to sell this house and clear out of town? Fine with me. I have some things to take to the dump. I thought I'd take some of yours." He gave her a challenging look. "But if you don't want my help—"

"Thank you."

He felt his expression soften. She looked dead on her feet already this morning—and even more beautiful even after having been crying. There was something vulnerable about her that he'd only seen a few times. Too bad the cameras had never been able to capture it. She would have been even more famous.

"You're welcome," he said quietly, his gaze still on her. It was hard not to touch her. To run his thumb over those full lips. To brush that errant lock of blond hair back from her soft cheek.

At a low rumble of a growl, his gaze was dragged away. He looked past her to where Sadie had entered the house and now stood just inside the kitchen, the hair standing up on the back of the puppy's neck. From where he stood, though, he couldn't see what the growling was about.

He stepped past Annabelle, worried that the dog had gotten into something she wasn't supposed to. As he entered the kitchen, he found Sadie hunkered down, a low snarl in her throat. What he couldn't see was what-

ever had her scared. She appeared to simply be growling at the wall.

"Your dog is freaking me out," Annabelle said as she
came up behind him.

ANNABELLE SHIVERED AT the eerie, spine-tingling noise
the dog was making. "What is wrong with her?"

"Good question. Any reason she would be growling
at your kitchen wall?"

"Do you believe in ghosts?" she asked Dawson in a
hushed voice.

"Ghosts?" He turned to look at her. "Seriously?"

Annabelle shook off the crazy thought, wishing she
hadn't brought it up. "Of course not, but there's a wall
that shouldn't be there." She explained about what Mary
Sue had told her.

"The plans must be wrong."

"That's what I thought, too, but now…" She glanced
at his dog. "Your dog seems to think there's something
behind that wall."

"Sadie?" The dog jumped in surprise and, whining,
ran to him to cower behind his boots.

Annabelle raised a brow. "I feel like your dog right
now."

Dawson was staring at the wall. "I've never seen her
act like that before," he said frowning. "Why would your
grandmother wall up an alcove?"

"That seems to be the question of the week." She
shrugged. "Makes no sense, huh?" She could feel his
gaze on her. When she met his eyes, she saw something
that made her soften dangerously inside. "I should get to
work." Turning, she headed for the third bedroom that

was nearly full of her grandmother's collectibles. She grabbed a couple of empty boxes on the way. Behind her, she heard Dawson talking to his pup. It made her smile since he was asking Sadie what was wrong with her as if he expected an answer.

DAWSON LOADED SADIE into his pickup, cracking the windows enough that he could hear her if she needed to get out. It was a crisp, cool November day, the air scented with dried leaves.

It didn't take him long to load all the boxes Annabelle had stacked at the edge of the porch into the back of his pickup. He stretched, thinking of her doing the same. She came out with more boxes full of what could only be considered junk.

"I'll take a load of boxes to the dump, then pick up more boxes," Dawson called up to the porch.

She put down the box and stretched. "Thanks. I was just going to make some coffee. You want a cup before you leave?"

He shook his head. "I won't be long." She nodded. He could feel her watching him as he drove away. What had made him think this would be easy?

By two in the afternoon, Annabelle had loaded all the empty boxes he'd picked up up on his way back from the dump. He'd helped with the last few and was glad to see his brother Luke arrive with some friends in the ranch flatbed truck.

It didn't take them long to load everything she had packed up. At the dump, he helped discard the contents of the boxes before Luke cut out with his friends. Dawson knew he could have called it a day, as well. There were plenty of boxes for Annabelle to continue pack-ing—if she felt like it. He didn't know about her, but it had been a long, tiring day.

But instead of going home, he drove back to her house, using the empty boxes as an excuse. Along with thoughts of Annabelle, he couldn't get the hidden alcove off his mind. After he'd parked and unloaded the empty boxes in the spot she'd cleared out in the living room, he went back outside.

Annabelle was busy working in one of the upstairs rooms. She'd only given him a tired wave when she'd seen him. He'd seen her surprise. She'd thought he wouldn't be back.

"Let me know when you have those boxes loaded," he'd called up. "I'll bring them down for you."

He wandered into the kitchen, the wall still bother-ing him. He tried to imagine why anyone would wall up an alcove. Especially Frannie Clementine. It had to have been the owner before her.

Behind him, he heard Annabelle come into the kitchen and pour herself a cup of coffee. She motioned to him. He declined. He had enough trouble sleeping as it was. The last thing he needed was coffee this late in the day.

"Still confused over the wall?" she asked with a chuckle. "I remembered that my grandmother had a hutch there when I was going up. There was definitely an alcove.

"So the plans are right. Why would my grandmother do that?"

He shook his head, but he suspected whatever was in that small space had enough of a smell that his pup was picking up on it. "Aren't you curious at all about what's in there?"

"No and I have no desire to tear into that wall, if that's what's on your mind. I just want to get this house ready to sell."

"There was only one other time that my dog acted like that, now that I think about it," he said, turning to look at her. "We stumbled onto a calf that had been torn apart by wolves."

"There is no dead calf killed by wolves in my wall."

He raised a brow. "There's something in there. Why else close off the alcove?"

"Why is everyone trying to scare me?" She put down her coffee cup. "It's late. We should probably call it a day."

"If I were you, I'd have to know what's in there."

"You aren't me," she snapped. "As you pointed out years ago, we are nothing alike."

His stomach knotted. It was the first time either of them had brought up that part of the past. "So true. You and I have never wanted the same things. And now you just want to get the house sold and get out of town."

"That's right."

"I won't do anything to slow you up." He stepped past her and started toward the front door.

"It's not that I didn't appreciate your help today," she said, following him out. "Thanks for taking boxes to the dump for me and for getting me more boxes."

"No problem."

"I just don't have time to remodel the kitchen," she said.

He nodded, wanting to take her in his arms and tell

her that everything was going to be all right. But he didn't think that was the case. Something was wrong at this house. Maybe there wasn't anything behind that wall. He hoped not. But he could see in her expression that she was running scared and had been for a while.

But he was the last person she wanted trying to comfort her.

He tipped the brim of his Stetson and headed for his truck, all the time mentally kicking himself for the emotions that had his heart aching.

ROB WALKED PAST the house as the last pickup pulled away. Out of the corner of his eye, he saw the young woman standing in the doorway. She pulled off the bandanna that had been covering her long blond hair. Her hair fell to below her shoulders as she turned back inside the house. He could hear her phone ringing as he continued on past.

At the corner, he turned and walked back toward the house. What he'd been able to find out about Francesca Clementine had left him shaken. Maybe it was a coincidence, but the woman had bought the house right after his uncle's Baby Doll had taken off with his loot from the heist.

Now Rob watched the woman inside the house on the phone. From what he could tell, she was alone. He was thinking of circling around to the back of the house when a neighbor came out onto her porch. She squinted in his direction. Small towns. This one was the worst. Everyone seemed to know each other, which meant he stood out like he was wearing a neon sign.

He gave a short nod at the woman and continued

walking. He could feel her watching him all the way to the end of the block before the busybody finally went back. It was the same woman who'd seen him last night around the Clementine house. He couldn't let her scare him off again. That his uncle might be right about this one had him excited. He would get into that house, one way or another. But what to do about the granddaughter?

INEZ GILBERT WAS a confirmed busybody. Anyone who didn't like it could just stuff it. At eighty-nine, she had no patience. Not that she'd had much when she was younger. But now she felt as if she didn't have a minute to waste on ignorant fools. And it seemed to her that the number of those people grew in relation to her advancing years.

She prided herself on being more observant than most people. When she was dead and gone, no one would be able to say that she'd let anyone pull the wool over her eyes. She believed that her advanced years had made her a student of the human condition. One look at a person, and she could size him or her up in a minute. She was hardly ever wrong.

That's why, when she'd seen the man walking down the street, looking hard at the Clementine place, she'd known. Something about the way he was walking, something about the way he was looking, something about the way he was dressed. Not to mention, she'd never seen him before last night and doubted he was from these parts.

Picking up the phone, she called the sheriff's office. The dispatcher tried to put her off, then tried to hand her off to one of the deputies.

"I want to speak to the sheriff," Inez said. "Don't make me come down there."

Finally she was put through to Sheriff McCall Crawford. Now there was a sharp woman. McCall had started out as a deputy, but bypassed several men on her way to sheriff. She was respected in the county and had won each election handily. Inez had made sure that everyone at the senior center voted for her. She'd also canvassed the neighborhood to make sure everyone got out and voted for the woman.

"Hi, Inez," McCall said when she came on the line. "I heard there was a problem in your neighborhood." She sounded friendly and not in the least upset that Inez hadn't wanted to talk to anyone but her.

"I saw a man walking past on the other side of the street. He was obviously a stranger, dressed all wrong, and he was staring at the Clementine place in a way that was suspicious."

"Was it possible he was interested in the house because it's for sale?"

Inez appreciated the diplomatic way the sheriff had put the question and smiled. "That stuffy little Mary Sue Linton put a For Sale sign out in the yard, so, yes, I'm aware. But he wasn't looking at the place like he was thinking what it might go for or if he might want to buy it."

"How was he looking at it?" McCall asked.

"Like he was looking for someone. And tonight wasn't the first time I've seen him sneaking around."

MCCALL HAD BEEN dealing with Inez Gilbert for years. Most of the department staff found her to be a pain in the neck. But Inez was smarter than they gave her credit for. The elderly woman noticed things, things that often were worth checking out.

"I'll tell you what, Inez. If you see him again, you call me right away. I'll tell the dispatchers to put you right through."

The woman let out a satisfied harrumph. "He's up to no good. Mark my words. I can tell just by looking at people."

"I know." McCall listened to Inez talk about fools for a while and then got off the line. One of the new deputies was passing by. "Martin," she said, motioning him in. "Do me a favor. When you're on duty could you keep an eye on the Clementine place?"

"On Millionaire's Row?"

She smiled, wondering how that area had gotten the name. Apparently a lot of people didn't know what a million would buy. "Let me know if you see anyone loitering around there."

After he left, she decided to call it a day. Her husband was making dinner tonight since it was his day off as a local game warden. Their daughter, Tracey, would have spent the day playing hard since she was on holiday until Monday.

McCall was looking forward to that time after dinner when Tracey was tucked away in bed for the night and she and her husband could just curl up on the couch together.

But as she was leaving, she couldn't help thinking about the man Inez had seen. The county had been quiet for a long while now. There were the usual disturbances that went with any community. But there had been little crime lately. Most of the calls her department got were barking dogs, kids misbehaving, speeding, car wrecks, underage drinking and minor thievery.

It was one of the joys of living here, she thought as she climbed into her patrol car. Her home was in the country, but she made a point of driving the couple of blocks to go down Millionaire's Row. She'd always liked the large houses with their wide porches, though most of them looked as if they could use a little work.

Still, the trees were huge and beautiful when grown out in the spring and summer. In the fall, the yards would be full of fallen leaves. Only a month ago, she'd seen some of the children playing in them and had thought of her own daughter. There was nothing more fun than piles of leaves. But while the leaves were gone now and the trees were stark against the November sky, the branches were so thick and full that they still provided privacy from the street.

She slowed as she neared the Clementine place. A sports car was parked in the driveway. She'd heard that one of Frannie's granddaughters have returned to town to get the house ready to sell. Maybe that's all the stranger was interested in, she thought. As she drove on by, she saw Inez peering out her front window.

McCall gave a flash of her lights and waved. Inez, always on duty, waved back.

ANNABELLE WATCHED DAWSON drive away, reminding herself why they'd broken up all those years ago. She could tell by the set of his jaw and the ramrod stiffness of his back that he was upset with her. Upset because she didn't want him to take a sledgehammer to her kitchen wall?

And why? Out of simple curiosity. Like she had time to remodel the kitchen before she sold the house.

She couldn't help being irritated with him. It hadn't been her idea for him to help her clean out the house.

But the moment she had the thought, all her irritation evaporated. The problem between them wasn't her kitchen wall. It was those old feelings mixed with the chemistry that had always arced between them like a live electrical wire. Being so close together most of the day had been hard on both of them.

She felt close to tears as she wandered back into the kitchen and opened the refrigerator. Of course Dawson had come to her rescue. She glanced toward the wall that shouldn't be there.

"What is it you have to hide, Grandma Frannie?" she asked the empty room.

Unfortunately, the refrigerator was almost as empty as the room. She had a few leftovers from her last grocery store trip, but nothing looked good. She closed the door; her stomach rumbled. Glancing at the clock, she saw that the grocery store was open for another twenty minutes.

But she didn't have the energy to drive the few blocks and shop. Turning out the kitchen light, she wandered down to her bedroom and threw herself onto the bed.

Another day or two and the house would be empty. A day or two of cleaning…maybe painting…

She couldn't think about that now. She was too tired. Unfortunately, her mind was still on Dawson. Pulling out her cell phone, she made the call, thankful when his phone went to voicemail.

"I'm sorry. Thank you for your help today. I really appreciated it." She disconnected.

Changing into a flannel nightgown she found in one of the chests of drawers, she crawled into bed. If her model friends could see her now, she thought, loving the feel of the warm flannel. Her last thought, though, was of Dawson as she closed her eyes and dropped off into an exhausted sleep.

Several hours later, she woke with a start. She listened, trying to understand what had awakened her. That's when she heard it. Someone was trying to break into the house.

ROB SWORE AS he saw a light come on at the house next door. That nosey old woman. She'd run him off last night, coming out on the porch with a shotgun, of all things, and yelling at him like he was a stray.

He moved into the shadows where he couldn't be seen. He'd been in town too long. His uncle called him every day, demanding he get into the house, no matter what he had to do.

"You don't understand," he'd tried to tell Bernie. "There's this old woman who lives next door—"

"You can't handle an old woman?" Bernie had demanded. "Am I going to have to come out there myself?"

He'd gotten off the line in the middle of his uncle's tirade. The old man knew nothing about small-town America. Every time he walked around the neighborhood, people stared at him. All day there were people coming and going from the Clementine place. Tonight, he'd told himself, he would get into the house. The problem was that if he had to kill the granddaughter, he feared her body would be found too quickly. It wouldn't leave him much time to search the place, and from what he'd seen looking in the windows, the house was a mess.

But he couldn't keep waiting. Maybe the granddaughter knew about the loot and was looking for it, as well. He couldn't take the chance that she would find it first.

He pried harder at the window and thought he almost had it when a light came on inside the house, making him swear under his breath.

"Move and I'll blow your manhood to kingdom come," said a weathered old woman's voice behind him at the same time he felt the business end of a shotgun shoved into his back.

He swung around, grabbing the barrel of the shotgun and knocking the old woman off her feet. She opened her mouth, but he was on her before she could scream. Clamping a hand over her mouth, he swept her up from the ground. Taking her and her damned shotgun, he headed through the bare-limbed trees that separated the two properties.

Chapter Ten

Dawson woke, head aching. With a groan, he rolled over onto this side and came face to face with Sadie. The look the pup gave him was one of disappointment. "Was I that bad last night?" he asked the dog.

Sadie whined and looked away.

He groaned again, feeling even worse. And all over a woman. Not just any woman. Annabelle Clementine.

Last night, after he'd left her house, he'd started to head home. But then he'd seen Jason's pickup parked in front of the Mint. He'd told himself that he could use a drink. Maybe two. Now he couldn't remember how he'd gotten home.

At the sound of someone in his kitchen, he felt his heart leap. Surely he hadn't gone back over to Annabelle's. And what? Had her drive him home? No.

Swinging his legs over the side of his bed, he saw that he was fully clothed. Hmm. He wasn't sure exactly if that was good or bad. Might depend on how he'd gotten home. He'd never been a drinker—let alone driven drunk. Someone must have helped him off with his boots, though. That meant someone had driven him home last night.

Padding to the kitchen, he peered around the door-jamb, not sure who he would find making coffee—just thankful someone was.

"Jason?"

His best friend turned to grimace at him. "You look like hell."

"I feel worse. Was I...?"

"Drunk?" His friend nodded.

"Morose?"

Jason laughed. "Do you mean did you go on and on about Annabelle?"

Dawson grimaced and headed back down the hall toward the bathroom. "Don't you get tired of being a fool?" he demanded of his image in the mirror. The answer was as plain as the look on his face.

"Talking to yourself again?" his brother asked from behind him, making him start.

"Knock much?"

"You left your door open. You look like hell."

"Thanks. I heard that already." He turned off the water after splashing some on his face and drying himself with a towel. "What are you doing here so early?"

"It's after ten."

He winced as he reached into the medicine cabinet, shook two aspirins into his hand and, chewing them, swallowed them dry.

His brother was grinning at him. "You butt dialed me last night from the bar."

His head began to ache even worse.

"It sounded like you were in trouble."

"Other than having the worst hangover ever, I'm fine."

Luke cocked an eyebrow at that. "So, what is going

on with you? If you're going back over to haul more boxes to the dump, I'm sorry but I can't help you today."

"Sure you are."

"That why you have such a hangover?" his brother teased. "Things didn't go well with Annabelle?"

He shot his brother a warning look and walked out of the bathroom to the kitchen where Jason handed him a cup of coffee and offered one to Luke, who heartily accepted.

"So how *are* things going with the two of you?" his brother asked as he pulled up a stool at the breakfast counter.

Dawson didn't even bother to look at Luke, let alone answer.

"Don't get him started," Jason said joining them. "Did I hear that your mother volunteered the two of you for the Christmas Stroll and Parade this year?"

Both groaned. "I hate to ask," Dawson said after taking a sip of his coffee.

"You're going as Santa," Jason said to him and then turned to Luke. "And you're going to be one of his elves."

"Of course I am," Luke said with a curse.

All Dawson could think was that by the time the Christmas Stroll and Parade rolled around, Annabelle would be long gone.

THE LAST PERSON Annabelle expected to see was Dawson. He arrived in his pickup, which she saw was full of more empty boxes. He began to unload them on her lawn. She watched, wondering what he thought he was doing, but at the same time thankful to see that many boxes. She'd been up since daylight, unable to sleep, and had made a half dozen trips to the porch with full boxes already this morning.

She hadn't expected to see him again--not after snapping at him yesterday about the stupid alcove wall. Even with the apology she'd left on his phone. It made her all the more suspicious as to why he was helping her.

Her head ached from lack of sleep. The house had been particularly noisy last night. At one point, she'd thought she heard someone breaking in. But when she looked out, she hadn't seen anyone. After that, she'd gotten up a couple of times only to find the wind whipping tree branches against the outside. Still, at one point, she'd stood at the dark window and could have sworn she'd seen a shadow scurry through the trees and away from Inez's house. The man Inez Gilbert had seen peeping in windows?

She had stared for a long time, but didn't see the shadow again. Still, it had kept her up. At one point, she'd even checked the doors and windows to make sure they were all locked.

Dawson brought a bunch of the boxes up onto the porch. He hadn't seen her standing in the doorway and started when he looked up and saw her. He looked as if he'd had a bad night, as well. He gave her a nod as he went back to pick up more of the boxes he'd unloaded from his truck. Jason and a couple of cowboys she didn't know drove up in pickups and got out. They headed for her, stopped at the edge of the porch for introductions then asked what they could do.

Today she wasn't about to argue. "I have some large things that I need taken down from upstairs to the charity shop," she told them. "Bed frames, side tables and some blankets."

They went to work while she finished filling boxes from upstairs. She'd hoped that she and Dawson might find a minute alone to talk, but he kept his head down loading the boxes she'd filled, seeming just to want to get the work done so he could leave.

On one rare occasion late in the day, both Jason and the crew had taken loads away and hadn't returned yet. She found Dawson on a water break next to the house.

"You don't have to bring your own water," she said as she watched him gulp the cold water from a bottle. It reminded her of when they were kids and shared a hose many times over the summer months.

"I'm fine," he said between gulps.

"You don't look fine." The words were out before she could call them back.

"I might have had too much to drink last night."

She couldn't help being shocked. "That's not like you. At least, not the Dawson Rogers I knew."

"PROBABLY WHY IT didn't take all that much to get me into this shape," Dawson said and finally smiled for the first time that day.

"I didn't expect you back here," she said.

He chuckled at that. "Didn't plan on coming back when I left." His gaze met hers. "I didn't get your message until this morning."

"I am sorry."

"You shouldn't be. We were both tired and I was butting in where I had no business."

She glanced toward the house. "I *am* curious about

what might be behind that wall." She chuckled. "Probably just dust bunnies. We'd both be disappointed if we knew."

"Probably," he said, although he knew that wasn't the case. Sadie didn't react like that over dust bunnies. "Maybe it's best if we don't know what's back there or why your grandmother sealed off the alcove. It will just be a mystery." Until the next homeowner realized the space was there and broke into it to find...to find what?

At the sound of Jason returning, they both went back to work. They worked all day. Jason had picked up hamburgers from Joe's In-n-Out for lunch. But that had been hours ago. It was getting dark by the time Jason and the cowboys he'd brought called it a day after loading the last of the boxes. Annabelle thanked them for their help and watched them drive off, leaving her alone with Dawson.

"Why don't I run by the store and get something for dinner?" he offered. He'd taken a peek in her refrigerator when she was out of the room. He doubted she ate much, being a model, but he also worried that she might still be short on cash.

She started to argue that it wasn't necessary, but he waved off her protests and headed for the store before it closed.

It was late. Very few cars were parked in the lot as he went in, not that he was paying much mind. He was bone weary, and he knew it had little to do with the physical exercise he'd had most of the day or even his hangover.

"So you're back from your hunting trip," said a familiar voice behind him.

Amy. With a mental head slap, he remembered telling

her that he'd call her when he got back. For a moment he couldn't think of anything to say. They had dated off and on for the past year. If he had to put a name to their relationship, he guessed it would have been called friendship with benefits.

Not that he thought of it that way. In truth, he didn't give it a lot of thought. That was what was nice about what they'd shared. It was...comfortable. He liked her. She liked him.

"Sorry, I'm afraid it slipped my mind," he said honestly as he turned to face her.

She raised an eyebrow. "Slipped your mind?" Divorced, Amy Baker worked at the local hardware store. He saw that she still had on her vest and, like him, had stopped after a long day of work to pick up a few groceries.

Amy studied him as if looking for something in particular. He could pretty much guess. If she'd heard about Annabelle Clementine returning to town, she was no doubt wondering, like a lot of other people, what was going on. Not that he and Amy had ever discussed his high school girlfriend. But Dawson knew that someone in town would have told her. It was hard to have a broken heart here without most of the county knowing about it.

"How was your Thanksgiving?" he asked, recalling that she planned to go to her aunt's up by the Canadian border and desperately wanting to change the subject.

Her expression made him feel guilty, but that followed quickly by anger at himself. He and Amy had an understanding. Both of them could date other people. Even if he was doing something he wasn't supposed to, he shouldn't have felt guilty.

He groaned inwardly as she said, "Fine," and turned her back on him to sort through the oranges.

Glancing around, he told himself that he really didn't want to get into anything here in the grocery store produce department. Like the post office, this was where you eventually saw everyone in town. It was also where rumors got started like wildfires.

"I'll call you later," he said to her back. She nodded without turning around.

He paid for the chicken wings, bean salad, rolls and a six-pack of beer he'd picked up for his dinner with Annabelle, telling himself he had nothing to feel guilty about.

But by the time he got back to the Clementine place, he was in a bad mood. Annabelle picked up on it right away.

"Your dog pee on your pickup seat?" she asked as he tossed the food he'd bought onto the kitchen table.

He shook his head. He certainly wasn't going to try to explain it to this woman. He wished he'd just gone home. What had possessed him to suggest getting them something to eat for dinner? He couldn't really leave Annabelle without any food, could he?

"Make yourself at home. I'm going to change," she said and left the room.

Change? He blinked. Change into something more comfortable? Had he given her the wrong impression by suggesting dinner? Now he was really wishing he'd followed his instincts and just left.

ANNABELLE WONDERED WHAT had happened at the grocery store. Clearly something, given Dawson's change of mood. She could tell he wished he hadn't suggested getting dinner. She'd smelled the spicy chicken wings the moment he'd walked in the door and heard her stomach rumble.

As she changed out of her dirty clothing, she wished she'd taken a shower while he was gone and changed then. Instead, she'd kept working. Her mind was set on getting this house ready to sell. It occupied all of her thoughts—except when Dawson was around.

"I'm so glad you got chicken wings," she called from the bedroom as she finished changing. No answer, but she didn't let that bother her. She was betting he got bean salad and rolls and beer. That was what he used to get when he planned one of their picnics out in the wilds. The man was a creature of habit. That used to drive her crazy. Now it felt…wonderful and sweet and made her heart ache.

She thought about him coming back this morning, even though he was clearly hungover. That, too, was like Dawson. He wasn't one to whine. Or to take a day off when there was work to do. That he'd come back at all to help her made her heart beat a little faster. It also made her feel guilty. She'd treated him poorly before she'd left and now he was overlooking that to help her.

To get you out of town as quickly as possible, she reminded herself. He wanted her gone. When an old high school friend called after hearing she was back in town, Annabelle had asked if Dawson had anyone in his life.

"I heard he's been seeing Amy Baker for a while," her friend had told her. "But I get the impression it isn't serious. Why? You aren't falling for him again, are you?"

"No, of course not. I'm just here to sell the house.

Dawson and I…well, lightning never strikes in the same place twice, right?"

"Wrong," her friend had said with a laugh. "Is there a storm brewing?"

When Annabelle walked into the kitchen, Dawson looked up in surprise. He blinked, taking in what she was wearing and then seeming to relax. Had he forgotten she was there?

"You changed," he said, looking almost embarrassed.

She frowned. "Is that a problem?" She'd put on the T-shirt and jeans that she'd purchased the other day.

The food he'd brought was spread out on the table. She saw that he'd opened a can of beer and was drinking it as he glanced at the contents of the metal box she'd left on the table. Dawson was going through the photos and yellowed newspaper clippings from inside it.

She sat down across from him.

"Help yourself," he said of the food. He stopped looking at the contents of the metal box to enjoy some of the food he'd brought, the two of them eating in companionable silence.

"So what do you make of these?" he asked after a while, as he slid his beer toward her and motioned to the box.

She took a drink before she said, "I haven't really looked at anything in it. I found it under the floorboards in my bedroom. When I opened it, I didn't recognize anyone. Must be from before Frannie moved in."

Dawson shot her a look before he pushed one of the photos in her direction. "Check this out." He went back to reading the newspaper clipping next to his paper plate.

She glanced at the old black-and-white photo. It ap-

peared to be four people in some kind of nightclub setting. Two women, two men. All were dressed to the
nines. Other than that, she couldn't imagine what he'd
found of interest.

As she pushed the photo back toward him, she saw
that he was frowning. He put the newspaper clipping
down and looked at her.

"What?" she asked.

"Did you see it?" he asked and nodded toward the
photo he'd given her.

"Apparently not." She was tired and the beer was
making her lethargic. She would much rather just sit
here with him than look through old photographs of
people she didn't know.

"Look hard at her," he said, putting his finger under
the face of the prettiest of the two women.

She picked up the photo. The woman's pale hair was
long and fell over one shoulder. Her figure was quite vo-
luptuous for a woman who was small in stature.

Then she looked into the woman's light eyes and felt
her heart begin to pound. "Frannie?"

Dawson chuckled. "Frannie was quite the looker in
her younger days, wouldn't you say?"

"That can't be her. This woman is blonde."

"Blonde like her granddaughter."

"But Frannie always had red hair."

He lifted a brow. "Well, at one time, she was a
blonde."

Annabelle stared at the photo. It was her grandmother.
She hadn't recognized Frannie because she'd looked so
different from the grandmother Annabelle had known.
And she didn't just look different, she was dressed dif-

ferently. Frannie had never worn makeup in all the years Annabelle had known her. But in the black-and-white photo, she was clearly wearing dark lipstick and mascara and eyeshadow.

It was a shock seeing Frannie so young—and sexy—and blonde. The young woman in the photo was smiling broadly and standing next to a handsome man in a pin-striped suit. Annabelle couldn't help but smile back at her grandmother. Frannie looked so happy. Was this the man Frannie had said was her alleged husband? Annabelle had been shocked to find out that Frannie had never married. So who was the mysterious man who'd fathered her son? Could this man be Annabelle's grandfather?

Annabelle speculated that Frannie's white lie about a husband who never existed might have been one reason they hadn't met her until their parents were killed and their grandmother insisted they come to Whitehorse to live with her.

"Even more interesting is the man with her." Dawson carefully smoothed out the old newspaper clipping. It was yellowed and cracked. "His name according to this is Bernard 'Bernie the Hawk' McDougal. He was an Irish mobster."

"What?" Annabelle quickly skimmed the newspaper clipping before staring at the man's mug shot. "He was arrested for a famous heist?"

"Arrested and released for lack of evidence," Dawson said. "The jewels were never found."

She picked up the photograph of her grandmother again.

"Wanna bet they were lovers?" he said. "Check out the way the man is looking at your grandmother."

"You're reading a lot into a photo." Even as she said it, though, she knew he was right. She couldn't help but think of a photo of her and Dawson that she'd kept all these years from their senior prom. The way Dawson was looking at her in the shot—the way she was looking at him... She knew what love looked like.

Her gaze rose to meet his and she wondered if he remembered the photograph. Or if he'd kept his copy. A lump formed in her throat, but it was nothing like the knot in her chest.

"Your grandmother was a gangster's moll," he said with a laugh. "Who would ever have suspected it?" He was grinning at her as he reached for the beer they'd been sharing—just as they had when they were lovers all those years ago. Their hands brushed. She started to pull away, but he caught her, entwining his warm fingers with her own. His grin disappeared. His eyes darkened and his breath seemed to catch.

Her own breath began to come quicker as she lost herself in the warmth of his gaze. She felt her lips part. His gaze shifted to her mouth. Her heart pounded so loudly she couldn't hear anything else. He was going to kiss her.

He gave a slight tug on her hand as he leaned toward her. She held her breath, remembering Dawson's kisses and yearning for this older, even sexier version of him to kiss her as he had on the dance floor that night at the bar.

He was a breath away. She closed her eyes as she closed the last of the distance. Her lips brushed over his, just a feather touch. She leaned in farther.

Her eyes came open abruptly as he let go of her hand. She blinked. He'd pulled away and was now shoving back his chair and rising.

"I've got to go," he said, his voice hoarse with emotion.

"Dawson." She'd wanted that kiss, needed it, and yet as she got to her feet, she knew kissing him again was the stupidest thing she could do. Hadn't Jason warned her not to lead his friend on? That was definitely not what she'd meant to do. As soon as this house sold, she was out of here.

So why did she feel like crying?

BACK AT THE RANCH, Dawson mentally kicked himself as he built a fire and fed Sadie. The pup quickly fell asleep in front of the crackling blaze while he paced, still angry with himself.

He should have been tired after all the boxes he'd loaded and unloaded today. But he felt antsy. At the sound of a vehicle pulling up out front, he moved to the window to see Amy park and get out. He swore under his breath as he opened the door before she could knock.

"I got tired of waiting by the phone," she said, as she stopped at the foot of the porch steps.

"I'm sorry. I've been...busy."

"I heard." She glanced past him into the house. "Is she here now?"

It wasn't like he had to ask whom she was referring to. "No. She's never been here."

Amy nodded and came up the steps. "I thought we should talk." She didn't give him a chance to tell her that he was tired and wasn't in the mood. Clearly she didn't care.

As he followed her inside, he realized that she felt he owed her an explanation. It surprised him, since what they had wasn't serious. At least, for him.

As she turned and he saw the tears in her eyes, he felt a start. It was his night for surprises. Clearly Amy had seen their so-called relationship a lot differently than he had. He thought of his mother's warning.

"Don't hurt that girl," his mother said when he and Amy had first started up after years of random dating.

"She knows it isn't serious," he'd said, and his mother had rolled her eyes.

"It's been serious for her since the first time you took her to your bed."

"It was her bed," he'd said, making his mother roll her eyes again. "Stop trying to get me married off."

"That's not what I'm doing. You shouldn't marry Amy. You should marry someone you can't live without."

"Is this reverse psychology?" he'd joked, uncomfortable with the conversation because there'd only been one woman who fit that bill. And while he and his mother could talk about anything, this was one topic he'd prefer not to discuss with her.

Now, as he looked at Amy, he knew that Willie had been right, as always. He'd thought he and Amy both knew that this wasn't going anywhere. "Amy, I'm sorry I didn't call you."

"This isn't about you not calling me when you returned from your hunting trip," she said. "Although you did say you would."

He nodded. "You're right. Something came up."

Amy let out a bitter laugh. "Something? Don't you mean *someone*?"

"Look, it isn't what you think."

She scoffed. "You didn't just say that."

He groaned inwardly, thinking the same thing.

"It's her, your high school sweetheart, the one who broke your heart."

Yep, he thought, that was the county grapevine's short version of him and Annabelle apparently.

"Annabelle—"

"I know her name," Amy snapped. "Annabelle Clementine. A supermodel no less. What I didn't know was that if she ever came back you would drop everything to be with her."

"That might be the way it looks, but…"

"I don't want to talk about her," Amy said with a shake of her head. She looked around the room for a moment. He could see that she was barely able to hold back the tears.

"I think I know what you want to hear," he said. Her watery gaze met his. "You know I like you." One tear broke loose and cascaded down her cheek. "I enjoy being with you."

"But you don't love me." She nodded. More tears followed.

"I thought that's how you felt about me, as well."

"You never suspected that I might want more?"

"I didn't have more to give," he said, hating himself. His mother had tried to warn him. He should have seen this coming. But he hadn't thought about the future. He'd been living day to day since Annabelle left. "I never wanted to hurt you."

"So you're back with her."

"Good God, no," he said, surprised that she would think that.

She made a swipe at the tears. "Then what is going on?"

"I'm helping her clean out her grandmother's house so she can get it sold and leave town."

Amy stared at him. "You really believe that."

"It's the truth."

She laughed and shook her head again. "And then what?"

"And then nothing."

"You're going to let her leave again?"

"*Let* Annabelle leave?" It was his turn to laugh. "You don't *let* a woman like Annabelle do anything. She's like a force of nature. She does whatever she wants, when she wants, and the best thing you can do is get out of her way before she mows you down."

Surprise registered on Amy's expression. "You make it sound as if you don't even like her."

He took a deep breath, held it for a moment as he considered what she'd said. As he let it out, he said, "Sometimes I want to strangle her. Other times…"

"You're still in love with her."

He started to deny it, but she cut him off.

"All these years? You never got over her. Were you just waiting for her to come back?"

"No." He shook his head adamantly. "I never thought she would come back. Why would I wait for her? Only a fool would…" He swore under his breath. "Like I said, it isn't what you think."

She lifted a brow, clearly not believing a word of it. "She's the one, the one you will always be in love with. The one that got away, the one you will compare all other women to and find them lacking. Is it possible you didn't realize that before she came back? Seriously?"

He felt as if he'd been blindsided. "Look, you have it all wrong."

She was shaking her head. "Stop lying to yourself and worse, to me. We're friends, right?" He nodded, glad she wasn't crying anymore. "So do something about this. If you love her, then don't let her leave again. Tell her."

He laughed and took a step back. "I did that thirteen years ago."

"If you don't, then you aren't the man I thought you were." With that, she turned and walked out, leaving him standing in his living room wondering why she couldn't understand how wrong she was.

"Annabelle doesn't love me. She never did love me. At least, not enough," he said as the door closed behind Amy. He listened to her pickup drive away before cussing Annabelle for coming back and messing up his life yet another time.

Chapter Eleven

Annabelle spread everything from the metal box out on the kitchen table after Dawson left. Once she'd recognized her grandmother in the one photo, she'd been able to find her in others. Bernie, the mobster, was in his share, as well, along with his "associates."

Her grandmother used to tell these outrageous stories of when she was young. She and her sisters had never believed a word of them.

But, it appeared, there'd been some truth to them—maybe more than Annabelle wanted to acknowledge. As she glanced through the contents of the metal box, she reminded herself where she'd found it. Was it coincidence that her grandmother had hidden it under the floorboard in the bedroom Annabelle had stayed in for years growing up? Did her grandmother assume Annabelle would choose to stay in that room when she came back to sell the house?

If the floorboard had been loose and something hidden under it from the time she was a girl until she left at eighteen, she would have noticed it. She was sure of that. Which meant her grandmother had left it for her—just as she'd left her the house. So there was a message in here.

But, for the life of her, she didn't know what it was. Frannie's name was never in the newspaper cutlines. Under one photo, she was referred to as Baby Doll. What was that about? Maybe the woman just looked like here grandmother.

Then why would Frannie have the photos and newspaper clippings?

As she read the news articles, it left little doubt that her grandmother had been involved in some dangerous business as the moll of mobster Bernie McDougal. These men that her grandmother had partied with were criminals. Could it be possible she hadn't known at the time?

Doubtful, Annabelle thought. Her grandmother had been a sharp woman. Annabelle suspected Frannie had known exactly what she was dealing with. She thought of the grandmother she'd known—a soft-spoken, ladylike and diminutive woman. Now, though, she realized there was a lot more to Frannie than anyone in Whitehorse had suspected.

In the clippings, she'd also discovered something that gave her a chill. The heist that Bernie McDougal and one of his associates had been hauled in for questioning about had never been solved—nor the rare jewels ever recovered. But what sent shivers up her spine was that it had been less than a year later that Frannie had bought this house in Whitehorse.

Annabelle recalled her grandmother saying that she used the money from her deceased husband's insurance policy to buy the house. Frannie had been pregnant and given birth not long after that to Annabelle's father, Walter Clementine, said to have been named after the father he'd never known.

Now Annabelle knew that the husband had been a lie. So who was the father of her baby? Carefully she put everything back into the metal box. She couldn't shake the feeling, as she glanced at the wall hiding the former alcove, that she'd only found one of her grandmother's secrets.

That her grandmother had known these men... It made her shudder. Worse, her grandmother had left this for her. Why? Was she trying to warn her?

At the sound of someone on her porch, she jumped. A moment later the doorbell rang. She stuck the metal box into one of the kitchen cupboards as the doorbell rang again. She felt jumpy, almost afraid to see who was standing on her doorstep.

Peering out through the red-and-white gingham curtains, she saw Mary Sue. The Realtor spotted her about the same time. Annabelle quickly dropped the curtain and opened the door.

"Is everything all right?" Mary Sue asked suspiciously.

"It's fine."

"You just had such a weird expression," the woman persisted.

"You startled me, that's all. So, do you have a half dozen prospective buyers to tell me about? How about one?"

Mary Sue shook her head. "I came by to see how you were faring. I heard Dawson and his friends have been helping you."

"No secrets in this town," Annabelle said under her breath as she stepped out of the way to let the Realtor see how much had been accomplished. "All but one of the bedrooms is empty. One bathroom is done and the other one getting there."

"You still have a lot of things to get rid of," Mary Sue noted as she took in the items piled up in the living room.

"These are all to be either sold or donated. I called the antique shop. Mary said she would come look to see if there is anything she can use. I wanted to wait until I had a chance to go through the kitchen."

"You are making progress, I'll give you that," the Realtor said, then *tsked* at the state of the walls in the emptied bedrooms. "Those are going to have to be painted."

Annabelle sighed. "Did you just come by to torment me?"

Mary Sue seemed surprised. "Is that what you think I'm doing?"

Annabelle didn't answer for a moment. "I'm just tired and out of sorts." Mary Sue would be, too, if she'd been working day and night to empty out this place. She hated to imagine how the Realtor would be if she'd just learned that her grandmother had left her a houseful of junk— and box full of disturbing secrets.

"So, you and Dawson…"

Annabelle gave her an impatient look. "Really? Have you had any interest in the house?"

Mary Sue shook her head. "It's a bad time of the year with Christmas coming."

Annabelle groaned. Before she could escort the Realtor out, she had to listen to Mary Sue's other suggestions regarding paint color, possible new appliances, even the replacing of all the carpet in the house with hardwood.

She let out a sigh of relief when she was able to close the door behind Mary Sue. That's when she noticed the dark car parked across the street and realized it wasn't the first time she'd seen it there.

It was, however, the first time she'd realized there was a figure sitting at the wheel behind the tinted glass.

DAWSON OFTEN WENT for a horseback ride to clear his head. Unfortunately, it hadn't done much good today. He kept thinking about his mother's earlier visit and what she'd said about Annabelle. As if Annabelle wasn't on his mind enough.

But he had made a decision, one he thought even his mother would support, he thought as he returned from his ride.

"We got Annabelle's house pretty much cleared out, but you're right, she needs more help." The words were barely out of Dawson's mouth before his mother took off her apron, tossed it down and said, "So, what are we doing standing around here? Let's pack up some food. I'll get your brother up to help and make a few calls."

When he hesitated, she asked, "That is what you want, right? Jason told me how hard you all have been working to help her get the house ready to sell so she can leave."

He nodded. "That's the plan, remember?"

Within minutes, his mother was on the phone lining up able-bodied men and a couple more trucks.

"I already helped," Luke said when he was rousted from bed.

"So I heard. But today we're getting everything out of the house to begin cleaning and painting," she said, making her youngest son groan. "Get a few of your friends to meet us at the Clementine place."

Luke groaned. "If I call them this early, they'll kill me."

"Tell them your mama said if they don't get up and meet us there—"

"Got it." He threw back his covers, then quickly pulled them over himself again. "Could I have a little privacy?"

"Like you have anything to hide," Dawson joked from the doorway.

He had no idea what kind of reception they were going to get once they reached Annabelle's grandmother's house, but he didn't have to worry.

The moment they drove up, Annabelle opened the door, looking both leery and surprised. She'd already filled a dozen more boxes and had them sitting at the end of the porch.

His mother was out of the truck in a shot, her arms full of food as she charged toward the door.

"Willie?" Annabelle said and looked to Dawson for clarification. As if he could control his mother once she set her mind to something.

"Point me to the kitchen." But his mother was already headed there by the time Dawson reached the edge of the porch.

"I'm going to need your keys to move your car," he said to Annabelle.

She looked a little dumbstruck as two more pickups arrived, both full of boxes. Luke trudged toward the house, a carton full of cleaning supplies in his arms.

As if sleepwalking, she reached back inside for her keys. When she dropped them into his palm, he gave her a quick nod.

But before he could turn away, he saw surprise and something more in her big blue eyes. Gratitude? Surely nothing more. That night outside the bar after he'd kissed her, she'd told him to stay out of her business. Then, last night, she'd seemed willing when he'd kissed her, before his senses had come back to him.

She couldn't be anymore confused than he was about last night. But, in his defense, she'd been real clear about him leaving her alone and he hadn't been listening. Still wasn't. But that didn't mean she hadn't been sincere in what she wanted—and didn't want—from him.

"Dawson," she began.

"Annabelle?" It was his mother calling. She seemed about to say something more to him, but turned back into the house as Willie asked where they should begin. Luke's friends simultaneously began to bring in the cardboard boxes.

Dawson didn't see much of Annabelle after that. He kept busy hauling the last loads to the dump. Willie had put Luke's friends to work filling boxes with old newspapers and magazines and dragging them out to the porch. If anyone could organize an army, it was his mother.

They broke for lunch. By then, Willie had managed to get both spare bedrooms and a bathroom cleaned. She put Luke and his friends to work painting.

"Neutrals," Willie said in response to Annabelle's surprise. "I called Mary Sue and asked her what we should paint the rooms. I just happened to have some paint. I hope you don't mind."

But Dawson could tell that she didn't believe his mother had never-opened gallons of neutral colors just sitting around anymore than he did.

"I can't tell you how grateful I am for all of this,"

Annabelle said, her voice breaking. "I don't know how to thank you."

Willie reached across the table to squeeze her hand. "No need. We're practically family." She shot Dawson a look that said they would have been family if it wasn't for him.

He lowered his head and sighed inwardly. His mother didn't think he'd done enough to try to stop Annabelle from leaving thirteen years ago. Maybe she was right about that. But ultimately, nothing on this earth could have kept Annie in Whitehorse—certainly not him.

ANNABELLE COULDN'T MISS the look that passed between mother and son. Dawson appeared uncomfortable, taking a sandwich from the plate his mother passed around and going out to the tiny back porch rather than eating it in the crowded kitchen.

"I'm sure this is your doing," Annabelle said when she joined him on the porch with a sandwich of her own. She sat down beside him to let her legs dangle over the side, much as she had when they were kids.

"My mother?" He shook his head. "You know how she is. She likes to help."

"And she just happened to have a lot of neutral-colored paint she wanted to get rid of."

He grinned over at her. "I told her how anxious you were to get the house sold…" He shrugged.

She looked off into the distance to the line of trees that marked the edge of the Milk River. The backyard was still lush in places, even after a hot summer and long fall. But she could tell the temperature was dropping. Soon the cold and snow would set in. She had to be out of here by then.

"How are you holding up?" he asked.

She smiled, knowing what she must look like in her grandmother's hand-me-down clothes, her hair under a bandanna, smelling of dust and old musty things. "I can see the floor now in all but a couple of the rooms. I'm feeling…better."

He nodded. "What about your grandmother, the photos, the newspaper clippings?"

Annabelle shook her head. "I still can't believe it. Frannie used to tell us stories about these outrageous parties she went to when she was, like, seventeen and all the crazy things men would buy her, furs and diamonds…" She laughed. "We never believed a word of it. I mean, look how she lived here in Whitehorse. I can assure you, there are no furs or diamonds that I've run across in this house."

"I would agree if I hadn't seen the photos."

She drew out the hem of the dirty sweatshirt she had on. "Most everything I've found in her closet looks like this, only with gaudier designs. Frannie didn't even own a car and she used what was left in her bank account to pay the utilities and taxes so I'd have time to sell this place." Her voice broke. "This house was all she had when she died."

She could feel the heat of his gaze as he looked over at her. "She had more than this house. Everyone in town loved her. She was always doing for others. She was rich in friends. To her, that was more important than furs and diamonds," he said as he finished his sandwich and got to his feet.

"You mean her values were better than mine."

He stopped and looked at her. "I wasn't comparing the two of you." He brushed again at the invisible chip on her shoulder.

"Last night…"

"I shouldn't have kissed you," he said quickly and looked away. "You've made it clear how you feel about me, this town, Montana in general."

Had she? "I'm not even sure how I feel about a lot of things," she said, looking up at him.

Willie called from the doorway. "I thought I would start cleaning the kitchen cabinets unless there is something else you'd rather I do."

"No, that's great," she said, pushing to her feet as Dawson hopped off the porch to walk around front. "I'll come help you."

DAWSON OFTEN FOUND himself in awe of his mother. Just watching her in action was a sight to see. The afternoon passed in a blur of activity. The house smelled like cleaning products and paint, which was much better than dust and decay.

"We paint the kitchen tomorrow and finish the rest of the rooms," Willie was saying. "I expect all of you back here after work tomorrow to help."

Luke's friends nodded. His mother commanded respect. He knew no cowboy stupid enough to go against Willie.

Annabelle started to object but his mother cut her off saying, "I'll bring my chocolate cake." As if anyone needed more incentive.

That got grins out of Luke's friends. Willie's chocolate cake was famous.

Dawson hadn't said two words to Annabelle since their talk on the back porch. Mary from the local antique shop had come up and taken what she wanted. After everything had been removed from the house except for a chair in the living room, the bed and dresser in Annabelle's old room, and the kitchen table and chairs, they called it a day.

Everyone began to leave. His mother packed up a few things to take home. When Dawson offered to carry them out to his pickup—since the two of them had ridden in together—his mother waved off his help. "I'm riding with Luke. See if there is anything else you can help Annabelle with."

As if he was fooled by that. Annabelle wasn't, either.

"Thank you, but you've done more than enough," she said as Willie left.

She and Dawson eyed each other in the silence that filled the house following his mother's exit.

"Look, I know you said—"

"Thank you." She met his gaze. "It would have taken me weeks to accomplish all of this…" Her voice broke.

He shrugged. "You needed help. That's what people do here for neighbors." Then he tipped his hat and left, headed straight for the bar. "See you tomorrow," he said over his shoulder.

Chapter Twelve

"What are you doing?"

At that moment, Annabelle was wondering why Mary Sue was calling her, let alone asking her such an inane question. There was music playing in the background and the sound of drunken voices.

"A few people from high school thought you might want to come down to the bar for a drink." She sounded as if those few people were holding a gun on her, forcing her to make this call. A few people from high school? "We're down at the Mint. If you're interested…" Mary Sue also sounded like she'd already had a drink or two. "You have something better to do?"

Now, that really was the question, wasn't it? "I just need to shower and change."

"Great. See you soon." Mary Sue disconnected.

Annabelle considered calling her back and declining. What had she been thinking, saying she would go? But really, did she have something better to do? Fall into bed exhausted. That also had its appeal, but she headed for the shower. When was the last time she'd been out with a bunch of women? She thought of her clubbing days and groaned inwardly. Those days were gone and she wasn't even sure she missed them.

Showered and changed, she pulled her hair up and drove down to the Mint. A glass of wine sounded perfect. Maybe two. Then back home to bed.

The moment she walked in, she spotted Mary Sue with a handful of young women she wasn't sure she recognized. But as she approached the table and each of the women greeted her, she began to remember them. Mary Sue had traveled in a different circle than Annabelle had in high school. But the school had been small enough that she'd still known everyone.

Mary Sue got her a glass of wine and some of the others pulled up a chair for her. There was the usual chatter around the table—men, mothers and work. Fortunately none of it was about her or why she was back in town. She figured Mary Sue had warned them not to try to interrogate her. She was just starting to relax when she saw Dawson nursing a beer alone at the end of the bar.

DAWSON LOOKED UP from his beer and saw her in the mirror over the bar. He swore under his breath. What was Annabelle doing here? Had she followed him?

He turned on his bar stool, surprised to see that she'd showered and changed, unlike him. She was sitting with a bunch of women, women she'd never associated with in high school. But they all seemed to be getting along as if old friends. Go figure.

He turned back to his beer, determined that she wasn't going to ruin it for him.

At the sound of a commotion and sudden raised voices, he turned, shocked to see that Annabelle was at the center of it. A bar patron who'd clearly had too much to drink was trying to pull Annabelle to her feet, demanding a dance.

"You think you're too good for us since you became some hoity-toity cover girl?" the man demanded in a loud, drunken voice. "You too good to dance with someone like me?"

Annabelle was trying quietly to tell the man that she was just there visiting with friends and didn't want to dance. "I appreciate you asking, but I'm really tired."

"Tired?" The man scoffed and jerked her to her feet and into his arms.

Dawson swore, put down his beer, slid off his bar stool and strode up behind the man. He recognized him as a cowhand from up north by the name of Clyde Brown. He laid a hand on the man's shoulder. "Let's leave the lady alone," he said.

"Lady?" Clyde scoffed as he looped his arm around Annabelle's waist and started to haul her toward the dance floor.

"Let her go," Dawson said quietly, afraid he could see how this was going to play out. Definitely wasn't what he'd had in mind when he'd come here for one beer and a little peace, if not quiet.

"Stay out of this if you know what's good for you, Rogers," Clyde snarled drunkenly.

And just as he'd figured, the cowhand shoved Annabelle. She crashed into the table edge, drinks going everywhere, as Clyde spun around, leading with his fist.

Dawson saw it coming long before the cowhand took the swing. He blocked it and grabbed the cowhand by the back of the collar. "I don't want to fight you. So let's just—"

"She ain't worth fightin' over?"

Dawson looked past the man at Annabelle. Before he could answer, Clyde broke free and took another swing.

From behind Dawson, he heard the cowhand's friends get up from where they'd been at the bar. He swore under his breath as he coldcocked Clyde and swung around to take on the rest.

Chapter Thirteen

Her face flaming from humiliation, Annabelle drove back toward her grandmother's house. She would never think of it as hers. It was her grandmother's, and she was suddenly angry that Frannie had left it to her. True, she needed the money from it to save herself, but right now she could overlook that.

In fact, the more she thought about it, the more she was convinced that Frannie had collected all that junk, filling the house full, just to keep her granddaughter in town for as long as possible. Not that that theory made any sense.

Within a block, she realized that the last place she wanted to be right now was in that house. She turned at the next street and headed east out of town. She had no idea where she was going. A part of her realized she was wasting precious gas, but at that moment, she didn't care.

The night was dark. There was no one on the highway. She drove mindlessly, wishing she never had to stop. The fact that she had nowhere to go after she sold the house terrified her. She had no plan, wouldn't have much money and had no idea what to do next.

At a sign for Nelson Reservoir, she turned off and

drove down to the lake. The water shimmered even in the blackness of the dark night. She got out and walked to the edge of the shore, thinking about throwing herself into the icy-cold water. The thought actually made her laugh. As bad as things were, she still wanted to live.

She thought of Dawson, probably still back at the bar fighting those men—and all because of her. She kept seeing the expression on his face when the man he called Clyde had asked if she was worth fighting over.

Annabelle shook away that image, still embarrassed. Dawson had fought the man for her. He'd come to her rescue. Again. She shook her head and breathed in the night air. Mary Sue had gotten her out of there as the bar had erupted into a half-dozen fistfights. She'd passed a patrol SUV, lights and sirens blaring, headed for the bar as she'd left.

If only someone would make an offer on the house. Now it was more than a desperate need for the money. She had to get out of this town. She had to get away from Dawson before she ruined his life as well as her own. Right now he could be sitting in a jail cell because of her. If so, she didn't even have the money to get him out. She owed him money for keeping her car from being re-possessed, as it was.

She groaned, suddenly chilled by the November air, and headed back to her car. Just the thought of Dawson choked her up. Why did he have to be so nice to her? She'd hurt him. Why couldn't he act like a jackass and make her glad that she'd left him as well as Whitehorse?

On the drive back, she reminded herself that the house was coming along nicely—thanks to Dawson and his family. Tomorrow most of the rooms would be finished,

then there was no reason Mary Sue couldn't start showing the house. By this time next week…

As she pulled into the drive, her headlights flashed
across the front of the house. Her breath caught in her
throat. She slammed on the brakes, her eyes widening
in alarm at the sight of someone inside the house. She
cut the lights and sat in the dark staring, telling herself
that as upset as she was, she had to have imagined—

The figure moved past the window.

Annabelle threw the sports car into Reverse and
stepped on the gas. The car roared backward and into
the street. At the sound of screeching brakes, headlights
filled the inside of her car. She had only an instant to
realize how close she'd come to being hit before her car
door was jerked open.

"WHAT THE HELL?" Dawson demanded as he reached in
and pulled her keys. "Are you drunk?"

Annabelle stumbled out from behind the wheel and
into his arms. He could feel her trembling. "There's
someone in the house."

"You can't just back up like that without looking," he
snapped before her words registered.

She turned her face up to him. It looked ghastly
white. Even her bow-shaped mouth was trembling. "In
the house. I saw someone."

Her actions began to make sense as he looked from
her to the house. "Stay here."

She nodded, those blue eyes wider than he'd ever
seen them.

He considered moving the cars out of the middle of
the street, but figured if she really had seen someone in

the house… He still had her keys in his hand. "A house key on here?"

She pointed to a large square one.

"Get back in your car out of the cold and stay there."

"Maybe you should call the police."

"I just had a long talk with the sheriff, so no thanks."

"Then be careful."

Was she actually worried about him? He'd fought four cowboys because of her and held his own pretty well. While her concern was touching, he knew it was just something a person said when they were sending someone into a house after an intruder.

As quietly as he could, he crossed the porch to the front door. He listened for a moment before slipping the key into the lock. Slowly he turned the knob.

The door swung open. A now familiar fresh-paint smell rushed out at him. He listened, heard nothing while he waited for his eyes to adjust to the semidarkness before he stepped in and turned on a light.

He figured if there really had been someone in the house, they were long gone by now. They would have heard the commotion out in the street. They would have seen Annabelle's headlights when she pulled in.

But he wasn't taking any chances as he moved quietly through the house, checking one room after another. There was no sign of anyone. He checked the back door, still locked—just as the front door had been. He checked windows, all locked.

He walked through the living room into the kitchen and turned on the overhead light. Again, no sign that anyone had been here.

He went to the wall concealing the alcove, recalling

Sadie's reaction. He'd just squatted down to inspect the white beadboard wainscoting when he heard a sound behind him.

Shooting to his feet, he spun around only to find Annabelle standing in the doorway. She still looked terrified. Her gaze met his. He shook his head, telling himself he shouldn't be surprised that she hadn't done what he told her to—stay in the car.

"Is he gone?" she asked and saw Dawson's expression.

"I couldn't find any sign of anyone being here. Everything is locked up tight. Nothing looks disturbed, not that there is much to disturb at this point."

"But I saw…" She swallowed and shook her head. "Someone." She met his gaze, hoping he would tell her it was possible. She could see that his knuckles were skinned and there was a cut on his cheek near his right eye, the skin around it bruised.

"The place was locked up tighter than a drum. If someone broke in… I didn't see it."

She hugged herself. "So, you're saying I imagined it."

He wasn't saying anything. He looked down at his boots then finally lifted his gaze to her. He saw her bristle. "It isn't that I don't believe you thought you saw something…

"Why are you here?" she demanded.

He felt himself balk at her sudden anger. Right now, he had no idea. "I thought that after what happened at the bar… I only wanted to check to make sure you were all right. I'll move your car."

She said something he didn't catch as he started past her and caught a hint of her perfume. It had the same effect on him that it had thirteen years ago. He increased his stride as he headed for the front door. Remembering how she felt in his arms only minutes ago in the middle of the street, he feared that if he even hesitated, it would only make him do or say something foolish.

"I'll bring you back your keys," he said as he walked out the open front door, thankful his senses were starting to clear in the fresh air of the porch. But as he turned, he saw that the keys he'd left in the door were gone and Annabelle had pulled her car into the drive, but his pickup still sat in the middle of the street. Something about that seemed to mock his behavior tonight.

Hearing her behind him, he said over his shoulder, "Lock up behind me." He almost added that if she had any more trouble tonight to call him. "Call the sheriff if you see anyone around the house again."

He was almost to his truck when he heard the front door of the house slam as if caught by the wind. He looked back to see her pass by the front window. All he caught was a glimpse of her, since she'd turned out all but one of the hall lights. But he could tell that she was crying.

The sight stirred his earlier protectiveness. "Damn it, Annie," he said under his breath. "Why do you have to keep doing this?"

The night had no answer. He saw a light come on in her old bedroom and felt an ache that threatened to double him over.

He had to get her out of Whitehorse. Get her house sold. Get her on the road. No matter what it took. Otherwise... She was going to get into his heart again.

And yet, even as he thought it, he feared it was too late.

ANNABELLE KNEW WHAT she'd seen. A man moving through the house. No ghost of her grandmother, even though, for a moment, there had seemed to be a white light around the figure. No doubt a reflection from her headlights. She didn't believe in ghosts.

She moved through the house searching every closet and cubbyhole, checking the windows and doors herself, turning on all the lights. Dawson was right. The house was empty. All the windows and doors had been locked.

He hadn't believed her. Worse, when she'd come into the house, she'd found him inspecting that stupid wall in the kitchen. Did he think the intruder had escaped through it, somehow?

Exasperated, tired, upset and generally irritable, she stood in the living room trying to decide if she was going to leave all the lights in the house on tonight. It seemed silly, but she was tempted. Angry with herself for being such a chicken, especially given that apparently she'd only imaged the intruder, she went through the house turning off lights until she reached her bedroom.

She was still annoyed with Dawson and realized she had no good reason to be. He'd worked here at the house all day, he'd saved her at the bar, he'd driven over to check on her, he'd braved coming into the house to look for the intruder…

The man just couldn't stop saving her. He must be getting sick of it. Hadn't he pretty much told her that the only reason he was helping her with the house was to get rid of her more quickly?

Well, it wouldn't be quick enough for either of them, she told herself as she started into her bedroom on the first floor and froze.

The loose floorboard where she'd discovered the metal box with Frannie's photos and newspaper clippings was sticking up just enough that only she would notice it. Her heart began to pound as she looked around the room. The board wasn't the only thing out of place.

Her pulse a steady panicked throb in her throat, she saw that someone had moved her bed.

Chapter Fourteen

Annabelle stood nailed to the spot, her mind racing as fast as her heart. *Someone had been in the house.* Dawson wouldn't have pried up the floorboard, but he might have moved her bed when he was searching before she came in.

The thought sent a chill through her, because when she'd searched the house minutes ago, she hadn't looked under the bed. She glanced toward the closet. All that was in it were her grandmother's ugly clothes. No trespasser.

Edging toward the bed, she stopped next to the disturbed floorboard. With her toe, she pushed it back down, knowing whoever had been in here hadn't escaped that way. Now that she was closer, she could see where the legs of her bed had scraped across the floor all the way to the wall. How strange. The bed had definitely been moved.

Slowly, she bent down to peer underneath.

At first, all she saw were dust bunnies, relieved not to find a man hunkered under there. But then she saw something that sent her already thundering heart into overdrive. A scrap of fabric was caught in the corner of one of the floorboards. *Another secret hiding place, Grandma Frannie?*

Rising, she went to the side of the bed. It was heavy, the headboard and footboard made of solid wood. But she got it to move an inch at a time until the bed finally stopped at the wall.

The scrap of fabric appeared to be a gray and white stripe. She touched the cloth. Not an ounce of dust on it. Nor were there any dust bunnies on a large portion of the floor.

As she moved closer, she saw a spot on the floor that had been carved out like…like a handhold. Blinking, she realized what she was seeing. A trapdoor.

She started to try to lift it, but quickly thought better of that. What if the man she'd seen was down there? She pulled out her phone. Her first thought was to call the sheriff. Her second was to call Dawson.

Annabelle was so tired of needing to be saved that she pocketed her phone and went into the kitchen to her grandmother's utility drawer. Willie had managed to get all the top cabinets and some of the lower ones cleared out and cleaned earlier today, but they'd decided to leave this drawer for now because it held all kinds of keys, screws, bolts, nuts and tools, all things that they might need before they were finished.

She brought out the hammer and hefted it, gauging its weight, then grabbed a small flashlight that she quickly found worked. Hurrying back into the bedroom, she found the trapdoor was just as she'd left it. If the intruder was down there, he hadn't tried to get away, because the scrap of fabric was still caught in the corner.

Leaning down, she grabbed the handhold and lifted.

The door was heavy but she managed without having to put down the hammer. It groaned upward. She saw that a table leg had been attached so the door could be propped open.

Cautiously she shone the flashlight beam into the gaping hole, surprised to find several wooden steps that dropped down into blackness. What was down there? The piece of cloth that had been caught in the door fluttered down into that darkness. She aimed the flashlight beam into the space, only to see what appeared to be a passageway.

Annabelle listened, chilled to her soul at the sight. *Oh, Grandma, what were you involved in?* She thought of Dawson earlier on the back porch painting Frannie as a saint. Did saints have hidden trapdoors under beds? Or secret passageways dug under their houses?

There was no way she was going down there. Not tonight. Maybe not ever. Exhaustion pulled at her. Slowly she closed the trapdoor. In the kitchen, she dug some nails out of the utility drawer. Back in the bedroom, she pounded four nails through the door and into the floorboards next to it. A crude job, at best, but effective. She put the hammer aside and pushed her bed back into place.

If someone was down there, he wasn't getting out. Not tonight. She told herself she would deal with it tomorrow.

Chapter Fifteen

Annabelle had been hoping to get Dawson alone to tell him about the trapdoor. It was proof that she hadn't been mistaken last night or overreacted or been trying to get his attention. Or whatever it was that he'd thought.

He arrived again with his mother and brother and a small crew armed with rollers and paintbrushes. Everyone fell into line with Willie cracking the whip. Drop cloths were put down, paint cans were popped open, rollers and brushes were handed out and in no time the once-dingy walls took on new life.

Annabelle and Willie emptied the rest of the cabinets in the kitchen and cleaned them in preparation for the painters. Dawson had hauled away the last of the junk. All that was left behind was what Annabelle would need to live here until the house sold.

Willie had asked if Annabelle wanted her to empty the closet in her bedroom of her grandmother's things, but she'd declined, saying she would do it later. The truth was, the clothes were the last of her grandmother's belongings. She'd kept the cookie jar where Frannie had put her "loose change" as well as a few other personal things including several boxes of Christmas tree ornaments, but the truth was, her grandmother hadn't had much worth hanging on to.

"Tell me," Willie said as they cleaned the last cupboards. "What was it like, modeling?" She sounded genuinely interested.

Annabelle rinsed out the rag she'd been using before she answered. "It was hard work. Hardly anyone believes that. They think you just stand there, turn one way then another, smile and go about your day. It was hours of shooting, often either in the cold or the heat. And that wasn't even the worst part."

She stopped, realizing that she'd said more than she'd originally planned. But Willie was looking at her expectantly, as if waiting for the rest.

"There is the not eating, but you get used to that. The working out every day of the week to keep in shape. The always being made up in expectation of someone snapping your photo on their cell phone and selling it to the tabloids, with an accompanying story about how sick you look, how fat, how tired, how ill-dressed. So you're always 'on' except when you're alone in your apartment."

"I'm guessing that still wasn't the worst part," Willie said.

Annabelle let out a bitter laugh. "No. There are the men who have power over your career and the desperate young faces who want your job. At first, it was wonderful, unbelievable. The parties, the money, the famous people you get to meet, seeing your photo on the cover of a magazine." She shook her head. "But none of it is real. Your photos are all doctored. That's not really you on the cover or in the ads. Because even if you look good, you don't look good enough without Photoshop."

She took a breath, shocked that she'd let all of that out—especially to Dawson's mother.

"So, you're going back after you sell the house?" Willie asked.

Tears stung her eyes. "I don't have a choice. I'll never work again at the level I did before, but it's all I know."

Willie scoffed at that. "We all have choices. Some are harder than others. What I'm hearing is that you feel trapped. Sounds like you're the only one who can change that. Just make sure you don't latch on to the first life raft that comes along. It wouldn't be fair to anyone to find yourself trapped in some other way, now would it?"

Just then, Luke came in to announce that the other rooms were done.

But Annabelle had gotten the message loud and clear. *Willie's son wasn't a consolation prize for the mistake she'd made with her life.*

After a quick lunch, Annabelle and Willie painted trim in the bathrooms, neither talking. Willie'd had her say. Annabelle didn't blame her for the warning.

Several of the crew had to leave, which left Dawson and Luke to paint the kitchen.

"I can't believe how different this house looks," Willie said after they'd cleaned their brushes and wandered through the finished rooms. She stopped at Annabelle's bedroom. "You sure we can't paint this room today? We can move the bed and—"

"I'd like to do this one myself," Annabelle said.

"Sure, sweetie, if that's what you want."

"I appreciate everything you've done," Annabelle said quickly.

Willie patted her arm. "Honey, we were glad to help. Now you can get it on the market."

She nodded, afraid she would cry. There was so much she wanted to say. She'd hurt this woman's son, and yet here was Willie helping her. Or maybe she wanted Annabelle out of town so she didn't hurt her son again.

WHEN THEY WERE finishing up for the day, all Dawson wanted to do was make a quick getaway. But his mother seemed to be dragging her feet. The house was coming along nicely. The only room that hadn't gotten painted was Annabelle's bedroom. According to his mother, she wanted to paint that one herself.

More than likely she was just ready for them all to clear out. He knew *he* was ready. Every moment he was around her, he was intensely aware of her. It wore him out. It was time to let them both get on with their lives.

He'd just picked up the cooler his mother had packed and started for the door, when Annabelle said, "Dawson, could I speak to you for a moment?"

He knew he must have looked like a deer caught in headlights.

"Privately?" She motioned him back into the house.

"I'll catch a ride with Luke again," his mother said quickly and grabbed up her belongings. "I need to talk to him anyway." She was out the door before Dawson could argue.

Now, with just the two of them alone in the house, he shot Annabelle a weary look as he put down the cooler. "If this is about last night…"

"There's something I need to show you," she said without preamble and headed for her bedroom.

He watched her go for a moment before following. At the bedroom door, he stopped. She was standing by the bed. For a moment, he thought she'd brought him in her to…to do what? Seduce him?

She shoved the bed with all her strength, sending it skidding across the floor until it hit the wall.

He blinked in shock, his mind racing. What the—

She pointed at the floor. His mind was still on Annabelle standing next to a bed in her bedroom and him thinking… His gaze dropped to the floor. He stared.

"Are those nails?" he asked. They were sixteen-penny nails, large enough that even with half of them embedded in the wood, the other half was sticking out a good three inches. All he could think was that she'd lost her mind—until he saw the handhold carved into the floor and realized he was looking at a trapdoor.

"What the hell?" he said as he moved closer.

She nodded at his surprise.

"Did you know that was under your bed?"

"Not until last night when I came back into my room and found my bed had been moved."

So they were back to her believing that someone was in her house last night?

"Remember the metal box I told you I found under the floorboards? That same floorboard had been pried up and hadn't been pushed back down all the way. I knew someone had been in here. When I knelt down, I saw that the dust bunnies under the bed had been disturbed. Also there were marks on the floor where the bed had been moved."

He had to give her credit, that was pretty observant of her. When he'd searched her house for an intruder, he hadn't noticed any of that. "It must just be an opening to the crawl space under the house. Did you—"

"I took a look, but no, I didn't go down there. But *someone* did. I found a piece of cloth caught on the trapdoor. It hadn't been there long since there was no dust on it."

He stared at the trapdoor with the nails sticking out of it for a moment. "I'm assuming you have a hammer."

She reached over to the bureau, retrieved the hammer and handed it to him. "That's not all. Remember the metal box with the photos and newspaper clippings? I had put it in an empty drawer in the kitchen. Well, it's gone."

He looked up at her. "But it didn't appear that anyone had broken into the house. Unless…" He glanced down at the trapdoor. "Sorry, I didn't believe you last night."

She nodded, seeming to let it go.

It took a few minutes to remove the nails. She'd hammered them down pretty good. He handed them to Annabelle, and after the last one, she gave him a flashlight. It was small and not all that powerful, but he figured he wouldn't be going far. He'd seen trapdoors in other homes that were merely a way to get down to the crawl space if needed.

That's why he was surprised when he shone the flashlight beam down into the hole and saw the footprints on what appeared to be steps. He glanced at Annabelle. She flashed him an impatient look that said maybe it was high time he started trusting her. Now that was definitely something he wasn't going to ponder right now.

"I'll go down and see—"

"I'm going with you." She had her arms crossed, and her jaw set, and determination burned in those blue eyes.

"I can tell you right now there are going to be spiders, cobwebs, maybe even mice and only God knows what else down there."

ANNABELLE DID HER best to hide her shudder. "I'm going."

He shook his head. "Suit yourself, but don't say I didn't warn you."

She still had the bandanna covering her hair and wore the baggy jeans and ugly sweatshirt. Perfect for a tour of the hidden space under the house.

Dawson took a tentative step onto the top stair, then dropped down the next three. The steps were wide apart. When he reached the earthen floor, he turned to offer her a hand. She hesitated only a moment before taking it. Even with his help, she had too much momentum and ended up in his arms.

He chuckled. "If that's all you wanted, we could have stayed up in your bedroom."

"Funny," she said, pushing herself off his rock-solid chest.

He turned to shine the flashlight beam under the house. "Huh?"

She too was surprised to see that they were standing in what appeared to be a narrow trench. "Isn't this awfully deep for a crawl space since we don't have to crawl?" she asked.

He shot her a look. As he shone the light toward the rear of the house—and the darkness, he said, "If you are still determined to come along, stay right behind me."

Once away from the trapdoor, the damp, earthy air

became close. The flashlight beam punched a small hole into the absolute blackness ahead. She grabbed hold of his tooled leather belt. When she tried to see around his broad shoulders, a spiderweb hit her in the face. She shuddered and wiped crazily at it with her free hand.

"You all right back there?" he asked, amusement in his tone.

"Fine."

He stopped. The flashlight beam flickered upward and she saw that they had reached the back of the house. "Watch your head," he said as he ducked under the edge of the foundation.

This time when she glanced past him she saw that this underground space didn't end under the house. It made a sharp right-hand turn and then appeared to keep going. They would have to either crouch down or crawl.

"What is this?" she whispered, although she doubted anyone could hear them this far underground. That thought sent a chill through her.

"It appears to be a tunnel."

"A tunnel? A tunnel to where?"

"Good question," he said. "I'm not sure you should go any farther. We have no idea how long it's been here. If it were to cave in—" She started to argue, but he stopped her. "One of us needs to be able to call for help if the other doesn't come back. You want to see where it goes? Or…" He turned her around. "Or do you want to make your way back to the bedroom? Just keep walking until you reach the light." As much as she hated to admit it, he made a good point. "Give me five minutes once you reach the bedroom. If I'm not back, call for help because part of your backyard would have caved in on me."

"Maybe you shouldn't—"

"Sure you can find your way back?"

She swallowed the lump in her throat and nodded. He gave her a little push and she started walking. It was pitch black all around her. She put out her hands. Spiderwebs brushed her fingers. She stumbled and had to grab hold of the dirt bank next to her. She thought she heard a scampering sound and wanted to run.

But she kept her gaze on the faint light ahead and walked as swiftly as possible. When she reached the steps up into her bedroom, she turned to look back. All she could see was darkness. Not even a faint flashlight beam.

She pulled herself up the steps into her bedroom, grabbed her cell phone and set the timer for five minutes. That's when she saw the spider on her sweatshirt sleeve.

Annabelle had been a runway model, but she'd never undressed that fast in her life. Opening the window, she tossed the clothes and bandanna, spider and all, out the window. She could still feel spiderwebs in her hair. Phone in hand, she streaked across the hall to the bathroom. Turning on the shower, she jumped in, letting the warm water wash away the dirt and dust and spiderwebs as quickly as possible. The alarm would be going off in a few minutes. If Dawson hadn't come back...

Dawson followed the tunnel, aware of the fresh prints in the soil ahead of him. Annabelle was right. Someone had recently been in this tunnel, which would explain how someone had gotten into the house without breaking in.

As he shone the flashlight into the blackness ahead,

his mind raced. How long had this tunnel been here? Had the first owners of the house dug it? For what?

He'd read stories about secret passageways. In Mexico, wealthy Spanish silver families years ago had tunnels dug under their houses to get their families and silver out in case of an attack by outlaws. But what would a family in Whitehorse have to fear? What would a sweet old lady like Frannie Clementine have to fear? Or to hide?

He thought of the newspaper clippings and the walled-up alcove. *Oh, Frannie, what secrets did you have?* Maybe more to the point, why leave the house just to Annabelle? *Was there something here that you wanted only her to find?*

His flashlight beam shone on what appeared to be more stairs ahead. Reaching the end of the tunnel, he climbed up a step to push on another trapdoor. It creaked open, but only a fraction of an inch. That was enough though to see where the tunnel ended—in the old garage behind the house. Someone had pushed several heavy bags of sand onto the door. To hide it?

When the alarm on her phone went off, Annabelle was just stepping from the shower and ready to call the sheriff for help if Dawson hadn't— She let out a shriek as the bathroom door swung open and jumped back into the shower to cover herself with the plastic curtain.

"You do realize that shower curtain is see-through, don't you?" Dawson drawled as he stepped into the steamy room and turned off her phone's alarm.

"You scared me half to death," she snapped. "I was

ready to call the sheriff so we could start digging for you. You could have knocked."

"I did. When I saw your clothes flung all over the yard, I got worried."

"There was a spider…"

He nodded, still looking at her. She had to give him credit, though, his gaze was on her eyes. But she could tell that he was enjoying himself. He'd caught her at a distinct disadvantage.

"Well?" she demanded.

"The tunnel kept going all the way to the old garage. There was another trapdoor. Someone had pulled several bags of sand over on it recently, I would suspect so no one else found it."

"I wasn't asking about that. I meant that you should leave the bathroom and let me get dressed."

He glanced around. "It seems you didn't remember to bring anything to wear. It's a good thing the tunnel didn't cave in on me."

"I was ready to call for help." She cocked her head at him. "A gentleman would leave."

He chuckled at that, his gaze locking with hers. "You and I are way past that, Annie."

Her heart did a dip-tee-doo at the sound of the pet name. He'd only called her that when they were alone and always when they were intimate. The heat of the shower had warmed her cheeks, but nothing like the sound of that cherished name on his lips.

Without breaking eye contact, he handed her a towel.

Her pulse throbbed under her skin as desire rippled through her. In his eyes, she could see that he remembered what they'd shared right down to the last kiss, the last caress, the last time they'd made love.

She let go of the shower curtain to pull the towel around her. When she did, his eyes definitely weren't on hers.

Chapter Sixteen

Rob walked along the edge of the Milk River. He could only assume it had gotten its name because it resembled chocolate milk. The river was more like a wide ditch. It backed up onto Frannie Clementine's property.

After the old lady had been a problem, he'd known he couldn't keep walking around the neighborhood. Unfortunately, there were a lot of old ladies like her. Driving past was almost as bad. He swore most of the neighbors spent their time at the window looking for trouble.

He'd gone through the metal box of photos and newspaper clippings last night. If he'd had any doubt that Francesca Clementine was his uncle's Baby Doll, he no longer did. He had to get back into that house, but it had been a beehive of activity. He'd watched box loads of belongings being hauled out.

After following one of the trucks, he'd realized with a sinking feeling that all of it was going to the dump. All but some old furniture that he'd seen dropped off at a local charity shop. What if the granddaughter didn't realize what she was throwing away?

He told himself that wasn't possible. She wouldn't

throw away priceless gems. He had to believe what he was looking for was still in the house.

Anxious, he wanted to end this. The motel in town was adequate but nothing like his home in New York. The weather was colder and he couldn't get any of the food he'd grown accustomed to in the city. It made him jumpy and irritable. Everywhere he went he saw cowboys and pickups. Last night he swore he heard mooing cows. He'd looked out his window to see a semi parked across the street. Sure enough, the back was loaded with cattle.

"I have to get out of here," he said to the wintry-looking landscape. The temperature had dropped and a fog had rolled in. Now everything was covered with frost. He kept slipping on the icy grass along the edge of the river. So help him, if he fell in, he was going to kill someone today.

Last night he'd seen the trapdoor in the old barely standing garage and thought he'd hit the jackpot. But once he'd dropped down in it, he realized it was a tunnel. Following it, he'd ended up in one of the bedrooms. It had taken all of his strength to move the bed aside enough that he could get the trapdoor all the way open.

Once inside, the house had proved to be uninteresting. He'd found the metal box with the photos and newspaper clippings, confirming what he already knew. Francesca had been Baby Doll. But that's all he found.

So what was the point of the tunnel? He hadn't had enough time to search the house well. He didn't think the loot was hidden in the tunnel. It seemed more like an escape route. The old lady must have had it installed in case someone discovered who she was, what she'd done and just how much stolen loot she had gotten away with.

Now he stopped at the back of the house. He could see only a portion of it through the dense, bare-limbed trees and the rock wall next to the river. On the other side was the old garage. He studied the property for a few long minutes trying to decide what to do next. From what he'd seen in the house, the crew who'd been helping the granddaughter should be about done.

The granddaughter would finally be alone. He was counting on it. The first step would be seeing what she knew. Then disposing of her. He could hide her body in the tunnel while he tore the house apart.

He'd been so sure that the woman in the obit wasn't his uncle's Baby Doll. Then he'd been certain that, if she was, she'd blown the loot long ago. Then he'd discovered the tunnel and that had changed everything. The way he saw it, Frannie Clementine had the tunnel dug as an escape route in case she was found out. She would have been afraid of what Bernie would do if he found her. The woman wasn't stupid.

But if she was that afraid, then Rob's instincts told him she probably lived on the cash and gold but wouldn't have dared fence the jewels. She would have known that Bernie and his associates were all waiting for even one of the pieces to surface. Which meant the gems were still in that house. All he had to do was find them.

"YOU KNOW WHAT this means," Dawson said, rising up on one elbow.

She looked into his eyes, her heart pounding. When she'd awakened, all she could think was that this was what everyone had tried to warn her about. But being with Dawson had felt so right. She still loved him. Had never stopped loving him.

That didn't mean she knew what she wanted to do with the rest of her life. She thought about Willie's warning.

"You know what we have to do now," he said.

A dozen thoughts raced through her mind. Her mouth went dry. Did he think because they'd made love and fallen asleep in each other's arms that it meant she was back? That they would take up where they'd left off? All her conflicted feelings for him aside, her life was a mess. She couldn't commit to a paint color if she had to, let alone what she wanted to do with the rest of her life right now.

"We have to bust open that wall in the kitchen."

She stared at him in disbelief. "What?" That was the last thing she'd expected him to say. He must have seen her relief because his brown eyes dimmed a little. His look said, *It's okay, Annie. I know you don't want me.*

Annabelle wanted to cry out that it wasn't true. She'd never wanted anyone the way she did him. But everything was so complicated right now. She would never know if he'd just been an easy way out. Worse, he'd never know if that hadn't been the case.

DAWSON HAD SEEN the panic on her face when they'd awakened in each other's arms. The passion was still there between them, the chemistry, even the love. Last night had proved it. But it wasn't enough to keep her in Montana, maybe especially with a Montana cowboy like him. She'd been out in the world. She'd lived a glam-

orous life. Being a ranchwoman was a far cry from the
way she'd been living in California.

"Annie, the tunnel, the metal box, all of it," he said,
hoping she didn't see his disappointment. Had he really
expected last night to change anything? "Who knows
what other secrets your grandmother had, but given what
we do know...we have to open that wall."

A laugh escaped her. He saw her relief and felt his
heart drop even more. Obviously last night hadn't
meant the same things to her that it had to him. Still, he
wouldn't have changed anything. They'd wanted each
other, needed each other. Even as he'd taken her in his
arms, he'd known it was temporary and he hadn't cared
one damn bit.

This morning...well, only a fool would have thought
that making love with her would change everything.

"We have to look at all the evidence," Dawson said as
he climbed out of bed and began pulling on his clothes.
So they weren't going to talk about last night. Apparently they were back to business as usual, which meant
getting this house sold and her gone.

"No woman has an escape tunnel unless she has
something to hide," he was saying.

She felt bereft as she watched him dress and leave
her bed. As much as she wanted to call him back, to try
to explain... "Maybe the original owner—"

"The original owner didn't have it dug. This was the
bedroom you grew up in, right? Was that escape hatch
under the bed?"

She shook her head. Nor had the board been pulled up
to hide a metal box. But there had been an alcove in the

kitchen that was now gone. She didn't want to believe that any of this was true because of what it said about her grandmother. What it said about Annabelle herself. There was a reason her grandmother had left only her the house, she was starting to realize.

"We're talking about Frannie," she said as she got up and quickly dressed. She saw that Dawson had retrieved her clothing from the yard, sans spider. She dropped it into the hamper and put on her own jeans and one of her new T-shirts. "You remember Frannie? Local do-gooder, tiny, sweet, always helping others."

"I remember her. But you're forgetting. Sweet Frannie had a past. She was a mobster's moll."

She turned her back to him as she dressed. "We don't know that," she argued over her shoulder. "Just because she had her photo taken with that mobster a few times…" She knew she was clutching at straws, but this was Frannie. The grandmother she wanted to believe had left her the house because they were so much alike.

Slowly she turned to look at Dawson. He was so handsome that sometimes it took her breath away. Big, strong, broad shouldered, slim hipped and all cowboy. But also tender and sweet and as trustworthy as the day was long. "You're determined to tear into that wall, aren't you?"

"Just as determined as you are not to touch it. I know you're scared…"

He had no idea. She swallowed. She'd come this far. "Okay."

"We have to open that wall," Dawson said. "We have to know what's back there. Maybe nothing."

"You don't believe that."

"No, I don't. All these secrets… You have to admit, walling up the alcove like that…"

She nodded.

"I promise to fix it better than new so you can sell the house. I'll do it quickly so it doesn't hold up the sale. If there is nothing behind it, you'll be gaining an alcove. It will add to the value of the house."

Annabelle mugged a face at him. "And if there is something behind that wall that shouldn't be?"

He shrugged. "Better to find out now than later."

She headed into the kitchen, suddenly scared. She hoped her grandmother had merely lost her marbles, decided she didn't like the alcove and had someone come in and wall it up. Or maybe she did the work herself. Her grandmother was a master at a lot of things around the house, as Annabelle recalled.

Now that she'd remembered the hutch that had been in the alcove…that meant that her grandmother had to have closed up the space sometime in the thirteen years that Annabelle had been gone.

"I have a sledgehammer in my toolbox in the back of the truck," Dawson said from behind her. "And a better flashlight."

Annabelle nodded and listened as he hurried out to his pickup. Her gaze was on the wall. In the morning light, it appeared innocent enough. It was what might be behind there that had her terrified. *Oh, Grandma, how many secrets do you have?* Maybe more important, what was Frannie expecting her to do about them?

Dawson returned quickly. He hesitated, looking over at her. She nodded and he hefted the sledgehammer.

"You want to do the honors?" he asked.

She shook her head. She didn't want to know what was behind there. She'd already learned enough disturbing things about Frannie and feared they were about to learn even more.

Dawson stepped back and swung the sledgehammer, making a huge hole in the Sheetrock. He swung again, making an even bigger hole. The third time, the Sheetrock crumbled enough that they could see into the hole.

He put down the sledgehammer and picked up the large flashlight he'd brought from his pickup. This one had a broad, strong light. Glancing at her, he said, "Ready?"

She nodded. There was no going back now. She stepped to the hole as Dawson shone the light into the darkness beyond it. The first thing that hit her was the smell.

He let out a curse. Annabelle couldn't speak. *Oh, Frannie, what have you done?*

Chapter Seventeen

Sheriff McCall Crawford stepped into the kitchen. She'd never been in Frannie Clementine's house. Few people had. While always up for helping others, she'd kept to herself the rest of the time. McCall had known the woman was a hoarder and her house was full to the brim. No wonder she didn't have friends over—not even her neighbor Inez Gilbert.

"In here," Dawson Rogers said now, as he motioned toward the large hole in the wall at the end of the room. McCall wondered if he and Annabelle Clementine were back together since her return. News of the supermodel's return had the entire county talking—and speculating.

He handed her a flashlight. McCall took it as she looked at Annabelle standing with her back to the kitchen counter, arms crossed around her, a scared, stony, shocked and worried look in her eyes.

Turning on the flashlight, McCall stepped to the hole and shone the light in. What she saw shouldn't have surprised her. When Dawson had called and said they'd found something at Frannie Clementine's house that they thought she should see, she hadn't been sure what to expect. Being in law enforcement she was seldom surprised.

At first, all she could see was the rotted, once-clear plastic the body had been wrapped in. Sometime over the years, the decaying body stuffed in the hole had burst the rotting plastic. It appeared that the gelatinous remains of the body had run out, soaking into the floorboards. The rest of the body had rotted along with the plastic and was now little more than a gluttenous blob and bones.

With a sigh, McCall straightened and looked at the granddaughter. "You have any idea who this might have been?" she asked.

Annabelle shook her head. Her blue eyes were wide with shock and fear and no doubt revulsion.

McCall looked to Dawson. "How about you?"

"Not a clue."

"Any reason you decided to look in this wall?" the sheriff asked and listened as he explained about his puppy's reaction. "So this used to be an alcove that you believe your grandmother walled up?"

"For obvious reasons," Dawson said before Annabelle could answer. As he did, he reached over and took the young woman's hand, making McCall wonder again what their relationship now was. Idle curiosity, since everyone in the county knew that she'd broken his heart when she left town all those years ago.

This latest discovery would only add to the intrigue, McCall thought as she looked past them to the window. A small crowd had gathered. Taking a quick inventory, she realized someone was missing.

"Has anyone see Inez lately?" she asked.

ANNABELLE LOOKED AS if she was in shock. "You can't stay here tonight," Dawson said, feeling guilty. He'd been determined to open up this wall even though he'd known she hadn't wanted to. Had he expected to find a body? Or was he thinking he might find the missing jewels from the Marco Polo exhibit heist they'd read about in the newspaper clippings Frannie had saved in the now missing metal box?

"I have a guest room," he added, seeing how anxious Annie already was.

"He's right," McCall said. "You can't stay here. In fact, I need you both to clear out while we take care of this." She turned to the deputy who came through the door. "Run over to the neighbor to the south and see if Inez is all right."

The deputy seemed surprised that Inez wasn't already over there finding out what was going on. Clearly so was the sheriff.

She looked to the two of them. Annabelle seemed rooted to the floor. "If you need to get a few personal things," the sheriff said, "do that. I'll let you know when you can get back into the house."

Dawson already had Annie's hand in his. Hers was freezing cold. He gave her a little shake. "The sheriff needs us out of here."

"Who is that?" she asked, motioning toward the former alcove.

"We won't know for a while," McCall said and looked to Dawson. "You'll see that she's okay?"

Those words finally seemed to bring Annabelle out of her stupor. She nodded, saying, "I'm fine," even though it was clear she wasn't. She numbly followed him out to his pickup. The street was full of people. Some called to him, asking what was going on. He merely shook his head and hurriedly loaded Annabelle into the passenger seat, then ran around to slide behind the wheel.

Annie was staring at all the gawking people. "Everyone is going to know what Frannie did."

He wanted to argue that they didn't know it had been Frannie's doing, but he doubted she would believe that any more than he did. Once they'd seen the photos of her with the mobster, they'd stopped being sure what Frannie might have done.

He drove toward his ranch. Annabelle stared out the side window, appearing to fight tears. "I'm sorry," he said.

"It's not your fault."

"I never should have opened that wall."

She finally looked over at him, her blue eyes swimming. "She had to have killed him and then closed off the alcove to hide his body." She shook her head as if trying to chase away the memory of what she'd seen. "This is why she left me the house and not my sisters."

He wasn't sure how that computed.

"I just don't know what I'm supposed to do with this," she said. "She wanted me to know about her past. She left it all for me, including what we found behind the wall."

"I doubt your grandmother meant for you to find the body," he argued.

She gave him a patient look. "Why do I feel as if all of this is a warning?"

NEWS OF THE discovery traveled like quicksilver through the town. Rob heard people talking about it everywhere he went. He wasn't sure what rumors to believe. But the bottom line was that a body had been found in the house—and no jewels, as far as he knew.

Back in his motel room, he called his uncle and told him.

"They have any idea who the man is?" Bernie asked.

What shocked Rob was that his uncle didn't sound all that surprised. "Not yet. Why? Do you think you know him?"

Silence, then finally Bernie said, "I might."

Rob swore. "Someone you had looking for her?"

"I had a lot of people looking for her. Mickey Frazer, remember him?"

"Wait. He disappeared like fifteen years ago?"

"Maybe less than that."

"I thought the speculation was that he got hit by the Italians."

His uncle chuckled. "I might have started that rumor since he was always fighting with a few of them."

Rob couldn't believe this. "So how did he end up dead in some wall in Whitehorse, Montana?"

"If I had to guess? He found Baby Doll and she did him in, stuffed him into a wall and covered up the whole thing before he could contact me with her location. If that was his plan. So, what about the jewels?"

"The place is now crawling with cops," Rob complained. He wasn't about to tell his uncle that part of the reason was the death of the neighbor, a woman named Inez Gilbert. She'd been found at the bottom of her basement stairs with a broken neck. "If any of the loot is left—"

"It's there and I want it, understand?"

Oh, Rob understood perfectly. "How do you expect me to find it—if it is there? They are still digging Mickey's remains out of that wall. If the gems were in there with him... Well, they're gone, okay?"

"She wouldn't have put them in the wall with a guy like Mickey Frazer. No, she would have hidden them somewhere else. Remember, the woman was smart, cagey. So find the jewels."

"I don't get it," Rob said. "Why take the jewels if she wasn't to sell them or fence them?"

"Truthfully, I think she thought she was saving me from a prison sentence. As it turned out, she probably was. The Feds turned the city upside down looking for those gems. They would have found them if Baby Doll hadn't absconded with them. Maybe she thought she was doing me a favor."

"Yeah, I bet that was it."

"Just find them."

Rob stared at his phone, realizing that his uncle had hung up on him. He cursed a blue streak as he disconnected. A thought struck him. Once the cops were through over at the house, he could get into it. The granddaughter wouldn't stay there now. He knew how to get in—and out—without notice. All he had to do was wait until the cops cleared out.

"WE GET AN ID on the body?" County Attorney Rand Bateman asked from McCall's doorway.

"Frannie made it easy. The man's leather wallet was in the hole with him." She picked up the plastic bag with the New York driver's license in it and held it up. "Michael James Frazer. From what I've been able to find out, he was involved in the Irish mob in New York City."

"Cause of death?"

"The coroner found blade marks on his ribs."

Rand shook his head. "Unbelievable."

"That's not the half of it." She motioned to her open computer. "Ever heard of the Marco Polo Heist?" He shook his head. "Me, either. Way before my time. But fifty-six years ago, it was big news. Several men died during the robbery. Only one was believed to have gotten away, Bernard 'Bernie the Hawk' McDougal, an Irish mob kingpin. The men killed all worked for him. There was never enough proof to arrest Bernie, but he was questioned about the heist, according to what I've found out so far."

"What could any of that have to do with Frannie Clementine?"

McCall leaned back in her chair. "Michael 'Mickey' Frazer would be seventy years old now if he had lived. But that's not the interesting part. Guess who he worked for?" She nodded. "Bernard McDougal. Although Bernie was suspected in the Marco Polo Heist, he was never convicted and the gems were never recovered. Now one of his men ends up dead walled up in Frannie's house. The coroner says he's been there for from ten to fifteen years."

Rand swore under his breath. "So the body wasn't in the house when Frannie bought it."

McCall shook her head. "In the wall we found newspapers she must have used to wipe up the blood. The dates on the papers bear out the fact that she was the owner of the house when the body went into the wall about twenty years ago. Frannie had to have known—even if she didn't personally put the body in the space and wall it up."

Rand had been standing, but now he pulled up a chair and sat down. "I knew Frannie Clementine most of my life. She went to our church. Hell, we had her over to dinner." He met her gaze. "I don't believe it. What did the granddaughter say?"

"She seemed to be in shock. I'm sure what we found took her by surprise, but I am curious what made them open the wall."

"Them?"

"Dawson Rogers was with her. He told me his puppy sensed something about the wall that scared her. There was a definite smell. Also, when Annabelle was getting the house ready to sell, she realized that an alcove had been walled over. I think they were just curious."

"How could Frannie have kept something like this a secret for...?"

"I don't think there would have been a smell since the body was wrapped in multiple plastic sheeting, trussed up like a turkey, but the plastic had rotted and the some of the contents had leaked out."

Rand cringed. "And the Gilbert woman?" he asked, as if anxious to change the subject.

"Apparent accident."

The county attorney eyed her questioningly.

McCall shook her head. She didn't want to admit that she had a feeling it hadn't been a sad mishap. Inez had been wearing a coat and boots, as if she'd been outside. Also, deputies hadn't been able to locate the old woman's shotgun. McCall knew for a fact that she kept it by the front door. Inez had bragged about it, saying she liked to have it handy. Now it was missing.

DAWSON WOKE WORRIED about Annie. He got up to find the guest room empty. He found her sitting at the computer in his office. She looked up, startled to see him in the doorway.

"I didn't think you'd mind," she said.

He shook his head. "What are you looking at in the middle of the night?"

"The sheriff, when she called earlier, asked me if I'd ever heard of a man named Michael 'Mickey' Frazer."

Dawson stepped into the room and sat down on the edge of his desk. "Is that who was in the wall?"

She nodded. "McCall had found out the Marco Polo Heist and that Mickey worked for Bernie McDougal. What she doesn't know is the connection between Frannie and Bernie. Without the photos…" She broke down. "Isn't it bad enough that everyone will know Frannie was a murderer? Do they have to know that she was a mobster's moll?"

"Annie." He wanted desperately to comfort her but he was trying to keep his distance. Making love the other night had been a mistake—at least, he could tell she thought so. He knew better than to let it happen again— for his own heart's sake if not hers.

"Worse, I don't understand is how deep my grandmother is involved in all this," she said between sobs. "She had to be the one who killed that man and put him in the alcove and then walled it up. Along with jewels taken in the Marco Polo Heist there was a whole lot of cash. Apparently the museum hadn't taken the deposit to the bank. Because the Marco Polo exhibit had been so popular, there were thousands of dollars in a safe that was blown open. And I thought my grandmother lived all those years on my grandfather's insurance policy."

"Annie, you can't let this—"

"She must have been in on the heist. She was definitely in New York City at the time. Robbery is nothing compared to murder and hiding a body in your house behind a wall."

Dawson reached over and shut off the computer. "Come on, it's almost daylight. Let's get out of here." She let him pull her to her feet. "Get changed. I'll saddle up the horses."

THE SUN ROSE fiery red over the prairie. Annabelle breathed in the sweet scents of the late-fall day. She could see her breath in the cold morning air, but it felt good to be on a horse again. Good to get away from her troubles for a while.

She looked over at Dawson. Now, there was someone who felt at home in the saddle, she thought. Past him the Little Rockies loomed up into a brilliant blue sky. The breeze carried the scent of the pines as well as the creek next to them. Only a few golden leaves still remained on the cottonwoods. Fall here had always been a beautiful time. She realized how much she'd missed the seasons, missed a lot about Montana.

Her gaze went to Dawson again. Her heart ached. She was surprised by how much she'd missed him. Her life in California had been filled with busy, long, stress-filled days trying to make something of herself. She'd forgotten what it was like to just relax and enjoy the day.

"Better?" Dawson said.

She nodded and looked away, realizing she'd been staring at him. He'd aged wonderfully. If anything, he was more handsome. There was a confidence to him that had also grown. Dawson Rogers knew who he was, what he wanted, what tomorrow would bring and he was good with that.

Tears burned her eyes; she turned to swipe at them.

"It's going to be all right," he said softly as he rode beside her. "Once the sheriff is finished at the house, I'll go in and make that kitchen like new. You'll get the house sold and—"

"Dawson," she said, her voice breaking as she turned toward him. "I don't care about the house, about any of that."

He swung off his horse. The next thing she knew his big hands were on her waist and he was lifting her down and into his arms. She let the tears come again, crying her heart out, soaking his jean jacket with her tears.

One hand smoothed her hair, while the other held her tightly to him. He said soothing words, whispered into her hair as he let her cry.

When she finally was able to stop, he handed her his bandanna. She wiped her eyes and blew her nose. He took the bandanna back, stuffing it into his pocket. She couldn't help but smile at him. He'd always been there for her. Always.

"I love you." The words came out on their own accord. She couldn't have stopped them even if she had wanted to. "I love you so much."

He nodded. "I love you, too." His voice sounded rough with emotion.

"The other day after we made love—"

"You don't have to explain," he said. "I know."

"You do?"

"We both got lost in the moment. I'm not sorry, but I know that it didn't change anything."

Hadn't it?

"Come on. Let's head back. I suspect the sheriff will be calling."

She looked into his face. There was so much she wanted to say to him. "I need to tell you—"

"You don't have to say it," he said, handing her the reins to her horse. "I know you appreciate my help. That's what old friends are for."

She took the reins, feeling her heart breaking all over again. She realized he wouldn't trust anything she said at this point. She'd just had her second emotional breakdown. Given what had been found in her grandmother's kitchen wall, of course, she would be emotional.

But it was Dawson, being back here with him, that was killing her. She hadn't known what she wanted, but looking at him right now, he was all she wanted.

"Is there someone else?" she asked as he gave her a boost up into her saddle.

He seemed to hesitate for a moment. "I've been seeing Amy Baker," he said, swinging up into his saddle. He reined his horse around. The sun had come up making the day shine. "That sun sure feels good, doesn't it? I'll make us some breakfast when we get back. You still love French toast?"

DAWSON HAD NEVER thought of himself as a coward, but he'd had to cut Annie off from whatever she was going to tell him. He couldn't bear the thought of her telling him that their lovemaking hadn't meant anything. That she was still heading back to her life in California once the house was sold.

Those were all things he already knew on an intellectual level, but he'd let his heart hope for a different outcome. Sometimes the way she looked at him, he would swear... But he knew that she'd been through so much, she probably didn't even know what she needed. He didn't want her making the wrong decision. But he didn't want her staying with him for the wrong reasons, either. He honestly didn't know what was right for her and he doubted she did either right now.

Back at the ranch, he'd sent her inside while he unsaddled their horses. Holding her earlier had made him want to throw down one of the horse blankets and make love to her out there in the wild. He wanted her so badly...

He pushed that thought as far back into his heart as he could. Once her house was sold... It was the mantra that kept playing in his head. But when he thought about her leaving, it almost knocked him to his knees.

"There you are."

He turned at the sound of his mother's voice.

"Are you all right?" she asked, closing the distance between them to look into his face as if she could read him like a child's book. "Oh, Dawson."

He shook his head, swallowing the lump in his throat. "I'll be fine."

She shook her head. "I heard what happened at the house. Annabelle's staying with you?" Her gaze searched his face.

"It isn't what you think. She's staying in the guest

room." He'd never seen his mother cry, but right now she looked close to tears. He put his arm around her. "Once the sheriff lets her back into the house, I'll go over and get the kitchen fixed and then the house should be able to go on the market."

Her mother was shaking her head. "Who's going to buy it knowing…"

He'd thought of that and was sure Annabelle had, too. "I might have to buy it."

Willie nodded. "Okay, son. You could use it as a rental, I suppose. You're that anxious to get her on her way?"

"I have no choice."

"I suppose not." She sounded as sad about that as he did.

ANNABELLE HAD SEEN Willie drive up and head out to where Dawson was unsaddling the horses. She watched them for a moment before stepping into the bathroom to check herself in the mirror. Her cheeks were still pink from the November air. Her eyes weren't as bad as she thought they would be considering all the crying she'd done earlier. She couldn't help being embarrassed. Dawson, as usual, had been kind and understanding. It was his tenderness that kept breaking her heart.

Her cell phone rang. She stared down at the number. Clarisa? It was one of the models she used to work with. Her phone rang again. She thought about not answering it. She'd spoken to hardly anyone she'd worked with since everything went south. Clarisa was one of the new, younger models, but a sweet girl who was just starting in the business.

The phone rang again. Curiosity made her take the call. "Hello?"

"Annabelle, I'm so glad I got you. I was worried you wouldn't pick up. So, have you heard?"

Apparently not. "Heard what?"

"About Chambers. More models have come forward after hearing what happened to you. At first, everyone was scared to speak up, but then they did, one after another." Clarisa was laughing. "Chambers was arrested yesterday on assault charges. Everyone is talking about it. It happened because of you."

She couldn't believe what she was hearing. When she'd reported Gordon Chambers, she hadn't been believed. Gordon owned the top modeling agency in Southern California. If you crossed Gordon, your career was over. Annabelle had dodged his advances until he'd offered her a modeling job she would have given her eyeteeth for—but not at the cost of sleeping with him.

She'd told him what he could do with his job and then gone to the authorities, for all the good it had done. Chambers had instantly blackballed her. Word went out. She'd known he could hurt her. She hadn't realized how badly. He was telling everyone that she was impossible to work with and denying her charges. That's all it took and she couldn't get another job.

"I have even more good news," Clarisa was saying. "I ran into Thomas Darrington the other day. He asked if I'd seen you. Apparently he'd heard about Gordon blackballing you. Anyway, I brought him up to speed. He said he wants you for a big spread he's going to be doing after the first of the year. Girl, I really think you can have just about any job you want now. A lot of people had the same problem with Gordon and you brought him down."

Only she hadn't brought him down. She'd only started the ball rolling. She took a breath and let it out. Her heart was pounding. She could go back. She had a job. She'd always liked working with Thomas Darrington, an up-and-comer in the business and someone she'd worked with before. Thomas had made her an offer she couldn't refuse. She could have her old life back. According to Clarisa, it was waiting for her.

"You need to take down Thomas's number and give him a call," her friend was saying. "He's really anxious to talk to you."

She found a notepad on Dawson's desk and wrote down the number. "Thank you for letting me know."

"I was afraid you hadn't heard," Clarisa said. "You were always so nice to me when some of those other models..." She laughed. "I hope you come back. Give me a call anytime. Also, I know a model who's looking for a roommate, if you're interested."

Annabelle disconnected and looked down at the number she'd written on the notepad. Next to it, she'd written *Thomas. Modeling job.* She still couldn't believe it. Just when she was at her lowest.

At the sound of Dawson's voice, she stuffed the note into her jeans pocket. As happy as she'd been just moments ago, she felt that awful pull on her heart. Could she really go back and leave here? Leave Dawson?

"Annabelle?"

Just the sound of his voice made her close her eyes for a moment, as if memorizing it. She loved him. He was all Montana cowboy. He'd never leave here. If she left him again, there would be no coming back.

Chapter Eighteen

Dawson noticed the change in Annabelle when he and his mother entered the house. They'd all congregated in the kitchen, with Willie talking about how it wouldn't take long to get the house back in order and on the market.

Annabelle was quiet, nodding, but saying little. When their eyes met, he saw pain in them. There seemed to be a sadness to her, a resignation. He told himself he was glad he'd stopped her when they were out on horseback. More than ever, he felt that she'd been about to tell him what he already knew. That she was leaving as soon as the house sold.

He whipped up French toast, talking his mother into staying and joining them. He didn't want to be alone with Annabelle. He told himself that if he kept busy...

They'd turned the conversation to the weather and the upcoming holidays when Annabelle's cell phone rang. She pulled it out and glanced at the screen as if she'd been expecting a call. At her frown, he surmised that it wasn't the one she'd been waiting for.

Excusing herself, she stepped away from the table. He and his mother both pretended not to listen, but it was clearly the sheriff calling to say they were finished at the house and she could move back in.

"You'll get the work done for her?" Willie asked.

He nodded as Annabelle returned to the table.

"Honey, you dropped something." His mother knelt to pick up what appeared to be a sheet from his office notepad. She glanced at the writing on it before handing it to Annabelle. Dawson couldn't miss what was written there. If he'd had any doubts, any hopes, they were dashed.

He watched Annabelle stuff the note into her pocket quickly. Her gaze locked with his for a moment and she seemed about to say something when Willie spoke.

"Dawson and I were just discussing your kitchen," his mother said. "Are we going to close off the alcove again or open it up?"

"You have both already done so much," Annabelle said.

"We finish what we start, isn't that right, Dawson?"

He was still looking into Annie's blue eyes, feeling his heart breaking all over again. He mentally cursed himself for letting it happen. Of course he'd fallen for her again. Hell, he'd never stopped loving her.

"I'll get right on it. The sooner the better," he said and got up to clear away the dishes.

"Let me help you with those," Annabelle said, but he quickly cut her off.

"I've got them."

"Yes," his mother said, as if seeing that he needed to be alone. "Annabelle, why don't you and I go back to the house and see what we need to pick up?"

Annabelle started to say something, but he heard his mother whisper, "Let's leave Dawson alone for a while, okay?"

Annabelle stared at Dawson's back. He'd seen the note. So had his mother. She wanted to tell him that she was torn, that she didn't know what she wanted, that she couldn't bear leaving him again. But she couldn't do that to him again. She'd put him through enough, so she left with Willie.

For much of the way into Whitehorse, neither of them spoke.

"Want to talk about it?" Willie finally asked.

"You saw that I've been offered a modeling job back in California. I'll admit that at first I was excited. I thought for sure I'd never get to work again."

"So it's good news."

She looked over at the older woman. "I can go back to that life. In fact, they want me back." She told Willie why she'd left and what had apparently happened.

"I'm so sorry," Willie said. "That must have been awful."

"Yes, it was. But the others came forward. They backed me up."

"So there is no reason you can't go back to the life you had."

"You know there is a reason," Annabelle said. "Just the thought of leaving Dawson again..." She had to look away as tears welled in her eyes. Determined not to break down again, she said. "I don't think I can leave him."

Willie looked over at her as they pulled up in front of the house behind Annabelle's car. "You love him."

"With all my heart. I always have. But I wanted to see what I could do outside of Whitehorse."

"What do you want now?" Willie asked, but before she could answer there was a tap on the window.

They both turned to see Mary Sue standing there as if waiting for them. Willie hesitated a moment, as if not wanting to quit their conversation, before she turned to put down her window.

Annabelle felt a moment of relief. What did she want to do?

"I thought you might need me," Mary Sue was saying. "The sheriff called me to say that the house was open. I suppose we'd better see how bad it is and decide what to do."

Willie agreed and put up her window. As Annabelle started to get out, the older woman touched her sleeve. "You know how I feel about you and about my son. Make the right decision for yourself. If you stay for the wrong reasons, you'll resent him and the life he has to offer you." She dropped her hand, smiling sadly. "I just want you both to be happy."

DAWSON HAD NO idea how much work undoing Frannie's remodeling in the kitchen would take. All he knew was that he had to do it quickly and then hope the house sold. If not, he would buy it. He'd already made up his mind. He would just have to do it through a subsidiary of the ranch corporation so Annabelle didn't know it was him buying it.

He wasn't far behind his mother. In fact, he drove up right as Annabelle was opening the house. Mary Sue was here, no doubt to see how bad it was going to be. That, or morbid curiosity. He imagined that would be the case for a lot of people once the house was on the market. Another reason he had to act quickly and probably buy the place. He didn't want Annie to have to go through that.

She opened the door and he saw her grimace. There was a definite smell. They all trailed inside. He pushed his way through, wanting to see how bad the kitchen was, to spare Annabelle if it was as bad as he suspected.

But she wasn't having any of that. She was right behind him. The alcove was wide open. The sheriff's department had made the opening larger to get the body out. It appeared that McCall had had someone clean up the floor. But the frame of the stained wall was still there. That was the first thing that would have to go.

He turned to find Annabelle staring at the hole. "Want it walled back up or opened?" he asked.

"Open. But I can't ask you to—"

"You aren't asking. I'm going to get my tools, tear the rest of this out, take up the floorboards. The flooring in the kitchen will have to be replaced but there isn't that much. It won't take long. I was thinking a nice hardwood floor." Before she could object because of the price, he added, "It will help sell the house, trust me."

She closed her mouth and nodded. "I do trust you. I already owe you so much."

"I'm sure money won't be a problem once you're back at work."

Annabelle didn't get a chance to reply as Mary Sue and Willie came into the kitchen. Mary Sue was complimenting everything that had been done. Willie offered to show her the rest of the house. The two of them left as Dawson headed for his pickup and tools.

She stood in the kitchen feeling almost dizzy. So

much had happened. The poor old woman next door had died after falling down her stairs. Not to mention Annabelle's grandmother had walled up a man in her kitchen.

"Is there anything I can—"

Dawson cut her off as he returned with his tools. "I've got it. I called for the subfloor sheeting and the lumber to be delivered. This won't take long."

She nodded and stepped out of his way as he strapped on his tool belt. He couldn't have looked more sexy, she thought and quickly moved out of his way.

From upstairs came voices. Willie and Mary Sue were visiting, discussing people they both knew. It seemed most people in Whitehorse were related to each other in some way.

Annabelle walked down to her bedroom. It was the last room of the house to be painted and cleaned out. She closed the door and called Chloe. "Hi," she said when her sister answered.

"What's wrong?"

She let out a nervous laugh. "You can tell by that one word?"

"I know you, remember?"

Yes, unfortunately, her sisters did know her. That's why they didn't like her. "Something's happened." She explained about the walled-up alcove and what had been found inside.

"You can't be serious. A man's body?"

"I'm afraid so. Would you let TJ know? From what the sheriff has told me, it's been in there for years. I remembered there used to be an alcove there. Do you remember it?"

"I suppose. It's just been so long. I'm not sure I would have remembered. You're saying this happened when?"

"After we all left home. That's what the coroner thinks so somewhere in the past thirteen years."

"How did he get into the wall?" Chloe asked.

Annabelle stifled a laugh. The question was so like her sister. *Oh, he just crawled into the alcove and curled up to die while Grandma built a wall around him.* "He was murdered, wrapped in plastic and walled up in the kitchen."

"They can't think Grandmother did that!" her sister cried.

"I'm afraid that's exactly what they think." Annabelle thought of the photos and the newspaper clippings. It was all going to come out. She figured warning her sisters was the kindest thing she could do.

She told Chloe about what she'd found under the floorboard and under her bed, along with what she found in the metal box.

"That is the most ridiculous thing I have ever heard," Chloe snapped when she was finished. "Our grandmother was not a mobster's girlfriend."

"The dead man worked for the mobster. The sheriff thinks the man followed Grandma from New York and that the reason she killed him probably has to do with the Marco Polo Heist, a famous robbery back in New York. They've never found the jewels or the money that was taken."

Chloe had fallen silent.

"I'm sorry to hit you with all of this, but it is going to come out," Annabelle said.

"What is that noise?"

"Dawson is in the kitchen removing the rest of the wall and putting down new flooring."

"That house is never going to sell."

Annabelle thought her sister was probably right about that. Murder houses weren't that popular. "I will probably be returning to California and keeping the house on the market. I've been offered a really good modeling job." Annabelle glanced in the direction of the kitchen. "Unless I decide to stay."

"You're thinking about staying? You have to stay at least until Christmas. TJ and I have already bought our tickets. We were going to surprise you. Surprise! We're coming up there to help you sell the house and have Christmas together. We were planning to be there a few days before Christmas Eve."

"Really?"

"Would that be all right or do you need to get to your job before then?"

"No, it would be wonderful." Annabelle was having trouble believing they really were coming back to help her so the three of them could have Christmas together, especially after she'd just told them the news.

"Now, more than ever, I feel like we should be together for the holidays," Chloe said.

Annabelle was fighting tears when she heard the knock at her bedroom door. "I couldn't be happier," she said, her voice breaking. "I have to go, but I will talk to you soon."

"Am I interrupting?" Willie asked when Annabelle opened the door, still fighting tears.

She shook her head. "That was my sister Chloe. She and TJ are coming up to spend Christmas with me."

"That's wonderful." Willie hugged Annabelle. "I'm happy for you." As she pulled back, she said, "Dawson thought things would go faster if you came out to the house and stayed at the ranch until he's finished."

She could see what the two of them were trying to do. "Thank you, but I'm staying here."

"Are you sure?" Willie asked, glancing over her shoulder toward the kitchen.

"I'm sure." Annabelle smiled. "My grandmother left me this house because she knew I was the one who could deal with all this."

"Yes, you're plenty strong," Dawson's mother agreed.

He called from the kitchen, wanting Annabelle to see if she liked the hardwood floor he'd ordered.

"I'm going to take off, then," Willie said. "If you change your mind…"

"I know where you live," Annabelle said with a smile. "Thank you again for everything."

"You bet," Willie said and called goodbye to her son as she left.

Dawson looked surprised. "I thought she was going to ask you to stay at the ranch."

"She did. I'm staying here."

He didn't look happy to hear that. "It's going to be noisy and dusty."

"I'll make do. My sisters are coming up for Christmas." She laughed at his surprise.

"So you're staying that long? What about the job offer?"

"It wouldn't start until after the holidays. But I'm not sure I'm going to take it, anyway. I still have to get the house sold."

"Maybe you'll get lucky and the house will sell and there won't be anything keeping you here after the holidays," he said and turned away to show her the flooring.

"It's beautiful. Thank you. I'm getting better at accepting help, don't you think?"

He glanced over at her. "You are."

"Who says people can't change?" With that, she turned and left him to it.

ROB COULDN'T BELIEVE how quickly the house had filled up again after the sheriff's department finished its investigation. He'd kept his ear to the ground, but it seemed there hadn't been anything else of interest found.

"I think the old girl got rid of the loot," he grumbled to himself. "Maybe she didn't even try to fence it. Could have sold it to a private collector. It wasn't like she hadn't met the kind of people who would have been interested. And now my uncle thinks she did him a favor? The foolish old coot definitely has dementia."

Still, he knew what his uncle would have said. Someone would have talked if they'd bought the gems. That was the problem with even the filthy rich, they liked to brag. If one of them had bought the jewels from Francesca Clementine, word would have gotten back to Bernie. And the old gal would have died a long time ago.

So she'd kept it for whatever reason. Hidden them like she had poor Mickey's body. He cringed at the thought of being walled up in a house like that. Sure, the goon was dead, but still.

Frannie, as everyone referred to her, had stiffed Bernie, gotten out of town and come out West telling everyone she was a widow. The woman probably couldn't have told the truth if her life depended on it. She couldn't have found a husband, gotten knocked up and become a widow that quickly, unless...

He frowned. Not long after arriving, she'd bought the house and given birth to a son, according to the local gossips he'd overhead at the café downstairs in the hotel. As far as anyone knew, she'd never had a full-time job other than raising her grandkids when they'd come to live with her when they were young. His frown deepened.

He stopped pacing to count on his fingers, then swore.

His uncle had wondered for over fifty years why she'd left like she had. He counted again to make sure before he picked up the phone. "You aren't going to like this," he said and then told Bernie. Let him do the math.

"I'M CALLING IT a day," Dawson said as he put away his tools. He'd looked up to find Annabelle standing in the doorway.

"I can't believe how much you got done," she said. "It looks great. I like that that stupid wall isn't still there."

"You sure you aren't going to have nightmares tonight?" he asked seriously as he closed his toolbox and straightened.

"No," she said, realizing it was true. "It's funny, but this house seemed more creepy with that wall. Now that's it's gone and what was behind it, I'm fine." She shook her head. "At least I know now why my grandmother left the house to me." She had to smile. "She said I was a lot like her."

"I hope not," Dawson said with a laugh.

"I guess we'll never know for sure what happened here. If McCall is right, then it all has to do with that museum exhibit on Marco Polo and the stolen jewels. I'd like to think the man's death was self-defense—and that grandmother did what she had to do to protect us all. If she was running from her mobster boyfriend… We already know that she was pregnant, probably with his child. It's funny. She always seemed so…content, as if she'd made her peace with the past and everything else."

"She did a good job of raising you girls and everyone in this community loved her."

"Well, they *did*. Wait until they learn about the man she kept in her wall."

"This town is pretty forgiving. Your grandmother did so much good in this community. That's what will be remembered."

"I hope so."

He stood for moment just looking at her. She felt the chemistry sparking between them and a whole lot of good past history making the kitchen suddenly seem too warm. "I should get goin'."

Annabelle stepped out of his way and let him walk out. She was staying for Christmas. There would be time to see how he felt about her maybe staying around. She watched him drive away and then closed the door and locked it.

"I WASN'T SURE you'd be back to the ranch tonight," Willie said as Dawson walked into her kitchen to find her standing over the stove.

"I don't know why not," he said and leaned in to see what she was busy stirring. "Chili?"

She nodded. "The way you and your brother like it."

"I thought we'd be eating leftover turkey for a few

weeks," he said as he leaned against the counter to watch. When his mother was fretting over something, she cooked. He didn't have to ask what was bothering her.

"That huge old turkey carcass got picked clean at Thanksgiving," Willie said. "That's what's nice about having a lot of people over. Not a lot of leftovers."

"You don't mind me using some of the ranch funds to buy Annabelle's house?"

"I think it's a good investment."

He wasn't so sure about that. "I figure the sale will go through pretty quickly so she should be able to leave right after the holidays."

"Sounds like you have it all worked out." Willie stopped stirring the chili to turn to face him. With a sigh, she said, "I'm worried about you."

"I'll be fine."

"She doesn't want to go." Willie made it sound as if it was hard for her to tell him that.

"What would make you think that?"

His mother gave him a look. "You live as long as I have and you know things. She just doesn't know how to tell you so neither of you think she's taking the easy way out."

He shook his head. "Don't take this wrong, but this time, you're wrong." He started to turn away but she caught his arm and pulled him back.

"I was thinking as I was making this chili. Maybe it's time for some sort of grand gesture, you know, like they do in movies, to let her know how you feel."

Dawson chuckled at that. "She knows how I feel, Mama." He hadn't called her that since he was a boy.

She let go of his arm. "You want some chili?"

"I'm not hungry, but thanks." With that he left and headed to his own home, knowing that without Annie there it would feel empty—just like he felt.

ANNABELLE WOKE WITH a start. For a moment, she thought the sound had come from under the bed, but Dawson had secured the trapdoor with the nails. No one was coming up through that door.

She lay in bed listening. There was a strange light coming through the curtains. She frowned and quietly climbed out of bed to look. After a longer than normal Indian summer, winter had come while she was sleeping.

The first blizzard of the season had blown in. She could tell that the temperature had dropped drastically from the ice that was forming on the inside of the old windows. The sky, which should have been dark, was a pale gray color as huge snowflakes whirled in the wind, sticking to anything they touched.

She shivered and climbed back into bed, telling herself she must have heard the wind. Gripping the covers under her chin, she lay still, listening to the wind—until she heard a sound that sent her pulse into overdrive. The front door had just blown open!

ROB HAD KNOWN his uncle was going to be furious.

"She was pregnant? Pregnant with my kid?"

"If you do the math—"

"I did the math. I had a son I knew nothing about? Where is he now?"

"Died in a car wreck with his wife when the youngest kid was, like, four or five, I heard. You can't believe the way people talk in these small towns. If you stay here long enough, you hear—"

"So that's my grandkid staying at the house," his uncle said, clearly not listening to him. "My grand-daughter. And Baby Doll kept this all from me." He was swearing again.

"So, what do you want me to do?"

"What I told you to do. Find the damned loot. But don't touch a hair on my granddaughter's head. You got that?"

He couldn't believe the old man was getting senti-mental in his old age.

"I got it. But what do I do if she catches me in the house?"

"Figure it out. But don't you hurt her. Not one hair."

He'd hung up doing some cussing of his own. Then he'd gotten dressed and started to leave the motel, only to find that a snowstorm had blown in. Just his luck. But he couldn't put this off any longer. He would break into the house and finish his search. If he was right, no way would the granddaughter be staying in the house—not after a body had been hauled out of it.

ANNABELLE SCRAMBLED OUT of bed and rushed into the living room to close the front door. She turned on a light and was about to bolt the door, when she heard a noise behind her. Turning quickly, she saw the snowy foot-prints melting on the floor a second before she came face-to-face with Lawrence Clarkston, the old man with the cane who'd sworn he was Frannie's beau. He'd lied, according to Inez. Worse, she'd noticed his car parked in front of the neighbor woman's house across the street.

She stared at him, shocked to see him standing in the empty living room. Even more surprised to see the gun in his hand. He motioned for her to step away from the door.

"Where's the jewels?" he demanded. "I know your grandmother still had them when she died. She might have spent the money, but she still had the gems."

Annabelle groaned. "I don't know anything about any jewels."

"My brother followed your mother out here. I never knew where she ended up. She'd changed her name, her looks, everything. I'm amazed Mickey was even able to get a lead on her. Bernie was losing his mind trying to find her. He's been looking for her for years. My brother finds her and she kills him!"

She didn't know what to say. "If you knew your brother found her—"

"He called, told me he'd found her but didn't give me any specifics. Damned fool. He thought he could keep the jewels for him, fence them and not have Bernie find out. I was trying to talk him out of it, telling him how dangerous it would be." He laughed. "Instead, Bernie's Baby Doll kills him?"

"He must have told you something since you showed up at my door days before the body was found," Annabelle said. She didn't know who or what to believe. This old man had lied to her once already.

"I've kept my ear to the ground for years. When I heard where Bernie was living now, I made sure I got a room down the hall. He doesn't know me from Adam, but I know him. He corrupted my brother. Mickey was a good guy before he met Bernie."

"So Bernie knows about Frannie?"

He nodded. "You know why they called him Bernie the Hawk? 'Cuz he had an eye for the ladies—until your grandmother came along. He fell so hard for that woman. My brother said anyone could have told him she was trouble, but no one had the guts. I laughed my ass off when I heard that she stole it all and disappeared."

Her mind was racing. She glanced around for a way out. Since they'd pretty much cleaned out the house, there was no handy weapon. The door was a few steps behind her, but she doubted she could turn and reach it before the man shot her.

"Look," he was saying. "Mickey wasn't all that bright. I thought he'd taken off with the jewels. But when I happened to see the newspaper in Bernie's trash at the rest home, I got curious. Bernie was all excited. Everyone at the home was talking about it. I went online, saw the Milk River Courier newspaper and checked out what Bernie had cut from it. The moment I saw your grandmother's face…" He smiled. "Bernie must have felt the same thing. Your grandmother was a looker. Played Bernie like a Stradivarius. Did you know she never told him her real name? He just called her Baby Doll."

The old man took a breath. "When I found out that Bernie had sent his worthless nephew, Robby, out here, I thought it was going to be another wild-goose chase. How wrong I was. So hand over the jewels and I'm out of here."

She started to tell him again that she really didn't know anything, when they both jumped at the sound of glass breaking.

Lawrence swore and said, "Stay right here." The moment he started toward her bedroom, she quickly unlocked the door. She didn't think the old man could move fast enough to catch her and once she was outside in the blizzard—

Annabelle had the door open and was almost outside when she slammed into a dark figure that appeared out of nowhere. She realized he must have thrown something at her bedroom window to distract the old man. This man wasn't old. He was big and strong and he literally lifted her up by her shoulders and thrust her back inside the house. He'd just slammed the door behind him when Lawrence came running into the room, gun firing.

The younger man pushed her out of the way and drew his own weapon, firing at the approaching target. The old man staggered and went down. "Larry the Loser? What the hell is he doing here?"

She watched in horror as the younger man walked over and picked up the gun the old man had dropped. He pocketed it. Everything had happened so fast that she hadn't even moved. Now, as she started to bolt for the door, he turned to point his gun at her.

"Tell me you aren't going to give me as much trouble as your grandmother did my uncle," the man said.

"Your uncle?" she managed to get out. This must be Robby, the guy old man had mentioned.

"Bernie. He said to say hello. You realize he's your grandfather, right?"

Annabelle felt as if she'd fallen down a rabbit hole. "Yes, my grandfather."

"So, just give me whatever is left that she took from my uncle and I'm out of your hair, so to speak."

She groaned. "I just told that man I don't know any-thing about any loot."

"You threw a lot of stuff away. You're sure you didn't come across some jewels? Rubies, pearls, diamonds, emeralds?"

"My grandmother didn't have anything like that. She didn't wear jewelry, so she didn't even have costume jewelry."

"Didn't wear jewelry?" He scoffed at that. "My uncle weighed down that woman with diamond necklaces and earrings. On her birthday, he gave her an emerald ring that set him back a small fortune. You're telling me she got rid of all of his gifts?"

"Apparently. I suspect that's how she lived as long as she did. I never saw any jewelry, ever." She took a step closer to the door.

He waved her back with the gun in his hand and a shake of his head. "We're still talking here."

MAKE A GRAND GESTURE. Dawson couldn't get the phrase out of his head. What exactly did his mother expect him to do? Show up like he had the last time, with an en-gagement ring and a bouquet of roses—both things he couldn't afford. That had been his grand gesture and look where it had gotten him.

No, he was fresh out of grand gestures. But as he drove through the blizzard toward home, he couldn't get Annabelle off his mind. He hadn't liked leaving her in that house alone.

He wasn't concerned with ghosts. He didn't think she would be, either. She was a strong woman and she was handling all of this remarkably well.

Still, when he reached the turn-off to his house, he kept going in the direction of town. He told himself it wouldn't hurt to drive by her place. It was late, since, after talking to his mother, he'd gone out to the barn and worked on his old tractor for a while. It had seemed a symbolic thing to do. Also the damned thing wasn't running again.

The snowstorm roared around him making it difficult to see where the road started and ended. He felt the need to drive faster, to get there quicker, and told himself he was letting his imagination run away with him. Maybe he was more spooked by what they'd found at the house than Annie was. Annie. He did much better when he thought of her as Annabelle.

Through the falling, whirling snow, he caught a glimpse of the lights of Whitehorse. He told himself she'd be in bed, sound asleep, not having given a thought to him.

But still, he sped up a little on the outskirts of town. It wasn't far now.

ROB STUDIED HER. He thought she was telling the truth. He'd been hanging around long enough to know that this woman had been some kind of supermodel until she fell on hard times and came back here to sell her grandmother's house. He'd even heard that her fancy sports car out in the yard was almost repossessed for lack of payment. Someone at the local bar had seen Dawson Rogers write the repo man a check. The car had already been hooked up to the wrecker. A few more minutes and it would have been gone.

"Look, I need to call my uncle with this news. He

won't be happy. Normally he would tell me to torture you until you told me the truth. But the fact that you are his flesh and blood and Baby Doll's granddaughter, I think he'll cut you some slack. You have to be honest with me, though, okay?"

Her mind had been racing. "You found the tunnel," she said as she was putting things together. "I would imagine you already looked down there and in the garage. I don't know of any more hiding places. I never knew any of this about my grandmother. It all came as a shock, including the dead man in the wall."

Rob was considering that when he heard a sound behind him. He spun, just not quickly enough. For a moment, he couldn't figure out what had hit him. But glancing over his shoulder, he saw the sword blade sticking out of his back. When he looked at the old man he'd thought he killed, he saw that he was holding the shell of his cane.

Rob lifted the gun to fire, but as he turned, it felt as if someone had cut his strings. Before he could get a shot off, he slumped to the floor at the old man's feet. "Bernie isn't going to like this, Larry," he choked out before everything went black.

ANNABELLE WATCHED ALL of this play out before her eyes as if in a bad dream. It wasn't until the younger man slumped to the floor that she found her feet.

She made a run for the door, but the old man was faster than he looked even wounded. He grabbed a handful of hair and jerked her back. His rancid breath washed over her face as he pulled her close and whispered, "He might have believed you, but I'm betting you're going to tell me where the loot is before this night is over because I could care less if you're Bernie's granddaughter."

She could hear the storm raging outside. The old man jerked her hair harder, making her cry out in pain. She could see that he was bleeding, but clearly the gunshot wasn't going to kill him. Apparently he'd been listening to her conversation with Rob.

"Let's go in this room down here," Larry said. "Your bedroom. I saw through the window that it's about the only room with stuff still in it. Is that where the loot is?"

"I told you just like I told the other man. There is no jewelry."

"Right," the old man said, giving her a hard shove. "Maybe I can help jog your memory."

She stumbled into her room, banging against the closet door where her grandmother's clothing still hung. Her mind raced to think if there was something in here that she could use for a weapon. She spotted her hammer on the dresser.

Larry went to the closet. Keeping one eye on her, he began to tear Frannie's clothes from their hangers. One gawdy sweatshirt after another hit the floor.

Annabelle inched a little closer to the dresser and the hammer sitting on top. Larry saw her out of the corner of his eye and lunged at her, throwing her across the bed. He smacked her across the face, holding her down as he reached to grab the cord on the blinds. She tried to kick him in the groin only to have him slap her harder.

The cord snapped off and he roughly rolled her onto her face on the bed and began to tie her hands together behind her back.

"You're hurting me," she cried out.

"I've only just begun. You try anything and I'll kill you because, according to you, you know nothing, right? I can hog-tie you and I will if you move again."

She rolled to her side and watched him as he went back to the closet. He pulled down boxes of old shoes, throwing them onto the growing pile until the closet was empty.

He was breathing hard when he came back over to where she lay. "Okay, girlie, now we're going to get down to business." He pulled a knife from a scabbard under his pants leg. She tried to recoil, but he grabbed her hair again as he laid the edge of the blade against her cheek. "You were your grandmother's favorite, according to the woman across the street who I visited for a while recently. These little old ladies are so helpful. If Frannie confided in anyone, it would have been you. Tell me where it is!"

DAWSON SAW THE lights on Annie's bedroom and the living room the moment he pulled up. He couldn't explain what had him so afraid. Just a bad feeling. He rushed up to the house and pounded on the door. She would think he was crazy. Think he was butting into her life. Again. But he didn't care. He had to see her. Had to see if she was all right.

The light in the bedroom went out.

"Oh, no, you don't," he said as he pounded harder. "Annie, you might as well open up, because I'm not going anywhere until you do!" he yelled.

The light came back on in the bedroom. A few minutes later, the door opened a crack.

Annabelle's pale face peered out. "What do you want?" she demanded, her voice cracking.

He noticed there was a red mark on the side of her face. Had she been asleep?

"You need to leave." Her blue eyes seemed to plead with him. "Please."

"I just had to be sure you were all right. I know it sounds crazy but… Could I come in for a moment?"

She shook her head. "No. Now, please go." She began to close the door.

As she was closing the door, his bad feeling was even stronger, now that he'd seen her. Before she could get the door all the way shut and locked, he slammed his hand into it, forcing her back so he could enter.

Bursting into the empty living room, he shoved to the side. As he turned, he found some old man holding a gun to Annie's temple.

"Close the door," the old man ordered. "Lock it. Play hero and she dies."

Off to the side, he could see a body with a sword sticking out of it. His throat constricted. He'd been right about Annie being in trouble. But now he might have made it worse.

ANNABELLE LET OUT a cry as the man jabbed the gun against her temple and twisted her arm behind her as he dragged her to him. He was much stronger and quicker than he looked.

"Close the door," Larry ordered. "Now!"

Dawson did as the man asked. "What's going on?" He sounded so calm.

"He thinks my grandmother had the jewels from the

heist and that I know where they are," she said, her voice breaking. If only Dawson had just left like she'd asked him. She couldn't bear the thought that he was going to die because of her.

"That's ridiculous," Dawson snapped. "She didn't even know about the heist or her grandmother's relationship with Bernie McDougal."

"Or about my brother being murdered and walled up in her grandmother's house?" the old man said.

"I was the one who wanted to know what was behind that wall. Let her go. She doesn't know anything."

"Maybe. Maybe not. But unless you want to see her die, you'll do exactly what I say." Larry motioned with the gun for Dawson to go down the hall toward her bedroom.

She didn't believe for a moment that he would let them go when he didn't find anything. Or even if he did.

Dawson was ahead of them as they started toward the bedroom. She feared what would happen once they reached there. Larry still had her arm pulled behind her, but the gun was no longer to her head. She knew it was risky, but she saw no other way. "Dawson!" she called and spun around, even though it hurt her arm.

She kicked Larry as hard as she could in his private parts. As she did, she grabbed the gun. The old man doubled over, but his grip on the gun was still too strong for her to wrestle it from him. She feared he would get off a shot at Dawson before she could. From behind her, she heard the sound of Dawson's boots on the old hardwood floor as he rushed toward them. As he did, he pulled the sword from Robby's body.

He drove the blade into the man's side, forcing him

back. Larry's grip on the gun gave. She jerked it from his hand as he stumbled back and dropped to the floor.

Dawson took the gun from her and held it on the man. It had all happened so fast. She felt dizzy, fear still coursing through her even with a sense of relief. Was it really over? Or would there be others who would come looking for the loot?

Trembling, she listened to Dawson make the call to the sheriff. Then he pulled her into his arms as they stood over the old man until they heard the sound of sirens. Moments later, deputies were streaming through the front door.

Chapter Nineteen

Annabelle didn't know how long she'd been asleep when she felt something warm and wet touch her cheek. Her eyes flew open. She jerked back, a laugh escaping her lips as Dawson's puppy gave her another kiss.

"Sadie, no," he cried as he rushed into the room. "She has been wanting to come see you for hours. I thought I'd closed the door all the way after I checked on you earlier. How are you?"

"Good, thanks to you."

"Well, when you're ready, I made you something special for breakfast." With that, he called the puppy, who scampered out and the door closed.

Annabelle looked around for her clothes and groaned when she realized that last night she'd thrown on one of her grandmother's sweatshirts and her jeans. She pulled on the sweatshirt, thinking about her grandmother. Was she really like Frannie? Her grandmother had been a survivor. Annabelle guessed she could say that about herself too.

"Something smells good," she said as she walked into Dawson's kitchen.

"I thought you might be hungry. You slept a long time. It's almost noon."

She couldn't believe it. Then again, last night she remembered his arm around her all the way out to his house. He'd helped her inside and into the bed. She remembered trying to thank him, but he'd already closed the door. The next thing she knew, she was waking to Sadie's kisses.

"You saved my life last night," she said, her voice breaking. "If you hadn't come back to look in on me…"

"For once my instincts were right," he said and turned back to dishing up the Mexican quiche he'd made.

The smell of it brought back other memories of the two of them. Dawson had always been a great cook. There wasn't anything the man couldn't do.

"Your instincts weren't wrong thirteen years ago," she said as he put a slice in front of her along with a bowl of fresh fruit. "I wanted so badly to marry you. The ring, the roses…" Her voice broke again. "But I couldn't."

He nodded, his brown eyes serious. "I know. There were things you had to do. I was incredibly selfish asking you to give up your dream."

"I'm not going back to modeling. I know you said you're seeing Amy now, but—"

"Annie, you can't make a decision like that so soon after everything that's happened."

"I'm not going to change my mind. Also, I'm going to give Amy Baker a run for her money. I want you back, Dawson."

He shook his head. "Annie."

"My life was so up in the air the night we made love. But I'm perfectly clear on what I want now. I love you.

I'll wait for you. I'll talk to Mary Sue about keeping the house and I think I can get a job down at the grocery store. If not there, then—"

He reached across the breakfast bar and took her face in his big hands. Bending, he kissed her. She forgot all about the quiche. All about everything except being in this man's arms again. She kissed him back as he swept her up and carried her to his bedroom.

They made love slowly until neither of them could stand it any longer. And then they let the chemistry burn between them in a fire that Annabelle knew would last the rest of their lives.

Later, lying naked in his arms, she looked up at him. He was her Montanan and she was finally home.

"WHEN I SAID maybe you needed a grand gesture," Willie cried when they came in the kitchen door, "I didn't mean almost getting yourself killed." She rushed to her son, cupping his face in her hands and just looking at him, as if too thankful to speak.

"But I got the girl," he said and smiled.

"Oh, you boys are going to be the death of me," Willie said and stepped to Annabelle and hugged her tightly. "You're staying."

She nodded. "I'm not going anywhere." Dawson put his arm around her.

Willie smiled at them. "I'm so glad the two of you are all right."

"The nightmare is over," Dawson said.

"I wish that were true. It won't be over until the jewels from the heist turn up," Annabelle said. "We can't even be sure that my grandmother had them. Obviously,

my grandfather still believes she does and so do his...
associates. He believes she stole them when she took
off without a word and disappeared. He's been looking
for her and the loot for more than fifty years. I doubt he
will stop now."

Willie shook her head, as if in wonder, and Annabelle realized she was staring at her ugly sweatshirt. "It
was my grandmother's. She has a closet full of them."

"I bet she does," the older woman said. "I've never
seen anything like it. I noticed you were wearing a clown
one the other day. What is this one?"

"A unicorn," Annie said with a groan.

"May I?" Willie asked as she began to pry at one of
the green stones that made up the ground the unicorn
was standing on. "It's been a while since I've seen an
emerald, but I'd swear this is one."

"What?" Dawson and Annie said in unison.

Willie handed the stone to her son. "I think we've
found what happened to the missing jewels. Your grandmother knew there would be others coming to find them,
so she hid them in broad daylight."

Dawson looked at Annie. "I think she's right. You say
there are a dozen of these in her closet?"

Annabelle nodded in disbelief. "We need to call the
sheriff."

"ARE YOU SURE you want to keep the house?" Dawson
asked as he finished setting up the last of the furniture
in the spare bedroom. Fortunately, they'd been able to
retrieve a lot of it from the charity shop, assuring them
it would only be temporary.

"My sisters are coming home for Christmas. I think

we need to stay here. At least for the holidays. This is where we were raised."

"I was planning to buy the house, anyway," he confessed as he stepped to her to take her in his arms and kiss her.

"Aren't you tired of rescuing me yet?"

"No chance."

They both turned at a knock on the door. A deliveryman stood on the porch. When Annabelle opened the door, he asked her to sign for the large envelope he held in his hand. She signed, curious.

After he left, she stepped back inside and showed Dawson. "It's from Bernie in New York. Do I dare open it?" She looked at him and then laughed, thinking of the wall over the alcove. Her future husband was even more curious than she was.

She tore into it to find a letter-sized envelope inside with a note attached to it.

I'm one of Bernie McDougal's nurses. He asked me to make sure you got this. It was his dying wish.

She looked up at Dawson and slowly opened the letter.

My dear granddaughter,
I'm sorry I'll never get to meet you.

But I wanted you to know how much I loved your grandmother. Whatever she might have done, it was to protect the child she was carrying and later her three granddaughters.

My nephew told me that everyone said you were the one most like your grandmother. In that case, I know you must be beautiful and have her spunk. So I also know that you will do just fine.

I wish you well. You will be safe now,
Bernie, your grandfather

Annabelle had tears in her eyes as she refolded the letter. She looked at Dawson. "Aren't you worried that I might have inherited some of my grandparent's genes?"

He laughed and pulled her to him. "I can handle it."

She smiled up into his handsome face. "I know you can, cowboy."

Annabelle cuddled against Dawson. She'd come home and there was no other place on earth that she wanted to be.

Her sisters would be here soon. It was going to be a wonderful Christmas, she thought, as she looked around the house Dawson and his mother had helped her get ready for her family.

Outside the snow continued to fall. Nothing like a white Christmas, she thought.

She only had one wish. That her grandmother were here to share it with them. Then again, she thought with a smile, knowing Frannie the way she did now, she figured she was here in spirit.

* * * * *

SHOTGUN BRIDE

This book is dedicated to the readers
who love the fictional town of Whitehorse, Montana,
and its residents as much as I do.
Say hello to the Corbett family.

Chapter One

Jerilyn Larch froze, one foot on the floor.

From the sagging motel bed, Earl Ray Pitts mumbled something, let out a snort and resumed snoring loudly.

Jerilyn released the breath she'd been holding and slipped out of the bed, knowing she'd called this one a little too close.

Gingerly she picked up each piece of her clothing from the grimy carpet and tiptoed into the bathroom to get dressed.

Jerilyn Larch hadn't just fallen on hard times. She'd hit rock bottom. While the Larch name had once meant something in this part of Arizona, it wasn't worth squat anymore.

The land was gone and so was the money. Worse, as her mother would have said, Jerilyn had hooked up with the wrong sort. She needed to get out of this ratty motel—out of this town—as quickly as possible and put some miles between her and the man still in the lumpy double bed.

Dressed, she peered out of the bathroom. Only a little of the gray dawn leaked through the cheap drapes. Earl Ray was still sleeping or at least pretending to. She could never tell for sure with him. The man had a mean streak that she knew all too well. He'd told her often enough that he'd kill her if she ever left him—or at least make her wish she was dead.

For days she'd been looking for a chance to escape.

She glanced around for his keys and caught sight of herself in the filmed-over mirror by the door, shocked by what she saw: a woman who looked much older than forty-two, a woman with nothing to lose. Jerilyn silently made a promise to herself. Her life was going to get better, starting today.

Spying the keys on the bureau, she carefully picked them up and hesitated for a moment before she scooped up Earl Ray's wallet.

Slipping out, she hustled to his Buick parked in front of the room. The car was old, the rear panels rusted, a real embarrassment. She wished that if she had to borrow a car, she could at least get one that was worth a damn. But beggars couldn't be choosers, and she had the keys to this one.

Jerilyn climbed behind the wheel and made a quick check of the wallet. Earl Ray didn't have enough money to get her far. She tossed the wallet on the seat and felt herself panic as she considered what her options were with little money, a car that probably wouldn't get her past town and nowhere to run.

Earl Ray would be furious. He was mean enough, but taking his money and his car and then leaving him high and dry in some tiny sand-blown desert town would push him over the edge. As if he needed a nudge.

As she sat there, a realization began to set in. Once she started this car and made a run for it, she'd have to look out for herself. And that frightened her almost more than Earl Ray did.

Jerilyn had always latched on to a man and let him make all the decisions for her. Earl Ray was a bastard, but maybe being on her own was worse. She glanced toward the motel room, wondering if she could slip back inside without him noticing she'd ever left.

As if in answer, the door banged open, and Earl Ray staggered out looking like this side of hell. The look on his face when he spotted her sitting behind the wheel of his car told her there would be no turning back.

Jerilyn stabbed the key into the ignition and cranked up the engine. The radio blasted on, drowning out whatever he was yelling.

Throwing the car into Reverse, she hit the gas as he lunged for the Buick. He fell face-first onto the gravel as she sped backward, nearly taking out a palm tree.

Slamming the car into Drive, she barely missed Earl Ray as she took off, tires spitting gravel as the vehicle fishtailed.

At the street, she stopped, opened the window and, after snatching out the cash, tossed his wallet in the dirt.

She might have hit bottom, but Jerilyn Larch was no thief. The three hundred and seventy-eight dollars she'd taken was money earned from putting up with him.

As for the car, well, she'd call him once this was over and let him know where to find it—no doubt abandoned beside some road where the engine had quit for good.

In her rearview mirror, she could see that Earl Ray was up on his feet and stumbling after her. Jerilyn hit the gas and didn't look back again. She knew he couldn't call the police to report the car stolen, not in his line of work as a thug between illegal crime jobs.

Maybe he wouldn't even come after her. Maybe all those threats had been nothing but bluster. Either way, she'd have to move quickly, staying one step ahead of him until she could escape the country.

She would ditch the car once she reached Montana—if the car made it that far. Otherwise, she'd hitchhike. It wouldn't be the first time. She just hoped it would be the last.

Montana. Jerilyn hadn't realized she'd made a decision where to go until that moment. She'd promised herself years ago that she wouldn't use what she considered her ace in the hole unless she was truly desperate.

Well, she was desperate now, she thought, as she reached into her shoulder bag and removed the small, beaded purse her grandmother had given her. Most of the beads were missing, the fabric beneath gray with age.

She nearly ran off the road as she unzipped the purse and pulled out the piece of yellowed paper.

She had to hold it for a moment just to make sure the note was still there and that she hadn't made it up like she had that rosy future she dreamed about all the time.

The writing had faded from age and too much handling, but as she held it up to the light, she saw with relief that she could still make out the words.

Guilt pierced her conscience, but she cast it aside as quickly as she had Earl Ray at the motel and the man before him. Jerilyn returned the note to her purse just as carefully as she had twenty-six years ago.

A male orderly had handed her the note the day she'd given birth. Sixteen and pregnant. Just a baby herself.

Her hips were too narrow, and the doctors had to take the baby, leaving her sterile and scarred in ways that had never healed.

Her mama had made it clear from the start that she couldn't keep the baby. Jerilyn was too young, too immature, to raise a child.

"You'd just mess up the poor baby's life as you have your own," her mother had predicted. "I'm doing that baby the biggest favor of its life."

Jerilyn hated her mother for those words. She knew the real truth. Her mama didn't want the Larch name tarnished by some illegitimate baby. That's why she made Jerilyn go away to Montana before anyone knew she was pregnant.

After the birth, she'd gotten only a glimpse of the tiny pink toes peeking out of the blanket before her mama handed the infant off to some old woman down the hall.

That same night, there was another young girl in labor. Later, Jerilyn had heard her crying as if her heart was also breaking.

"Your baby is with a good family, a family with money and status, a family like ours was before you disgraced us all," her mama had said when Jerilyn begged for information about her baby. "The less you know the better. Just forget you ever had it."

As if her mama had ever let her forget. The Larch family seemed to be cursed after that. Her father made some bad investments and everything went downhill from there. Of course, her mother blamed her although no one knew about the tiny little baby girl she'd been forced to give up.

That was the first time Jerilyn had known heartbreak, but definitely not the last.

The adoption had all been done in secret. There was no paperwork and no chance of Jerilyn ever finding out what had happened to her little girl.

At least that's what her mama had thought until her dying day.

But her mama had no idea what she was capable of when she put her mind to it. Jerilyn had paid the sympathetic orderly to get her information, and he came back with a scrap of yellow paper.

On the paper was written:

Baby girl: Madeline "Maddie" Cavanaugh to Sarah and Roy Cavanaugh, Old Town Whitehorse, Montana.

Now Jerilyn was about to right the terrible wrong her mother had forced her to commit.

"I'm finally going to find my girl," she said as she steered the Buick north toward Montana. Jerilyn hoped that her mama had been right about one thing—that her baby had gone to a good family, a generous one with money and status.

Being a friendly family would help, too, but if not, Jerilyn imagined they would pay to get rid of her. Jerilyn hated what she was about to do, but in a way she'd felt as if it was out of her hands, as if it had been destined since she was sixteen.

EARL RAY LISTENED to the knock of his old Buick's engine as it faded away in the distance. What the hell was the woman thinking? No one was that stupid, were they?

He waited, hoping the car blew a rod before it disappeared from view, or that Jerilyn had the good sense to turn around and come back.

Otherwise there was going to be serious trouble.

Earl Ray accepted partial responsibility for the situation. Last night at the bar he'd seen a man he'd thought he recognized. Worrying that it was someone after him and the little black book, he'd slipped the leather notebook into Jerilyn's shoulder bag.

When he'd realized there was nothing to worry about, he decided to leave the book in her purse until he could retrieve it without Jerilyn being any the wiser. Jerilyn was the last person he wanted knowing anything about the book—or its contents.

Unfortunately, he'd let himself drink too much and had forgotten about retrieving it. Now the stupid broad had taken off with the book, not even realizing that she had it.

At least he didn't think she did.

Either way, she had something equivalent to a bomb in her purse. That book was his ticket out of this miserable existence he'd been living. There was only one problem. If the book fell into the wrong hands, he was a dead man.

Earl Ray let out a string of expletives. If he could have gotten his hands on Jerilyn, he would have wrung her neck. The good news was that she couldn't get far in that pile of rusted junk.

As he started back toward the room, he realized he should have known she was going to take off. In the past when she became weepy drunk, she'd take out that little coin purse of hers and look at a scrap of faded paper. Lately, she'd been looking at it more and more.

The first time he'd seen her crying over the note, he'd waited until she passed out and dug the damned thing out of her purse, thinking the dumb broad was crying over some man.

It didn't take a genius to figure out what the note was about—or where Jerilyn was now headed. This had been coming for some time, and Earl Ray prided himself on knowing women.

He limped into his motel room and closed the door behind him. Luckily, he knew where he could scrape up some money and help. He picked up the phone and dialed his associates Bubba and Dude, his anger ebbing a little as he realized the three of them could beat Jerilyn to Montana.

Earl Ray smiled. He couldn't wait to see her face.

Chapter Two

"I say we settle this with a horse race."

"The hell we will," Dalton Corbett said, pushing his brother Jud out of the way in order to get to the bar in the main house on the Trails West Ranch.

Jud might have been the youngest of the Corbett brothers—three minutes behind his fraternal twin, Dalton—but in no way was he the smallest. Not at six foot three! The Hollywood stuntman was like all the Corbett brothers: tall and broad-shouldered, handsome as sin and wild as the West Texas wind.

Jud shoved Dalton back, and the two commenced pushing and jostling just as they'd done as boys.

"Hell, let's just shoot it out," Shane said. He stepped past the two to grab a glass and a bottle of bourbon from behind the bar before settling into one of the deep leather chairs. He looked out a bank of windows onto the rolling prairie of Montana. Only the purple silhouette of the Little Rockies broke the wide expanse of open range.

Shane wondered what the hell his father had been thinking, moving here. Grayson Corbett hadn't been thinking clearly, that was the only thing that could explain it. That and the fact that his father, at the ripe old age of fifty-five, had fallen in love again.

"The only fair way to do this is to have the oldest brother go first," Lantry Corbett suggested, since he was the second to the oldest and the divorce lawyer.

Russell stood up from where he'd been sitting. "We'll draw straws." He was the oldest of the five Corbett brothers and considered the least wild of the bunch, which wasn't saying much.

Jud and Dalton quit wrestling to look at Russell. "Straws?" they asked in unison.

"Why not beans?" Shane suggested, thinking of the Texas Rangers who were caught in Mexico back in the 1800s. "A white bean, you're spared. A black bean, you're not."

"Drawing straws is the only fair way," Russell insisted, ignoring Shane's sarcasm. "We leave it up to chance."

"Or destiny," Jud added.

"*Destiny?* You've been hanging out with those Hollywood types too long," Lantry said. He grabbed a beer from behind the well-stocked bar and pulled up a chair in front of the window next to Shane.

"What do *you* say?" Lantry asked him.

Shane was disgusted with the whole mess. He poured himself a glass of bourbon and downed it before he finally spoke. "This is emotional blackmail, and I don't want any part of it."

His brothers all looked at him in surprise.

"It was our mother's dying wish," Russell said.

"Yeah, and bad karma if we ignore it," Jud said.

"*Destiny? Karma?*" Shane scoffed.

"It isn't just about Mom," Russell said quietly. "Can't you see what this is really about? Dad wants us here in Montana with him. He's not always going to be around."

"Well, I think he was a fool to leave Texas," Shane said.

Russell shook his head. "He did it for Kate. He loves her and would do anything for her. Look how happy Dad is. All those years of being lonely without Mom. I'm glad he found Kate."

"Kate found him," Shane corrected. "Just to keep the record straight."

This marriage and the move to Montana had been all her doing. Anyone could see that. She'd gone to Texas to find their father, playing on the one thing they had in common—Grayson's deceased wife. Kate and Rebecca had grown up together on this ranch.

No one was fool enough to think that buying the Trails West Ranch in Montana hadn't been Kate's idea. The ranch had been in her family for decades, until her father died and it was lost.

"Kate isn't the only one with history here," Russell argued. "Let's not forget that our mother was born and raised here." Rebecca Wade's father had been the fore-man of the ranch. She and Kate had been like sisters. "This place means a lot to both Dad and Kate and should to all of us, as well."

"We're doing this for Dad," Russell continued. "And Mom. It's what she wanted."

Shane shook his head as he watched Russell step over to the bar, pick up the knife their father had used to slice up limes for margaritas, and proceed to cut five straws into five different lengths.

Taking another drink, Shane swore under his breath as a hush fell over the room. He couldn't believe they were really going to do this.

Russell mixed up the pieces in his hand, leveling off the cut straws at the top, hiding their lengths in his massive fist.

"This is crazy," Lantry said, looking to Shane for help. Shane knew that he was considered the sensible brother. After all, he was the Texas Ranger. Or at least had been.

Russell held out the cut straws. "Who wants to go first?"

"Not me," Jud said quickly. "I'm leaving mine up to destiny. I'll take the last straw."

"Hell, I'll go first," Dalton said, and drew one, palming it until the others had drawn.

Lantry went next, although he didn't seem any happier about it than Shane. Part con artist and charmer—if there was a way out of this, Lantry, the lawyer would find it.

"Shane?" Russell held his closed fist out to him.

"I don't want any part of this," Shane said with a curse.

"If you get the longest straw, you have five years before you have to do anything," Russell said, always the pragmatist. "By then Dad may be gone, too. You can ignore both of their dying wishes and do whatever the hell you please. In the meantime, take a damned straw."

Shane snatched one of the cut straws from his brother's hand, tossed it on the table without looking at it and poured himself another drink.

"You lucky bastard," Dalton said. "Shane got the longest one."

Russell turned to the youngest of the brothers. "Well, Jud, you still sure you want to go last?"

Jud stared down at the tops of the two remaining straws. "Yeah."

Russell drew one, and Jud took the only remaining straw.

"Okay, let's get this over with," Lantry said. He held out his straw to compare it to the others.

Shane was the only one who didn't join in. As he took a drink, he heard Jud swear and smiled to himself. The youngest of them had drawn the shortest straw. Maybe there was something to this karma business after all.

"Can't argue with destiny, Jud," he said. His brother collapsed into a chair beside him to brood or, more than likely, try to figure out an angle to get out of this. The brothers all had that in common—they all looked for a way out of whatever situation they found themselves in.

Shane had gotten the longest straw. Not that it mattered. This whole thing was ludicrous, and he wasn't going to be blackmailed into anything—especially marriage.

"Okay," Russell said. "Jud, you have one year in which to find a suitable wife. Lantry is next, then Dalton, me and Shane."

"I say we do it over. Best two out of three," Jud suggested. All four brothers turned on him. "Okay, okay. I suppose it's time I started thinking about settling down."

They all laughed. Of the five of them, Jud was the wildest when it came to horses—and women. The Hollywood stuntman settle down with one woman anytime soon? Not likely. On every film he was involved in, he usually had a couple of girlfriends.

"I told you this wasn't going to work," Shane said. "It's not the way to find a woman to spend the rest of your life with."

"Come on, none of us would marry unless forced to," Lantry said with a laugh. "Look at Dad. After Mom's death, he had all kinds of chances to marry, and he didn't."

"Not till Kate," Jud said.

"Maybe Kate reminds him of our mother," Dalton said.

Russell shook his head. "Kate is nothing like our mother." As the oldest at thirty-two, Russell had the best memory of their mother. "Anyway, Dad always said there was no one like Mom."

Shane said nothing. He'd only been around Kate at the wedding, but there was something about her that had made him suspicious, even before she talked their father into selling his place in Texas and moving to this isolated part of Montana to buy back her family's home ranch.

Kate was a woman with secrets. Shane had been a lawman for too long not to recognize it. Kate was hiding something. Something big. And Shane feared that when the truth came out, Grayson Corbett would be devastated.

"I'll have you know that I've already found the perfect woman," Jud announced. "Her name is Maddie Cavanaugh. She's exactly what mother said she wanted for us—a Montana girl."

The rest of them laughed, but Shane watched his little brother, thinking he might actually be telling the truth.

Jud did attract women the way magnets attracted tacks. And Jud had been in town for over a week now.

"Dad and Kate are going to love Maddie," Jud said with a grin. "I predict wedding bells in the very near future."

Shane got to his feet. He couldn't take any more of this. "Have you all lost your minds? Who gives a damn what's in some stupid letter? Our mother didn't live long enough to know any of us well enough to determine what kind of woman we should marry. Why should we let her tell us how to live our lives from the grave?" He shook his head.

JERILYN DROVE AS far as she could. She'd been running on fear and large doses of caffeine. Now after fifteen hours at the wheel her nerves were fried and she had the jitters so bad she was forced to stop for what was left of the night.

She pulled over beside a park in some small town and climbed into the back of the car to sleep, telling herself that she'd put enough miles between her and Earl Ray. There was no way he could find her, especially without a car and without knowing which direction she was headed. She'd never told him about the daughter she'd been forced to give up at sixteen. She'd never told anyone.

And she was sure he hadn't called the cops. No, Earl Ray would call some of his low-life buddies and probably get drunk. That was his answer to everything.

It was when he sobered up that she would have to worry. Then he'd be hungover and furious. But why come looking for her at all? He could just pick up another down-on-her-luck woman at any bar. Those were the only kind of women who put up with Earl Ray.

Her stomach growled, but with gas being so expensive, she had gone without food. In the morning, though, she'd have to get something to eat. She had to take care of herself if she hoped to get to Montana.

As she curled up to sleep, she thought about her little baby girl. Jerilyn tried to picture what Maddie would look like now and hoped her daughter had blond hair and blue eyes just like her real mama.

Jerilyn wished she could get some new clothes before she met her and maybe even buy her daughter a gift. Flowers, maybe, or chocolates.

Her stomach growled again, and she tried to sleep, but every little sound startled her. Finally sometime before dawn, Jerilyn fell into a deep sleep and dreamed about her reunion with her daughter.

GRAYSON CORBETT STOOD at the window watching his wife. *His wife.* He smiled at the thought. Falling in love had come as a surprise.

He'd never thought there would be anyone but Rebecca. In all those years since her death, he never met a woman who stirred his heart or tempted him to remarry.

Until Kate.

She'd come into his life so late. That was his only regret. At fifty-five, he hated that he wouldn't have an entire lifetime with her. But if Rebecca had taught him anything, it was not to count on more than this moment in time.

He and Rebecca had married young and started a family right away. They'd both wanted lots of kids, but

Grayson lost the love of his life right after the twins were born.

He'd never expected to love again.

As he studied Kate's slim back now, he ached at the sight of the way she hugged herself as she looked out across the land—her family's land.

He'd hoped getting her family ranch back would take away that haunted look he'd sometimes glimpsed in her eyes.

But there was more to her sadness than the loss of mere land. Something powerful had a hold on her. Whatever it was, Kate kept it to herself.

Grayson hoped he could gain her trust and that she would open up to him. So far that hadn't happened.

"Dad?"

Grayson turned to find his youngest son standing in the doorway. He motioned Jud in, smiling in spite of himself. Having his sons all under the same roof again, even for a short period of time, brought him more joy than they could imagine.

"I thought you'd want to know we talked and came to a decision," Jud said.

Grayson held his breath, worried that his foolish plan hadn't worked. He was torn between guilt and hope.

"We drew straws," Jud said.

So like his sons. He smiled. "Straws, huh? How did you come out?"

Jud shook his head, grinning. "Wouldn't you know it? I got the shortest."

"What do you plan to do?"

"What choice do I have?"

Grayson hated forcing his sons into this, but if he

hoped to live long enough to see grandchildren, what choice did he have?

"Think of it as a nudge," he'd told Kate when he'd revealed his plan to her after finding the letter.

"Oh, Grayson," she'd said, looking worried. "Are you sure about this?"

Hell, no. But he knew his sons too well. Threats and bribes wouldn't have worked. All five sons were successful, and telling them they'd lose their inheritance if they didn't marry wouldn't work. Making an old-man's plea to them wouldn't have worked, either.

He'd raised strong-willed, highly independent men. They were all more like him than Rebecca.

It wasn't until he found the letters Rebecca had left to be given to each son on his wedding day that Grayson seized on the idea. For years, he hadn't touched anything of Rebecca's. Not until the move to Montana. He'd been shocked to find the letters—and grateful. Rebecca, even from the grave, had helped him decide what to do about their wild, incorrigible sons.

Along with a letter to each of the boys, Rebecca had left him a letter, as well. In it, her dying wish had been that the boys marry before the age of thirty-five. She half jokingly had said she hoped that they would marry a Montana cowgirl—just as their father had.

"Don't look so guilty," Kate said when he'd told her he'd called the boys to Montana for a family meeting. "You only want the best for your sons."

Grayson hadn't been so sure. He'd felt as if he was being selfish by using Rebecca's dying wish.

"Honey," Kate had said. "Your boys are like you, strong—stubborn and independent to a fault."

He knew she was right. The boys had grown up without a mother and in a house without a woman's touch. They'd seen him live for years without the love of a good woman and with everything on his own terms.

But since he'd fallen for Kate, he'd come to realize how important love and marriage were for a man. He wanted the same for his sons, and he wanted his sons to settle in Montana, close enough that they could be a family again.

"How are they taking all of this?" Grayson asked his son.

Jud laughed. "As expected."

He laughed, as well. "I can just imagine." Russell would take command as the oldest. Lantry would look for a loophole. Shane would rebel. Dalton would try to charm his way out of it. And Jud…

Grayson studied his youngest son. The wildest one. What would Jud do?

A TRAIL OF DUST rose on the horizon. Kate Wade Corbett watched the three riders cut across the wide prairie.

The Corbett brothers were racing each other to the corrals. Competition was in their blood.

All five brothers were so much like Grayson. No wonder none of them wanted to settle down. She hoped that her husband's plan worked, but she couldn't help being doubtful.

"Hello."

Kate smiled as she felt Grayson's warm breath on her neck. As he put his arms around her, she leaned back into him and breathed in his masculine scent.

"The boys drew straws to see who would get married first," Grayson whispered.

Boys. He still thought of them as boys, but they were grown men. Too bad they often didn't act like it, she thought as dust billowed up, and the breeze carried their shouts and laughter.

"Jud got the shortest straw," he said. "He says he's met someone he thinks we'll like."

She sighed and chuckled softly. "And you believe him?"

"Still skeptical, huh?"

Kate turned in his arms to cup his smooth-shaven jaw and look into those incredible blue eyes. "Wouldn't it have been easier just to tell them the truth?"

He shook his head, smiling down at her before gently giving her a kiss. "I just want them to be as happy as I am," he said as they turned to watch the finish of the race.

In a cloud of dust and cheers and curses, Dalton reached the corrals first. Lantry and Russell finished neck and neck. As the dust settled, Kate spotted Shane sitting in the shade of the bunkhouse. She hadn't noticed him before, but she now had the distinct feeling that he'd been watching her and his father.

Shane, she feared, saw more than the others. Of the five, he worried her the most.

Chapter Three

Jud Corbett wasn't about to tell his brothers, but he'd known this was coming. He was working on a film just to the north in Canada and had overheard Kate and his father discussing the family meeting on one of his visits.

At first he'd told himself that his brothers wouldn't go along with any crazy marriage pact, but that was before he heard about the letters from their mother. While none of the brothers would want to disappoint the old man, ignoring wishes of the mother they'd heard about their whole lives would be impossible.

Jud had known that this whole situation would be a train wreck. That was why he had immediately started looking for the perfect girl-next-door to bring home. He knew his father and Kate would only approve of a woman unlike the kind he normally dated.

He'd found her on a local online dating service's Web site. The moment he'd seen Maddie Cavanaugh's face, he'd known she was perfect.

Imagine his disappointment when he'd found out that the woman's photo and personal profile had been put up on the site by accident. According to Arlene Evans, who ran the service, Maddie Cavanaugh wasn't even in the area anymore.

But a few days ago, Jud had seen Maddie coming out of the Whitehorse Drugstore. Her photo on the Web site hadn't done her justice.

Her long blond hair was pulled up in a ponytail. A pair of silver loops dangled from each earlobe. She wore no makeup. Freckles were sprinkled across her cheeks and the bridge of her nose like tiny stars in a Montana night sky.

Her slim figure was clad in a Western shirt, jeans and boots, which looked at home on her. She had pushed her sunglasses up into her hair to glance down at the book she was holding. When she raised her head, she'd looked right at him with a pair of wondrous big blue eyes, which held an innocence that took his breath away.

Jud was within a few feet of her when she glanced at her watch and then took off toward her pickup, which was parked across the street. He watched her go, chuckling to himself.

He knew he was considered the wildest of the Corbett brothers. Earning his reputation had taken hard work since his four older brothers had sown more than their share of wild oats.

But as he stared after Maddie Cavanaugh, Jud knew he had found the perfect bride.

AT A GAS STATION on her way north, Jerilyn was in the process of digging in her large shoulder bag, looking for what was left of Earl Ray's money when she found it.

"What's this?" Frowning, she pulled out a small black notebook. The leather was worn, and she gingerly peeked between the covers, wondering how it had gotten into her bag.

Inside were names, numbers and dates. Her stomach roiled as she recognized some of the names, names from the news. She dropped the book onto the car seat as if the pages had scorched her fingers and covered her mouth to keep from screaming.

For a few minutes, Jerilyn couldn't think, couldn't do anything but panic. While she had no idea what exactly the names and numbers meant, she had to get this book back to Earl Ray.

Otherwise...

She swallowed and looked down the long highway she'd just driven and reassured herself that Earl Ray didn't have a clue where she was going.

She knew, now more than ever, that he wouldn't go to the cops because they were the last people he wanted seeing this little notebook. No, the book was worth much more to those members of organized crime who'd been in the news. This book would put them behind bars for life. No wonder she and Earl Ray had been living in dumpy motels under assumed names for weeks.

She hadn't believed him when he kept saying his ship was about to come in and that they'd be eating lobster tail and living in penthouses.

But now that she'd found this book, she realized Earl Ray had just been waiting around for the right buyer. How had he gotten his hands on this?

Jerilyn felt herself growing calmer as she realized that she not only had something that Earl Ray wanted—she had something worth a bunch of money. This book could be her backup plan. If things didn't work out with Maddie's family, she could always make a deal with Earl Ray.

Of course, any negotiations with Earl Ray would be dangerous—much more dangerous than meeting her daughter's family and convincing them to help her financially.

Jerilyn tucked the book back into her bag. Once she got to Montana, she'd have to find a safe place to hide it until she decided what to do.

MADDIE WAS LATE. It wasn't the first time and wouldn't be the last. She'd picked up a novel in the drugstore, started reading and couldn't put it down. The next thing she knew she'd lost track of time.

As she sped down the street toward the restaurant, she hoped her cousin Laci wouldn't be angry with her. Maddie felt terrible about being late to her own welcome-home party. She'd stopped by the drugstore to buy a nice card to thank Laci for throwing her the party and ended up in the fiction section. She should have known better.

When she pulled up across the street from Northern Lights, the restaurant co-owned by Laci and her husband, Bridger Duvall, she saw all the cars.

She felt a wave of panic. All of her friends and neighbors and family from around Whitehorse were here. These people all knew about her broken engagement to Bo Evans, and for a moment Maddie thought about driving on past. How could she face everyone?

For years now, she'd been away at college and had avoided coming back. But she'd missed her cousins Laci and Laney, along with this part of Montana. Not to mention her horse, which her cousins had been boarding for her.

Maddie wished she'd never agreed to this party, though. But Laci was very persuasive; she loved cooking and throwing parties. As Maddie pulled into a parking spot, she tried to talk herself out of running away.

Just then Laney appeared at her side window. One look in her cousin's eyes and Maddie saw that she understood her fears.

Maddie cut the engine and rolled down the window. "I'm such a coward."

"No, you're not," Laney said, giving her a sympathetic smile. "All those people in there have missed you. They love you, Maddie, and are so excited to have you home."

Maddie's eyes brimmed with tears as her cousin opened the pickup door.

"Laci and I will be right there with you. I promise you will have a good time."

Maddie nodded and bolstered her courage by reminding herself that Bo Evans had left town. She knew, though, that he wasn't the only reason she hadn't returned for so long. No, the real reason she'd fled Old Town Whitehorse was a secret she prayed would never come out.

JUD KNEW HE had to act quickly. His brothers could stand around arguing about their mother's motives for forcing marriage on them, but it seemed pretty transparent to Jud that the old man wanted his sons to settle in Montana or he would have never told them about the letters.

If there were even any letters left from their mother to be read on each of their wedding days. Maybe her dying wish really hadn't been that her sons find wives.

None of that really mattered to Jud.

He was doing this for his father. Come hell or high water, Jud intended to give the old man what he wanted—a wedding. Just not the wedding everyone was expecting.

In a town the size of Whitehorse, it didn't take Jud but a matter of minutes to find out where Maddie Cavanaugh had gone. Crashing the welcome-home party had been child's play, since most everyone in town had been invited.

Seeing her again reinforced his belief that she was exactly what he was looking for, and yet he hesitated. Unlike the other women he'd been with, Maddie didn't have obvious sexual appeal. She was understated. That's what she was. Sweet-looking. Real.

She was also completely wrong for him, and he suspected she would know it soon enough.

He'd known even before he reached her that she would turn him down for a date. He would have been disappointed if she hadn't.

"Maybe some other time," he'd said, looking regretful as he backed off. But as he left, he saw out of the corner of his eye that she was watching him leave. Her cousins were at her side, whispering something to her. No doubt encouraging her.

Smiling to himself, he left, betting himself he'd have a date with her before the day was out.

Maddie Cavanaugh wasn't getting away. Too much was at stake here.

"SO TELL US about this Maddie Cavanaugh," Lantry said at breakfast several mornings later.

Jud grinned. He was going out for lunch with Maddie and planned to take her to the theatre in town tonight. But while he had to return to his film in Canada tomorrow, he had another date with her to the rodeo the day after. "You'll see for yourself when you meet her."

"We've been waiting to meet her," Lantry said. "Come on, fess up, there isn't any Maddie Cavanaugh. You made her up, thinking it would buy you time."

"I couldn't make up a woman like Maddie," Jud said in all seriousness, then concentrated on his breakfast. Juanita had served huevos rancheros with homemade tortillas and beans, his favorite.

"So when are you going to bring her out to meet Dad and Kate?" Dalton asked from the end of the table. "Or isn't that Hollywood charm of yours working?"

"All in good time," Jud said. "When you're serious about a woman you need to take things slow. You'll learn that if you ever date a woman more than once."

Lantry cocked his head at his brother and narrowed his eyes. "You've never been secretive about any of the women you were dating. Quite the contrary. You're up to something."

"Just true love," Jud said with a grin.

TWO DAYS LATER, Shane had his feet propped up on the porch railing and his hat pulled down low against the afternoon sun. He appeared to be asleep, but Grayson knew better.

"You still planning to go back to the Texas Rangers?" he asked quietly.

Shane didn't stir. "Why wouldn't I?"

Grayson suspected his son's wounds ran much deeper than the gunshot wound he'd suffered a month ago. "Montana could use a good lawman."

Shane chuckled and pushed back his Stetson to look at his father. "Subtle."

"Kate says I need to be more direct."

"You're plenty direct the way you are," he said, sitting up.

Grayson smiled. "I get the feeling you're ticked off at me."

"You think?"

"What's wrong with wanting my family close by?"

"You're the one who moved to Montana."

"You goin' to hold that against me?"

Shane sighed. "What's going on, Dad? It isn't like you to sell lock, stock and barrel and leave Texas the way you did."

Grayson shook his head. "Love changes everything, son. I hope you find that out for yourself one day."

"No, thanks. Not if it makes me change everything about myself."

"Is that what you think happened to me?"

"You've got to admit this letter thing is beneath you."

Grayson leaned back his chair and stared out across the summer-green prairie. This land, with its rolling grassland that ran to coulees filled with juniper and scrub pine and rocky outcroppings before dropping into the Missouri River gorge, had drawn him the first time he'd seen it.

He loved the sweet summer scents, loved the way the place was steeped in history, loved riding across the great expanse of country, the grasses, tall and green, undulating in the breeze.

But mostly he loved this place because it had once been Kate's and was now hers again. He'd given her the ranch, but it was so little compared to what she'd given him. His heart swelled at the mere thought of his wife.

But his marriage and this move had put more than miles between him and his sons. He couldn't bear the thought that he might lose them because of it.

"It's selfish of me," he said to Shane. "To want to uproot you boys to make an old man happy."

Shane laughed. "Blackmail first, now guilt?" He shook his head. "Hell, why don't you pull out all the stops and tell us you're— " Shane stopped as if the word *dying* had caught in his throat. Swallowing, he said, "Does this really mean that much to you?"

"Yes," Grayson said, meeting his son's gaze and holding it. "It means that much to me."

Shane looked into his father's eyes, his pulse drumming in his ears. His next breath came hard as he realized he might have stumbled onto the truth. "You aren't...sick, are you?"

He couldn't bring himself to say the *D* word. He'd come too close to saying it only moments before. Grayson looked as healthy as a horse, but there was no denying he'd aged. His hair had grayed and there were deep lines furrowing his brow.

"I'm fine," Grayson said and looked away. "I don't want you to feel..."

"Trapped?"

"No." His father's gaze came back to him, his eyes

shiny. "I raised you boys to be your own men. I would never want to do anything to change that."

Shane swore under his breath. He'd told himself his father wasn't going to make him feel guilty about not going along with this stupid marriage pact, and yet he felt guilty as hell right now.

The phone rang inside the house. Neither man moved. After the second ring, Juanita picked up. Shane could hear her and knew even before she stepped to the porch doorway that the call was for him.

"It's Jud," she said, handing him the phone. "He says it's urgent."

KATE HAD BEEN into the town of Whitehorse as few times as possible since her return to Montana. She'd let Juanita take care of the shopping and was happy to stay out at the ranch, venturing out only to ride the property and marvel at how fortunate she was to have a man like Grayson Corbett in love with her.

But she couldn't keep making excuses for avoiding town without someone getting suspicious. So she'd started venturing in a few times, making the trips short.

She knew that she'd eventually come face-to-face with her past.

Today she'd gone into the hardware store to pick up an extension cord, and as she came out she practically ran into a tall, slim, older cowboy waiting on the sidewalk.

Even after all these years, Chester Bailey hadn't changed much. He was still a good-looking man. His blond hair was graying at the temples and there were lines around his blue eyes, but she had no problem recognizing him.

"Kate?" He sounded incredulous. *"Kate Wade?"*

"It's Corbett now," she said. "Hello, Chester."

He stared at her, shaking his head as if he couldn't believe his eyes. "I heard someone had bought your folks' ranch... Corbett." He smiled. "So that's you."

She nodded. "How have you been?"

"Good. I suppose you heard. Lila and I are divorced."

She hadn't heard because until recently she'd made a point of putting Whitehorse behind her. "I'm sorry," she said. "You were married a long time."

He nodded, head dipping. "Over thirty years."

Kate felt all those old emotions stir inside her and wished she'd never come to town. Never come back here. As she stood there, she was afraid of what she would say next and terrified of what Chester might reply.

Fortunately, she didn't have to worry. A middle-aged woman came out of the local clothing store, laughing with a friend. She and the friend parted company, and the woman headed toward Chester.

Kate saw at once that this was who Chester had been waiting for. The blonde was younger than Chester, her hair short and curly, her smile coming easily.

"Hi," Kate said, as the woman took Chester's arm. She noted that the woman wasn't wearing a wedding ring. A girlfriend?

"Susie, this is Kate... Corbett."

Susie's face brightened. "Corbett? You bought the old Trails West Ranch. I've always admired that place. I'm so glad someone is living there again."

Kate waited for Chester to tell his girlfriend that the ranch used to belong to Kate's family, that she'd grown up here, that the two of them had known each other.

When Chester told his girlfriend none of that, Kate said, "Thank you."

"Well, welcome to Whitehorse," Susie said. "You're going to love it here. Everyone is so friendly. Stop by the Hi-Line Café. Chester and I own the place."

"Best chicken-fried steak in town," Chester said, seeming a little embarrassed, since it was clear that he'd never told his girlfriend about Kate. Nor, apparently, was he going to.

"I'll do that sometime," Kate said. She took a step backward, relieved for the chance to escape.

She walked briskly to her SUV and sat behind the wheel, trying to quit shaking. Seeing Chester had brought it all back.

Why had she let Grayson move them here? She'd been shocked when he'd told her about her present on their one-month anniversary.

"I bought you something," he'd said, seeming shy and excited.

She'd laughed. "Whatever it is, I know I'm going to love it."

"Well, you used to love it."

Her heart had begun to pound even before he said the words: "I bought you Trails West."

She'd realized her mistake at once. From the first day when she'd shown up at Grayson's Texas ranch, he'd wanted to hear all about the years she'd lived in Montana. She'd told him what it was like growing up with Rebecca and how they'd been close as sisters until Rebecca went to college in Texas, where she met and married him.

Kate had also told Grayson about her father's death

and losing the ranch. What she hadn't told him was the rest of it.

"Grayson, you shouldn't have," she'd said, unable to hold back the tears as he handed her the deed to the ranch.

He'd thought they were tears of joy, and he had been so happy to give her the ranch that she couldn't tell him it was the last thing she wanted.

Her second shock had come a few months later, when he'd surprised her with the news that he'd bought up property around Trails West and was selling out in Texas. Grayson didn't do anything halfway. It was why he'd been so successful.

"I love the country up there, so I'm not doing this just for you," he'd told her.

Kate knew that his sons believed she'd talked him into moving to Montana and blamed her. She was at fault, no doubt about that. She should have spoken up right away and put an end to this before it got completely out of hand.

But she loved Grayson too much.

And she had to admit it was great being back on the ranch. All the wonderful memories of her father and her childhood were here.

Grayson loved hearing about her memories of life on the ranch with Rebecca. She knew it helped give Rebecca a new life for him. Surprisingly, it seemed to free him, as well. He suddenly felt ready to finally go through Rebecca's things. That's when they'd found the letters Rebecca had left for her sons.

As Kate started the SUV, wanting nothing more than to return to the ranch and Grayson, her heart swelled as she thought about his capacity for love. She didn't deserve him. She didn't deserve any of this, she thought as she drove out of Whitehorse.

Her life was a fairy tale, perfect in every way. Except for one—Chester Bailey and the lie between them. When Grayson learned the truth, she feared her fairy tale would turn into a nightmare.

Chapter Four

After Jud's "urgent" call, Shane hooked up the horse trailer, cursing the whole while. As he climbed into the cab of the truck, he realized he was winded. He told himself it was from anger at his brother for roping him into babysitting Jud's girlfriend.

But there was no denying the truth. It was from this small amount of exertion, which meant he'd only been kidding himself about being ready to go back to his job as a Texas Ranger—and this scared him more than he wanted to admit.

He'd expected to bounce right back. It wasn't like it was the first time he'd been shot. He'd tried to tell himself that this time was no different.

"Like hell," he grumbled, as he started the pickup. Every night since the shooting, he'd relived it in his nightmares. This time wasn't just different. This time had changed everything. The mere thought of not being able to go back made him furious, especially after all the years he'd worked toward becoming a Texas Ranger.

He quickly turned his anger back to Jud, not wanting to deal with the other issue. He feared it wasn't being shot that was the problem. Something was missing, and he knew he wasn't in the right frame of mind to even consider what that something might be.

"I'm in a terrible bind," Jud had said when he'd called from the set of his latest movie. "Shooting has run over and I promised Maddie—"

"Maddie? This woman you just met? I'm sure she'll understand."

"She can't round up another horse trailer at this late notice," Jud argued. "Hers is in the shop, and the rodeo is in a few hours."

"Nice that you waited until the last minute."

"I'd hoped I could get out of here and not let her down."

Shane fought to curb his temper. He didn't want to get involved in this little love affair Jud had going with a local girl. If that's what it was. The family had yet to meet her—and Jud was acting odder than usual. In fact, Lantry was convinced the woman didn't even exist, and that Jud was up to something other than romance.

Shane tended to agree with Lantry. It wasn't like Jud not to talk about the woman he was dating. Jud was probably just humoring their father, making it look as if he was keeping up his end of the marriage pact. Even if this woman existed, Shane didn't believe for a moment that Jud had any intention of marrying her.

Because of that, going to pick her up made him more than a little uncomfortable. Shane didn't want to be within a hundred miles when Jud broke this poor young woman's heart.

"Just tell me where I need to go," Shane had finally said. He was angry with his brother, but he felt he needed to meet this woman and decide for himself what his brother was up to.

"She's staying with her cousins on a ranch outside of Old Town Whitehorse. I owe you, Shane. I really appreciate this."

Right, Shane thought, as he drove out of the Trails West Ranch, dust billowing up behind his pickup and horse trailer.

It crossed his mind that standing up Maddie Cavanaugh might be Jud's way of letting her down easily. If so, Shane would wring his brother's neck when he saw him.

The land stretched out to the horizon, golden in the afternoon sun. Shane had seen some of the country when he'd driven up from Texas. To the south was the rugged terrain of the Breaks, where the Missouri River cut a gorge through the plains on its way to the Mississippi, the Louisiana delta and finally the Gulf of Mexico.

The Breaks had been home to many an outlaw in Montana's past, the miles of wilderness providing hideouts along the river. Butch Cassidy and the Sundance Kid had allegedly robbed a train outside of Whitehorse before taking off for South America.

Maybe his father hadn't been foolish to buy a ranch up here. But the fact that the ranch had belonged to Kate's family still bothered Shane. Plus, the Trails West Ranch was to hell and gone, south of Whitehorse near the Breaks, out in the middle of nowhere. The closest airport and real city were a good three hours away.

Grayson couldn't have moved farther away from Texas without leaving the country. At least he'd stayed in the lower forty-eight. Shane guessed he should be thankful for that.

Fortunately, Grayson and Kate had talked Juanita into moving up with them, so at least the food was familiar— Tex-Mex, homemade tortillas every morning and barbecued brisket and Texas beans on warm evenings.

Shane was also thankful for a place to recuperate. If truth be told, he'd wanted out of Texas for a while. The memories of his ordeal had ridden shotgun with him the whole trip, but it was easier here, easier to worry about his father and Kate and this stupid marriage pact than to face what he'd left in Texas. Or was it lost in Texas— what he may have *lost* in Texas—being able to return as a Ranger.

Once Shane hit the main highway, he wound his way north to town. Whitehorse was small and Western, all pickups and cowboy hats and boots. A dozen trucks were parked along Main Street, the town bustling because of the Whitehorse Days celebration.

He turned on the radio and got drumming on the Native American station. It made him think of yesterday, when the daily polka came on the radio. Kate and his father danced around the kitchen, laughing and kicking up their heels. The sight had left a lump in his throat.

How could he be suspicious of Kate when she clearly made his father so happy? Sometimes he hated the lawman in himself.

Whitehorse was so small it was easy to run out of town. Shane quickly found himself in the country again. The road turned to gravel, the country dotted with cattle. Five miles later, he spotted a sign for Old Town Whitehorse barely sticking up out of the tall grass.

The first settlement of Whitehorse had been nearer

the Missouri River, but when the railroad came through, the town migrated north, taking the name with it.

Locals now referred to the original settlement as Old Town Whitehorse. These days it was little more than a ghost town.

At one time, there'd been a gas station but that building was sitting empty, the pumps long gone. There was a community center—every ranching community up here had one—and a one-room schoolhouse that still looked as if it was being used.

Past that, there were a few houses. One large one was boarded up and had a Condemned sign nailed to the door.

As Shane kept going, he circled around what was left of the town and headed west. He hadn't gone far when he saw the sign to the Cavanaugh place. Jud had told him that Maddie was staying with her great-aunt and uncle, Titus and Pearl Cavanaugh, both descendents of early homesteaders.

Titus was as close to a mayor as Old Town Whitehorse had. He provided a church service every Sunday morning at the community center and saw to the hiring of a schoolteacher when needed.

Pearl, who was recovering from a stroke, was involved with the Whitehorse Sewing Circle, which her mother and her husband's had started years ago. The women of the community still got together to make quilts for every new baby and every newlywed in the area.

Jud had provided more information than Shane had wanted or needed to hear. He just wanted to see Maddie for himself and make up his own mind. Then he planned to stay as far away from Jud's affairs as possible—just as he'd always done.

Shane told himself that once he got Maddie and her horse to the fairgrounds, he'd leave the horse trailer, go back to the ranch and not give Maddie another thought. Jud had promised to make it down in time to drive Maddie and her horse home from the rodeo.

As Shane parked and walked toward the Cavanaugh house, he spotted a blond cowgirl waiting on the front porch. He was instantly taken aback. Was this Maddie Cavanaugh? If so, then she was nothing like the women Jud dated.

She was cute enough—curvy but slim, blond and blue-eyed. She had a fresh-faced innocence about her. Maybe it was the freckles. Or the wide blue eyes. She just looked too damned sweet for Jud's tastes.

Shane noticed that she was dressed in jeans, boots and a blue-checked shirt. Her long blond hair was plaited in a single braid that snaked out from under her Western straw hat. She apparently was waiting for him. He gave her points for that. There was nothing he disliked more than a woman who made a man wait just because she could.

"Maddie?"

She nodded and smiled.

"I'm Shane. Jud's brother."

He'd half-expected her to be in a snit since Jud had stood her up, but she didn't seem upset in the least as he headed up the steps toward her. If anything, she looked curious. Was it possible Jud hadn't called to tell her of the change in plans?

"Jud couldn't make it," Shane said. "He sent me."

Maddie eyed him for a moment. "You should have just called. I could have gotten someone to take my horse in."

He knew he hadn't sounded very friendly. He'd sounded put out. He wanted to tell her that it wasn't her—that it was Jud and this stupid marriage pact and knowing this so-called relationship was going to end badly.

"I don't mind," Shane said, although clearly he did, and he could tell she knew it. "Ready?" Her eyes were a shade lighter than his own, piercing in a way that made him feel she could see right through him.

Maddie seemed to be making up her mind whether or not to let him take her into town.

He shoved back his hat and chewed at his cheek, wishing he could think of something to say. His brothers were the smooth talkers, not him.

After a few seconds, she rose, brushed off the seat of her jeans, not looking any happier about this than he was. "Since you came all this way, I'll get my horse."

Part of him wished she would just send him packing. But at the same time, he'd have felt badly. Shane hated feeling he was involved in Jud's deception.

After they loaded her horse, Maddie climbed into the pickup cab. He tried to think of something to say on the way into town, but fortunately, she seemed fine without talking.

She gazed out the window as if soaking up her surroundings. He recalled that Jud had said she'd been away and had only just returned.

"Did I tell you Jud got tied up with a movie?" he asked.

"He'd said he might."

So Jud had already set up his excuse to get out of this. Shane silently cursed his brother.

"That's my brother," he said, wishing he could bring himself to tell her about Jud and save her a lot of heartache. Feeling Maddie's gaze on him, he glanced in her direction and saw something in her blue eyes that surprised him.

Earlier her eyes had been in shadow under the brim of the Western hat she had snugged down over her blond hair. She'd seemed so young, so innocent, so downright naïve. He'd thought this freckle-faced cowgirl from a forgotten part of Montana was a sitting duck for just about any man. Especially Jud Corbett. But now he had a clear view as she met his gaze dead-on. What he saw in all that blue wasn't dewy-eyed innocence, though. There was intelligence there, and pain.

He had to reevaluate his first impression. Was it possible that Maddie couldn't be easily taken in by his Hollywood stuntman brother Jud?

For her sake, Shane certainly hoped so.

JERILYN HAD NEVER made New Year's resolutions, planned for the future or worked toward a career.

Once her family money was gone, she depended on whatever man she was with to take care of her. If she thought ahead at all, it was only to consider what to eat or drink within the next few minutes.

That was why she had a moment of uncertainty as she drove into Whitehorse. She realized she lacked a plan and she didn't have a clue how to find her daughter.

On the way into town, she drove under a banner that read: *Welcome to Whitehorse Days*.

Apparently it was a rodeo.

She drove through town, a little surprised at how small it was. The bars seemed to be hopping. A dozen pickups lined the main street, and everyone seemed to be dressed in Western attire.

Was it possible that the couple who had adopted her baby were ranchers? She liked the idea of a huge ranch and lots of cattle.

Her mother had sworn the baby had gone to a good family. That meant wealth in Jerilyn's mind, but what if she was wrong? What if Maddie's folks couldn't help her?

Jerilyn parked in front of a bar and sat for a moment, wishing Earl Ray was here with her. At least he'd know what to do next. Now she felt lost, afraid and alone. More and more, Jerilyn realized taking off on her own had been a mistake.

The neon of the bar lights flashed across the cracked windshield of Earl Ray's old Buick. Jerilyn couldn't believe the car had made it this far. But now she was broke, the engine was making a loud noise and a light on the dashboard had been blinking for the past twenty miles or so.

She'd ignored it, just hoping the car would get her to Whitehorse. Now here she was, sitting in the dark, cold and tired, and thinking she might have acted a little impulsively.

The bar door opened. A man came out, bringing with him the sound of music and laughter. Past his dark silhouette, she caught sight of the brightly lit bottles lined up behind the bar and a few patrons who were sitting on the bar stools.

That glimpse inside the bar drew Jerilyn with a familiar tug. Pulling the keys, she climbed out and headed toward the flashing bar lights.

As she opened the glass-front door, she saw her reflection. The bar better be dark, she thought, since she didn't look her best after so many hours in the car.

She smoothed a hand over her long, straight blond hair, bit her lips to give them a little color and stepped in.

The jukebox cranked out a familiar country-and-western tune, and the smell of stale beer wafted toward her like a welcoming committee. Jerilyn took it all in, the music, the smells, the crowded room.

She could almost taste the cold beer she was on the verge of ordering. Feeling as if she'd come home, Jerilyn sauntered over to the bar and slid her narrow behind up onto a stool.

Leaning her skinny arms on the cool, slick surface of the bar, she smiled at the middle-aged, balding bartender and ordered herself a bottle of light beer. As he dug in the cooler, she glanced at the four men lined up on the bar stools and gave them a look that was universal at every bar she'd ever been in.

The bartender put down a cocktail napkin and a cold glass to go with her bottle of beer. She took her time pouring the beer into the glass and then, closing her eyes, she drank in the cold, familiar brew and let out a contented sigh.

She'd had only two gulps of her beer before one of the men told the bartender to give her another. She tilted her glass in the man's direction, smiling her thanks.

By the time the bartender set a fresh bottle in front of her, the man had come down the bar to take the stool next to hers. It was like a dance, and Jerilyn knew the steps by heart.

Everything is going to be all right now, she told herself, as she smiled over at him.

Jerilyn took a sip of her beer, licked the foam from her lips and asked, "So are you from around here?"

SHANE HADN'T PLANNED on it, but he ended up staying for the rodeo. It wasn't like he had anything else to do. In truth, he was curious about Maddie. He wanted to see her ride. According to the program, she was entered in the women's barrel-racing event.

He knew he shouldn't have been surprised, but she was damned good on a horse. Maybe Maddie and Jud had more in common than he'd first thought. Jud was a trick rider and did a lot of Westerns along with his other stunt work. He loved horses, and it was clear that Maddie did, as well.

"I didn't know the Cavanaugh girl was back in town," said a woman who was seated in front of Shane on the bleachers. "I hope it's not because of that awful Bo Evans."

Shane couldn't help but wonder who Bo Evans was as he watched the next young woman ride.

The other rider came in with a slightly better time than Maddie. Shane was disappointed and knew Maddie must be, too. When the bucking-horse portion of the rodeo began, he decided to stay a little longer. He hadn't been to a rodeo in years. The smell of hot dogs, burgers and traveling tacos rose up to the stands where he was sitting. In the stalls, wild horses kicked up dust under the lights. Darkness lurked beyond, and he found himself lulled by the sound of the announcer's voice and the hooting and hollering of the crowd.

Rodeos and cowboys, it seemed, were the same all over the country. Shane felt strangely at home, even though he didn't know a soul in the whole place except for Maddie Cavanaugh, who was now talking with some of the other cowgirls.

As if she felt him looking at her, she turned, her gaze moving over the crowd on the bleachers until she found him.

He tried to look away, but her eyes held his, and he felt his heart kick up a beat, no doubt from being caught watching her.

She looked surprised to see him. Probably because he'd made it pretty clear he would be leaving as soon as he dropped off her and her horse.

Shane mentally kicked himself for being such a jackass. As she wandered off with her friends, he turned his attention back to the wild horse race, which was so chaotic and absorbing that he didn't even notice Jud sit down next to him until the event was almost over.

"Hey, this is some race," Shane said and then remembered he was angry at his brother. "So you made it."

"Got out earlier than I'd thought. I'm surprised you stayed for the rodeo." Jud was studying him. "Did you think I was going to stand up Maddie and make you bail me out again?"

The thought had crossed Shane's mind. "She said she'd find a ride if you didn't make it."

Jud smiled. "Yeah, she's pretty independent. Part of her charm. So what do you think of her?"

Shane just shrugged as the wild horse race ended and a band nearby struck up a boot-stomping song.

Jud grinned over at him. "I think she's amazing, a real Montana cowgirl and just about the prettiest little thing. But she's got some backbone, too. I like that about her."

Shane had to bite his tongue. Maddie seemed like a nice young woman who deserved better than his Romeo brother. For a moment, he concentrated on watching the riders rounding up the wild horses, then rose. No reason to stay any longer.

"I need to find Maddie and tell her I'm here," Jud said. "If you see her on your way out, would you tell her I'm looking for her?"

"Yeah, sure." His intention had been to get the hell out of there, but the crowd moved in the direction of the music, and Shane found himself caught up in it. He couldn't remember the last time he'd been to an outdoor dance and found himself drawn to the country-and-western music being cranked out by the band.

Maddie was standing at the edge of the makeshift dance floor. She was tapping her toe to the song, looking like a woman who wanted to dance. Shane was glad Jud had at least made it in time for this.

He hesitated about giving her Jud's message. Then, feeling foolish, he told himself it was the least he could do, since he hadn't been very nice to her earlier. Maybe he'd even compliment her on her ride.

As he neared, the lights strung through the trees glittered above her head, and her upturned face glowed. Her

Western straw hat was pushed back; her blond hair now splayed loose around her shoulders.

She seemed to be watching the other dancers and enjoying herself. Shane was almost to her when she suddenly tensed. All the joy washed away, her freckles popping out as the blood seemed to drain from her face.

Shane quickly followed her gaze and saw a cowboy in a black hat push himself away from the flatbed truck being used as a portable beer garden and start toward her.

Maddie took a step back, eyes wide, glancing around as if searching for a place to hide.

Without thinking, Shane stepped in front of her, cutting off the cowboy who was almost to her.

"Dance," Shane said, taking Maddie's hand and pulling her to him as he swung her away from the cowboy and out onto the dance floor.

Shane felt her trembling, and the lights caught the disquiet in her eyes. He drew her protectively closer as he two-stepped her to the other side of the dance floor.

The cowboy was where they'd left him, glaring across at them.

"Who was that?" Shane asked.

"Nobody." She met his gaze, and he felt another tremor quake through her.

Instinctively, he drew her closer, wanting to protect her. She felt good in his arms, soft and very female. Shane couldn't remember the last time he'd danced.

Maddie's scent drifted on the night breeze. She smelled like summer, sweet and sunny. His hand on her back felt warm, comfortable, as if they had been dancing together for years. He breathed her and the night in, feeling more vulnerable than he had in weeks.

He spotted the cowboy standing at the edge of the crowd. The lights glittered and reflected off the cowboy's large silver belt buckle, which featured letters *B-O*. The infamous Bo Evans?

Maddie's warm fingers on Shane's shoulder tightened, and he could feel the pounding of her heart.

"Don't worry," Shane said, his voice sounding husky. "I won't let him bother you, if that's what you're afraid of."

She glanced up at him, her blue eyes widening a little as she met his gaze. She frowned as if she didn't know who he was talking about.

"That cowboy. The one—"

She emitted a soft chuckle. "I'm not worried about him." Her gaze seemed to soften at his confusion. Her lips curled up in a wry smile before she shook her head and looked away.

He knew she was scared. Why deny it? When her gaze came back to his, her lips parted as if she was going to tell him the truth. His breath caught in his throat as her eyes locked with his.

Shane started when he was tapped on the shoulder. Instantly he stiffened, expecting to see Bo Evans. There was no way he was turning Maddie over to the man. No matter what she said about not being afraid of him.

"You're not trying to steal my woman, are you, cowboy?" Jud grinned as he cut in, glancing from Shane to Maddie. Shane let go of Maddie, and she stepped back as if she was as relieved as he was for the interruption.

Shane felt oddly shaken. What had happened on the dance floor? *Nothing,* he thought.

When Shane turned back, he spotted Bo Evans watching Jud and Maddie dance. Trouble. Wondering what Maddie had to fear from him gave Shane something to think about other than what he'd felt out on the dance floor just before Jud cut in.

Bo Evans watched the bitch dancing with one man then another. Both strangers.

"Who is that?" he asked, grabbing the arm of a local girl at the edge of the dance floor.

She looked startled. "Who?"

"The man dancing with Maddie Cavanaugh."

The girl smiled as if speaking of a teen idol. *"Jud Corbett."*

"Who the hell is that?" Bo asked, hating the way she had made it sound as if anyone with a brain should know that.

"He's a Hollywood stuntman. He's working in Canada now, but he'll be shooting a movie here next month."

"Stuntman?" Bo repeated, and turned his attention back to Maddie. How was it that Maddie seemed to know this Jud Corbett? "How long's he been in town?"

The girl shrugged. "His family bought up a whole bunch of land including, my dad said, the old Trails West Ranch."

Bo scowled. He left town for a few months and everything changed. What was Maddie doing back here anyway? He'd been shocked to see her. He'd thought she'd never show her face around here again. Obviously she didn't have the good sense to stay away.

Just seeing her made him feel things he didn't want to feel. Like anger and desire.

The worst part was he didn't want to feel a damned thing for Maddie. The bitch had broken his heart, and made him look bad.

The song ended and Bo waited, hoping Jud Corbett left Maddie alone again. No such luck. The two walked toward a fancy pickup parked a few rows down from Bo's beater car.

Bo followed them as far as his car, cursing the way his life had been going. First Maddie had left, then his own mother turned against him. Not only had she refused to give him any money anymore but she'd forced him out of the house. Then she'd threatened to sell the place—his inheritance, and not give him a dime. She'd told him to get a job and earn his own money.

And now Maddie was back in town and dating a stuntman?

He was surrounded by heartless bitches, he thought, as he saw two men leaning against his car.

Bo knew at once that he either owed them money or he'd ripped them off. Since they didn't look familiar, they'd probably been sent by the person he'd ticked off. Not that it mattered. He was dead meat either way.

He started to veer off, pretending he hadn't seen them and that it wasn't his heap of a car they were leaning against.

But the bigger of the two pushed himself off the car and stepped in front of Bo, blocking his way.

The man dropped one huge paw of a hand on Bo's shoulder. "Mr. Evans?" The man had a deep voice, and the strong hand on Bo's shoulder felt capable of creating a lot of pain.

While lying came as easily as breathing, Bo sensed this was the one time in his life that the truth might be less painful. "Yes?"

"A word with you," the man said, and nodded toward his buddy.

"Sure," Bo said, sounding a hell of a lot more cheerful than he felt. He glanced around, but the parking lot was empty. Everyone who hadn't already left was still at the dance. Even the stuntman and Maddie were gone.

"Let's take a ride," the second man said. He was only a little smaller than the first guy, but he looked meaner. He wore a John Deere cap and a sullen expression.

Taking a ride with this twosome was the last thing Bo wanted to do, but the big one flashed a gun before he shoved him behind the wheel and climbed into the seat behind him.

The guy wearing the John Deere cap slid into the passenger seat. "You probably know somewhere quiet we can go to talk."

Bo contemplated his options as he tried unsuccessfully to put the key in the ignition.

"Calm down," the man next to him said with a chuckle. He took the keys from Bo and slid a key into the ignition. "Me and my friend, Dude, here, just want to talk to you. Isn't that right, Dude?"

"That's right, Earl Ray," the big man said with a chuckle.

Sure. Dude and Earl Ray? Were these guys for real?

Bo silently cursed Maddie. If all his attention hadn't been on her and the stuntman, he would have seen these two sooner and avoided what was sure as hell going to be an ugly ending to the night—if not his life.

He got the car going and drove out of town toward Bowdoin, a wildlife refuge only a few minutes out of Whitehorse. He hadn't planned to go out there. Hell, he'd just started driving out of town, not knowing where to go, too nervous to think.

But now he realized that Bowdoin was a good place to take these guys. There was at least one armed federal warden out there. With luck, the game warden would see Bo's old beater and become suspicious and come investigate.

There was a good chance of that happening since Bo and his car were known in the area for all the wrong reasons.

He drove down the narrow paved road that had been patched too many times and turned into the refuge, avoiding the headquarters building. He didn't want the two men to think he was up to anything.

When he got down the dirt road, through a stand of Russian olive trees and around a narrow turn beside an expanse of cattails, Bo felt the big hand of Dude drop onto his shoulder again.

"Pull over."

Bo pulled into a wide spot. Earl Ray reached across the seat and pulled out the keys.

"Cut your lights."

Bo did as he was told, his heart lodged in his throat. He hoped they did whatever they planned to do quickly. Would they shoot him right here in the car? And then what—walk all the way back to town?

No, they'd tell him to get out, and then they'd shoot, stab or pulverize him.

He saw the flicker of headlights in his rearview mirror and felt a surge of hope. The warden would be armed and suspicious of Bo Evans out here with these two bad-looking guys.

But the vehicle didn't approach. Instead, it slowed, its headlights going out as the driver pulled over thirty yards back up the road. Not the game warden, Bo realized with a sinking feeling. He hadn't even thought to check to see if they'd been followed. No doubt it was Dude and Earl Ray's ride home.

A trickle of sweat ran down Bo's cheek. "Can't you at least tell me what this is about?" he asked, hating that his voice sounded whiny and scared spitless.

"It's about your old girlfriend," Earl Ray said, pushing back the John Deere cap. "Excuse me, former fiancée."

Bo shot a look at the man. An almost full moon hung over the refuge, spilling a silver sheen over the landscape as well as the car.

"What?" Bo's mind raced. Why would these guys care about Maddie?

"Maddie Cavanaugh. You do remember her, right?"

Bo nodded numbly. "But what—"

"We need your help finding her."

He stared at the man. "You have to be kidding."

"Do I look like I'm kidding?" Earl Ray asked. Bo felt Dude's big paw on his shoulder again.

He winced at the pain as the big man's fingers dug into his flesh. "I thought you were joking because she was at the dance tonight."

"I thought she didn't live here anymore."

"So did I. I guess she's back."

"Where can we find her?"

"How should I know?" Bo quickly changed his tone. "I mean, it isn't like we're close, you know. I didn't even know she was back in town until tonight."

"Then you don't know where she's staying?"

"But I can find out," he added quickly. "Why would you want Maddie, though?"

Earl Ray just stared at him with that blank don't-mess-with-me look that Bo himself tried to perfect.

"The breakup wasn't friendly?" Earl Ray asked.

"The bitch broke my heart."

"Then you might be persuaded to help us?"

"What's in it for me?" Bo braced himself for more pain from the man in the back, but was surprised when both men laughed.

"You are everything we heard you were when we asked around town about you," Earl Ray said. "A man after my own heart. Did I mention we are willing to compensate you?"

Compensation. Music to Bo's ears. "Let's talk money, then," Bo said, relaxing now.

Chapter Five

"What did you say to her?" Jud demanded the next morning.

"What?" Shane looked up as his youngest brother sat down at the breakfast table. His mind had been a thousand miles away. In Texas.

"Maddie. What did you say to her?"

"Oh, her," Shane said, and went back to his breakfast.

"What do you mean, 'Oh, her'?" Jud demanded.

Shane looked up at him again, wondering who'd put a burr under his saddle this morning. "Look, I didn't say anything to her. I just picked her up and took her to the rodeo grounds like you asked me to."

"So you didn't talk to her?"

Shane put down his fork. "What is your problem?"

"I got the impression that you were rude to her. She was upset after dancing with you."

Shane recalled the dance. The memory hadn't gotten far away. "I wasn't the one who upset her. It was some cowboy. Bo Evans. I suspect he's an old boyfriend."

He didn't add that the cowboy had followed Jud and Maddie to the parking lot when they'd left the rodeo dance last night. Shane had feared there might be trou-

ble, so he'd tailed Bo. And there might have been—
if there hadn't been two thugs waiting for the cowboy
by his car. The three had left together, but the meeting
hadn't looked cordial.

"Maddie's a nice girl."

"Yeah," Shane said, locking eyes with his brother.

"You got something to say?" Jud challenged.

Shane picked up his fork and returned to his breakfast, even though he wasn't hungry anymore. The memory of the dance, the feel of her in his arms, had put him
off his feed. Something about the woman had gotten to
him. He didn't want to see her hurt.

And Maddie Cavanaugh was headed for trouble. If
not from her old boyfriend, Bo, then from Jud. And
Shane would hate to see that happen.

But, he reminded himself, Maddie was none of his
business.

"I have to return to the set today," Jud said. "But I'll
be back as soon as I can."

Shane said nothing, but he hoped his brother would
get tired of this long-distance romance with Maddie. The
woman deserved better. And if Shane was right about
Bo, Maddie already had her share of heartbreak from
falling for the wrong man.

MADDIE CAVANAUGH WOKE to the smell of pancakes.
She rolled over, smiling to herself at the thought of her
cousin's breakfasts. That was one of the joys of coming home.

Home. She did feel at home here. She'd made so many
excuses not to come back to Old Town Whitehorse. Her

childhood home was sold and gone, not that she ever wanted to return to it. Nothing but bad memories there.

She'd missed her cousins and hadn't realized how much she'd missed the land. Just being able to ride her horse across the open country and down to the Missouri Breaks gave her a sense of freedom and hope.

It was good to be back at a place she knew so well.

At the sound of murmured voices, Maddie got up and dressed. Her great-aunt had seen to it that her room was furnished with some of her own things. Maddie hadn't given a thought to any of her possessions when she'd left. None of it had mattered.

But now she was thankful that her favorite things from childhood had been saved. Tears welled in her eyes as she picked up a cherished doll from a shelf in the closet. Behind it, in a clear plastic bag, was her handmade baby quilt that, as far as she knew, had never been used.

Maddie started to reach for the quilt, then pulled her hand back at the thought of her mother. She didn't know why the quilt would remind her of her mother. Sarah Cavanaugh had never belonged to the Whitehorse Sewing Circle. As far as she knew, her mother had never sewn anything in her life, let alone helped make her birth quilt.

Sarah was more about putting on a good face. That was why she bought such expensive things for their home, things Maddie's father, Roy, couldn't afford. The baby quilt she'd bagged up and put in the attic. Maddie always thought her mother would have thrown it away if she hadn't feared the Whitehorse Sewing Circle women would find out and think her ungrateful for not appreciating the gift for her baby daughter.

Maddie hadn't realized the strain on her parents' marriage or how obsessed her mother was about being a pillar of Old Town Whitehorse society. It all seemed ludicrous to Maddie, but her mother would have done anything to feel that people looked up to her.

That part of Maddie's life was still painful. She could never forgive her mother for what she'd done, and that made her both sad and filled with guilt. How could she not love her own mother?

Pushing those thoughts as far away as possible, Maddie headed for the kitchen. As she wandered into the bright, warm room, she felt the weight of the past lift from her shoulders. These people were her family.

Her cousin Laci was busy making pancakes, looking funny in the apron that billowed out from her very pregnant belly. She had a spatula in her hand and a big smile on her face.

Aunt Pearl was at the table, her cane leaning against her chair. She'd recovered well from her stroke but still had trouble getting around.

Maddie went to place a kiss on her great-aunt's cheek.

"Laney's on her way over," Laci said of her sister. Laney and her husband, Nick, a deputy sheriff, lived in the house they'd built up the road. "There's choke-cherry syrup, real butter, bacon and ham to go with the pancakes."

"Of course," Maddie said with a laugh, as she joined her great-aunt at the table. Laci, who had always cooked huge meals, shared her love of cooking with her husband. The two now owned the Northern Lights restaurant and lived in the apartment over it. But Laci spent a lot of time here taking care of her grandparents.

Maddie breathed in the familiar scents and told herself that coming back hadn't been a mistake. She even liked the waitressing job at Northern Lights. Laci had offered to teach her to cook, but Maddie preferred to serve food until she decided what she wanted to do with her life.

"Who was that I saw you dancing with last night?" Laci asked, giving Maddie a playful nudge as she slipped a plate of pancakes in front of her.

"Jud Corbett. He's the stuntman you and Laney talked me into going out with."

"Not him. The tall, dark and seriously awesome one."

Definitely serious, Maddie thought. She swallowed and checked her expression before looking up. "That was Jud's brother, Shane." She could feel her great-aunt's gaze on her. Her cheeks heated at the memory of being in Shane's arms on the dance floor. There had been that moment, right before Jud had cut in...

"Shane saved me from Bo," Maddie blurted out, as if she needed an excuse for dancing with Shane.

"Bo's back?" Aunt Pearl asked in her stilted post-stroke cadence.

"I'm afraid so, but it's fine." In fact, she was surprised Bo hadn't been her first thought this morning. For so long, he had been. She'd been shaken and upset at just the sight of him, but after dancing with Shane and then Jud, she'd actually forgotten about Bo. She had thought he'd left town. Obviously he was back, as well.

"I can handle Bo," she said, seeing Laci's concern and wishing she hadn't brought him up.

"Of course you can," Aunt Pearl said.

"Good morning, everyone!" Laney called. She entered the kitchen, looking just as pregnant as her sister.

"Did you have fun last night?" she asked Maddie, as she passed her chair. Apparently everyone in town had seen her dancing with the Corbett brothers.

"She saw Bo," Laci said.

Laney stopped in midstep and turned to look back at Maddie, worry furrowing her brow.

"It was fine," Maddie assured her. "Shane Corbett cut him off and danced with me until Jud arrived. I didn't see Bo after that. Really, I haven't given him a thought."

"So you didn't talk to Bo?" Laney asked.

"There is nothing to say. Bo is history." That at least was true. Bo was part of her bad memories. "I can't believe you two are due at almost the same time," Maddie said, changing the subject. "I won't be surprised if you have your babies on the same day. Do you have names picked out yet?"

She cut her pancakes and took a bite as she listened to her cousins laughing and joking.

"We both want to name our babies Jack," Laci was saying. "So the first one who delivers gets the name."

Maddie laughed, feeling blessed. She was home with her family. She tried not to think about what a disappointment her parents had been. That was the past. And the future? A certain Corbett came to mind at the thought.

LATER THAT MORNING, as Maddie headed for work, she took the long way so she wouldn't have to drive by her old house or Geraldine Shaw's place. Geraldine had been the mother she'd never had, and Maddie mourned her death.

She hadn't gone far when she glanced in her rearview mirror and saw a rusted red car coming up fast behind her.

She'd known even before she caught a glimpse of Bo's face behind the wheel that it would be him. He leaned on the horn, startling her.

The gravel road was narrow. She'd have to pull over or almost drive into the ditch to let him pass. She had no intention of doing either.

He laid on the horn again. When she glanced in her rearview mirror, she saw that he'd rolled down his window and was motioning for her to pull over.

There was a time when she would have been afraid not to do as Bo demanded.

But that time had long since passed. She sped up, willing herself not to look in the mirror, not to react to his incessant honking.

He stayed right with her all five miles to town, riding her back bumper the whole way. She could almost feel his anger and frustration. Bo wouldn't forget this. The next time she ran into him—

She shuddered and shoved the thought away. At the edge of town, she headed for Main Street, wondering how far Bo would go.

As she slowed, she saw that he was still right behind her. She pulled into the sheriff's department parking lot, remembering another time she'd come here looking for help. Bo had stopped her that time.

She cut the engine and got out, not looking in his direction even when she heard his car come to a screeching stop in the middle of the street.

"Maddie! Hey, I'm talking to you!"

She couldn't possibly miss the fury and frustration in

his voice as she started toward the sheriff's office. Nor could she pretend Bo wasn't scaring her.

"I want to talk to you, bitch!" he yelled, as she reached the entrance. His engine revved as she pulled open the outer door and stepped into the tiny alcove. Out of the corner of her eye, she saw his car take off, tires smoking, engine clanking.

Maddie leaned against the closed door, fighting tears. She knew that if she reported the incident to the sheriff, he'd talk to Bo and warn him to leave her alone.

That would just make things worse. She knew Bo Evans. Her coming here had made him angry enough. She couldn't depend on anyone to protect her from him. He would get to her. It was just a matter of time.

Maddie knew she'd eventually have to face him. It was the only way to put an end to his harassment.

But as she waited just inside the outer door, she told herself she had an advantage.

Unlike Bo, Maddie had changed. She wasn't the woman who had let Bo mistreat her. That woman was gone. But Bo Evans didn't know that. Not yet, anyway.

SHANE COULDN'T BELIEVE what he was doing. He'd sworn he wouldn't get involved in his brother's love life.

In fact, when Jud called this morning, Shane had told him no.

"I just need you to drop something off at the restaurant," Jud had said.

"Sorry."

"I wouldn't ask, but it's Maddie's wallet. It must have fallen out of her purse last night. I doubt she's even realized I have it, but she will the moment she needs to buy gas. I left the wallet on the table by the front door. I'm really sorry to have to ask you to do this."

Shane had sworn under his breath. "Maybe Dad can do it."

"He's already left," Jud said. "Neither Juanita or Kate are going into town today. They're doing some canning, so they're tied up. I know it's a lot to ask…"

That was just it. Dropping off the wallet wasn't a lot to ask, and Jud knew it.

"This is the last time," Shane said.

"I doubt you'll ever have to return her wallet again," Jud said. "Thanks for doing this, Shane. I won't forget it."

He'd felt like a heel, making such a big deal out of dropping off a wallet.

But as he drove into Whitehorse, he still wanted to kick himself from here to Sunday for agreeing to do it. He had a feeling he was the last person Maddie wanted to see after the way he'd acted at the rodeo.

He told himself that with any luck it would take no more than a few minutes, and she wouldn't even have to see him. He'd just drop off the wallet and hightail it back to the ranch.

But as he turned down the street, he saw Maddie pull up in front of the sheriff's office and Bo Evan's battered red car pull up in the middle of the street right behind her.

Shane pulled over a few parking spots down, got out and walked down the street toward them. He couldn't hear what the cowboy yelled at Maddie as she exited her truck, but Shane was glad she had the sense to enter the sheriff's office rather than confront the man.

Shane got a good view of Bo's furious face right before the cowboy gunned the engine and took off.

What bothered Shane was that Bo didn't go far. He pulled over down the block.

The last thing Shane wanted to do was get involved. Hell, he wanted nothing to do with any of this. But whether or not Jud was serious about Maddie, Shane couldn't just sit back and let something bad happen to her.

Cursing under his breath, he walked down the street to where Bo was sitting in his beat-up car. The cowboy had his gaze on his rearview mirror, obviously waiting for Maddie to leave the sheriff's office.

Shane had run across men like this one too many times during his law-enforcement career.

All of Bo's attention was on the front door of the sheriff's department, so the bastard didn't even notice him until Shane jerked open the car door and dragged Bo out.

"Hey! What the—"

Shane slammed him against the side of the car. "I don't know what your story is or who the hell you are, and I don't care. Leave Maddie Cavanaugh alone."

"I'm Bo Evans, her…fiancé, you dumb bastard."

"You're not her fiancé anymore."

The cowboy puffed up even more, plainly yearning for a fight. "Yeah? Says who?"

"Says the young woman. It's clear she wants nothing to do with you. Now leave her alone. I'm asking you nicely. I won't be so nice next time."

"I recognize you," Bo said, squinting at Shane. "You danced with Maddie at the rodeo. You a cop or somethin'?"

"Or something." Shane started to turn his back on Bo, knowing that only then would the cowboy make his move. Men like Bo Evans were so predictable.

Sure enough Bo came at him with a roundhouse swing. Shane blocked it and caught him in the midsection with an elbow. Bo doubled over, falling back against his car.

"Don't let me catch you near Maddie again." Shane turned and walked back down the street. That had been a fool's errand. Men like Bo Evans didn't take no for an answer. While Shane meant what he said, he doubted Bo was going to take the threat seriously.

Shane then saw Maddie approach the Northern Lights restaurant. There hadn't been time for her to report Bo to the sheriff. Shane guessed that going into the sheriff's office had been just a ruse on her part. She'd never intended to report her former fiancé.

He hoped to hell Maddie knew what she was doing. Bo Evans was dangerous. But he suspected she already knew that.

Just before she ducked into the restaurant, Shane saw her look up the street to where Bo was still parked. Then her glance shifted to Shane. She frowned as if she knew what he'd been up to—and wasn't happy about him butting into her business.

Bo Evans fought to catch his breath as he watched the man walk away. For a moment, he thought about going after the cocky bastard or maybe pressing assault charges.

Yeah. Like the sheriff would believe anything he told

him. No, Bo knew if there was going to be any justice he'd have to get it himself. And he would.

Just as he would get his hands on Maddie.

A deadly mixture of frustration, anger and pain swelled inside him to the point where he thought he might explode. Turning, he proceeded to kick the rusting metal panels of his car until his feet hurt more than his pride, then slam his fist down onto the already dented roof until his knuckles bled.

His rage having run its course, Bo fell against the side of his car.

All he had wanted to do was talk to Maddie.

At least that's what he'd convinced himself he'd planned to do. Not harm her. Hell, maybe he was planning to warn her about the men who were after her.

But that was before the bitch had gone to the sheriff. Now all bets were off. Maddie deserved whatever happened to her. He could have saved her. He liked that her safety had been in his hands. Still was.

But now he was going to feed her to the dogs.

Bo wiped the blood from his hands on his jeans and considered what to do next. He was glad he'd told Earl Ray and Dude that he'd bring them Maddie. They were waiting at a motel down by the Milk River. They'd offered him money, which he damned well intended to collect.

Maddie Cavanaugh would rue the day she crossed Bo Evans, he thought as he plotted how he was going to get to her.

As MADDIE LET the door close behind her, she called hello to Laci's husband, Bridger, who was busy cooking in the back of the restaurant and went to change into her uniform for her lunch shift.

She refused to think about Bo. He wasn't going to spoil this for her. She was home and she was staying.

And as for Shane Corbett...

As if she'd conjured him up, Shane pushed open the door to the restaurant, making her realize that she'd forgotten to lock it behind her.

"We don't open for another twenty minutes," she said, trying to sound calmer than she felt. She was angry with herself for leaving the door open. Angrier still that she'd let Bo upset her to the point that she'd forgotten.

And then there was Shane.

What brought him by this time? she wondered.

"I didn't come by for lunch," Shane said, looking ill at ease. He wore jeans, boots and a red-and-blue checked shirt that brought out the blue in his eyes.

Maggie hated that the man unnerved her as much as she hated that every time she turned around he was there rescuing her.

"I just stopped by to drop off your wallet," Shane said, digging into his pocket. "I guess you dropped it in Jud's rig. He asked me to bring it by, thought you'd need it."

Maddie felt her cheeks burn with irritation. She'd dropped her wallet and Jud sent his big brother to return it? "Thank you," she managed to say, and stepped forward to take it from him.

"No problem."

"If that's all, I need to get my tables set up before the lunch crowd arrives," she said.

"Sure," he said backing toward the door as if anxious to escape.

Fortunately the door closed behind him before he heard her swear, something she seldom did. Didn't the man see what was going on? Apparently not.

Maddie knew she shouldn't be irritated with Shane. This was all Jud's doing. She couldn't wait to see Jud and give him a piece of her mind.

The lunch shift passed quickly, the restaurant so busy it kept her mind off Bo. And Shane. And Jud.

Maddie was surprised how many of the patrons she didn't know. The town had grown since she'd left.

When her shift was over, she changed from her uniform back into jeans, boots and a Western shirt, hesitating before she left to glance out the front restaurant windows.

A few large white cumulous clouds floated in the blue sky. Maddie loved summer days and couldn't wait to get back out to the Cavanaugh's ranch so she could ride her horse before her next shift. Her cousins had been boarding it there for her since she left town.

She didn't see Bo's car, but she knew that didn't mean anything. If she knew Bo, which she did, his next attack would be without warning.

As she passed a preset table for the dinner meal, Maddie slipped one of the steak knives into her purse.

Chapter Six

For the rest of the afternoon, all Shane wanted was to sit in the shade on the porch and read a book he'd picked up on Montana.

But the window to the living room was open, and he couldn't help but overhear the conversation between Kate and his father.

"I think I'll just stay around here," Kate said. "I have some things I want to do. You don't mind, do you?"

"Of course not," Grayson said. "I just worry about you staying out here on the ranch all the time."

"I love it here. There is really no other place I want to be."

Shane heard his father's voice soften even more and knew he was holding his new bride.

"I'll see you later then," Grayson said. "Don't overdo it. I worry about you sometimes."

Grayson was no fool. He must have noticed that Kate had been unusually quiet when she returned from town the other day. Shane remembered his father commenting on how pale she appeared and asking if she was feeling ill.

"I'm fine," Kate had said. "I think it was the heat. It's so much hotter in town than out here."

Now Grayson came out the front door, hesitating when he spotted his son. Shane watched him look back into the house, then come over to the porch rocker.

"Russell and I are driving up to Loring," Grayson said. "Interested in coming along?"

Shane shook his head. "Thanks, but I really want to finish this book." He hoped his father didn't push it. To his relief, Grayson didn't.

His father studied the cover of the Montana history book and then him. "Kate's running a little tired. She's staying home. Would you mind, since you're going to be here, just keeping an eye on her?"

Shane groaned inwardly. The last thing he needed was his father asking him to keep an eye on Kate. He'd already been doing that behind both of their backs.

"Sure. No problem," he said.

His father laid a hand on his shoulder. "Thanks. I didn't realize how hard it would be on her, coming back here, you know?"

Shane nodded, although he didn't know. What was it about coming back here that was so hard? Obviously Grayson believed it was because Kate's father had died here and the family had lost the ranch.

Shane suspected there was more to it and was even more convinced when not thirty minutes after Grayson had left, Kate came out carrying her purse and car keys.

"I need to run into town," Kate said. "Need to pick up something I forgot."

"Would you like me to go for you?" Shane asked putting down his book, trying hard not to let her see that he was on to her.

"No, but thank you," she said, as she hurried down the steps. "I won't be long."

"Drive carefully," he called after her.

Shane gave her over a few minutes' start before he headed for his pickup.

CHESTER BAILEY LOOKED UP as he came out of the Hi-Line Café, his footsteps faltering when he saw Kate.

"Running into each other two times in the same amount of days must be a record," Chester said, clearly flustered.

"This time it wasn't accidental," Kate said. "I need to talk to you."

Chester glanced back at the café, as if he were afraid Susie would see them together. "Sure. About what?"

Kate took a breath and let it out slowly. "Is there somewhere we could go?"

He looked at her as if she'd just suggested they get a motel.

"A place we could talk in private. How about the park?"

"The park?" Chester repeated.

"Trafton Park." Kate felt her patience slipping. The park was on the Milk River, just a few blocks away. "I'll meet you there."

He nodded, but she wondered if he would show up, given the way he was acting.

Kate got back in her SUV and drove to the park. She pulled under the shade of one of the large old cotton-woods and got out to sit at a picnic table. The day was pure Montana June—only a few clouds in the crystalline blue sky, the temperature just warm enough to be pleasant.

She fidgeted, trying to talk herself out of what she was about to do when Chester pulled up in his truck. He couldn't have looked more awkward as he climbed out and joined her, taking a seat on the opposite side of the picnic table.

"What's this about, Kate?" he asked, his voice wavering a little.

She stared at him, wondering what she'd seen in him all those years ago. She hadn't been that young or that naïve. But she had been hurting, and for a while Chester had made her feel better.

Now she knew it hadn't been honor or loyalty that had motivated him to make the decision he had. It had been cowardice. Chester Bailey was a man who always took the easy way out.

Or was that just her anger toward the man who'd hurt her?

"What do you think this is about?" she snapped, unable to contain that anger any longer. She knew she wasn't being fair, since most of that anger was directed at herself.

He looked as if she'd slapped him.

"I'm sorry, but I've been struggling with the past," she said, unable to keep the sarcasm out of her tone.

He sighed. "Kate, all that was so long ago, who can even remember—"

"*I* remember." She'd told herself she wasn't going to do this. "I remember being pregnant and scared and completely alone."

"You know why I couldn't—"

"Yes." She reminded herself that she hadn't asked him here to dredge up the past hurt—at least not between them. "I need to tell you something." This was going to be harder than she thought. "I didn't lose the baby."

He stared at her. *"What?"*

"I didn't lose the baby." All those years ago she'd sent him a note telling him she'd miscarried. She hadn't wanted him to know the truth because he'd made it clear he didn't care. "I gave the baby up for adoption."

He shook his head, his look one of shock. "You lied to me?"

"It was a baby girl. That's all I know except that she was adopted by someone from around here."

"I don't believe you."

"It's true. I left right away but you might've even gotten to watch her grow up. Your own daughter, right here in Whitehorse."

"I can't do this, Kate." He started for his truck, running away as he always had.

"I'm going to find her." Her words surprised her. She'd stayed away all these years, keeping busy with a newspaper career, not looking back. But then she'd found that damned box of photographs of her and Rebecca from their time on the Trails West Ranch, and since she was going to be in Austin anyway, she'd taken them by Grayson Corbett's ranch.

Chester turned back toward her, the desperation in his face making him look older than he was. "After all these years of believing our baby died and now... How could you have done that to me? Did you hate me that much?"

"Yes," she said honestly.

He stared at her, the raw pain in his face filling her with guilt. Then he turned and left without looking back.

Kate covered her face with her hands as she listened to the crunch of the pickup's tires on the gravel.

SHANE WATCHED KATE from a distance. He hated this, but protecting his father was second nature. Grayson had clearly been under Kate's spell from the beginning. Buying the Trails West Ranch and moving to Montana had been impulsive—and wasn't like his father. Grayson had always been so careful in his business dealings, amassing a fortune.

That was another thing that worried Shane about Kate. She had shown up on Grayson's doorstep out of the blue with the excuse that she'd found a box of old photographs of Rebecca.

It had happened too fast. The courtship, the marriage and this move. On top of that, since coming to Montana Kate had been acting oddly.

Shane had noticed how hesitant she seemed about going into town. Now he thought he knew why as he watched the man leave. Then, the other day she'd run into that older man outside the store. Shane had seen how nervous and awkward she'd been. It was clear Kate and the man knew each other.

Now Shane knew it was time to find out who this man from Kate's past was—and, if possible, what he'd meant to her.

He followed the man back to a café on the edge of the town. Getting out, he went into the Hi-Line café, ordered a cup of coffee and struck up a conversation with the waitress, a young high-school student.

He'd found out that the man's name was Chester Bailey. Bailey's daughter, Eve, was married to Sheriff Carter Jackson and lived on the home ranch south of Old Town Whitehorse. Another daughter, McKenna, raised paint horses with her husband on a separate place to the west of the old Bailey place. A third daughter, Faith Bailey, lived in Bozeman.

Chester and Lila, who had been married for thirty years, were divorced. Lila had remarried and was now living in Florida.

Chester and the other owner of the café, Susie, were an item. Chester was a former rancher—a little shy but sweet, according to the waitress who apparently knew everyone in town.

Angry with himself butting into his stepmother's business, Shane finished his coffee and left. He drove around for a while then, as if his pickup had a mind of its own, he drove down Main Street past the Northern Lights restaurant and saw Maddie's pickup parked across the street.

He checked his watch. The restaurant should just now be reopening for the evening. His stomach growled, and while common sense told him to keep on going, he turned in and parked.

After all, he had to eat. He wasn't going to be able to pass the physical to return to the Texas Rangers unless he took better care of himself.

The truth was he couldn't get Maddie off his mind. He told himself he had to warn her about Bo Evans. And while he was at it, maybe warn her about Jud. Then he could wash his hands of the whole mess with a clear conscience.

Maddie looked up as Shane entered the restaurant. Surprise registered in her gaze and was followed instantly by irritation.

"I'll be right with you. Sit wherever you'd like," she called to him, as she disappeared into the kitchen.

The place was empty. He chose a table in the corner so he could face the door, an old habit.

Maddie smiled politely as she returned with a menu, a glass of iced water and a small basket of warm, thickly sliced bread.

His stomach growled at the smell of the bread. Her smile broadened as she heard it.

"The special this evening is tomato-cheese ravioli with Italian salad," she said.

He handed her back the unopened menu as his stomach rumbled again. "The special it is." He smiled, embarrassed more by his own nervousness than his hungry stomach. This woman unnerved him.

"You won't be sorry," she said, as she took the menu. "Enjoy the bread. In the basket, there's honey butter in a small crock. Your supper will be right up."

As she turned and walked away, Shane told himself that she made him edgy because of her relationship with his brother—or lack of one. Jud had hardly seen Maddie. He bet his little brother had a woman or two on the set. He always did.

The bread with the honey butter was nothing short of amazing. He had the place to himself and almost hoped more diners would come in so he wouldn't be tempted to try to talk to Maddie about Bo and Jud.

Maddie brought out his meal, the ravioli smelling

heavenly. For a guy born and raised on Tex-Mex, he was surprised by how much he enjoyed his Italian supper.

He'd finished every bite and eaten his salad and all the bread when Maddie came back to see if he wanted dessert.

"We have a flourless chocolate torte that my cousin makes," she said. "It's worth every calorie."

"I'll take it and some coffee if you'll sit with me for a few minutes," he said.

She hesitated, clearly uncertain even though she wasn't busy. "All right," she said after a moment. She left, returning with the torte and two cups of coffee.

As she took the chair across from him, he noted that the freckles on her face seemed to stand out more than they had earlier. Her eyes were a bright, clear blue. And when she peered at him over the rim of her coffee cup, her gaze seemed almost challenging.

"I want to talk to you about Jud," he said, and could have kicked himself.

She slowly put down the cup, her eyebrow lifting as she cocked her head at him.

"The thing about Jud is that he's young and impulsive," Shane said.

Still Maddie said nothing, that blue gaze of hers never wavering. She seemed to be waiting for him to dig himself in deeper.

"He has a tendency to sweep a woman off her feet, especially when he's doing his Hollywood stuntman thing." Shane wished she would say something, but when she still didn't, he stumbled on: "What I'm trying to say is that I just don't want to see you get hurt."

"You're worried about your brother hurting me?" Maddie asked, sounding almost amused.

"You wouldn't be the first woman he's led on," Shane said, suddenly feeling horribly disloyal. "But this time it's different because you aren't even his type."

"I see. So you're saying there isn't any way Jud could be serious about someone like me?"

"No—" Shane rubbed the back of his neck "—it's more complicated than that."

She crossed her arms over her chest, clearly waiting for him to continue.

He sighed. Maddie deserved the truth, didn't she? He just didn't want to be the one to tell her. If he thought for an instant that Jud might be serious about her he wouldn't have started this to begin with.

"Look, I'm going to be straight with you," he said. "My mother died right after Jud and Dalton were born. I barely remember her, but my father was heartbroken. Until he met Kate Wade, he'd always said there was no other woman for him."

Maddie had an "And your point is?" look on her face.

He rushed on. "All these years, my father couldn't bring himself to go through my mother's things. Until—"

"Kate?" Maddie offered.

"Yeah. So when he finally did go through her things he found some letters. One for each of her sons to be read on our wedding days. My mother also left a letter for my father. Apparently she feared he would raise us to be like him, wild and untethered. She was afraid that since we wouldn't have a mother, we wouldn't appreciate the need for a woman in our lives until it was too late."

Maddie's eyes widened. "You have to be kidding."

"Afraid not. She wanted my father to do everything in his power to see that we were each married before the age of thirty-five. Right now my oldest brother is thirty-two and unmarried. Her dying wish was that we would each marry a Montana cowgirl, just like she had been when she met my father." He rushed on before he lost his courage. "So we drew straws to see who would get married first."

"Jud drew the shortest straw."

Shane nodded, waiting for his words to sink in. So far Maddie's reaction had been one of almost amusement.

"What straw did you draw?"

He stared at her for a moment, surprised by the unexpected question. "The longest one, but I think the whole thing is ludicrous and I have no intention of going along with it."

"You think Jud is, though."

"The thing is, even if it wasn't our mother's dying wish, Jud doesn't want to hurt our father. Since he moved up here, Dad seems determined to get us all to settle here, preferably on the Trails West Ranch."

"I see." She picked up her coffee cup and took a sip before putting it down again.

He'd expected her to be heartbroken or at least angry. "I just felt you should know what's going on."

She smiled at that. "I had a pretty good idea what was going on, but you've definitely helped me see it more clearly." She looked up, meeting his gaze. "Anything else you'd like to share with me?"

Shane swallowed. Warning her about Jud hadn't worked. He might as well give the other matter a shot.

"I saw Bo Evans harassing you the other day," he said.

Her expression didn't change.

"I wouldn't say anything but I'm worried about you."

Another cock of her eyebrow and that amused look. "You are?"

"The man is dangerous. But I suspect you already know that. I think you need to get a restraining order against him."

She smiled as she ran her finger along the rim of her coffee cup. "You really think that would deter Bo?"

"No, but it would let him know you mean business and make the sheriff aware of the problem."

Maddie chuckled as she looked at him. He found himself hypnotized by the tiny gold flecks floating in all that blue. "I'm touched by your concern. Really," Maddie said, although her tone suggested otherwise.

"I was a Texas Ranger." *Was.* He started to correct himself but continued. "I guess butting into other people's business is in my blood."

Maddie smiled at that. "So you're just telling me these things as a lawman. I see." She rose and started to clear the table.

He touched her hand to stop her, feeling he'd made a mess of this and wanting to fix it, needing to fix it, but not having a clue how.

He felt her tremble at his touch.

"I'm not Bo Evans," he said, thinking that explained her reaction.

"I never thought you were. But the truth is, you don't know anything about me, and while I appreciate your warnings, I can take care of myself."

He feared she was wrong on both counts. He did know a lot about her and sensed even more. And he wasn't all that sure that anyone could take care of themselves when it came to Bo Evans.

Shane knew his butting in had a lot to do with the rodeo dance and that intimate moment when he'd felt a primitive connection between them.

It had scared him. Maybe scared her, too. But she was still his brother's girlfriend, and he was out of line.

"You're right, it's none of my business."

He watched her bite down on her lower lip. As she studied him, her blue eyes sparked with something he took for anger. When she opened her mouth, he'd expected her to light into him again.

"Did you like the torte?" she asked, as she brushed a lock of blond hair back from her freckled face.

Shane looked down at his plate, surprised to find the torte gone. He didn't remember eating it but could still taste the rich dark chocolate on his tongue. "It was just as wonderful as you said it was."

She smiled almost ruefully before she left him alone at the table feeling like a fool. "I'll get your check."

MADDIE LET OUT an oath the minute she was out of Shane's sight. Something she'd been doing too often lately.

"Problems?" Bridger Duvall asked as she came into the kitchen.

"If I told you, you wouldn't believe me," she said, remembering the way Jud Corbett had chased her, determined to get a date with her. It was all starting to make sense. "Why are men so…so…"

"Clueless?" Bridger asked with a grin.

Maddie smiled. "When it comes to women? Yes."

"I'd love to argue the point, but I remember how I fought admitting that I'd fallen in love with Laci. Can you imagine? The truth was she stole my heart the first time I tasted something she'd cooked. It was love at first bite."

Maddie laughed. "The two of you are made for each other. At least you realized that."

"It took me a while," he admitted. "She knew before I did."

Men, Maddie thought, as she shook her head and dug out Shane's bill. And he thought he knew his brother so well. She laughed at the thought.

"So this problem you're having with a man, I assume it's Jud Corbett?" Bridger asked.

"The moment I laid eyes on Jud, I knew exactly what to expect," she said truthfully. It was one of the reasons she hadn't wanted to go out with him. But she knew Laci and Laney were worried about how she hadn't dated since Bo.

"Time to get back on that horse that bucked you off," Laci had said, then handed her a cookie.

Maddie had laughed, and warmed by the cookie, agreed to go out with Jud, knowing she could never fall for the man.

Now she knew that he only asked her out because he'd drawn the shortest straw in some stupid marriage pact and had come up with a way out. At least now she knew what he was up to.

"Give the man a little time," Bridger suggested. "He'll come around."

Maddie pushed open the kitchen door to glance out at

Shane. "We can only hope," she said under her breath, as she went out to give him his check.

She was suddenly furious with both Corbett brothers.

"What is wrong with you Corbetts?" she demanded when she reached the table.

"Where would you like me to start? It could take a while."

"You Corbett brothers wouldn't know what to do with a Montana cowgirl if you had one," she snapped.

Shane wisely said nothing.

She took a deep breath and let it out. "I hope you enjoyed your supper," she said slapping the bill down on his table. "Have a nice day."

With that she turned and stormed back toward the kitchen, feeling her face heat with embarrassment. On the way, she kicked the leg of one of the chairs, wishing it was Shane Corbett's shin.

FROM ACROSS THE STREET, Bo Evans cursed Maddie to hell and gone as he watched her with the Texas Ranger.

He'd known Shane Corbett was the law before he'd asked around and found out his name—and profession. The man carried himself with the same superiority that Bo had hated in every lawman he'd ever met. But he'd been surprised to find out that Corbett was a Texas Ranger on medical leave after being shot during an arrest.

Bo would have loved to shake the hand of the man who'd shot Shane. Unfortunately that man was dead, and Shane was alive and in Whitehorse and apparently interested in Maddie.

"Big mistake," Bo said under his breath, as he watched Shane come out of the restaurant. "Big mistake."

Bo waited until Shane drove away before he got out of his car and started across the street. He thought about going into the restaurant, backing Maddie up against the wall… He could feel his hands on her soft curves. Oh, what he wanted to do to that bitch.

But reason won out for a change, and he entered the hardware store a few doors down. He had to bide his time, think things out. Plan.

"Can I help you?" the girl behind the counter asked.

"Duct tape."

She pointed him down an aisle, where he found both duct tape and some rope used for clotheslines. A glint of metal caught his eye as he started toward the cash register. He back-stepped, smiling as he picked up a dangerous-looking pair of hedge trimmers.

"What you couldn't do with these," he said to himself, as he snapped the blades open and closed, and thought about what he was going to do to Maddie once it got dark.

Chapter Seven

Jerilyn woke in the afternoon, hung over and confused. It took her a moment to recall where she was. At first she thought she was still with Earl Ray and sat up in bed with a start. Then she remembered she was with the man she'd picked up at the bar last night.

She could hear Buck Jones in the kitchen and smell the scent of coffee. Lying back down, she snuggled under the covers. The bedroom had a slight chill to it that reminded her she'd made it to Montana. The wallpaper in the room was covered in faded tiny yellow flowers. There was an old bureau and an antique mirror.

That was the extent of a woman's touch in the room. Jerilyn suspected the house had belonged to Buck's mother and that he hadn't changed a thing since her death.

The moment she'd seen Buck's pickup she knew he wasn't going to be much help financially. When she'd checked the contents of his wallet in the middle of the night, she'd found twenty-three dollars and some coupons for groceries. Not a good sign. Even the house was small, and from what she'd seen of Whitehorse it wouldn't bring much.

But Buck had been kind and more than a little helpful.

"Maddie Cavanaugh? Sure, I know her. Well, know *of* her," he'd said after they'd left the bar and come to his house. "She's been away at college until just recently."

"Her parents nice?"

He'd hesitated, and she'd felt her stomach roil. "Sarah's always been a little uppity, you know. Roy's nice enough. Quiet. Like a lot of ranchers."

Uppity was good.

"They have a pretty big ranch?"

"Good-sized. Brought enough when Roy sold it that he was able to relocate to Arizona, I heard."

"They don't still live here?" she asked, sounding as if she might cry.

"Divorced. Been a few years now." He shook his head. "Why the interest in the Cavanaughs?"

Jerilyn had licked her lips and decided on the truth. It was going to come out anyway. "Maddie is my natural-born child."

Buck had stared at her as if she'd grown horns. "Are you saying…"

She'd nodded. "I was sixteen," she'd said, and poured out her story, crying a little as she'd told it.

"I'm so sorry. Maddie was adopted, huh?" He shook his head. "And you've never met her?"

"My mother told me she went to a good family. I didn't want to interfere. I wasn't even supposed to know what happened to her. I guess I was afraid, too, that she might not like me."

Now as the smell of coffee grew stronger, Jerilyn sat up in bed, and Buck brought her a cup along with a stale muffin. She thanked him and sipped the hot, strong coffee and nibbled at the muffin. She was hungry.

Buck's brown eyes softened as he gazed at her. "I've been thinkin'. I bet Maddie would want to meet you."

"I don't know," Jerilyn said. "You didn't say what happened to her adoptive mother."

"Don't know. There was talk, but then there's always talk in Whitehorse. I know a lot of people were glad to see her get her comeuppance."

This didn't sound good.

"I heard she'd been involved in some blackmail scheme, but no charges were ever filed. After the divorce Sarah just up and left town, but definitely with her tail tucked between her legs, if you know what I mean."

Jerilyn knew only too well. So there was no money. Unless Maddie... "You said my daughter is back from college?"

"Yep. She's waitressing down at the Northern Lights restaurant."

A *waitress?* "There's no other family?"

"There's her cousins, Laci and Laney, and her Great Aunt Pearl and Uncle Titus."

"They're well off financially? I mean, I wouldn't want to think that my baby girl wasn't well taken care of," she added quickly.

Buck patted her hand. "No one around here's rich by any standards. Some's got a lot of land. Most just scrape by. Maddie's cousin Laney's married to a deputy. Her cousin Laci and her husband just started the restaurant. Both women are pregnant, big as houses."

"And the great aunt and uncle?"

"Pearl's doing better after her stroke. Titus, well, he's

still preaching on Sundays down in Old Town White-horse."

Jerilyn felt her heart sink, and now her tears were real. She'd come so far, hoping that someone would be able to help her get back on her feet. But she still had Earl Ray's little black book as a last resort, she reminded herself.

"You know if you're afraid about meeting your daughter, we could go together for dinner at the restaurant," Buck suggested. "That way you could see her before you said anything about who you were."

"I don't know." What would be the point now that she knew Maddie's circumstances? Jerilyn took the tissue Buck offered her and dried her tears. So much for her ace in the hole. Just another disappointment.

But she guessed it wouldn't hurt to at least see her daughter. She had come this far. She wouldn't tell Maddie who she was. No reason to. It sounded as if the girl had gone through enough without finding out that her birth mother was no better than her adoptive one.

"You going to be all right?" Buck asked.

She nodded. If her mother hadn't already been dead, Jerilyn would have driven back to Arizona just to confront the old bat.

Shoving down her anger, she rose from bed and headed for the shower, turning to glance back at Buck, who was still sitting on the edge of the bed. "You don't happen to have anything I could wear. Someone stole my clothes out of the back of my car."

If Buck knew she was lying, he didn't let on. She hadn't really expected him to have something she could wear. She was just opening the door to hit him up for money. She'd seen a clothing store on Main Street.

"My sister left some clothes here," Buck said. "She's your size. You're sure welcome to anything that fits."

"Thanks," she said. Hand-me-downs? Nothing was going her way. "You've been great."

Buck grinned bashfully and ducked his head as he went to get the clothing.

Jerilyn stepped into the shower. Was she really going to see her daughter after all these years? It wasn't going to be the reunion she'd hoped for, but she'd hit Buck up for money for dinner and a present for Maddie. She could just leave the gift anonymously at the restaurant.

And then what?

Jerilyn didn't know. She couldn't see herself staying here with Buck. Maybe she could find someone at the bar who had a hankering to go to Vegas. Or she could do something with Earl Ray's little black book.

EARL RAY WAS BETTING he knew Jerilyn, knew her so well he could guess what she'd do next. The woman was predictable, though he had been surprised that she'd taken off on her own.

That wasn't like her. Jerilyn didn't like to think for herself. If he was right, that meant she would already have some man thinking for her. If she didn't, she would soon enough.

That was why the minute Earl Ray had gotten to town, he'd checked out the bars—all six of them. Which one would Jerilyn pick? It was anyone's guess.

He'd thought about asking the bartenders to keep a look out for her and let him know if she showed up.

But Jerilyn had a way of making some men go all protective. He didn't want a well-meaning bartender to warn her that he was asking about her around town. Earl Ray wanted to surprise her.

His plan was to get what she was looking for— Maddie Cavanaugh—and use her as bait to reel back in Jerilyn and his black book.

So, Earl Ray decided to bide his time, stay low to the ground and wait. Wait for Bo Evans to bring him Maddie Cavanaugh.

But he and his two buddies, Bubba and Dude, were holed up in a motel on the edge of town, and his patience was running thin. All Bubba did was complain about Dude, who spent all his time watching television.

Earl Ray wasn't sure how much more of this he could take. If Bo didn't come through—and soon—he was going to have to have another talk with him. Only this time, he might have to let Bubba and Dude work over the slimy bastard.

KATE COULDN'T HAVE been more shocked when she picked up the phone later that evening and heard Chester's voice.

"I think we should talk," he said, sounding as if that was the last thing he wanted to do. "Not on the phone. Meet me at our old place."

There was only one thing they had to talk about. She was trembling inside, a quaking that started at her heart and moved through her bones to ripple across her flesh. Meet at their old place?

"Kate?"

"Yes," she managed to say. "I can be there in thirty minutes."

Chester was silent for a long moment, no doubt remembering the times when they'd had this same conversation. Except back then, they'd both been excited to see each other.

"Fine," he said. "Thirty minutes."

She could hear in his tone how he hated this situation as much as she did.

Kate hung up. She glanced over her shoulder, even though she knew Grayson had driven up to the Loring Colony with Russell to see about buying some pigs from the Hutterites. They would stay for supper. Juanita had gone into town and none of the boys were around.

For a moment, Kate was overwhelmed with guilt. *You have to tell Grayson. You have to tell him everything.*

But she knew she couldn't. Not yet. She was too ashamed. Too afraid of how he would take it.

As she drove to the deserted ranch south of Whitehorse, every instinct told her to turn around, go home and forget the past. But coming back to Montana and the ranch had made that impossible.

The old barn was on a narrow, rutted road. As she came up over a rise in the sprawling grasslands that ran to the horizon, she spotted the weathered structure and was surprised that it looked just as it had all those years ago. Maybe a little more weathered, a few more boards missing, but too much the same.

Her heart did that little jump, and her stomach tensed, remembering the thrill of forbidden love.

She'd loved Chester. Hadn't she? From the beginning, she'd known he wasn't free. That had been part of the allure.

The memory brought a wave of guilt and regret for

how cavalier she'd been about sleeping with another woman's husband.

Chester's blue pickup was parked in the shade of the building. As Kate pulled in, she began to quake with a fear that immobilized her.

Chester climbed out of his pickup and stood next to it. In the past, he would have been waiting for her in the barn, in the little secret spot they'd made into a love nest.

She killed her engine and leaving the keys in the ignition, got out. A slight breeze carried the smell of hay and weathering wood.

The scent transported her at rocket speed back to the past. For a moment she had to hold on to the door of her SUV for support. All these years of lying to herself ended in a rush of truth that made her eyes fill with tears.

She swallowed, terrified that she would sob uncontrollably, like she had the last time they had met here.

"I thought we could sit over there out of the sun," Chester said, motioning to an old flatbed pickup that had been abandoned next to the barn.

She nodded wordlessly and, taking a deep breath and letting it out slowly, followed him. He dusted off a spot for her. The thoughtful gesture was almost her undoing.

"I'm sorry, Kate."

The pain she heard in his voice further weakened her. She sat down on the flatbed and stared out across the open country, remembering how one afternoon they'd danced on the worn wood of the old flatbed trailer while a slow country-and-western song poured out of the speakers in Chester's pick up—the dance as forbidden as their affair.

"I never wanted... I should have..." Chester shook his head as if the words were too hollow to even speak.

"It was a long time ago," she said, not trusting herself to look at him.

"If I had it to do over, I swear I would do it differently," he said, as he sat down next to her.

Easy to say after your marriage ended in divorce, she thought, but held her tongue. There was no rewriting history for either of them.

Kate wet her lips, swallowed the lump in her throat and finally met his gaze. "Have you found out what happened to our baby?"

He shook his head looking miserable.

Why had he asked her out here then? "But you must have some idea how we can find her." It was a local adoption, a secret one. The midwife had known someone who would take care of everything. Unfortunately, she was now deceased.

Chester lowered his head and poked in the dirt with the toe of his boot. "All these years, I wondered if things would have been different if you hadn't lost the baby."

"You wouldn't have left Lila."

He cursed under his breath as he swung his head to look at her, his gaze piercing her. "How do you know that?"

"Because you had made your choice." Her chest hurt as she looked into his eyes. "You could have had me and our baby girl, but you chose Lila and her ranch instead, since I no longer had Trails West."

Kate knew she was being cruel. She blamed him for the way things had turned out. That wasn't fair and she knew it. But even after all these years, she was still angry. Still hurting. She'd given up her baby and had regretted it every day since.

"We were so young," he said quietly.

"Not so young." She'd been twenty-four, old enough that she could have gotten a job and raised her baby on her own.

"It's easy to look back from this age and say that but, Kate, you were in no shape to raise a baby. You'd just lost your father, your home. You'd lost so much, and I let you down." Chester was shaking his head. "You did what you thought best for our baby. You need to forgive yourself."

His kindness brought tears to her eyes again, only this time no amount of willpower could hold them back. Chester knew her better than she'd thought.

"I have to find her." She was crying now, hating that she was. "I have to see her. I have to know that what I did was the right thing."

"Are you sure about this, Kate? What if things didn't work out so well? You'll only have more regrets."

"I shouldn't expect you to understand. You have children. Three daughters."

He nodded. "We adopted. Lila couldn't conceive. So this daughter of ours is also my only flesh-and-blood child."

Gulping back sobs, she looked into his eyes, saw the pain and the regret.

"Don't you think I hated myself for letting you deal with everything alone? For letting you go?" He reached over and touched her hand.

She flinched, startled by his touch, but didn't pull away. "Will you help me find her?"

He nodded.

"Your daughters are adopted?" She could see that he knew where she was going with this. "Through the same people probably."

"Maybe."

"Lila never knew about you and me or the baby, did she?"

Chester shook his head. Then he let go of her hand and rose to his feet. "Do you want me to call you when I know something?"

"I'll call you." She immediately regretted her words.

Chester's gaze narrowed. "Grayson doesn't know?"

She didn't answer as she got up and walked to her SUV. She made a point of not looking at the barn or remembering the way the sun slanted through the worn wood, warming the straw bed on which her younger self once laid naked in this man's arms.

As JERILYN STEPPED into the Northern Lights restaurant that evening, she felt self-conscious and glanced down at her clothing.

Buck had come through with some pretty nice stuff that fit well. Much better clothes than anything Jerilyn had owned in a long time.

But still she felt nervous. She checked her hair. She'd pulled it up and was glad she did. This place was nice. Her daughter must make good tips.

Jerilyn pushed the thought away as she saw a cute girl come out of the kitchen. Blond, freckled, blue-eyed. Jerilyn felt all the air rush from her lungs and her legs turn to water. This had to be her.

"Will someone be joining you?" the girl asked. Not a girl. A young woman.

Jerilyn swallowed, nodded, then corrected herself. "Just me."

Maddie smiled. "Right this way."

Jerilyn followed, heart pounding, to a table by the window and sat down heavily. Maddie brought her water, a menu and breadsticks.

Jerilyn watched her walk away, then opened the menu, instantly relieved that she'd asked Buck for an extra twenty. He'd also given her the keys to his pickup, which was now parked out front.

Some friends of Buck's had come by to go gopher hunting. She'd insisted he go, telling him she was nervous enough without him hanging around.

After he'd left, she'd watched some television then went through his house looking in all the cubbyholes. For a while she'd pretended he was rich but didn't trust banks. That fairy tale ended when she didn't find anything more than two dollars and twenty-nine cents in spare change.

She'd waited until the last hour and a half before the restaurant closed before drinking a couple of beers just to get up her courage, then going out. Buck had given her money to buy Maddie a gift, but Jerilyn hadn't made it downtown to look for anything before the stores closed. Not that she would have known what to buy, anyway.

When Maddie returned, Jerilyn ordered three appetizers and a glass of wine and tried to relax.

Only a couple of tables were occupied, the diners at them all about to leave.

She tried to think of something to say to Maddie when she returned with the appetizers.

"Are you from around here?" Jerilyn asked.

"Born and raised," Maddie said with a smile. Jerilyn had always hated her own freckles and wondered if Maddie felt the same about hers. Maddie seemed comfortable in her skin, and Jerilyn was jealous.

"So what is there to do around here?" Jerilyn asked, when Maddie refilled her water glass.

"Well, it depends on what you enjoy. There are two museums, one about the history of the area, the other about dinosaurs." Maddie cocked her head. "You're probably not interested in fishing, right? But there is a hot spring just outside of town if you like to swim or just soak. How long are you planning to be in town? There is a county fair coming up."

Jerilyn couldn't help but laugh. "What do you do here? It doesn't sound like there's much going on."

Maddie smiled at the question. "I spend a lot of time on my horse. But there's always something happening. Last night there was a rodeo and dance..."

"You like it here, then?" Jerilyn hadn't meant to sound so surprised.

It was Maddie's turn to laugh. "I do. I take it this is your first time in Whitehorse."

"My second time," Jerilyn said truthfully. "I'm from Arizona."

"Well, June's a good time to be in Montana. You probably wouldn't like winter here."

"No," Jerilyn agreed. Last time she was in Whitehorse it hadn't been winter, but she remembered it had felt cold and bleak.

"Let me know if I can get you anything else," Maddie said.

"Thank you. I will." Jerilyn picked at the food, suddenly not hungry. She watched her daughter clear the now-empty tables and heard her humming to herself.

Maddie seemed happy, content, doing okay. What hurt was that Jerilyn could see that her mother had been right. If she had raised this girl, Maddie would have ended up in a foster home or maybe worse, given the type of men she had shacked up with over the years.

She'd always told herself that if she'd kept her baby things would have been different. But as she watched Maddie, she knew she would have been a lousy mother and that her daughter had been better off without her—would always be better off without her. That hurt more than she wanted to admit.

Jerilyn finished her appetizers, paid her bill and left Maddie a large tip. As she stepped outside, her daughter thanked her for coming in and put up the Closed sign behind her.

FINALLY EARL RAY couldn't take it anymore. He decided to leave Bubba and Dude at the motel. The two were scary-looking. Not that Earl Ray was any beauty, but when the three of them were together, they could be mistaken for thugs.

He promised himself that once he got the book and sold it to the highest bidder, he'd buy himself an expensive suit, a nice car and always keep a wad of spending money in his pocket. People would look up to him then. Maybe he'd even find himself a nice woman, a lady. Not another ditz like Jerilyn Larch.

"I'm going to go get myself a beer," Earl Ray told his heavies. He was sure the two had real names, although he'd never asked.

"Whatever." Dude was sprawled on one of the motel beds watching poker on TV.

"Bring me back something to eat," Bubba said from where he was doing push-ups on the floor.

"Sure." Earl Ray already had his story worked out. He'd tell the bartenders that Jerilyn was his sister and their mother was dying. He had to get her back to Arizona before the old gal croaked or Jerilyn would never forgive him.

He hit pay dirt in the third bar.

"Yeah, I saw her," the bartender said after Earl Ray had described Jerilyn. "She was in here last night."

"Do you know where I can find her? Time is of the essence." He'd thrown a twenty-dollar bill down on the bar when he'd ordered a draft beer. He stood now, making it clear he'd be leaving the rest of the twenty as a tip.

"Buck Jones might know. The two of them were talking some last night."

Knowing Jerilyn, she'd gone home with the man. That would explain why he hadn't seen her car at any of the few motels in town.

"Where does he live?"

The bartender hesitated, picked up the twenty, then said, "He lives in a house over by the old high school. Well, where the old high school used to be. It burned down about ten years ago."

Fascinating, Earl Ray thought.

"It's a blue and white place, on the corner."

"You know the name of the street?"

"Fourth. Fourth and Third, I think."

Great directions. Earl Ray thanked him and headed for Buck Jones's house.

AFTER SEEING HER DAUGHTER, Jerilyn felt restless. Just the thought of going back to Buck's little house was too depressing for words. She walked down the dark street, noting how quiet it was. Why would anyone want to live here? The only sign of life was a few pickups parked in front of the bars on the next block.

One thing was for certain. She couldn't stay in Whitehorse, but she knew Earl Ray's car would never get her back to Arizona—as if there was anything waiting for her there even if the car would make it. Something other than trouble.

She stopped in front of a clothing store and was admiring a spaghetti-strap top in the window, when out of the corner of her eye she saw a set of headlights cut through the darkness. She watched as an older model car pulled up at the corner, motor running. She could see a dark-colored cowboy hat silhouetted against the street lights. The cowboy appeared to be waiting for someone.

The lights inside the Northern Lights restaurant blinked out an instant before the front door opened and Maddie emerged. Jerilyn turned to watch her leave, telling herself it would be the last time she saw her daughter.

Maddie stopped under the eave, hugging herself, as if looking for someone. When she noticed the car parked along the side street, she stepped from under the eave as if to run across the street.

Jerilyn didn't see the cowboy get out of the car. She'd been too busy watching Maddie.

He ran up before Maddie reached the edge of the sidewalk. For a moment, Jerilyn thought it was just Maddie's boyfriend who'd come to pick her up.

Maddie must not have seen or heard the cowboy coming. He grabbed her arm roughly and pulled her toward his waiting car.

Jerilyn watched, frowning, as Maddie didn't seem to want to go with him. Jerilyn opened her mouth to yell at him, taking a couple of steps in their direction.

Maddie was struggling to free herself and digging in her shoulder bag for something. Mace? But before Maddie could get whatever she was after, the cowboy punched her. As she slumped in his arms, he hurriedly dragged her toward the waiting car.

Jerilyn was running now, yelling after him. But the man didn't turn as he opened the back door of the car and put something over her mouth before he tossed Maddie in. After slamming the door, he leaped into the front seat. The engine revved, and before Jerilyn could reach the corner, the car sped off down the dark street.

She had to call the police. But she had no cell phone. She turned, looking for someone to help. But there was no one, and the closest bar was down the next block.

Racing over to the restaurant door, Jerilyn saw only a dim light in the back. Everyone must have gone home.

Jerilyn turned to look down the street. She could still hear the roar of the cowboy's car as it headed out of town.

Realizing there was nothing else to do, she ran to Buck's pickup. Her fingers trembled as she inserted the key in the ignition and got the motor running. As she whipped out of the parking space and went after her daughter, all Jerilyn could see of the car was the faint red glow of its taillights in the distance.

Chapter Eight

Bo couldn't believe he'd pulled it off. Now he had to find somewhere to pull over and take care of Maddie.

He listened. No sound from the backseat. She was still out, but for how long? He watched his speed. All he needed was to get picked up by the state Highway Patrol.

He just hoped to hell he hadn't overdone the chloroform and killed her. That would take all the fun out of it—not to mention the profit. He had a feeling the men waiting at the motel wanted Maddie alive.

The cell phone Earl Ray gave him vibrated in his jacket pocket. Bo checked and, sure enough, it was from Earl Ray. The guy had left three messages so far today. He must be really anxious to get Maddie. If Earl Ray was that desperate, he would probably pay more for her.

Putting the phone back in his pocket without taking the call, Bo reached into the backseat to hold his hand in front of Maddie's face.

To his relief, he felt her warm breath. Good. He figured he'd deliver her tomorrow. Maybe he'd call Earl Ray later just to keep the bastard from calling him all the time.

Right now Bo just wanted some time alone with his

former fiancée. As much as he didn't want to admit it, he'd never gotten over Maddie. Since she'd left town, there hadn't been anyone else who'd interested him for more than a night or two.

As he turned south on Highway 191, he kicked up his speed to seventy, wishing Montana hadn't done away with its no-speed-limit law—especially up in this part of the state, where there was nothing but open country for miles on end.

He'd had all afternoon to figure out where to take her. Whitehorse gave way to rolling prairie dotted with antelope and cattle. The full moon perched in the starry sky illuminated the countryside, making everything seem surreal as he sped along the open highway.

Bo could see the dark silhouette of the Little Rockies in the distance. It was the only distinguishing feature in the area, a landmark that could be seen for miles. He got a kick out of the fact that Lewis and Clark had thought the mountains were the Rockies and had to rename them the Little Rockies after they found the real thing.

Behind him, Bo noticed a set of headlights. He didn't think too much about it, but he decided to take the back way to the cabin his friend Cody's family had in the Missouri Breaks. He needed to stop and take care of Maddie first, though. She could be coming to at any time. He didn't kid himself that when she regained consciousness she would be hell on wheels.

As the turnoff appeared in his headlights Bo slowed, noting that the vehicle behind him also braked. He watched in his rearview mirror as the older model pickup turned onto the same road he'd taken.

He still didn't think much of it since he recognized

it as belonging to Buck Jones. Buck had a friend who lived down this road. Bo sped up, leaving Buck behind.

Over the next rise, Bo couldn't see the lights from the pickup behind him. He took the first turnoff he found. It dropped down into a coulee of scrub pine. He cut the lights and engine and waited for Buck to go by.

As soon as he saw the pickup disappear down the road, he popped the trunk lid and got out to get the duct tape. Once he had Maddie bound up, she would be all his, he thought with relish.

As he started to dig around in the dark for the duct tape, he heard the worn backseat springs groan.

Bo froze. Maddie was awake.

MADDIE CAME TO SLOWLY. Her cheek hurt, and her head throbbed. At first she didn't know where she was, but as the car rolled over a bump and slowed, it all came back to her.

Bo. She cracked one eye open and saw she was in the back of his car. From where she lay, she was able to see Bo behind the wheel, his Western hat cocked back. From what she could tell, the passenger seat was empty. That was a relief. He was alone.

Without moving, she glanced around for her purse but didn't see it. There was trash on the floorboard and an unpleasant smell that she didn't even want to speculate on.

She didn't dare move as he stopped the car. Closing her eyes tight, she'd waited. She knew Bo had something in mind. Even if he planned to kill her, he wouldn't do it quickly. That wasn't his style.

She told herself that she had the advantage in that he didn't know she was conscious.

His car door opened and she tensed, expecting him to open the back door to pull her out. Instead, she heard the trunk lid come up. Bo had left the driver's side door open as he walked back to the trunk.

She had to find her purse—and the knife inside it. The dome light was burned out, but the full moon shone into the car.

Fortunately, with the trunk lid up, Bo wouldn't be able to see her. She pushed herself up on one elbow, careful not to make a sound, and spotted her purse. As she listened to him rummaging around in the trunk, Maddie had considered jumping out and running, but she knew she wouldn't stand a chance against Bo. He was strong and fast, and she felt wobbly and weak from what he'd done to her.

No, her best hope was getting to her purse. She raised herself up further and could see it on the floor in front of the passenger seat. The flap on the shoulder bag was open. Had Bo found the steak knife? Or had the bag come open during the struggle?

If she could get the knife without Bo hearing her…

"MADDIE'S MISSING."

"What?" Shane blinked and fought to wake up. The phone had dragged him up out of the nightmare that had haunted his sleep for months. He glanced at the clock beside his bed. Just past eleven. "Jud? What in the—"

"Maddie. I've tried to locate her from here, but it's impossible, and even if I left right now, I couldn't get there fast enough, not if—"

"Whoa." Shane sat up in the bed, some of the dark fog of the dream burning off. "I'm not getting in the middle of this long-distance romance again. Stop leading this woman on." Shane started to hang up.

"Shane, no one has seen Maddie since she left the restaurant at about nine-thirty tonight. Her pickup is still parked across the street. She never made it home."

He heard real concern in his brother's voice.

"Her cousins are afraid something has happened to her," Jud continued. "The sheriff has a deputy out looking for her, but that country is so huge. She could be anywhere."

Shane groaned as he swung his feet over the side of the bed, the phone still at his ear. He couldn't help thinking about Bo Evans.

"Maybe a friend picked her up and she lost track of time."

"She would have called," Jud said. "The cousins are worried about some old boyfriend of hers. They say he's trouble. Shane, I'm afraid she's in danger. I know she's all wrong for me and me for her. But damn it, Shane, I don't want to see anything happen to her."

Shane swore under his breath.

"Please. You're trained in this sort of thing. I know if anyone can find her, you can. I promise I'll break it off as soon as I know she's all right. Just find her and make sure she's okay. That's all I ask."

"That's all you ask?" Shane said and swore. "Just give me the information." He wrote down the cousins' names and numbers. He already knew what Bo drove.

"The one cousin, Laci, lives over the restaurant with

her husband, Bridger. Unfortunately, neither of them heard anything or saw her lock up and leave."

"I'll see what I can do." He hung up. Shane was even more worried than Jud. He'd met Bo Evans. If Bo had Maddie, then God help her.

JERILYN TOPPED ANOTHER HILL. No sign of the car's red taillights. Was it possible he'd turned off? She had tried to stay back far enough that the cowboy wouldn't see she was following him. Now she realized that had been a mistake.

She thought about turning around and going back, but she had no idea which of the turnoffs he might have taken, so she kept going, thinking he might still be ahead of her.

The horizon filled with the dark fringe of pine trees. One of the roads headed up the side of the hill. She could see the bare bones of a house under construction. There were no lights on, no vehicles around. She turned in.

Her headlights moved across the grayed wood of an abandoned house. She turned around and noticed that she had a good view of the road she'd come down. He had to be behind her. He'd pulled off. Probably afraid she was following him. Maybe if she waited…

Jerilyn cut her lights, telling herself turning off had been impulsive and crazy—just like her. But from here she could see the road both to the north and south.

If she was right, he'd be coming up that road soon. She refused to think about what would happen if she was wrong. The bastard had her daughter. She couldn't let that man hurt her daughter, could she?

While she waited, Jerilyn realized that Maddie's cousins were bound to get worried when the girl didn't return home. They'd call the sheriff. The whole county would be looking for Maddie Cavanaugh.

Everyone would think she'd been kidnapped.

Maybe that was why the cowboy had grabbed Maddie. No, the way he'd taken her looked more personal than financial. From what Jerilyn could tell, Maddie had known him. And anyway, there wasn't any ransom money to get, right?

But Jerilyn couldn't help wondering what the owners of that nice restaurant might pay to get Maddie back.

It was just a random thought, she told herself. Just something to amuse herself while she waited. Kidnap her own daughter? What a crazy thought.

Bo FOUND THE DUCT TAPE and stood listening for the springs to groan again. Maybe Maddie had just stirred. It would take her a while to really come to, wouldn't it? And if she was conscious, wouldn't she have tried to get away by now?

He couldn't be sure. This Maddie was different from the one to whom he'd been engaged.

"Maddie Cavanaugh's all wrong for you," his mother had told him time and time again. "I know her mother and I've heard things about Maddie. Believe me, the girl's got some head problems. You don't want to be taking that on. A woman like that, you never know what she'll do."

Not that he ever paid any attention to his mother's advice. He'd seen how Arlene's life had gone, and he had no plan to mess his up in the same way. He wanted no part of farming, ranching or work of any kind. Nor did he really want to get married.

He'd only asked Maddie to marry him because he couldn't stand the thought of any other man being with her—and he'd stolen the engagement ring for her.

Now Maddie had changed. And so had his mother. Bo still couldn't believe that his own mother had put him out of the house. He'd once been her favorite. He could do nothing wrong. And then Arlene had met some stupid man and turned on her only son.

"You're twenty-five, Bo," she'd said the last time he'd seen her. "Do something with your life. Don't waste it. If there is one thing I've learned, it's that you're never too old to change. I'm doing this for your own good. Someday you'll thank me."

Bo had laughed. "When hell freezes over," he'd told her, enjoying the hurt he'd seen in her eyes.

But she hadn't relented, and he hated her for it just as he hated Maddie for what she'd done to him.

Bo realized he should have brought a flashlight. There used to be one in the trunk, but the batteries would probably be shot. He felt around, his hand brushing cool plastic. The flashlight. He tested it, putting his palm over the light end. If Maddie was playing possum, he was about to find out.

As he started to slam the trunk, he stopped himself. Cautiously, he moved around the side of the car. The backseat was in shadow, too dark to see if she was awake and just lying there waiting. He felt the hair rise on the back of his neck as he reached for the back-door handle on the passenger side—the side closest to her pretty little head.

MADDIE HAD HEARD the groan of the seat springs as she'd retrieved the knife from her purse, and she feared Bo had, too.

Lying back down, she curled around the steak knife and waited, her blood thrumming in her veins.

The door by her head suddenly swung open. She felt the cold night breeze rustle her hair, but she willed herself not to move.

She could feel Bo standing over her, staring down at her. She felt dirty just thinking of the way he would be looking at her.

She heard a snap and almost flinched as she sensed a flashlight beam flicker over her. She held her breath, anticipating his touch.

Still, when his warm palm brushed her shoulder, she winced. He must not have felt it, because his free hand moved over her shoulder and slowly down her arm as the dim flashlight beam wavered a little.

His hand slowed, then brushed across her left breast. Revulsion washed over her as his hand cupped her breast and squeezed.

It was all Maddie could do not to pull the knife and go for his throat. But she knew he had her at a disadvantage. With him behind her like he was, she knew he could see it coming. She had to wait.

He lifted his hand from her breast and the flashlight beam blinked out. With a groan, the door slammed shut. She had expected him to try to rape her. Now she didn't know what to think.

The other passenger door suddenly opened and Maddie heard a sound that took her only an instant to recognize.

Tape being ripped off a roll.

She knew it was now or never as he grabbed her ankles.

SHANE DROVE THROUGH the moonlit night toward Whitehorse, telling himself that Maddie would probably turn
up before he reached the city limits.

There was no traffic on the road at this hour. The
moon was huge as it hung in the sky.

He hoped Maddie had just gone off with a friend,
but every instinct told him it wasn't something Maddie
would do without letting her family know.

Whitehorse was dead. There were just a couple of
vehicles in front of the only bar still open at this hour
on a weekday night. Down the street, there was a lone
pickup parked across from the Northern Lights restaurant. Maddie's.

Shane parked and walked across the street to circle
the truck. To his relief he saw no sign of a struggle near
the truck: no blood, no scuff marks, no spilled contents
of a purse.

Cupping his hands over his eyes, he looked inside
the cab. Nothing out of the ordinary. Covering his hand
with his sleeve, he tried the door. Locked.

As he glanced toward the front door to the restaurant, he saw the light on inside and the woman waiting
anxiously for him.

She unlocked the door as he neared. "Are you Shane?"

He nodded.

"I'm Laci Cavanaugh Duvall, Maddie's cousin."

Shane took her hand. It was ice cold. "You called
the sheriff?"

She nodded. "My brother-in-law, Deputy Nick Giovanni, is out looking for Maddie. So is my husband, Bridger."

"Do they know about Bo Evans?"

She scowled. "Everyone knows about Bo Evans."

"Bo's been harassing Maddie lately. Did she tell you that?"

"She never said a word," Laci said, shaking her head and looking close to tears. "She said she saw him but that was all."

"Is it possible she went off with him?"

"No! She'd never go near him."

"They used to be engaged, I heard."

"That was a long time ago," Laci said. "For a while, Maddie was under his spell. Or should I say under his thumb?"

"Maybe she's fallen under it again."

Laci shook her head adamantly. "Bo abused her. She was going through something, and he took advantage of her vulnerability. But Maddie isn't that girl anymore. She's strong and determined. She'd never go back to Bo, and he knows it."

Shane liked Laci's conviction, but he also knew that sometimes people got caught up in things that were bad for them. He couldn't help but think of Kate and wonder what she was caught up in.

"We need to find out where Bo is," Shane said. "Your brother-in-law needs to question him right away."

"I was hoping Maddie was with your brother, Jud," Laci said. "I thought maybe he had come down from his movie shoot to surprise her."

"She's not with Jud."

"I know. I guess I just can't stand the thought that

she might be with Bo," Laci said. "Jud said you were a Texas Ranger. Can you help find her?"

He didn't tell her that he was on a medical leave or that he didn't feel up to this. If Maddie was in trouble, she needed someone who wasn't wounded both physically and emotionally.

Instead, Shane said, "I'll try. Can you get hold of your brother-in-law? Maybe he's already found Bo."

Laci pulled out her cell phone and stepped away for a moment, her free hand resting on the baby she carried inside her.

Shane couldn't bear the thought that Maddie might never know her niece or nephew—or vice versa.

"Nick has been looking for Bo," Laci said after she got off the phone. "The problem is Bo no longer has a permanent residence here. But Nick heard that three men driving a car with Arizona plates have been asking about how to find Bo. He's looking into that."

Shane thought of the two men he'd seen Bo with the night of the rodeo dance. They'd apparently found him.

"What about Bo's friends?"

"He has only one that I know of—Cody Barnes. He lives in a trailer over by the river," Laci said. "But I'm sure Nick has already talked to him."

"It won't hurt to talk to him again," Shane said, then asked for the directions to Cody's place and Laci's cellphone number.

As he left, Shane looked to the table where he'd had lunch earlier that day. He recalled the way the sunshine had streamed into the room from the front window and set fire to Maddie's hair. She had more red in her blond hair than her cousin. More fire in her than maybe any of them knew.

He could only hope that was true because he feared tonight Maddie might need all the strength she could muster.

MADDIE ROSE UP from the backseat of Bo's car, lunging as she thrust the knife. At the last second, she pulled to the right, unable to put the blade into another human being's heart. But the blade connected with flesh, and as Bo shrieked, she recoiled in horror at what she'd done.

"You bitch!" Bo screamed. A dark stain blossomed across his shirtsleeve, where she'd stabbed his upper arm. He stumbled backward into the darkness. "You crazy bitch! *You stabbed me!*"

With momentum still carrying her forward, Maddie stumbled from the car, dropping to one knee in the dirt, the knife in her hand. As Bo started to lunge for her, she brandished the knife to keep him back, still shocked by what she'd done.

"Are you friggin' crazy?" Bo demanded. He had dropped the flashlight at his feet. The beam cut a swath of pale light in his direction. He held up both hands in surrender, but Maddie wasn't fooled.

She knew that if he got the knife away from her, he'd use it on her. With relief, she saw that he didn't seem to be badly hurt. She'd only managed to make him more angry. But he was also scared of her, she saw, and realized she could use that to get away from him.

"Damn, Maddie, why did you have to go and do that?" he asked, sounding as shocked as she was that she'd actually cut him.

"This from the man who abducted me and nearly broke my jaw?" She abhorred violence, and yet here she was with a bloody steak knife in her hand.

She wanted to cry but knew if she did, Bo would see it as a sign of weakness. She held the knife in front of her, forcing him back another step.

"What else was I to do but kidnap you? You wouldn't talk to me. All I wanted to do was talk to you."

"I don't want to talk to you. I never wanted to see you again. Wasn't that clear enough?" Her anger scared her. She was shaking, still appalled that she'd stabbed him.

"How can you say that?" he whined. "I loved you."

She shook her head. "That wasn't love."

"Like you know all about love?" he said, getting angry again as he grabbed his upper arm and winced in pain. "You stabbed me!"

Maddie had seen that the car keys were still in the ignition. She edged backward to slam the car door and saw Bo tense.

"What are you doing, Maddie?" he asked warily.

She didn't answer as she moved toward the back of the car.

"I don't blame you for being a little upset with me, but you need to get me to a doctor. I'm going to bleed to death if you don't."

She said nothing as she slammed the trunk, keeping the knife so he could see it.

"Maddie, you know how I am," he whined. "If you had just talked to me…"

She edged around the car. "Stay where you are."

He nodded as though the idea of coming after her had never crossed his mind.

She knew once she got behind the wheel, she would have to move quickly. It worried her that Bo seemed to be giving up so easily. It wasn't like him.

At the open driver-side door, she glanced at him over the roof of the car. He was standing where she'd left him, which surprised her.

"You're just going to leave me out here to die?" he asked, his voice laced with fury.

When she and Bo were together, his mood swings used to scare her. Watching him now, she was even more terrified by how quickly he could change. She knew if she didn't get away from him tonight, he would hurt her. Hurt her bad.

She ducked into the car, slammed the door and hit the door locks as she reached for the key in the ignition.

To her shock, the passenger-side door flew open as the engine turned over, and belatedly she realized why Bo had stayed where he was. He'd known that the locks didn't work.

She shifted the car into First and hit the gas, but Bo managed to get in. The flashlight hit her in the side of the face and knocked her against the window. Stunned by the blow, her foot came up off the gas pedal, the car lurching forward.

Bo was on her before she could get control again. He grabbed the steering wheel with one hand and harshly twisted the knife from her hand with the other.

Pinning her against the driver-side door, he shut off the engine and slammed his foot down on the brake. The car came to a jarring stop, throwing her forward into the steering wheel.

His hands were on her throat as he banged her head against the door window and screamed obscenities.

Maddie felt her eyes bulge, her throat rasping as she frantically tried to fight him off and breathe.

"Stupid bitch. Stupid damned bitch," Bo cursed, his eyes wild with rage.

She felt blackness encroaching on her vision. Her hand found the door handle, but to her disappointment, the door refused to open. Unlike the passenger-side door, this one had locked.

As she felt herself slipping away, her other hand reached for Bo. She raked her fingernails down his face, determined to fight him till the brutal end.

EARL RAY PITTS didn't believe in coincidences. When he'd gone by Buck Jones's house, he'd found his stolen car in the drive, but no sign of Jerilyn—or Buck Jones.

When he'd tried to get hold of Bo Evans, the little bastard didn't answer.

Something was up. Earl Ray could feel it.

"Let's go," he told Dude and Bubba when he got back at the motel. He grabbed the remote control and shut off the television. "What's your problem, Dude? Don't you have cable TV at home?"

"Hey, I'm going to miss one of my favorite shows."

"What did you bring me to eat?" Bubba asked.

Earl Ray tossed him a bag of chips from the vending machine outside and headed for the door.

"Where are we going?" Dude asked as they followed.

"We're going to find Bo Evans." He didn't tell Dude that the cell phone he gave Bo had a GPS on it. The phone and Bo Evans were to the south in what was called the Missouri Breaks. As for Jerilyn—who the hell knew where that broad was?

Earl Ray climbed in the passenger side of the rented SUV and ordered Dude to drive south. Bubba slid into the back.

As they left Whitehorse, Earl Ray couldn't help but think about the first time he'd laid eyes on Jerilyn. She'd been sitting at a bar, playing with a lock of her blond hair the way teenagers do. She'd seemed young and exciting.

It wasn't until later he realized she was neither. She was a woman trapped in the past. A girl who never grew up. Earl Ray hadn't understood it until he'd seen the note in her purse. He was no psychiatrist, but he'd put his money on her problems having something to do with the baby she gave up.

"I thought we were looking for Jerilyn," Dude said, as they left town and the country began to change.

"Just drive and try not to think." His instincts had kept him alive this long. For Earl Ray that was good enough. He'd been right about Jerilyn coming to Montana. He knew he would be right about Bo Evans.

JERILYN MUST HAVE DOZED. She sat up with a start, blinded by a set of headlights coming up the hill on the other road. For a moment, she thought she was still on the way to Montana.

Automatically she hunkered down in the seat, even though she was sure the driver of the car wouldn't notice the pickup parked beside the abandoned house.

The car drove past, silhouetted in the moonlight. The cowboy and his old junker. He wasn't wearing his hat, she noted. Nor was there any sign of Maddie as the car disappeared over the rise.

Was it possible he'd left Maddie back up the road?

Jerilyn doubted it. She was all too familiar with men like the one who'd grabbed her daughter. They dealt in meanness and pain. It was what they knew, what they reveled in. The man who'd grabbed Maddie had some reason he'd chanced taking her off the street. He wouldn't have dumped her that quickly. No, a man like that wouldn't be finished with her already. She was putting her money on Maddie still being in that car. Otherwise, wouldn't the cowboy have gone back toward town?

Jerilyn waited a few heartbeats, then started the pickup. The moon seemed brighter now. She could make out shapes even in the distance. The cowboy would get suspicious if her headlights suddenly showed up in his rearview mirror again. She'd have to drive without lights and remember not to touch her brakes.

Tentatively she pulled back onto the road. With the moon high and bright, it was almost like daylight. She sped up as her confidence grew. Over the next rise, she saw the cowboy's taillights and, keeping them in view, followed at a safe distance.

As she drove, Jerilyn let her mind wander. It circled back to an earlier thought, one that had nagged at her until she had fallen asleep. *What was in this for her?* She could be risking her life. Shouldn't she get something other than gratitude and maybe her name and photo in the paper for saving Maddie?

It didn't seem fair. She was flat broke and needed all the help she could get. The rest of the world had been so much luckier in life than her.

"Buck won't call the sheriff right away," Jerilyn said aloud, working out the details as she drove under the vast canopy of the Big Sky. "He'll be a little concerned about his pickup. After all, he is a man. But he won't call the sheriff. Not with my car sitting in front of his house. He trusts me—or at least wants to. He'll wait a day or two. Maybe more since he's the kind of man who still has faith in women. The fool."

Ahead, Jerilyn saw the taillights glow brighter as the cowboy hit his brakes. She didn't dare touch her own. Shifting down, she slowed the pickup as the car ahead of her turned off onto a narrow road and disappeared.

She coasted to a stop up the road from where he'd turned off and pulled over in a stand of pines. Cutting the engine, she rolled down her window. The only sound was the tick of the pickup's engine as it cooled.

As she dropped open the glove box, Jerilyn let out a pleased cry of surprise before she carefully pulled out the pistol.

She'd known Buck was practical. Organized, too, it seemed, because behind the .22 was a full box of ammunition.

THE TAPE AROUND Maddie's wrists and ankles was cutting off her circulation. She had tried not to panic at having the duct tape over her mouth. When Bo had finally stopped choking her, she'd gasped for breath, her throat on fire and her lungs crying out for oxygen.

He'd held her down, taping first her wrists, then her ankles, all the time his weight painfully pressing her down.

"Bo, think about what you're doing," she'd said, trying to reason with him even though she knew it was futile. "No good can come of this."

He'd slapped a piece of tape over her mouth. She was filled with terror at the thought of what Bo would do with her now. He'd crossed some line and they both knew it.

As the car rolled to a stop, Maddie saw a wall of dark pines outside the window. The front seat creaked. She heard Bo sigh. Was he starting to realize how foolish this had been?

The driver-side door let out a tortured groan as it opened. Maddie felt a shaft of even colder night air rush in and braced herself.

The back car door opened. She closed her eyes, not wanting to even look at him. Her face hurt from where he'd hit her, first with his fist and then with the flashlight. Her throat felt raw and bruised, and it was all she could do to fight back tears of both pain and fear.

She no longer had any doubt about the seriousness of her situation. The flashlight had split the skin over her right eye. She could still taste the blood and feel it clotted on her cheek and eyelashes. But at least it was no longer running down into her eye and blinding her.

She fought for calm. Bo fed off fear, and she didn't need to give him any more reason to hurt her.

As she felt his hands slip under her shoulders, she tried not to recoil at his touch. He dragged her out and stood her up, leaning her against the side of the car as he bent to bring his shoulder up under her, then carried her like a sack of potatoes.

She caught sight of a small, dark cabin and realized she should have known where he would bring her. Just the sight of the cabin triggered memories of the times Bo had brought her here when they'd been engaged. The cabin was isolated and seldom used. No phone. Miles from another human being. Maddie willed herself not to think about that now. Bo would want her to panic and try to get away.

At the door to the cabin, he stood her up against the wall. She watched him feel around on the ledge for the key, praying someone in the Barnes family had moved it and realizing as he found the key that it wouldn't have mattered. Bo would have simply broken a window to get in.

As he unlocked and opened the door, Maddie watched, knowing she stood no chance against him with her ankles and wrists bound.

A light blinked on inside, and Bo was in front of her again. Their eyes met for an instant, and Maddie cringed at the sick anticipation she saw there.

Lifting her, he carried her inside and dropped her unceremoniously on a weathered, old couch. She strained against the tape as she heard him go back out to the car, pop the trunk again, then slam it shut. What could he have gone back for?

Her question was answered moments later when he returned to sit down on the edge of the coffee table in front of the couch.

Her heart dropped at the sight of what he held in his hands. Hedge trimmers. The blades were long and shiny, and they looked sharp as razors.

A small sound of terror escaped from behind her taped mouth as Bo reached down and grabbed her blouse, ripping it open.

Smiling, he slipped one cold, thin blade under the front of her bra. "Snip, snip," he said, and snapped the blades closed, cutting her bra and exposing her breasts.

Chapter Nine

As Shane was leaving the Northern Lights restaurant, he noticed a man coming down the street. What caught his eye was the way the man was looking at Maddie's truck.

The man drew closer, then started to turn around and go back the way he'd come.

"Just a minute!" Shane called out as he strode down the sidewalk to him.

"Yes?" The man was in his fifties, wearing worn jeans and boots and a canvas jacket that was stained with blood left over from hunting season. Or grease. Or both.

"I noticed you're interested in that pickup," Shane said motioning to Maddie's truck.

The man laughed, sounding embarrassed. "I thought it was mine. Same year. Looked like the same color from a distance."

"You've lost your truck?" It was clear that the man had had a few drinks, but he didn't appear drunk enough to have lost his pickup.

"My girlfriend borrowed it to go out to dinner." He squinted at Shane. "I don't think I've seen you around."

"Shane Corbett. I'm staying out at the—"

"Trails West Ranch," the man said, nodding and smiling. "You must be the son who's a Texas Ranger, the one who got shot." He grinned. "Noticed you limping a little. Name's Buck Jones." He extended his hand. "Sorry, but there are no secrets in a town this size."

"I guess not," Shane said with a laugh, although he disagreed. Everyone had secrets, and small towns hoarded them. "You say your girlfriend borrowed your truck?"

"My girlfriend. I guess you could call her that," he said, smiling shyly. "I was a little worried about her. I could see how nervous she was." Buck seemed to notice Shane's questioning look. "She was going to meet her daughter at the restaurant. Her daughter waitresses there."

Shane's ears perked up. "Which waitress is that?"

"Maddie Cavanaugh."

"I thought Maddie's mother wasn't around here anymore." Hadn't Jud told him there was bad blood between Maddie and her mother?

Buck was shaking his head. "Not that mother. Jerilyn, the woman who has my truck, is Maddie's birth mother."

"Maddie was adopted?" Jud hadn't mentioned this.

"Apparently so," Buck said. "Jerilyn gave her up at birth and hadn't seen her since. She was going to the restaurant to introduce herself. I wanted to go with her, but she said she had to do it alone."

Shane couldn't believe what he was hearing. This definitely put a whole new spin on things. "Then you don't know if this Jerilyn…"

"Larch. Jerilyn Larch from Arizona."

Arizona? "You don't know if she told her daughter who she was?"

Buck shook his head. "I hope things went as she'd wanted."

"Your truck isn't the only thing missing," Shane said. "No one has seen Maddie since she left the restaurant tonight. Her cousins are worried about her. I think you'd better talk to the sheriff. His deputy, Nick Giovanni, is out looking for Maddie. If Jerilyn and Maddie are together…"

Buck nodded his head. "I'll give the dispatcher a call and have Nick be on the lookout for my pickup. They probably just went for a ride together to talk."

Shane wished he believed that.

THE WALK TO the turnoff where Jerilyn had seen the car disappear didn't take her but a few minutes. At the mouth of the narrow side road stood a pine tree with a small wooden sign tacked to it.

She had to step closer to read it. *Barnes.* The road into the Barneses' place looked as if no one had been here for a while. Grass grew ankle deep, and there was only the one set of tracks in the dust from where the cowboy's car had gone in.

Jerilyn hadn't walked far up the road when she saw a light glowing through the pines. A little farther and she saw the bastard's beat-up old car.

She caught her breath and rubbed her knee, which she'd scraped when she fell down just moments before on the road in to the cabin. Her hand was also scraped and bleeding, and she felt a little nauseous now that she was here, since she didn't have any kind of a plan.

Inching toward the light burning in the cabin, Jerilyn figured she'd take a look in the window and then decide what to do.

As she passed the car, she had a thought. The moonlight glimmered off the keys dangling from the ignition. Jerilyn eased the car door open, cringing at the sound it made.

Her thought had been to start the engine. The cowboy would come running out, and Maddie could get away. But as Jerilyn began to slide behind the wheel, she spotted the knife on the driver-side floorboard. Picking it up, she saw a smear of blood on the blade and quickly dropped it.

"Oh hell," she whispered, as she looked toward the house. Her pulse began to pound when she realized that Maddie might not be able to escape on her own.

Jerilyn pulled the keys from the ignition, pocketed them and slid back out, leaving the car door open so that the noise of closing it wouldn't call attention to her. She shivered as she moved toward the cabin, aware that this might be the craziest thing she'd ever done.

But her baby girl was in there.

And Maddie's great aunt and uncle would be so happy if Jerilyn saved her from this bastard.

Pulling the .22 from her pocket, she wondered just how grateful they would be. Enough that they'd at least buy her a bus ticket out of town.

She couldn't hear any sounds coming from the cabin, but she wasn't taking any chances. At the window, she leaned against the side of the log building to catch her breath. The higher altitude was killing her. That and the lousy condition she was in from years of boozing, smoking and bad eating habits.

After a few moments, she slid closer to the window and peered in through a crack in the curtain. Her fingers tightened on the gun in her hand.

The cowboy stood over Maddie, who lay bound and gagged on a couch in the center of the room, her shirt open. He held what looked like hedge trimmers and was snapping the blades in the air over Maddie's bare breasts.

Jerilyn thought of all the men she'd known who seemed just like this one. Seeing her daughter's terrified expression, she felt sick to her stomach as she gripped the .22 and edged toward the door.

SHANE CALLED LACI from his truck. "Was Maddie the only waitress working at the restaurant tonight?"

"Yes."

"Did you see her after her last customer left?" he asked.

"I came back down for a minute earlier. Why?"

"Did she seem upset?" Shane asked.

"No, and I would have been able to tell. Why? Did one of the customers give her a hard time or something?"

Shane repeated the description Buck had given him of Jerilyn Larch and asked if Laci knew if Maddie had waited on the woman.

"Now that you mention it, I remember there was a woman who fits that description," Laci said. "She ordered three appetizers just before closing. I glanced out from the kitchen, a little surprised that the woman was alone."

So she was alone. "Did you see Maddie talking to her?"

"Yes."

"Is there any chance Maddie might have left with her?"

"*What?* Why would Maddie do that? I'm sure she didn't know her. She wasn't local. Why are you asking me all these questions about this woman?"

Shane rubbed a hand over his face. "Was Maddie adopted?"

"*Adopted?* No, of course not."

"You know that for a fact?"

"No, I mean, I remember my aunt had a hard pregnancy. She had to have a lot of bed rest so we didn't see much of her."

He could hear Laci wavering. "It's possible that this Jerilyn Larch might have told Maddie that she was her birth mother."

"*What?* Is that true?"

"I don't know. What would Maddie have done?" he asked.

"I… I don't know. Maddie's been through so much." Laci was crying. "Where is this woman?"

"Apparently she and the pickup she borrowed are also missing but the sheriff's department has been notified. They're looking for the pickup she was driving."

"You think Maddie might be with her?" Laci asked.

"Maybe. I'm going over to Buck's now. Apparently Jerilyn Larch left her car at his house. I'm hoping there is something in it to give us a clue where the woman has gone."

Bo Evans felt the cell phone vibrate in his pocket. This was the fourth time in a matter of minutes, and it was getting damned annoying.

Worried that something might have happened to change Earl Ray's mind about the deal they'd made, Bo swore and laid the hedge clippers on the coffee table in front of the couch.

He stroked a hand over Maddie's bare breasts, pinching a nipple, before he reached into his pocket and took out the phone. Bo figured he'd keep the phone after this was over. He couldn't afford one of his own. Hell, he could hardly afford gas for his old beater car.

The messages were all the same. Except for the last one. "Listen, you sniveling little bastard. You stop whatever the hell it is you're doing and call me. *Now.* If I don't hear from you, I'm going to come looking for you. You don't want that to happen—trust me."

Bo wanted to tell Earl Ray to take a flying leap, but he needed the money the man had promised him. All he had to do was give him Maddie, which he intended to do. First thing in the morning.

"I gotta take this, sweetheart," he said to Maddie. "Don't worry, I won't be long—and then we can have some fun. I know you can't wait." He laughed as he left the room. No reason to let Maddie know what he had planned for her with Earl Ray.

In the back room, he hit speed dial. Earl Ray thought of everything. The man answered on the first ring.

"Why the hell haven't you been answering my calls?"

"I've been a little busy," Bo said, trying to keep his voice down. "You want Maddie, don't you?"

"What are you saying? That you have her?"

"That's right."

"Then why haven't you called?"

Bo looked to the ceiling. He wanted to say, "I'm not

ready to hand her over yet." Instead, he said, "I was thinking of renegotiating the deal we made, since it seems you want her pretty bad."

"You should give that some thought."

"I have. Double the money and I'll bring her to you tomorrow morning."

"If you have her, why not deliver her tonight?"

Bo considered. "Because I already have her, but I'm not in town. It has to be in the morning or no deal."

"You really are a stupid bastard," Earl Ray said.

"Hey, no name calling or the deal is off." Bo held his breath, afraid for a moment that Earl Ray had hung up on him. "You want her, up the ante."

"Tomorrow morning. But leave your phone on. Don't make me leave any more messages."

Bo heard something in the man's voice that told him Earl Ray wasn't bluffing. He was anxious to get back to Maddie, but, he reminded himself, they had all night. This time tomorrow, he'd be in the money after a fulfilling night with his former fiancée. Life didn't get any better than this.

"You can have Maddie at ten."

"Let's make it eight. I'm tired of waiting."

Eight? That still gave Bo plenty of time with Maddie. "Sure, why not?"

JERILYN HAD WAITED until she saw the cowboy put down the hedge trimmers to check his cell phone and then leave the room.

On the couch, Maddie strained to loosen the tape binding her. She managed to get into a sitting position, glancing over her shoulder toward the back of the cabin.

Jerilyn could only assume by the frantic way Maddie worked that she could hear the man talking on the cell phone and knew she didn't have much time left before he came back.

Now or never, Jerilyn thought, as she reached for the doorknob and turned it. She slipped inside, closing the door quietly behind her. She could hear the man in a room at the back talking quietly on the phone.

The couch was only a few steps away, but Jerilyn was afraid the floor would creak or that the man would finish his call too quickly.

As she stepped carefully in front of the couch, Maddie looked up, and her eyes widened in shock. Jerilyn pressed a finger to her lips, her gaze going to the hallway that led to the room where the man was still on the phone.

Maddie's gaze flicked from Jerilyn's face to the .22 gripped in her hand. Jerilyn hurriedly pocketed the gun and picked up the hedge trimmers from the coffee table. Moving to Maddie, she opened the trimmers and worked the blades between the girl's taped ankles.

The tape was thick, and it took a few moments before she could cut through it. Maddie held up her bound hands behind her, trying to pull the tape apart so Jerilyn could get the blades between them. As the tape sliced apart, Maddie reached at once for the duct tape across her mouth.

Jerilyn touched her fingers to her own lips in warning.

Maddie nodded in understanding, then ripped off the tape and got to her feet. Jerilyn showed her the car keys she'd taken, and Maddie nodded again.

As they headed for the door, Jerilyn pulled the .22 from her pocket. Maddie, she noticed, had picked up the hedge trimmers and tried to cover her nakedness before making her way out the door.

SHANE WALKED AROUND the old Buick with the Arizona plates once before he opened the unlocked passenger-side door. The car's old-dirty-socks smell rose to his nostrils and he grimaced. From what he could tell, Jerilyn Larch had been living in the car.

His worry increased as he opened the glove box and took out the car registration. The Buick was registered to an Earl Ray Pitts of Bullhead City, Arizona.

Had she borrowed the car? Stolen it? And where was Mr. Pitts? He thought about the two men he'd seen with Bo Evans. Definitely not from Whitehorse.

Unfortunately, he found nothing in the car to help him locate Jerilyn or Earl Ray Pitts. As he was leaving, he called the sheriff's department, and the dispatcher put him through to Nick. Shane passed along what he knew to the deputy, including the plate number on the car.

"Any luck turning up Bo Evans?" he asked the deputy.

"Unfortunately, no. Bo's bad news. You still think Maddie's with him? What about this woman who claims to be her mother?"

"Either way I don't think Maddie left of her own free will."

"I checked with Bo's mother," Nick said. "She hasn't seen him. He isn't staying with her. She made that pretty clear. And his friend Cody swears he hasn't seen him."

Shane turned down a side road. Cody Barnes's trailer appeared in the pickup's headlights. "I'm on my way to talk to Cody myself. You have my cell number. Call me if you hear anything."

Shane disconnected as he pulled into the drive and cut his lights. A beat-up SUV sat in front of the lit-up trailer.

As he walked up to the trailer, Shane heard the throb of loud music. He didn't bother to knock. He just swung open the door catching Cody by surprise.

Cody wore a knitted skull cap down to his eyes, worn jeans and a dirty, oversized sweatshirt with Got A Quarter? across the front.

Shane strode to the boom box and yanked out the cord, sending the trailer into a sudden deafening silence.

"What the hell?" Cody yelled.

He was standing in front of the stove, a spatula in his hand and what smelled like hamburger sizzling in a skillet in front of him.

"I'm looking for Bo Evans," Shane said.

"He's not here. I already told the deputy that. Who the hell are you?"

"Shane Corbett. Bo's been staying with you, right?" he asked, stepping down the hall past two clothes-strewn bedrooms.

"He had no place to go, so I said he could stay for a while." Cody sounded defensive. "But I haven't seen him tonight, okay?" The burger in the skillet began to burn.

"If Bo isn't planning to stay here tonight, where would he go?"

"Beats me." Cody looked as if he'd been at the bar earlier tonight.

"You just told me that Bo's options are so limited that he's staying with you. Where would he go if he wanted to be alone with his girlfriend?"

"Maddie?" Cody looked shocked. He shut off the burner and moved the skillet off to one side. "They're back together?"

"Why wouldn't they be?"

"Are you kidding? She dumped him, said she never wanted to see him again."

"Maybe that's why Maddie's cousins are worried about her and asked me to find her. Where would Bo take her so they could be completely alone? If you know where he is and don't tell me and he does something to Maddie—"

Cody's expression changed. "He used to take her to my folks' cabin down in the Breaks. I'm sure he still knows where we hide the key."

GRAYSON WOKE TO find the spot next to him in the bed empty. He glanced at the clock, saw how late it was and went to find his wife.

He found Kate standing in the living room staring out into the night. Her slim body was silhouetted against the night sky, her shoulders slumped, her head down, her fingers pressed against the glass.

For so long, he'd turned away. Pretended nothing was wrong. He'd given her space, praying she would come to him when she was ready.

But Grayson realized he could no longer do that. He loved this woman. She was in obvious pain, and he couldn't let her suffer alone any longer.

As he stepped toward her, he feared she was about to break his heart, but nothing could stop him. Not this time.

She didn't seem to hear him come up behind her and

started at the touch of his fingertips on her shoulder. As she turned, he pulled her in, holding her tightly to him. She felt stiff at first, almost breakable. Then with a moan, she softened in his arms, leaning into him, her arms coming around him, holding on as if against a fierce, cold wind.

They stood like that for a long time, neither speaking. Grayson waited until he felt some of her strength return. Then, taking her shoulders in his hands, he stepped back to look into her eyes.

"Tell me," he said, his voice a hoarse whisper.

KATE GAZED INTO her husband's wonderful, open face, tears brimming in her eyes.

"Tell me," he repeated, his hands cupping her shoulders and tightening slightly, his gaze holding hers captive.

She swallowed, afraid yet unable to keep this from him any longer.

"It's just you and me," he said.

She nodded and bit her lip at the compassion she saw in his expression. "Could we sit down?"

He led her over to the couch and sat next to her, holding her hands in his.

She took a deep breath and let it out. "I... I had a baby." The words tumbled out, falling over each other. "It was the year Dad died. I was so alone, so scared, still mourning my father's death and the loss of the ranch. I felt like everything I'd loved was gone."

"What about the father of the baby?" he asked quietly.

"He was otherwise engaged," she said, guilt-ridden

for what she'd done to all of their lives. "I was so selfish, Grayson, so stupid."

"No, Kate," he said, emotion making his voice tight as he pulled her to him. "You were young and obviously needed someone. Honey, I'm so sorry."

She was crying now, needing to let it all out. "The baby's father…"

Grayson pulled back to look at her, his eyes widened a little as if he knew what she was going to say.

"He still lives around here," she said, and felt him tense. "I hated him for not standing by me when I needed him. Hated him and loved him."

"Have you seen him since you've been back?"

She nodded.

"Are you still in love with him?"

She heard how hard the words were for Grayson to say. "No." She'd said it too quickly. "I don't know how I feel about him," she said truthfully. "But I do know how I feel about you. *I love you.* This isn't about him."

Grayson studied her openly. "What *is* it about, Kate?"

"The baby I gave up twenty-six years ago. I have to find her."

Chapter Ten

Once outside the cabin, Jerilyn ran to the car, anxious to get away and fearful the cowboy could come busting out of the house at any time.

She had the gun, but she'd also seen the look in that man's eyes. She wasn't sure the .22 would stop him before he took it away from her.

Sliding behind the steering wheel, Jerilyn inserted the key into the ignition as Maddie opened the passenger-side door and awkwardly climbed in with the hedge trimmers gripped in both her hands.

"You all right?" Jerilyn asked, noticing that Maddie seemed a little dazed.

But she nodded and slammed the door as Jerilyn started the engine and threw the car into Reverse.

"Who are you?"

Jerilyn shot her a look as she backed the car up and bumped into a small pine tree. "My name's Jerilyn Larch." She shifted into first gear and glanced toward the cabin. She imagined the cowboy had heard the car engine, raced into the living room and discovered that Maddie was gone.

"Jerilyn Larch?" Maddie repeated blankly as if trying to place the name.

As she hit the gas, Jerilyn saw the cowboy come flying out the front door.

"The door locks don't work," Maddie said, her voice high as the man lunged for the car, grabbing the handle on the passenger-side door.

Jerilyn watched her daughter grip the hedge trimmers in her hands, ready to run them through the man if he managed to get the door open.

But the car was moving too fast. He couldn't get his footing. Still he held on, letting the car drag him along the bumpy road. Jerilyn knew how to put an end to this. She cut the wheel toward a stand of ponderosa pines along the edge of the narrow lane.

There was a loud thud and a cry as the man was nailed by one tree and then another.

When Jerilyn looked in the rearview mirror, she saw him lying unmoving on the side of the road and looking like nothing more than a bundle of dirty clothing. Served him right.

"Who was that man?" she asked.

"Bo Evans." Maddie's voice sounded hoarse as she glanced over her shoulder to where the man lay beside the road.

Jerilyn had seen the bruises on her neck. "Your boyfriend?"

"Former. A low point in my life."

Jerilyn nodded. "I hear ya." She thought about Earl Ray and realized he was no better than this Bo Evans. "I thought I saw a jacket behind the seat."

Maddie reached back to get it. Jerilyn watched her

glance again to where Bo lay in a crumpled heap and then quickly turn to the front as she pulled the jacket on and zipped it up, covering her nakedness.

Jerilyn sped up, wondering what she was going to do now that she had her daughter.

MADDIE DIDN'T WANT to think about Bo Evans as she looked over at the woman behind the wheel. As a precaution she leaned the hedge trimmers against the seat within easy reach.

She realized that Jerilyn had been in the restaurant just before closing. She'd eaten alone at the table by the window. She'd also left a very large tip. Too large a tip.

Maddie remembered that she had felt the woman watching her. Jerilyn had given her the creeps just as she did now, even though Maddie knew she should be grateful. The woman had saved her from Bo.

"How did you find me?" Maddie asked.

The blonde glanced over at her for a moment. "I saw him grab you outside the restaurant. There wasn't anyone around to help, so I followed the car."

The explanation seemed plausible enough. So why didn't she feel safe?

Her uneasy feeling amped up when Jerilyn turned south instead of heading back toward town.

"Whitehorse is back the other way," Maddie said, reminding herself that the woman had said earlier that she wasn't from around here. She didn't know the area.

"I have to get my pickup. It's just up the road. It was faster to take his car and make sure he couldn't use it to come after us," Jerilyn said. "Not that he's going anywhere ever again."

Maddie thought of the body she'd seen beside the road. Was Bo really dead? She tried to feel something but came up empty.

Everything about this felt all wrong, she thought, as she looked at the woman behind the wheel, a woman she'd never seen before tonight. Why would a complete stranger risk her life to save her?

And what woman just happened to carry around a .22 pistol?

"Relax," Jerilyn said, smiling over at her as if she could feel Maddie's growing anxiety. "I'm a friend."

She had her doubts about that.

"So what did you do to tick off this Bo Evans?" Jerilyn asked as she drove.

Maddie bristled. "Nothing. He was born that way. I just made the mistake of thinking for a while that I deserved being mistreated." She realized that was probably the most honest she'd ever been about her time with Bo.

"I know just what you mean. My ex, Earl Ray, he could be such a bastard. But then he'd be real sweet, you know?"

Maddie knew. Like some of the women Maddie had met in her support group, Jerilyn had the look of an abused woman. The dullness in the eyes. The lines on her face were a sign of a lot of hard miles. The gravelly whiskey voice. This woman had spent some quality time down on her luck.

She watched Jerilyn glance in the rearview mirror as if afraid they were being followed.

"You have any idea who he called back there?" Jerilyn asked.

Maddie had forgotten about the call Bo had made.

She'd been too busy trying to get away. "I wasn't paying any attention."

"I heard him say something like, 'You can have her in the morning.' Have any idea what that might have been about?"

"No." Bo couldn't have been talking about her, could he?

Jerilyn shot her a worried look. "Is there anyone who might pay to get their hands on you?"

"Why would you even ask me that?"

"Because I heard your old boyfriend say something about negotiating more money for you."

Maddie stared at the woman. Her head ached from being banged around by Bo and exhaustion dragged at her. She just wanted to go home, get a hot bath, go to bed and put all of this behind her.

Jerilyn slowed the car and turned into the pines. For a minute, Maddie didn't see the older pickup parked off the road. It was the same year as her own and almost the same color. Jerilyn parked next to the truck and shut off the lights and engine.

"We'll take my pickup from here." She glanced over at Maddie. "That your purse on the floor? Grab it and come on."

Maddie gripped the hedge trimmers and didn't move. The plates on the pickup were local, but Jerilyn had said she was from Arizona. So whose truck was it?

"Why don't you drive?" Jerilyn asked as she handed her the keys.

Maddie didn't take them. Every instinct told her not to get into that pickup with this woman.

Jerilyn reached into her pocket and pulled out the .22,

leveling it at Maddie's head. "I need you to do what I say, okay? The last thing I want to do is hurt you."

"I don't understand. What is it you want from me?" Maddie asked, hearing the tears on the edge of her words. She'd been through so much tonight, and now this?

"We need to talk," Jerilyn said. "That's all. Then I'll get you home safe and sound. Let's just go someplace where we don't have to worry about anyone bothering us."

Who would bother them? "Talk about what?"

The blonde only smiled and motioned with the gun for Maddie to take the keys and purse and get out of the car.

SHANE DROVE THE two-lane highway through rolling grasslands silvered by the moonlight. The land stretched to the far reaches of the horizon, unbroken except for the black etched outline of the Little Rockies off to the west.

His headlights picked up several sets of eyes ahead. He slowed and saw a half-dozen deer grazing in the barrow pit. One of the deer bolted across the road, bounding through the path of the pickup's headlights, just inches in front of his grill.

Once past the deer, Shane sped up again, feeling the night slipping away and his fears for Maddie growing with each tick of the clock. Over the next hill, he spotted a large herd of antelope, their hides gleaming white and gold in the moonlight. The animals looked as if they should have been in Africa not Montana.

He hadn't seen another car since he left Whitehorse, which wasn't that surprising for the time of the night and

where he was: No Man's Land. Right now he felt the full
weight of this isolated country. There hadn't been any
ranch lights for miles. No sense of another human. He
could see why this part of the state was said to be the
loneliest on earth.

As he neared the Missouri Breaks, the land rose in
rough limestone buttes and dipped into thousands of juniper– and scrub-pine–filled coulees. Ponderosa pines
stood along the buttes, etched black against the night sky.

"There's other ways to get there," Cody had said.
"Lots of back roads, passable as long as they're dry, but
this would be the fastest way to get to the cabin."

Shane felt the land dropping toward the river. Pine
trees popped up in his headlights like sentinels and
bluffs rose up, glowing in the moonlight. He felt as
though he were on another planet as he dipped down
into the rugged Breaks, all the time thinking that the
Barneses' cabin couldn't be in a more isolated place.

MADDIE STARED AT the gun in the woman's hand, then
climbed out of the car. Jerilyn slid out right after her,
and they walked over to the pickup.

"Why can't we talk here?" Maddie asked.

Jerilyn shook her head, and with the pistol trained
on her, climbed into the driver's side, pulling Maddie
after her.

"You do know how to drive a stick shift, don't you?"
Jerilyn asked, when Maddie had settled behind the
wheel. "After all, you are a Montana girl, although you
should have been an Arizona girl."

Maddie started the engine, her head swimming.

"Go back up the road we came on until you see the turnoff that will take us down to that fishing access."

Maddie hesitated until she felt the barrel of the .22 dig into her side. The road to the river would only take them deeper into the Breaks and farther from help.

"You would have liked growing up in Arizona."

"I don't think so."

Her answer seemed to upset Jerilyn. "You would have been happy in Arizona. I would have seen that you were happy."

Maddie's alarm shot up to a whole new level at the absurdity of this argument—and the fact that Jerilyn was now crying.

Maddie had suspected the woman wasn't stable. No normal woman would have followed Bo's car into the Breaks after seeing her waitress abducted.

"I would have been a good mother to you," Jerilyn said through her tears. "I really would have."

"I'm sure you would have," Maddie said, trying to calm the woman. "But I had a mother."

"That woman wasn't your mother," Jerilyn cried. *"I was!"*

As Maddie drove down the road deeper into the Breaks, she thought she'd misheard the woman.

"I'm your mother, your real mother, your birth mother."

She shot Jerilyn a look.

"Didn't you notice the resemblance?"

"There are a lot of women with our same coloring," Maddie said, and then wished she'd bitten her tongue.

"I knew you were my daughter the minute I saw you at the restaurant." She sounded proud of that. "I figured your adoptive parents wouldn't tell you. I asked the orderly about them. Your mother couldn't have babies so she took mine. I was only sixteen, just a baby myself, but I could have raised you if my mama had let me."

Maddie tried to concentrate on her driving as the road got more rough and narrow. Of course Sarah Cavanaugh had given birth to her. There was no reason to doubt that, not after hearing her whole life how terrible the birth had been and how much she owed her mother.

"The orderly who told me about your mother got their names and yours for me," Jerilyn was saying. "Roy and Sarah Cavanaugh. That's how I found out that they'd named you Madeline but called you Maddie."

Maddie almost drove off the road.

"See, I really am your mother," Jerilyn was saying. "I've always wanted to come see you, but my mama was sure I would screw up your life like I had mine."

No, this couldn't be true. "If you really were my mother, you wouldn't be pointing a gun at me."

Jerilyn laughed. "It's the only way I can get you to listen to what I have to tell you."

"That's not true."

Jerilyn's face twisted into one of anger. "Why are you driving so slow?" she demanded. "Speed up or we'll never get far enough away."

"Away from what?"

"Just drive. I know you probably won't believe this, but I came from a family with a good name, lots of money, property and status. It's not my fault that things changed, and that now I need my daughter's help."

Maddie shot her another look. "I don't have any money if that's what you're after."

"But your cousins do. I saw that fancy restaurant. At those prices, your cousin must do just fine."

"You're kidnapping me?"

EARL RAY COULDN'T HELP being excited. He'd have the little black notebook back soon. He thought about the first thing he'd buy himself with all that money. A ticket out of the country, if he was smart.

He didn't like to think about the people he'd taken the book from or what they would do if they found out he had it.

Instead, he thought about Jerilyn and the look on her face when he showed up with her precious daughter. Talk about priceless.

When he'd gone by Buck Jones's house, he'd found his damned stolen car in the drive, but no sign of Jerilyn—or Buck. One of the neighbors had confirmed what Earl Ray had suspected.

Jerilyn had left alone in Buck's truck.

Jerilyn was looking for Maddie, and now Bo Evans swore he had her. Earl Ray thought he might be seeing Jerilyn sooner than he first thought.

As they drove south, he tracked the location of the cell phone he'd given Bo. He felt anxious.

He'd miss Jerilyn, but he couldn't see her in his life anymore. In fact, if she'd found the little black book, he couldn't see her in anyone's life anymore, including her own. He couldn't have her loud mouth telling everyone about the book, and who'd stolen it.

The woman wasn't completely stupid. If she'd found the book, she would know it was worth something. He hated to think she might try to make her own deal for it.

"Not on your life," Earl Ray said under his breath.

"You say somethin'?" Dude asked from behind the wheel.

"We're getting close to where we have to turn. You'd better slow down."

As Dude turned onto an even narrower dirt road, Earl Ray checked his gun, anxious to give Bo Evans what he had coming to him.

MADDIE HAD TO do something. They were driving deeper into the Breaks, farther and farther away from the chance of finding help and escaping this dangerous woman.

As the pickup topped a small rise in the road, Maddie saw the moon reflected in a small pond up ahead just off the right side of the road. When she'd gotten into the pickup, she'd buckled her seat belt and deactivated the passenger-side air bag after noticing Jerilyn hadn't buckled up. Jerilyn sat sideways on the seat, the .22 pistol trained on her.

As Maddie dropped down the hill, she told herself what she was planning was risky, but staying in this pickup with this crazy woman could be more dangerous.

The pond didn't look very deep, but Maddie put down her window just in case.

"What's wrong with you? It's freezing out there," Jerilyn complained.

"I just need a little air."

"Put that window up! What's that?"

The pickup started swerving back and forth in the ruts. "I think we have a flat tire!"

"Stop the truck!"

"I'm trying."

"Hit the brakes!" Jerilyn yelled, taking the pistol off her as she swung around to look at the road ahead. "Look out!"

Maddie had swerved and braked a little pretending they had a flat. As they came down the hill, she swerved and headed straight for the pond.

The pickup bounced over the uneven earth beside the road and hit the water, the front end breaking the moon-slick surface and sending up a spray over the windshield and in through Maddie's open window. The front of the truck plowed through the water for a dozen yards before finally coming to a stop, the tires sinking into the mud.

Out of the corner of her eye, she saw Jerilyn hit the windshield with a thud. Maddie knew she had to move fast. Even before the truck came to a full stop, she unsnapped her seat belt and reached for the door handle.

Chapter Eleven

Grayson held Kate until she fell back to sleep. Then, unable to sleep, he got up and wandered through the empty house. Shane's truck wasn't in front of his cabin. That in itself was odd. But Shane was a grown man. If he decided to stay out all night that was fine. Juanita lived in one of the guesthouses some distance from the ranch house. He'd wanted them all to have plenty of room. He'd wanted Trails West to be a haven for them all.

Out on the porch, Grayson dropped into a chair and looked across the moonlight-drenched land. He feared his plan to get his sons to Montana wasn't going to work, no matter how much he yearned for it. All this space, all these added cabins he'd had built for family and company, and yet he and Kate were probably going to end up here alone.

He'd told himself that he'd bought this place for Kate. But a part of him had hoped to find a little of his Rebecca still here. Sometimes he thought he could hear her laughter on the breeze or look up and see her riding across the prairie toward him. He knew how much she'd loved living here, riding her horse over these rolling plains.

He had a photograph of her astride a pretty paint horse at the age of eleven, all pigtails and grin.

Even with the memories of Rebecca so strong here, the move had only strengthened his love for Kate. She was his connection to the past and the present—the bridge that had helped him heal. Their love for each other was what he'd hoped would bring the family together. His family.

Now to find out that Kate had a twenty-six-year-old daughter... A daughter she gave up. A daughter she had with a man who still lived in Whitehorse.

Grayson hated that the news had kicked his feet out from under him. He'd known Kate had had lovers. But this mystery lover shared a child with her. That was something Grayson could never do with her, and he found himself unable to hold back the surge of jealousy he felt toward the man.

He didn't turn as he heard the front door open and Kate pad across the porch to him. He didn't want her to see him like this. Hell, right now he could barely stand himself. He thought he was a better man.

But the moment she touched his arm, he felt that eternal connection between them. This was his Kate. She loved him. And God knew he loved her.

She curled up on his lap, and he held her to him.

"I'm so sorry," she whispered. "I should have told you long before now."

"It's why you never came back here, isn't it?" he asked after a moment.

She nodded.

So he'd opened this can of worms by buying the ranch

and not even thinking to discuss it with her. He chuckled at his own foolishness.

"Can you ever forgive me?" she asked softly, as the breeze teased at her hair.

"There is nothing to forgive." He drew back, so he could see her face in the moonlight. "We'll find your daughter. No matter what it takes, if that's what you want."

Tears welled in her eyes, and she bent to cover his mouth with her own. He deepened the kiss as he rose. Grayson renewed his resolve that this ranch would one day ring with the voices and laughter of their family, and carried his wife back into the house.

EVEN THOUGH THERE was only a little water against it, it took all of Maddie's strength to push open the pickup door.

As she slipped out, she glanced back at Jerilyn, who lay crumpled on the floorboard breathing but not moving. No sign of the gun.

Maddie dropped into the pond. The cold water took her breath away, even though it was only waist deep.

She sank in the mud and had to struggle to take a step. Behind her Jerilyn called out her name.

"Maddie?"

She heard Jerilyn and tried to hurry. The moon shone down, making her a perfect target.

Jerilyn couldn't be her mother. No mother would threaten to shoot her daughter. Maddie felt a chill at both the thought and the cold pond water. Sarah Cavanaugh had been a terrible mother. But Jerilyn? If Maddie had been adopted, she would have known, wouldn't she?

She shuddered as she recalled how cold and distant Sarah had been. Nothing like a real mother. But Maddie had Geraldine next door, and Sarah hadn't seemed to mind that she found love and affection at the older woman's house instead of her own.

"Maddie! Come back here! You have to help me!"

Maddie was almost to the shore. She could hear Jerilyn still banging around in the cab of the pickup as if looking for something. The gun?

"You did that on purpose!" Jerilyn was yelling. "You drove into this damned pond. You little beast. You could have killed us both!"

Maddie heard Jerilyn open the passenger-side door and splash down into the water. Something metallic banged against the side of the truck. She had apparently found the gun. As Jerilyn worked her way along the side of the truck, Maddie could hear the steady tap of the gun in her hand.

She tried to hurry, thankful the pickup was between her and Jerilyn, but with each step, the mud sucked down her boots and the snowmelt pond water lapped up, freezing cold.

"Don't leave me," Jerilyn screamed after her. *"You have to help me. I'm your mother!"* The woman sounded close to hysterical.

Maddie didn't look back as she reached the shore. Across the narrow dirt road, the pines were thick, the land dropping off toward Old Town Whitehorse. Country Maddie knew.

She ran toward the road, knowing that for a few moments she would be silhouetted against the moonlight and provide a clear target if Jerilyn was serious about shooting her.

"Maddie!"

A bullet whizzed past her ear as she raced across the road and headed for the shelter of the pines. She reached the trees as the sound of another .22 gunshot filled the air. Maddie dove deeper into the pines, afraid Jerilyn was chasing her.

She caught her foot on a tree root and fell headfirst, skidding across the long-dried ponderosa pine needles to crash into the trunk of a pine.

Her shoulder was on fire from hitting the tree. Dragging herself up into a sitting position under the tree boughs, she took a few moments to let the pain subside and catch her breath. From the shadows of the big pine tree, she could see the road and the crazy woman standing in the middle of it.

Jerilyn was squinting into the pines. She didn't seem to be wearing shoes. Earlier she'd been wearing some low-heeled pumps. They were no doubt stuck in the mud of the pond.

Maddie didn't dare move, fearing Jerilyn would see her the moment she stepped out in the moonlight. The ponderosa boughs formed a protective shelter from the light, the ground under them dark and soft with dried needles.

Holding her breath, she tried to move her shoulder. It didn't feel broken. The skin on her hands burned from where she'd scraped them when she fell, and she had a stitch in her side from slogging out of the pond and running into the trees.

She leaned back against the tree trunk, prepared to run again if Jerilyn made a move toward her.

But Maddie told herself that the woman couldn't see her, and that as long as she stayed where she was, hidden under this pine, she was safe. She prayed that was true as she tried to catch her breath, her terror making her side ache with each gasp. She was hurt, weak and exhausted and felt frighteningly fragile, afraid she couldn't take much more before she broke.

As her breathing slowed, she heard the growl of a car engine coming up the road. Suddenly the glow of headlights washed over the pines.

Maddie shrank back as she saw Jerilyn move to the edge of the road and hide the .22 behind her back.

Maddie wanted to scream. Someone who could help her was coming up the road. People in this part of the state wouldn't hesitate to stop the moment they saw a pickup in the pond. But the person wouldn't know Jerilyn was crazy—or that she was armed and dangerous.

The car slowed as it approached, the taillights flashing red. Maddie couldn't let an innocent, well-meaning person get killed because of her. She pushed herself away from the trunk of the pine, and on hands and knees she began to crawl out into the moonlight.

EARL RAY HAD never been so glad to see anyone. Here was Jerilyn standing beside the road looking like a drowned rat.

He didn't even have to ask what had happened, given that the pickup was partially submerged in the pond beside the road, the driver-side door hanging open.

He lowered his window. "Kind of hard on other people's cars, aren't you?"

"Earl Ray." She said his name as if she'd just seen him a few minutes before—as if she hadn't stolen his car and money, left him in a fleabag motel in the desert and forced him to come a thousand miles to find her sorry behind.

"What the hell is wrong with you, woman?" he demanded, losing his temper as she bent down to look in his open window.

"Not a damned thing you can't fix," she said with a smile. "Aren't you glad to see me, Earl Ray?"

"Where's my notebook? I know you found it."

"I did," she said, nodding, a change coming over her eyes. "Is that all you care about, your stupid notebook?"

"Where is it, Jerilyn?" He grabbed hold of a fistful of her mud-covered blouse.

"I threw it out the window of the car on my way to Montana."

He only had an instant to shove her back and duck as she thrust a .22 pistol through the window.

The shot echoed through the rented SUV but did nothing to blot out Dude's shriek of pain. She kept firing blindly. Earl Ray heard Bubba let out a curse and slump heavily against the backseat.

Earl Ray threw open his door as Jerilyn took off across the road toward the pond, her last shot going wild. He clambered out after her, not sure he hadn't been hit until he was on his feet. At the edge of the road, Jerilyn turned as if to fire back at him.

But he was right behind her.

"You're a lousy bastard, Earl Ray Pitts. I hope you rot in hell."

He tackled her, his momentum driving them off the road and into the soft mud at the edge of the pond. He fell on top of her, Jerilyn still screaming obscenities. The sound of the gunshot came as a complete surprise.

Hot liquid splattered across his face, and he swore, certain this time she'd hit him. His hands went for her throat. The crazy broad wasn't going to shoot him again.

Everything had gone quiet. Dude had even stopped shrieking. Earl Ray doubted that was a good sign.

He tightened his fingers around Jerilyn's scrawny throat, not realizing why it was suddenly so quiet until he looked at her face. Her cheek was caked with mud, and her eyes were more vacant than usual.

It took him a moment to understand what had happened. When he'd tackled her, driving her down into the soft mud, the .22 had been between them and she'd fired. His weight had flattened the gun between their bodies, forcing the barrel to be pointed right at Jerilyn's throat. A straight shot to her brain.

"Oh hell." He jerked his hands from her neck and stared down at his warm, bloodstained fingers.

Scrambling to his feet, he told himself he hadn't meant to kill her. He'd planned to let Dude or Bubba do it—after he got his notebook. Now everything was screwed.

He staggered back, wiping the blood on his pants and trying to calm down. He swore as he wiped his sleeve over his face and realized he was sweating. *Jerilyn was dead.*

Earl Ray glanced up the road, thankful it was still the

middle of the night. All he needed was some rancher to come along. As far as they were from civilization, he doubted the road got much use, but he couldn't chance it.

"Dude!" he called to the SUV. "Bubba!" Neither answered. He looked at the pickup out in the pond. He was going to have to go out there himself. She could have been lying about the notebook, he told himself. It could still be in her purse.

The water was freezing and the glue-like mud took one of his shoes with the first step. He retrieved it, stepped back to the shore and took off the other shoe before wading out again.

Both of the pickup's doors were open. He worked his way out to the driver's side and peered in.

The purse on the seat wasn't the one Jerilyn had in Arizona. When had she had time to buy a new one? He dug through the contents, using the dome light. No little black book.

He let out a curse. This wasn't Jerilyn's purse. Squinting at the driver's license, he saw that it belonged to Madeline Cavanaugh. Maddie Cavanaugh?

The hair stood up on the back of his neck. He'd been so upset it hadn't registered that both doors of the pickup had been open. That's because there'd been a passenger. That's why Maddie's purse was in this pickup with Jerilyn?

He let out another curse and quickly searched the rest of the pickup. Jerilyn's purse was on the floorboard, down in the murky water. He rummaged through it, hoping he could save the book and the writing inside.

But his little black book wasn't in her purse.

"She wouldn't have thrown it out," he said to himself. She wasn't that dumb. Or was she?

He felt along the floorboard, thinking maybe the book had fallen out. All he found was a pair of hedge trimmers. He didn't even want to think about what they were for as he backed out of the pickup's cab and started toward shore.

A thought struck him. What if Jerilyn had shown Maddie his black book and told her to keep it if anything ever happened to her?

He tore off his muddy socks and pulled on his shoes. Climbing back up to the road, he looked toward the woods and saw what he knew would be there. Footprints in the soft earth at the edge of the road and tracks heading into the woods.

Maddie Cavanaugh was out there somewhere. He could almost feel her presence, and there was little doubt in his mind that she would have heard the gunshots and the screams. She was a potential witness to murder.

But he was more worried about what Jerilyn might have given her for safekeeping.

MADDIE HAD BEEN partway out of the trees when she'd heard Jerilyn call by name the man who'd pulled over—Earl Ray. She'd said her boyfriend's name was Earl Ray. That had barely sunk in when she'd heard the shots and the shrieks and Jerilyn screaming. She'd ducked back under the pine, afraid that they would see her if she ran.

Now she huddled under the dark boughs, praying that Earl Ray and whoever else had stopped for Jerilyn would just drive off.

Then a twig snapped, and a large dark shape appeared at the edge of the pines.

Her heart lodged in her throat as he called her name.

"Maddie? I know you're out there. Why don't you come on out? I won't hurt you. I'm a friend of your mother's."

A shudder quaked through her. He knew she was out here. Knew her name. Thought Jerilyn was her mother. But she didn't believe for a moment he was a friend.

Maddie held her breath, forcing herself not to move. Where was Jerilyn? What about the other sounds she'd heard? Her every instinct told her that Jerilyn was dead. So were the others, the ones this man had called Dude and Bubba.

She could see the man but was sure that he couldn't see her.

A cell phone rang, the sound coming from his car. He ignored it. "Come on, Maddie. I'll give you a ride back to town. You've had a rough night. I know you're anxious to see your family."

The cell phone rang again. He let out a curse and turned back toward the road.

She waited until he reached the SUV before she leapt to her feet and ran. Her heart was pounding too hard to hear if he came after her.

OVER THE SOUND of his ringing cell phone, Earl Ray thought he'd heard something move in the woods. But when he'd swung around and looked, he saw nothing but moonlight and shadows in the trees.

He found the cell phone where he'd dropped it. Only one person had this number.

"What the hell do you want?" he snapped.

"I'm hurt," Bo said. "I need you to come get me and take me to a doctor."

Earl Ray laughed. "But I don't know where you are. Too bad you didn't give me Maddie tonight like I asked you to," he said through gritted teeth. "You still have her, right?"

Silence. "I did. But someone took her," Bo finally admitted.

Earl Ray walked around the SUV. His first thought was to leave Bo wherever he was and let the bastard die. But as desperate as the kid sounded, he'd probably do something stupid like call for an ambulance.

Cursing under his breath, Earl Ray opened the driver-side door. Dude was sitting behind the wheel, blood pooled in his lap. Bubba didn't look much better in the backseat.

With distaste, Earl Ray leaned over Dude, unbuckled his seatbelt and pulled with his free hand. Dude tumbled out on the road. Once out of the car, Dude was fairly easy to kick off into the barrow pit. Bubba, he pulled out and rolled down the slope into the trees.

"Tell me where I can find you," Earl Ray said to Bo. He listened with little interest, since he was already close by and just needed the last detailed directions to find Bo.

According to what Bo told him, the cabin was just down the road.

"Are you alone?" Earl Ray asked.

"Yes. Don't worry. I'll find Maddie for you. I swear. Just get me medical attention first."

"Yeah, sure. I'll be right there." Earl Ray disconnected as he spotted a set of headlights in the distance headed up the road.

THE SKY TO the east opened a crack at the first sign of daylight. Shane noticed the shimmering orange glow along the horizon but it was still dark here in the mountains. Ahead the land dropped toward the Missouri River, the pine trees taller and thicker on each side of the road.

A few miles down the road, his headlights picked up the shine of chrome just off the road. Shane slowed, his pulse rate jumping up at the sight of the pickup in the middle of the small pond off the side of the road.

"Buck Jones's pickup." Shane swore under his breath as he brought his truck to a stop, grabbed his flashlight and jumped out. Both truck doors were hanging open, and even from the road he could see that the cab was empty. No sign of Jerilyn or Maddie.

As he looked down for footprints in the soft earth around the pond, Shane spotted a body half-buried in the mud at the edge of the water. For one heart-stopping moment, all he saw was the mud-caked blond hair. Maddie.

He shone the flashlight beam in the woman's face. It was Jerilyn. She matched the description Buck had given him.

The beam shone on the gunshot wound under her chin. Shane felt an icy cold fear brush the back of his neck as he examined the ground around the body.

Footprints. Too large to be Maddie's. Was it possible

Maddie hadn't been with Jerilyn? That the woman had picked up a man?

As he directed his flashlight beam along the edge of the road he found two other bodies, both too large to be Maddie. Shane searched the ground for more tracks and finally found smaller boot prints coming out of the pond. He followed them across the road, where the tracks were much farther apart. The woman had been running.

Unfortunately, the boot tracks ended in the fallen pine needles of the forest.

He flashed the light out over the ponderosa pines.

"Maddie?" He called again, louder. "It's Shane. Shane Corbett."

No answer.

As he walked over to the bodies, he recognized one of the men as the same one he'd seen talking to Bo Evans the night of the rodeo dance.

Climbing back into his truck, Shane used his cell to call the sheriff's office and report what he'd found. He'd hoped when he called that the dispatcher would tell him that Maddie had been found, alive and safe, but he'd known better the moment he'd seen the tracks going into the woods and not coming out again.

The dispatcher told him to stay at the scene until the sheriff got there. A search-and-rescue helicopter would be called in to help search once dawn broke.

Shane couldn't just sit there and wait. Not when his every instinct told him that Maddie was out there some-where—most likely along with two very dangerous men.

EARL RAY TURNED at the tree with the Barnes sign tacked on it and followed the directions Bo had given him. After he'd seen another vehicle headed this way, he needed to get Bo and find Maddie and the notebook as quickly as possible.

As he drove toward the cabin, he noticed a piece of clothing stuck to the bark of a tree along the edge of the road. The cloth looked soaked with blood. He slowed. There were tracks, as if something had been dragged. Several twigs were snapped off the trees and there was a scrape on one of the pines where the bark had been rubbed off. It all looked fresh—including what appeared to be droplets of blood in the dust.

There were more scuff marks in front of the cabin. And more blood. What the hell had gone on here tonight?

Earl Ray could only imagine, given who was involved. But he had to wonder how Bo had apparently gotten the worst of it.

He drew his gun. It was no little peashooter like the one Jerilyn had used to kill Dude and Bubba and herself. This was a man's gun for a man's job. Earl Ray didn't bother to shut off the engine as he got out.

An owl hooted, making him tense as he neared the cabin entrance. The door was ajar, a smear of blood on the steps, and from inside came the sound of moaning.

"Bo?" Earl Ray called.

"In here."

Earl Ray smiled as he stepped inside. "Ready for that ride I promised you?"

MADDIE DIDN'T KNOW how far she'd run. Time had lost all meaning to her. She ran because that was all she could do, sprinting down the mountainside through the trees, pale light flickering in the boughs as the day began to dawn. Even when she felt the hitch in her side again, even when she thought she couldn't run another step, she kept going.

She thought she knew where she was, that the occasional rock butte or tall pine looked familiar. She had headed in the direction of the Breaks to the south of Old Town Whitehorse. As a girl, she'd ridden her horse all through this country and knew a place where she would be safe.

She ran as if the killer were right behind her. But she knew she was also running from what Jerilyn had told her. She didn't look back, not since she'd scrambled from the shelter of the pine. She feared falling —or worse, seeing Earl Ray Pitts right behind her.

For all she knew, he was practically breathing down her neck. With each running stride, she expected to hear him or feel the burning fire of a bullet as it slammed into her back.

She ran blind through the pines, tears streaming down her face, everything a blur. Over the sound of her ragged breathing and the thunder of her pulse, she didn't hear the vehicle, didn't see the headlights or even realize she had reached a road until the lights flashed over her, catching her like a deer in their glare.

Maddie stumbled and fell, sprawling across the dirt road directly in front of the vehicle.

Chapter Twelve

The sun glowed behind the pines to the east, blindingly bright as it spread across the country, highlighting the rocky bluffs and making the ponderosa pines shimmer.

Shane caught the movement out of the corner of his eye only a heartbeat before the person came running out of the woods and onto the road in front of his truck.

In that instant, he saw the head of blond hair. Saw the woman look up in surprise. Saw the look of sheer terror in her blue eyes. *Maddie.*

Shane slammed on his brakes and turned the wheel hard to the left. The pickup left the road, skidding off and down the incline into the pines.

The tree came up fast. The front of the pickup crashed into the thick trunk, the heavy boughs slamming against the windshield as his air bag exploded in his face.

ALL MADDIE HAD seen was the grill of the vehicle coming at her. Earl Ray. When she'd seen the vehicle bearing down on her, all she could think was that this killer had found her.

Maddie scrambled to her feet. As she did, her hand brushed a weathered tree limb lying at the edge of the road. She snatched it up and took off running down the road as she heard a door open.

This time, she heard him behind her. Heard the pounding of his shoes on the hard road. He was gaining on her. In fact, he was right behind her, calling her name just as he had earlier.

She swung around, using the limb like a club. Only at the last minute did it register that she knew this man.

"Maddie!" Shane ducked the limb, lunged at her and took her down at the edge of the road. They tumbled into the soft earth and tall green grass.

She struggled under him for a moment, all her adrenaline still pumping.

"It's okay. *It's me. Maddie, it's Shane.*"

She blinked up into the bright day, finally focusing on his face. It really was Shane Corbett.

"I... I..." Her voice broke, and all the fight went out of her. He rolled off her and brushed back a lock of her hair from her face. She saw his expression and knew what she must look like with her bruised, cut face.

"Who did this to you?" he asked, his voice low, husky and tinged with fury.

She shook her head. What did it matter? His warm hand felt so good against her skin as he gently cupped her jaw, his thumb pad brushing her cheek, his eyes full of compassion. She leaned into his hand and closed her eyes and whispered, "Bo."

She heard Shane curse under his breath. He helped her to her feet, and she saw his pickup, wrecked down in the trees. She shivered, realizing they had no way to drive out of here and that Earl Ray must still be looking for her.

"He's looking for me." She hadn't realized she'd spoken the words out loud until Shane told her not to worry.

"I've called the sheriff. He should be on his way along with a couple of his deputies. They've sent a search-and-rescue chopper, as well."

She nodded but didn't believe everything was going to be all right. Her nerves were on end, and she swore she could hear another vehicle driving along the road. But she'd thought that ever since she'd bolted from her hiding place under the pine. She'd thought she could feel Earl Ray's hot breath on her neck.

She saw Shane reach for something, but he came up empty-handed. "What is it?" she asked, her voice cracking.

"My cell phone. I'm sure it's in the truck. I probably lost it when I hit the tree. Where's Bo now?" Shane asked. He cocked his head, as if he were also listening to something in the distance.

"He's dead." At least he'd looked dead the last time she'd seen him. She gazed into Shane's clear blue eyes and remembered being in his arms on the night of the dance—remembered that fear and excitement. Shane had thought her reactions were because of her fear of Bo.

She no longer had to fear Bo, but that didn't mean this was over. "There's this man," she said. "Earl Ray. He killed this blond woman who said she was my real mother." The words tumbled out. She looked into Shane's handsome face, saw the distress there. "He's after me. He knows I went into the woods. He knows I saw."

Shane nodded and pulled her into his arms again. "The sheriff will find him."

Her limbs trembled. She couldn't remember ever feel-

ing this weak and exhausted or this relieved to see anyone. She leaned into him, feeling his warmth and his
strength and wishing she could stay right here forever.

Shane was here to rescue her. That's what the Texas
Ranger did. At lunch when he'd tried to warn her about
Jud and Bo, he'd wanted to protect her, but she'd been
so certain she could take care of herself—that she had
no other choice. Now her eyes burned with tears. It took
all of her strength not to cry.

Suddenly, the roar of an engine filled the air, and before she could take another breath the front end of an
SUV appeared over a rise in the road.

SHANE THOUGHT HE'D heard a vehicle coming. It would be
the sheriff or one of his deputies. One of them would get
Maddie somewhere safe while he and the others made
sure Bo Evans was really dead and tracked down Earl
Ray Pitts.

The driver had seen them in the road. Shane waited
for the vehicle to slow. Instead, he heard the driver give
the SUV more gas as it bore down on them.

Shane grabbed Maddie and dove for the ditch. Behind him, all he heard was flying gravel as the driver
skidded to a stop.

He and Maddie hit the dirt and rolled. At the edge of
the pines, Shane pulled Maddie to her feet and, taking
her hand, ran deeper into the woods.

A car door slammed. An instant later a bullet whizzed
through the air next to them. Behind them, Shane heard
a twig break. Another bullet zinged past, struck a tree
and showered them with bark and dust.

He zigzagged them through the pines, running hard

to put as much distance as possible between themselves and the shooter, ignoring the pain in his legs.

Shane knew Maddie had to be exhausted. He'd felt her trembling in his arms back there on the road when he'd first caught up to her, and he'd seen the defeat in her eyes those few seconds before she'd recognized him.

They had a little lead on the shooter, but not much. If they hoped to survive, they had to outrun him. Shane wished he had his gun. But he hadn't touched it since he'd left the hospital. He'd been a fool to leave it in Texas and an even bigger fool not to take one of his father's before he'd left the ranch.

But just the thought of firing a gun again...

He felt her lag behind and saw that she was limping badly. He knew she couldn't go much farther, yet he pulled her along because there was no time for stopping.

"This way," Maddie cried, pulling on his arm as she motioned toward the sheer face of a rock butte off to their right. The sun had caught on the limestone, making it glow golden in the morning light.

As they neared the butte, all Shane could see was a solid wall of rock. "Maddie, we have to keep going," he whispered, as he gasped for breath. He was limping a little, too, a reminder of the last time he'd had to face a criminal with a gun.

"I can't." She was limping too badly now, grimacing with each step. She motioned for him to follow as she made her way to the rock wall.

He went after her, hoping she didn't plan to climb up the face of the cliff. As he neared, Maddie disappeared into a narrow crevice between the rocks. The crack was so well hidden he hadn't seen it.

Shane glanced back the way they'd come. He couldn't see anyone, but he knew they weren't far behind. Maddie had said Bo was dead, but that didn't mean that Earl Ray Pitts was alone.

"Come on," Maddie called, sounding as if she were deep inside the rock.

Hoping she knew what she was doing and that he would fit, he squeezed into the crevice. Because of his size, it was hard to wend his way through the crack. He felt Maddie reach for his hand and guide him in.

To his surprise, the crack opened into a hollow not yet touched by the sun. The space was small, the rock floor filled with several deep, tiny pools that held rainwater. Maddie bent down to cup the clear water and bring it to her lips. He knelt down beside her and did the same.

From what he could tell, they had reached a dead end. The only way out of there was back the way they'd come.

"Maddie, we can't stay here," he whispered. "If they find us, it will be like shooting fish in a barrel."

She gave him a tired smile and touched her fingers to her lips as she got to her feet with a grimace and limped over to another crack in the rocks, this one making a V as it soared upward. She motioned him to follow and began to climb, using the crack for leverage. He could see that she was using the last of her strength and feared the hurt ankle wouldn't hold. One thing was clear. She wouldn't be able to make another run for her life.

"Maddie?"

She disappeared from view again, but he could hear her still climbing. He grasped hold of the rocks and climbed after her.

MADDIE CLIMBED INTO the cave entrance and stumbled to her knees, her ankle killing her. She couldn't go another step. Tears sprung to her eyes as she crawled over to a corner and rested her back against the cool rock wall.

Shane climbed up through the hole, his eyes widening as he took in the room in the rocks. A shaft of sunlight poured down through a man-sized hole like a chimney above them. He could see blue sky.

"The whole area is a honeycomb of caves," she said. "I found this one quite by accident. I'd seen the opening from the top of the butte and knew there had to be another way to get into here."

"Who knows about this place?" Shane asked, looking worried.

"I never told anyone about it," she said. It was her secret place. She'd never brought anyone here before. Strange, but it seemed right that she was sharing it for the first time with Shane Corbett.

He sat down, leaning against the wall across from her. Sunlight spilled at their feet, making the room glow with warmth and light. "Nice digs."

She barely had enough energy to return his smile, but when she looked into his eyes she felt a shiver of desire—much as she had the night of the rodeo dance when he'd held her.

Like now, Shane took her reaction for something it wasn't. He'd thought when she'd trembled in his arms at the dance it was from fear of Bo.

Now he thought she was cold. He removed his jacket and reached across the small space to wrap his body-warmed cloth around her. They were so close she could feel his breath on her cheek—so close it would have been impossible not to kiss him. She'd secretly wanted to for long enough.

Maddie brushed her mouth over his, closing her eyes as she felt an incredible tingle from her lips to the tip of her toes. Chemistry. She'd heard about it, but had only felt it the first time she'd seen Shane—the day he came by to pick up her and her horse.

It had scared her then, just as it did now. The difference was that now she felt she had nothing to lose.

"Maddie?" He drew back to look at her.

She cupped his handsome face in the palms of her hands and breathed in the masculine scent of him, drawn like metal to magnet. "Shhhhh."

She saw something spark in his gaze. Had Shane felt the chemistry the first time he'd seen her that day at her house? He'd been so serious, clearly annoyed at his brother and upset because he'd thought Jud was leading her on.

Clueless, as her cousin-in-law Bridger had said.

She leaned into Shane now and kissed him again, tasting him, teasing his lips open. Desire sparked through her; a bolt of electricity jump-started her heart and made her forget her pain, her exhaustion, everything but Shane Corbett.

Maddie lost herself in the pleasure of his mouth, his tongue, his taste.

When he drew back to look at her again, there was a kind of wonder in his gaze.

She smiled and touched his cheek, a day's stubble rough under her fingertips. Everything about this man stirred a passion in her like nothing she'd ever known.

"I'm not sure I understand what's going on," he said.

"Don't you, Shane?"

"Jud—"

"Jud set you up. Set us up."

"What?"

She chuckled as she ran her fingertips along his solid square jaw to his sensual lips. "Weren't you even a little suspicious when he kept throwing us together?"

He frowned.

"I wasn't sure what he was up to until you told me about the marriage pact and that he'd drawn the shortest straw." She smiled. "And I'll bet he promised a wedding, right?"

"How did you know?"

"What would be the best way to give your father what he wanted without having to get married? Find a woman for one of your brothers. Does that sound anything like the Jud you know and love?"

Shane let out a curse. "I knew he was up to something, but I never dreamed…" He met her gaze. "Apparently you know him better than I do."

"I spotted the kind of cowboy he was the first time I saw him. The only reason I went out with him was that my cousins were worried about me. I'd do anything for them. Even date your brother. I knew I couldn't fall for Jud. He wasn't my type, and I didn't believe for a moment he was interested in me."

"I still can't believe Jud would—"

"Believe it. I should have seen it right away," she said. "When Jud and I went out, he ended up talking about you the entire time, what a great brother you were."

Shane laughed. "The little son of a… He said he'd found the perfect woman."

She cocked a brow at that.

"He was right." Shane leaned toward her again. "You *are* perfect."

Perfect for you, Shane Corbett.

He pulled her close, deepening the kiss. His body felt wonderfully strong and warm, and his touch was tender. "I don't want to hurt you," he said, gently touching her bruised face.

"You won't hurt me," she said. Shane Corbett, the Texas Ranger, a man who saved women in distress. She loved that he was shy, and while she knew he'd had his share of women, he was nothing like Jud.

"Are you sure about this?"

She'd never been more sure about anything in her life. While she'd never tell him, Jud was a pretty good matchmaker.

In answer to Shane's question, she wrapped her arms around his neck and pulled him to her. Their lips touched, and an electrical shot sparked through her. She knew Shane had felt it. She heard him groan. His hands cupped her buttocks as he pulled her onto his lap.

SHANE TRAILED KISSES down Maddie's slim throat. His brother and his plot were completely forgotten as he realized he'd wanted this woman from the first time he'd laid eyes on her.

He unzipped the lightweight jacket she wore to reveal her small, perfect breasts. He felt his desire spiral upward like the shaft of sunlight above them.

"Maddie," he whispered, as his mouth dropped to draw a nipple and suck the tip into a hard nub. She shuddered and drew him closer, her back arching.

Shane didn't remember removing the rest of her clothing or his own. He lost himself in her, rocketed higher and higher by her responses to his touch and his to hers. The feeling that they'd always known each other only grew as they finally came, both in sync, as if this had been written in the stars.

Later, when they lay spent in each other's arms, he couldn't help but think about Jud and his belief in destiny. Lying here with Maddie, Shane thought his brother might be right. This had felt destined since the first time he'd seen Maddie sitting on that porch. A Montana cowgirl.

"This was what you were afraid of, wasn't it?" he whispered against her hair. "The night of the rodeo dance. I thought it was Bo you were frightened of, but it was this."

She nodded against his chest. "I had never felt the emotions you evoked in me. Being in your arms… I wasn't ready for those kinds of feelings."

"But you are now?"

She smiled as she gazed up at him. "Almost getting killed changes a person. When I thought I might die before I ever got the chance to kiss you…"

"Tell me what happened to you," he whispered.

Safe in his arms, she told him about Bo abducting her and taking her to the cabin, and about the blond woman from the restaurant saving her.

"She was crazy. She said she was my real mother, that she'd given me up at birth." Maddie must have sensed something in his silence. She leaned up on one elbow and looked at him. "Don't tell me that I share any genes with that woman. *She kidnapped me. What mother kidnaps her own daughter and holds her at gunpoint?*"

He heard her voice break and knew how hard this was for her. "We don't know for certain that Jerilyn Larch is your mother. We won't know until we can run DNA tests."

"I'm afraid because she looks like me."

"A lot of women have blond hair and blue eyes. Like my mother. Like my stepmother Kate. Like your cousins."

Maddie nodded still worried.

"Bo wasn't the only one who hurt you, was he?" he said and, seeing Maddie's reaction, he knew he'd guessed right. "What made you leave and not come back for so long?"

Maddie took a ragged breath. "I just needed to get away." There was an edge to her voice, a don't-mess-with-me tone that he took for fear.

"Who hurt you?"

"Where do you want me to begin? My former fiancé just tried to… Well, who knows what he planned to do to me. My alleged birth mother just tried to kidnap me for ransom and shot at me. My mother, my possibly adoptive mother, Sarah Cavanaugh…" Maddie looked away.

"What did she do?" he asked quietly.

"Do you really want to hear all this?"

"Yes. I want you to be able to put all this behind you. No more secrets. I think keeping this secret is what puts that haunted look in your eyes." The same haunted look he'd seen recently in Kate's eyes. "Trust me, Maddie?"

She softened in his arms. "I'll bet you made a good Texas Ranger."

He liked to think so, but he'd certainly had his doubts, especially recently. As for Maddie, he suspected Bo Evans had just been a symptom. Bo wasn't the kind of man that a woman like Maddie Cavanaugh would go out with unless something had happened to hurt her, to make her feel unworthy of a good man who would love her.

"You can tell me."

He felt her weaken as she looked into his eyes.

"It's a long story," she said at last, and laid her head back on his chest.

"We have time." The cave was hidden well enough, and they should be able to hear anyone coming. Besides, he believed that the only way to get rid of a ghost was to shed light on it.

"My mother, at least the woman I called my mother, Sarah Cavanaugh, was cold and uncaring." Her voice broke. "I spent most of my childhood at the farm next door. Geraldine Shaw was older and very kind to me. She taught me to sew and cook. I loved being in her house because it was warm and cozy. My house was cold like my mother, a showplace, even though we never had any-one over to see it. Geraldine was killed. That's when it came out about Geraldine's husband, Ollie."

Maddie swallowed. He felt her tense against his chest, and her fingers tightened on his rib cage. "I helped her bury Ollie in the rose garden after she killed him. She hit him with a lamp because he was trying to rape me. He had Alzheimer's and he didn't know what he was doing. Neither of us wanted any of this to come out, so we did what we had to do."

Shane sucked in a pained breath as he pulled her tighter against him. "I'm sorry."

She nodded against his chest. "It gets worse," she said in a whisper. "Nick Giovanni was the new deputy in town at the time. The sheriff was in Florida. Nick discovered that someone had been blackmailing Geraldine, bleeding her dry. The blackmailer knew what had happened. I had no idea, but once I heard, I knew she'd been paying the blackmailer to protect me."

Shane felt his heart lodge in his throat as Maddie pulled back to look into his face.

"The blackmailer was my mother, Sarah Cavanaugh."

"Maddie." He drew her closer, stroking her long hair.

"My own mother—a blackmailer," she said, crying now. "Using something horrible that had happened to her daughter and taking advantage of the nice lady next door just for money. But maybe she wasn't my mother. Maybe my real mother is a kidnapper."

He let her cry it out. When she stopped, she lifted her head to look at him. Her smile was enough to break his heart. Shane Corbett knew at that moment that he would love this woman until the day he died.

They made love again as if the world outside this cavern no longer existed. Wrapped in Shane's arms, Maddie fell into a peaceful slumber on the pile of clothing. He told himself that by now the sheriff and his deputies would have found not only Jerilyn but also the other dead men, including Bo, and arrested Earl Ray Pitts.

It was over. Maddie was safe. Shane tried not to think about the future, especially about returning to the Texas Rangers. He felt healed emotionally and knew that had been Maddie's doing. He drew her closer, unable to face leaving her or Montana.

He'd barely finished the thought when a *whoop, whoop, whoop* filled the air. The cave went dark as a helicopter passed overhead, blocking out the sun.

Chapter Thirteen

"That's search-and-rescue looking for us," Maddie said, her eyes flashing open. She sat up abruptly and winced as she reached to rub her ankle. "We have to get up there."

Shane could see that her ankle was swollen and bruised, and as she reached for her clothes, she grimaced with pain.

"You're going to have to go without me," she said.

"I'll help you. I'm not leaving you here alone," he said, as he quickly dressed.

"No, the fastest way is to climb up the shaft," she said. "There is no way I can make it, but you won't have any trouble. There are footholds in the rocks. I think the Native Americans used this cave. You'll come out on top of the bluff. The view is incredible, and the chopper should be able to spot you up there."

He knelt down beside her. "Maddie…"

"I'll be fine." She gave him a quick kiss. "Go."

He pulled her to him and kissed her hard on the mouth. "I don't want you out of my sight until I know that Earl Ray Pitts is caught."

She smiled up at him, touching his cheek with her

warm fingers. "You'll be right above me. If I need you, I'll yell. Once you flag down the helicopter, we can get out of here. I'm sure Earl Ray has already been arrested."

Shane hoped she was right. He told himself that Earl Ray was too big to get through the crack in the rocks and that he didn't even know about the cave. But Shane couldn't help but worry.

"Go and signal them. I'm starved," she said, giving him a playful push.

He laughed as he brushed his fingertips across her lips, knowing that if he kissed her again he wouldn't be able to go at all. "I'll be back with help as quick as I can. Don't try to climb out."

"Don't worry, I'm not going anywhere."

Maddie watched from below as Shane climbed up toward the sunlight. She smiled, remembering his kiss, his touch, their amazing lovemaking. The man could be as tender as he was powerful. Just the thought made her heart beat a little faster.

Hadn't she known that if she got close to Shane she'd fall for him like a rock off a cliff? She'd felt it the moment she saw him: that incredible chemistry, flashing like fireflies in the dark.

After Bo, she'd thought she'd never be ready to trust another man with her heart. Now she knew that it had just taken the right man. There'd been men at college who'd asked her out, but she'd felt no excitement, no rush of emotions. Just the sound of Shane's voice made her pulse buzz.

Maddie finished dressing, and not even her aching ankle could take away the euphoria she felt. Shane was almost to the top of the shaft and soon they would be back home. *But then what?*

Jud had told her that Shane was on a medical leave from the Texas Rangers, recuperating after being wounded.

"I'm hoping he decides not to go back to the Rangers," Jud had said. "Dad really wants him to stay here in Montana."

"As young as he is, he must have started training to get into the Rangers right out of high school."

"Yeah, he went straight into law enforcement while getting his degree. He always wanted to be a Ranger." There'd been a twinkle in Jud's eyes. "But if Shane found the right woman, a Montana cowgirl, I bet he'd think twice about going back to Texas. After he was shot, I think his priorities might have changed."

Talking about Shane and his love life had made her uncomfortable. Even then, she'd known she hadn't wanted to be the woman who kept Shane Corbett from his dreams. She could never let him give up the career he loved for her.

Shane reached the top of the shaft, called down to say he made it, and slipped over the rim and onto the bluff, disappearing from view.

Her heart lurched in her chest as she stared up after him, suddenly terribly afraid. She'd fallen in love with a man who would be returning to Texas to a job that could get him killed. *Had almost gotten him killed.*

She thought she heard the *whoop, whoop, whoop* of the chopper in the distance and another sound, this one much closer by—the sprinkle of tiny rocks.

Someone was coming up through the crack in the limestone—the same way she and Shane had climbed into the cave.

SHANE SPOTTED THE helicopter over the Missouri River gorge. The chopper was flying low, no doubt searching for them. Or Earl Ray Pitts.

He moved to the edge of the bluff and waved his arms. Maddie was right. The view was breathtaking. He could see far down the river, limestone buttes towering on each side, the water slick with the sheen of the sun.

He thought about Maddie, twenty-five feet below him, and felt his heart soar at the memory of her in his arms. Was it possible that she was right about Jud setting them up? He didn't think his brother was that clever.

But if it was true, he owed his brother. Shane had never thought he'd ever meet anyone who could steal his heart, let alone his soul. He had fallen for Maddie so fast and yet fought it each step of the way. Until now.

He saw the chopper turn. The pilot must have seen him waving his arms, for the helicopter headed for him, the sound of the blades growing louder as it neared.

Shane couldn't wait to get back to Maddie. With help, they could get her out of the cave without further injuring her ankle. He just wanted to take her someplace safe, feed her and let her get some rest.

He thought of Juanita's cooking. He'd take her to the ranch. He couldn't stand the idea of being away from her, especially not until he was sure Bo Evans was dead and Earl Ray Pitts was locked up for good.

Eventually he wanted to get her in a real bed, he thought with a grin. But he would always remember this cave and the way the light played on Maddie's face. He was still amazed at what he felt for her. No woman had ever gotten to him the way she had. Shane smiled to himself.

The *whoop, whoop, whoop* of the approaching helicopter got louder, covering the sound of the man approaching from behind him.

MADDIE ROSE FROM where she'd been sitting to stand on her one good leg and lean against the rock face. Someone was definitely coming.

Through the shaft overhead, she could hear the chopper approaching. The pilot must have spotted Shane. But how did the person coming up through the crack in the rocks know she was here? There wouldn't have been time for search-and-rescue to see Shane and send someone up from below.

It had to be someone who knew about the cave, she thought, as she reached down and cupped a palm-sized rock in her hand.

Bo Evans slipped into the room and stopped when he saw her, looking around as if to assure himself that she was alone. She realized he must have been waiting until he heard Shane call down from the top of the bluff.

The look in Bo's eyes made her heart sink. She'd seen meanness there enough times. Last night she'd seen a sick kind of dangerous lust. But what she saw now was a cold, empty hatred that terrified her.

"You left me for dead," he said, his voice as dead as his eyes. His clothes were caked with blood and dirt, and he moved oddly, holding his side with one hand. But he was still moving. Moving toward her.

Maddie said nothing. She knew there was nothing she could say to Bo. He'd always turned things around, skewing the truth to make him come out the victim. What had worried her was that he believed his own lies. They became more real to him than the truth.

"You made me fall for you and then you dumped me," he said, in that same inflectionless tone. "You deserve everything you get. I could have saved you. All you had to do was be just a little nice to me."

More lies. She knew now that it had been the vulnerability she saw in Bo that had made her stay with him as long as she had. That and the fact that, like her, he was flawed.

But she hadn't been able to save Bo.

All she could do now was try to save herself.

"What? No last words?" he asked.

She felt the rock in her hand and feared that she wouldn't be able to use it, as Bo moved in his odd shuffle toward her.

Maddie clutched the rock, knowing it had come down to either her or him. Bo had reached some new low that there would be no coming back from. That he'd brought his life to this point, he would never accept. He would blame everyone else. Call it bad luck. Finding peace only when he breathed his last breath.

His face twisted into something both evil and sad. "This is all your fault, Maddie. You only brought it on yourself."

He reached for her.

Maddie swung. The rock connected with Bo's head. He staggered back, looking confused, but still on his feet.

THE BLOW FROM behind stunned Shane. He dropped to one knee on the smooth surface of the bluff as the chopper noise grew louder and louder, the sun glittering off the blades.

The kick to his kidneys dropped him all the way to the rock, but unlike the first blow, this one didn't come as a surprise. Shane quickly got back on his feet to face Earl Ray Pitts—the man he'd seen with Bo Evans the night of the rodeo dance—and the gun pointed at his heart.

"Just give me my property and I'll be gone," the big man said, motioning with the gun, an eye on the approaching chopper.

"What property would that be?"

"A small, black leather notebook." Earl Ray was studying him intently. "I know Jerilyn gave it to Maddie."

"I don't know what you're talking about, but I have a feeling you aren't going anywhere," Shane said. "I would imagine the sheriff is anxious to talk to you about Jerilyn's murder."

"It was an accident. The stupid broad fired the gun, trying to kill me, and ended up shooting herself. She shot and killed both of my men."

"I'm sure the sheriff will be glad to hear that." Shane could hear the helicopter. It was almost to him. He waited, knowing Earl Ray would look toward it.

When he did, Shane sprung, kicking the gun from Earl Ray's hand. The weapon skittered across the smooth rock. They both lunged for it, but before either of them could reach it, the pistol slipped over the edge of the shaft and dropped down into the cave.

Earl Ray leaped to his feet, charging like a mad bull, driving Shane to the brink of the cliff. Below was nothing but air for a good hundred feet, then a pile of huge boulders at the edge of the river.

The sound of the helicopter was deafening as it hovered just over their heads. Shane and Earl Ray teetered on the brink of the cliff, both struggling. Shane feared that Earl Ray wanted to take the coward's way out—the rocks below—rather than prison. Locked as they were in a death grip, it looked as if Earl Ray would take Shane with him.

He thought of Maddie and found renewed strength. Earl Ray was pushing him hard. He knew he stood only one chance against the man. Shane broke contact and, dropping to his knees, let Earl Ray's pressure tip him forward. Off balance, Shane levered the man over his back and over the cliff.

Shane felt Earl Ray grasping for something to hang on to. His fingers tried to clutch at Shane's sleeve, but Shane was already clambering away from the edge of the cliff.

Earl Ray dropped over the edge of the bluff. The chopper blades overhead drowned out the man's screams.

Bo SHOOK HIS head as if counteracting the effects of being struck by the rock. His right eye looked bloodshot, and the cut from where the rock had broken the skin on his cheekbone began to bleed.

But he stayed on his feet. For a moment he stood looking at Maddie as if he wasn't sure who she was. "You thought I didn't know about this cave." He let out a thin laugh. "I used to come here and get high when I was a kid. Then one day I saw you near here and knew you'd found my secret place. I hated you for taking it from me back then, and now I have even more reason to hate you."

Maddie gripped the rock in her hand until her fingers ached. He would come at her again, only this time he'd be expecting her to try to hit him again. He was stronger, larger, meaner than her. And the look in his eyes said he no longer had anything to lose.

A noise from above made them both look toward the shaft of light pouring into the room of the cave—and both started as the pistol hit the rock floor and bounced a couple of times before settling between them.

Maddie moved on pure instinct, hurling the rock at Bo as she lunged for the gun.

Bo let out a cry as the rock found its mark. She closed her hands around the grip of the pistol as Bo fell to the floor beside her. She rolled, her back to him, as she fought to keep the gun away from him.

He grabbed a handful of her hair, jerking her head back, and reached with his other hand for the gun.

She remembered the side he'd been holding when he came into the cave and drove her elbow back into him. Bo howled in pain. His one hand released her hair, his other drew back as if to clutch his wounded side.

Maddie rolled over, coming up with the gun gripped in both her hands. She was looking Bo Evans in the face. Her finger touched the cold steel of the trigger. She couldn't do it. Just like with the knife. She couldn't take another person's life.

"Can't do it, can you?" Bo bared his teeth, rearing back, fist clenched as he swung at her face.

Maddie fired twice, the shots echoing like thunder

in the cave Then Bo Evans flopped face-first onto the rock floor of the cave.

From overhead, she heard Shane calling her name.

Chapter Fourteen

When Shane came into the room, Maddie looked up from the chair where she'd been waiting. She couldn't hide how nervous she was about the DNA results. She couldn't hide anything from Shane Corbett.

"Jerilyn Larch wasn't your mother," he said, stepping to her chair to pull her up into his arms.

Maddie hugged him tightly, fighting tears of relief. After a moment, she drew back. "But I don't understand. She knew so much about me."

"From what the sheriff has been able to find out, Jerilyn wasn't the only one to give birth that night at the hospital. Obviously, she got the wrong information."

Maddie blinked back tears as she looked into Shane's handsome face. Since that day in the cave, he'd been there for her every step of the way.

Sometimes at night she woke, imagining she heard the sound of the gun's report and could see Bo's face the instant before he died. Shane held her, soothing her with his words and touch. He was the one person who understood what she was feeling. He'd been fighting his own demons since killing the man who'd shot him in Texas.

"But Jerilyn was *someone's* mother," Maddie said.

"She gave up her baby here in Whitehorse twenty-six years ago."

He nodded. "Honey, according to the sheriff, there were a group of older women who helped find homes for babies that the mothers couldn't keep. A secret adoption ring. The women took no money. They just wanted the babies to go to good homes. They truly believed they were helping both the mothers and the babies."

Maddie pulled away to walk to the window. Past the glass, the bright summer sun cast a golden glow over the land. In the green pasture, she could see her horse. Shane had brought it out to Trails West so she could ride once her ankle was better. The two of them had ridden every day since then, exploring the countryside, having picnics in the pines, talking for hours, or not talking at all. They'd become as close as any two people ever could.

"You're telling me that I was one of those babies," she said, not turning around.

"Your DNA also doesn't match Roy or Sarah Cavanaugh's."

She turned to look at him. "Then the other woman who gave birth that night was my mother?"

"That seems to be the case," Shane said quietly.

"So I have no idea who my mother or father was, where I came from, who I really am."

"We both know who you really are," he said, joining her at the window. "A strong, intelligent, very sexy woman. What more do we need to know?"

She smiled, loving him more than words could ever express. "What if that's not good enough?"

"There might be a way to find out who your biological mother was and, from there, your biological father, if that's what you want to do. Do you still have the White-horse Sewing Circle baby quilt that you were given when you were born?"

Maddie frowned. "Yes, but why would…" Her eyes widened. "Are you telling me the older women who ran this adoption ring belonged to the Whitehorse Sewing Circle?"

"At least one member did. Probably more were involved. According to the sheriff, there is something in the stitches that tell who your birth mother was. The sheriff told me that the adoption ring is Whitehorse's long-time secret. No one knew about the clues in the quilt until recently."

Maddie couldn't believe this. She thought of how her mother had hated that quilt, had hidden it in the back of the closet, never using it. Now it made sense. In fact, so many things in her life were finally starting to make sense.

"I can't help but be relieved that Sarah wasn't my real mother, since she was such a terrible mother. Jeri-lyn certainly wasn't a step up. But I'm not sure I'm quite ready to find my biological mother," she said, smiling up at Shane.

"I'll support you no matter what you decide," he said, returning her smile. "There's something else. Buck Jones found a small leather notebook hidden in a sugar canister at his house. He turned it over to the sheriff, who turned it over to the FBI. Apparently Earl Ray Pitts followed Jerilyn to Montana to retrieve this notebook. According to what the FBI has told the sheriff, the information in it could bring down a large segment of organized crime in Arizona and parts of Nevada."

"I heard Earl Ray ask Jerilyn about the book. That's why he killed her?"

"Earl Ray swore to me that it was an accident and that Jerilyn killed both of his men."

Maddie shivered and Shane drew her close, wrapping her in his arms. She snuggled against him.

"You did what you had to do," he said softly, as if he knew she was thinking of Bo.

She nodded. "It's just hard to think that I took his life."

"It's one of the reasons I'm not going back to the Texas Rangers."

She pulled back and looked at him in surprise.

He smiled. "You're the other reason."

"But you love being a Texas Ranger."

"*Loved.* I thought it was being shot that made me hesitant about returning. I'd worked so hard to get where I was, and yet I felt something was missing in my life." His gaze locked with hers. "I no longer feel that way. Nor do I feel driven to climb the ranks of the Texas Rangers."

"Are you sure about this, Shane?"

He nodded and smiled. "The sheriff has an opening for another deputy and said I have the job if I want it." Shane took her shoulders in his big hands. "I told him it would depend on you."

"Me?"

"I love you, Maddie Cavanaugh."

"Could you say that again?" She'd waited to hear those words for so long.

He chuckled. "I don't take these words lightly. That's why I haven't said them until I could completely commit to you. I love you, Maddie Cavanaugh."

She smiled through her tears. "Oh Shane." To her surprise, Shane dropped to one knee. As he did, he opened his hand. In his palm rested a small velvet box.

Maddie blinked at her tears. "Shane?"

He opened the jewelry box. Inside was a beautiful diamond ring. "It belonged to my mother. As the first of the Corbett brothers to propose marriage, it is to go to my fiancée."

"Oh, Shane, I love it!" The ring was beautiful, and the fact that it had belonged to his mother made it all the more magnificent to her.

As he took her left hand, he said, "I haven't had time to have the ring sized, but—"

Both of them let out a gasp as the ring slid onto her finger—a perfect fit. Maddie met his eyes, hers overflowing. Shane looked as shaken as she felt. It was as if their love was meant to be. As if it were written in the stars. But neither of them believed in that, did they?

"Will you marry me?" he asked, his voice breaking.

She nodded and pulled him to his feet to wrap her arms around him. "Oh, yes, Shane Corbett. I so love you."

The room behind them filled with applause and cheers as they both turned to find Shane's family gathered just inside the doorway.

"SOME THINGS ARE just destined to be, wouldn't you say?" Jud asked, grinning as he came into the room.

Shane saw that his other brothers were also grinning. Behind them his father looked close to tears. Kate was smiling, and everyone was looking as if they couldn't be happier—especially Jud.

"I have a bone to pick with you," Shane said to his brother. Jud had made himself scarce for weeks. He'd said he couldn't leave the film shoot in Canada, but Shane knew better.

"Just say thanks and let's leave it at that," Jud said, still grinning.

"Do you know what he did to me?" Shane asked the rest of his family.

"Are you kidding? He's been bragging about it ever since word spread that you'd asked Dad for the ring," Russell said.

"Yeah, let me guess who spread the word," Shane said, looking at his brother.

Jud laughed. "Took you long enough to figure it out. Hey, I'm a man of my word. I promised a wedding. I just didn't say it was going to be mine. The minute I saw Maddie, I knew she was perfect—for you. I knew it would be love at first sight."

Shane couldn't help but laugh.

"But I certainly hadn't planned on her being kidnapped," Jud added.

"I'm glad to hear that," Shane said.

"But you have to admit, you did come into her life right when she needed you—no matter what you say about destiny."

Shane scoffed. But he wasn't about to deny that he might never have met Maddie if things hadn't unfolded the way they had with his father remarrying and moving to Montana, and him getting wounded and ending up recuperating at Trails West.

"Well? Aren't you going to thank me?" Jud asked.

Shane shot him a warning look. "Don't push your luck. You still drew the shortest straw. You're the next one to get married."

"Hell, big brother, I have a whole year," Jud said. "A lot can happen in a year."

"This calls for champagne," Grayson said, as he and Kate came into the room to give Maddie a hug.

Shane watched as Kate hugged Maddie. He couldn't miss the tears in Kate's eyes as she pulled back to gaze into Maddie's face. "Welcome to the family, Maddie," she said, her voice breaking.

"About that champagne," Lantry said, going behind the bar to get one of the bottles that were chilling.

"I could use a stiff drink. I've had to listen to Jud brag for hours about his plan working," Dalton said, taking a stool at the bar.

Juanita came in with a tray of tiny tacos along with her homemade salsa, followed by Maddie's cousins and their husbands and Pearl and Titus Cavanaugh.

Shane watched his family, listening to the sound of laughter and the popping of several bottles of champagne. His gaze went to Maddie. Her face shone, those blue eyes brighter than he'd ever seen them. She'd been through so much, but she was strong. He had no doubt that she could take whatever life threw at her after this. Maybe even finding out who her birth mother really was, if that was what she decided to do.

Out of the corner of his eye, he saw his father move to Kate and put his arm around her. She was crying, her fingers pressed to her lips, her gaze on Maddie.

Shane felt a shiver move up his spine as he noticed how much the two women looked alike. They could almost be mother and daughter.

* * * * *

SPECIAL EXCERPT FROM

⬦ HARLEQUIN®
™

INTRIGUE

Author Tessa Jane Clementine, known by her readers as TJ St. Clair, is receiving threatening letters from a man claiming to be her biggest fan. Silas Walker, a handsome loner, is the only person who can protect her, but can she trust him?

Read on for a sneak preview of
Rogue Gunslinger
by New York Times *bestselling author B.J. Daniels.*

Chapter One

The old antique Royal typewriter clacked with each angry stroke of the keys. Shaking fingers pounded out livid words onto the old discolored paper. As the fury built, the fingers moved faster and faster until the keys all tangled together in a metal knot that lay suspended over the paper.

With a curse of frustration, the metal arms were tugged apart and the sound of the typewriter resumed in the small room. Angry words burst across the page, some letters darker than others as the keystrokes hit like a hammer. Other letters appeared lighter, some dropping down a half line as the fingers slipped from the worn keys. A bell sounded at the end of each line as the carriage was returned with a clang, until the paper was ripped from the typewriter.

Read in a cold, dark rage, the paper was folded hurriedly, the edges uneven, and stuffed into the envelope already addressed in the black typewritten letters:

Author TJ St. Clair
Whitehorse, Montana

The stamp slapped on, the envelope sealed, the fingers still shaking with expectation for when the novelist opened it. The fan rose and smiled. Wouldn't Ms. St. Clair, aka Tessa Jane Clementine, love this one.

***

TJ St. Clair hated conference calls. Especially this conference call.

"I know it's tough with your book coming out before Christmas," said Rachel the marketing coordinator, her voice sounding hollow on speakerphone in TJ's small New York City apartment.

"But I don't have to tell you how important it is to do as much promo as you can this week to get those sales where you want them," Sherry from Publicity and Events added.

TJ held her head and said nothing for a moment. "I'm going home for the holidays to be with my sisters, who I haven't seen in months." She started to say she knew how important promoting her book was, but in truth she often questioned if a lot of the events really made that much difference—let alone all the social media. If readers spent as much time as TJ had to on social media, she questioned how they could have time to read books.

"It's the threatening letters you've been getting, isn't it?" her agent Clara said.

She glanced toward the window, hating to admit that the letters had more than spooked her. "That is definitely part of it. They have been getting more…detailed and more threatening."

"I'm so sorry, TJ," Clara said and everyone added in words of sympathy.

"You've spoken to the police?" her editor, Dan French, asked.

"There is nothing they can do until…until the fan acts on the threats. That's another reason I want to go to Montana."

For a few beats there was silence. "All right. I can speak to Marketing," Dan said. "We'll do what we can from this end."

Don't miss
Rogue Gunslinger by B.J. Daniels,
available October 2018 wherever
Harlequin® Intrigue books and ebooks are sold.

www.Harlequin.com

INTRIGUE

EDGE-OF-YOUR-SEAT INTRIGUE,
FEARLESS ROMANCE.

Save **$1.00**

on the purchase of ANY
Harlequin® Intrigue book.

Available wherever books are sold,
including most bookstores, supermarkets,
drugstores and discount stores.

✂ -

Save **$1.00**

on the purchase of any Harlequin® Intrigue book.

Coupon valid until October 31, 2018.
Redeemable at participating outlets in the U.S. and Canada only.
Not redeemable at Barnes & Noble stores. Limit one coupon per customer.